I0822503

PUSS ON THE LOOSE

PUSS ON THE LOOSE

JEREMY TAYLOR

Andean Publishing
New York City

Andean Publishing
1420 York Avenue
New York, NY 10021

Published by Andean Publishing

www.andeanpublishing.com
Puss on the Loose/ Jeremy Taylor
1 2 3 4 5 6 7 8 9 10

Identifiers:
Library of Congress Control Number: 2024907715
ISBN: 979-8-9905189-0-2
Printed in the United States of America

To Grandma

PUSS ON THE LOOSE

PROLOGUE

I was holding a baby in my arms, someone else's baby, a baby I'd kidnapped. I wondered how I'd ended up in such a mess, hundreds of miles away from home, absolutely broke, with the FBI on my tail. (I'm really not comfortable with that expression as I'm not a dog—woof woof—but what else am I to say?) Me stealing, not babies but in general, took off in my childhood upon meeting my first gaggle of imaginary friends. All I wanted was to show the imaginary friends how cool I was by being . . . well, "imaginative" for the lack of a better word. If taking a pair of sandals in a shoe store without paying isn't imaginative at eleven, I don't know what is. It all started after my baby sister passed away from sepsis. Getting in trouble with the law at eleven would not result in much (except getting my ass belted by Daddy, which did happen often). But kidnapping a baby was a crazier, more adult (for the lack of a better word) thing to do. Please don't blame my being schizophrenic or overweight or sometimes high. Even without the diagnosis, my mind played tricks on me from time to time. Blame loneliness that stems from depression that stems from friends being busy that stems from smartphone-usage that stems from loneliness. Oh lord, I'm jumping all over the place and can't concentrate. When I kidnapped Lykke, my mind was playing tricks on me, and now lying in bed at the monastery a week later, I have time to go down memory lane. Let me start from the beginning so I could tell you exactly how it happened. And then you decide whether it was my fault. My story began when a different toddler had been kidnapped a month prior. That, you could say, was the catalyst.

"A TODDLER NAMED SIA SHIRTLEY WAS KIDNAPPED FROM Central Park early this morning," the anchor, Will Blab, said. It was Wednesday, March 14. I was so surprised by the news that I told myself, *Chloe, we're not in freaking Kansas anymore*. Which we were not—we were in New York. I remember that Wednesday because that's the day I applied for a job as a flight attendant, bought new boots, and also got my period. Did I say I bought new boots or *boobs*? No, I meant boots. Because that's what I bought—boots. Anyway, it seemed surreal, the kidnapping thing. And it was dry, really unpleasant. In New York, during winter, the heaters run nonstop. There's no moisture in the air, and my "vagin," that's French for "vagina," was so dry it resembled the Grand Canyon. Pretty—sure—but at what *price*? In fact, I was itching all over with my hand stuck in my briefs, and for a brief (see what I did there?) moment, I imagined having an STD. I even went to Sam Sung, my OBG-YN, for a checkup, who confirmed, quoting, "Nope—no STDs, just dry skin, Chloe."

Oh, right, Sia. Starting that Wednesday, every newspaper ran a story on Sia Shirtley, a two-year-old wonder of Armenian origin. She had chubby cheeks and a nose that was cute as a button. That Wednesday, after shopping for a pair of boots (not boobs) and a sexy red thong for my boyfriend,

I spent the day watching the news while eating a red velvet cake that was leftover from the previous night. I'm so anxious thinking about that day that I can't even think straight. The red thong was for me, not for my boyfriend. He was going to enjoy them on *me* since he was the one asking me to purchase a pair. Later that night, when Mom came home from work, she switched the news to *Dr. Phil*. Mom told me she felt a sore throat coming in and sent me to the store to buy some cold medicine. That's how I broke in my new boots. It never occurred to me until later why she couldn't pick up some on her way from work.

The next day, Sia's babysitter got arrested. Like, she was in handcuffs and all. The babysitter—Hembadoon Okeke—was a young black girl from Nigeria, who was a nineteen-year-old, live-in Au Pair—which is like a nanny, I learned, but on the books.

Sia's case had become about racism, and our senator proposed new immigration laws. At the same time, white folks (including my mother) started saying racial slurs. Racism bothers me in general, and while I don't believe I am in any way a racist, I noticed a shift in my attitude. Once, I even made a bad racist joke in the safety of my own head and instantly regretted it. My shrink tells me it's okay to have some negative thoughts sometimes, and I should not be ashamed to have them. It started bothering me to no end that my social circle consisted mainly of white women. Why is it called a circle? That question bugged me for thirty-one years! And now, with the Hembadoon at fault, I was afraid the racial affairs would only get worse. Would other people's "circles" only get tighter? I wondered.

From day one, I was heavily invested in the Shirtley case. I bought myself a bag of Doritos to have to snack on while in front of the TV. I also bought Cannoli chips because I love shoving things in my mouth in times of distress. And what distress there was. I despised Hembadoon. The dumb-dumb failed to notify the authorities and instead had been searching for the missing baby herself. Her argument against why she hadn't alerted the police immediately following the *incident*, Hembadoon said she was afraid of getting deported. What a nut case. I hated Hembadoon, and her greasy face and the fifteen bead necklaces she was wearing that were all interlaced and were made out of all sorts of colorful stones. She was pretty, I'll give her that. Everyone initially thought Hembadoon was in cahoots with the abductor. Thankfully, there were witnesses, and soon enough, the authorities released the kidnapper's composite to the public. We learned the kidnapper was a female. Still, her age varied from thirty to forty-five, a colossal inconsistency because she had been disguising herself continuously like a real pro, and each witness was seeing a "different" version of her.

When the Shirtleys realized the investigation was going nowhere, they printed out hundreds of T-shirts bearing Sia's face on them with HAVE YOU SIA ME? written underneath. I thought the name pun was brilliant. I picked a T-shirt for myself, one for each of my friends, and an extra small one for Mom—not because she could fit into it—but because she would be offended had I got her the small size. *Chloe*, she would say, *this is going to look baggy on me!* After I picked up the T-shirts, several volunteers were giving out in Central Park, I had an appointment with my psychiatrist, Dr. Pepper.

In some circles, Dr. Pepper could be called handsome. He's tall with salt-and-pepper hair. But more on the "oversalted" side. He has a booty that could double as a flotation device, and every time he bends over, I laugh, afraid his butt would burst. He has a chiseled chin, ears that belong on a labradoodle, and a pompadour that I call a pompadouroodle. Still, his age was a mystery to me, but he didn't look his age. Regardless of what age that was.

I'd been seeing him for a long time, right after my very first schizophrenic "episode" that brought hallucinations. I don't understand why they call them episodes as if I am a TV show. An "episode" occurs after overstimulation of the brain, whether positive or negative overstimulation. During my latest "episode," for example, I was upset about going to a high school reunion in the shape I was in (which was no shape at all—just a bunch of fat jiggling around). My medication had to be adjusted twice because some were not working or had insane side effects. So I had appointments with Dr. Pepper about once a month and, also, saw a shrink, Dr. Black, weekly.

The third and last doctor in my life was Dr. Clemens, my family doctor, and cardiologist. (And some suspect also a chiropractor, or as someone you'd call a Jack of all trades. The funny thing about Dr. Clemens, his first name is, in fact, Jack! Surreal, right? Well, not really . . . If he were named Jessica, then that would be surreal.) My daddy died from a heart attack ten years ago, and I'm at high risk for coronary heart disease since I'm overweight (by clinical standards; by my standards, I think I'm just fine). That's why regular monitoring from Dr. Clemens was mandatory. In essence, I was tossed around, you could say like a salad, from one doctor to the next.

I was in my psychiatrist, Dr. Pepper's office, relaxing in a comfortable mauve leather chair in the waiting room, catching up on my reading. Lately,

I'd been obsessed with the Russian classics suggested by my Russian friend Natalia. I was halfway through *The Master and Margarita*. I bought the book because it had a picture of a black cat on the cover who resembled my puss Anubis, and at the time, I was hungry and wondered if Margarita was related to the pizza.

My butt cheeks, like two hungry coyotes, kept chewing my panties all day. I repeatedly unglued them every five minutes, which made me look like a perverted woman with a voracious butt.

Mom sent me a text message.

Chloe, could you pick up a magnesium supplement? I may be deficient. I had a charley horse this morning.

Okay. I typed the words quickly into my cellphone. The phone case was a black cat with ears sticking out, a present from my friend Calyssa. I liked everything with cats on it. If the Shirtleys lost a cat, I wouldn't mind wearing a T-shirt with the face of their cat on it.

Mom texted with, *I'm jealous Josephine and Analise are going to Greece.*

I hate feta cheese, I countered, thrown by the non sequitur, *and wouldn't be able to eat anything there. Plus, I thought aunty was vegan, no?* No wonder my cousin was named Analise: she was a complete pain in the ass with all her pretentious vegan diet!

Well, they don't have to eat cheese, sweetie. She'll eat grape leaves.

Dr. Pepper stuck his head out from behind the door to his office. "Chloe, are you ready?"

I nodded and sent a concluding text back to Mom.

Gotta go.

I entered the room and plopped my full weight down on yet another leather chair, while Dr. Pepper closed the door behind him and took a seat across from me. Today he was wearing a green tie that matched his eyes, and it appeared he was growing some stubble, which looked great on him.

He adjusted his glasses. "What's new, Chloe?"

"My lipids test came back."

"And?"

"My blood pressure was one hundred and forty-five by ninety-five. My cholesterol was two hundred and fifty, and my triglycerides were four hundred."

"That's bananas. How did it get that high?"

"Because of Clozapine. Dr. Clemens wants me off it immediately. It messes with my triglycerides. I am taking a statin drug too, but my lipids, he said, look like an excerpt from a Steven King's novel. But the funny thing is, he doesn't strike me like the reading kind."

"Chloe," Dr. Pepper said, "I understand your concern with your lipids panel, but you can not—under *any* circumstances—go off Clozapine."

"Dr. Clemens said if I don't, I will have a heart attack."

"He is mistaken about that. You're only thirty-one; you can't be at risk for a heart attack."

"My daddy died from a heart attack at forty, which puts me at higher risk."

Dr. Pepper breathed out. He does this weird thing where he wrinkles his nose, so he did that. "I know. Triglycerides, cholesterol, and high blood pressure can be taken care of without going off Clozapine. You need an exercise routine and a healthier diet. If you go off this medication, we'll have to start from scratch. You will start seeing hallucinations, including seeing Matilda." He was referring to my dead sister. "Do you want that to happen?"

"It was nice seeing her," I said.

"She was merely a hallucination, Chloe. Remember, a schizophrenic episode can happen out of nowhere and last for a day, a week, or longer." When he said the word "episode," I secretly giggled. "If you get depressed or overly excited, the hallucinations will return."

Blah blah blah. Dr. Pepper sure liked to talk. Maybe he thought I was *his* shrink—and at that thought, I laughed so hard I peed a little in my pants. After a few seconds of silence where he left me alone to contemplate what he'd said, he caught me staring at a dimple in his chin and said, "You understand that, right?"

I nodded but didn't know what I had agreed to.

"Good. Glad we're on the same page." He switched gears. "Last time you mentioned your goals, and one of them was to move out of your mom's apartment and live on your own. How's that going, by the way?"

"I applied for a job as a flight attendant."

"Do you think you can handle living alone?"

"Yes, if I get this job. Plus, I've been saving from babysitting."

"That's remarkable, Chloe. You see, a person in your condition might want to blame their disease, their parents, or the world for their misfortunes. But you've been headstrong. If you go off Clozapine, you'll have another schizophrenic episode, and your mom will have to take care of you. If you don't take that medication, your dreams will be just that: merely dreams and not reality."

"Okay," I said. I had no idea how to respond. I was confused by what the two doctors were saying—one said to stop Clozapine, the other said the opposite. I needed more time to assess the situation, and have you ever noticed that there's an "ass" in assess? I hate rushing, so assessing was mandatory.

"Do you want to talk about Anubis?" Dr. Pepper asked and took off his glasses, folding them. "How is he doing after being diagnosed with diabetes?"

"He hates being shot with insulin twice a day."

"Have you asked the vet if it was normal for a cat to be diabetic?"

"The vet promised me it was rare but not unusual and soothed me by saying that one in every million cats gets it."

"How do you feel about having a cat who is diabetic?"

"I don't know. It's expensive, though. But it also means if Anubis eats any food without getting an insulin shot, he will feel sick or even die."

"What made you take him to the vet?"

"Well, he peed all over the place and was always thirsty. It took us months to realize something was wrong."

"What I want to point out here is that you saw something unusual in his behavior and took action. That's how you know if your own actions are unusual. You're becoming more responsible for your cat, your future, your medication. How does that make you feel?"

"Empowered? Like I can get away with murder? You know what I mean?"

"Hm," Dr. Pepper said, writing something in his notepad, "an interesting choice of words."

THE VERY NEXT DAY, I HAD AN APPOINTMENT WITH MY SHRINK, Dr. Black. All the doctors work in the same area near where I live in Murray Hill—very convenient. We also have a grocery store that's open twenty-four hours a day and a diner where they serve damn good burgers. Dr. Black was such an oxymoron, because everything in his office, from the way he dressed to the furniture, was white, including the chair in which I was sitting.

I was wearing my Sia T-shirt, and as soon as Dr. Black asked me about it, I told him that I hated Hembadoon and that it worried me so much that I barely slept the past couple of nights.

We also discussed the war between my cardiologist and my psychiatrist.

I, of course, thought the cute Dr. Pepper would win. Dr. Black could not comment on whether I should be taking Clozapine or nor, but he clearly had an opinion because one of his brows rose in a non-committal/non-verbal way of saying that I really should be taking it.

"Do you still feel isolated?" he asked. I nodded, and he continued. "I think you should tell your friends about your schizophrenia. You'll be able to break that barrier, and that might help you feel more connected to them."

"I already feel stupid for telling them about my high cholesterol and triglycerides."

"You shouldn't feel like you can't tell your friends the truth."

"I *won't* have any friends if they know the truth."

"Chloe, don't be afraid to show some vulnerability."

"People *hate* the truth."

"Trust me, if you open up, they'll understand."

"I'm just so tired of everything."

"What are you tired of, Chloe?"

"I want to live alone, have a daughter, have a career. But I can't. I mean, why do some people have everything while the rest of us suffer? That's unfair."

Dr. Black offered me a box of tissues, and I wiped my tears, then blew my nose.

"Look at it the other way, Chloe," he said. "You've applied for a job, and you've been seeing Kim for two months. That's a good start."

"True, but Kim's not husband material."

"Why do you say that?"

"When we first met, his pick-up line was, 'Wanna see my nuts?' He was referring to a shell game with hazelnuts, which he put under three metal shot glasses. I wouldn't want my husband to be goofy like that."

"But didn't you—"

"Then," I interjected, "he asked if I wanted to touch his belly button. He pulled open his vest, and there was a large button saying 'Belly' on it. I don't want my husband to be corny like that."

"I think what you're trying to do here, Chloe, is to set yourself up for failure. That way, when things don't work out with Kim, you have a reason to shift the blame and focus on the negative. Remember, the more requirements you have about a particular man—whether it's how much money he has or whether he's well endowed—the fewer chances you have at establishing a meaningful relationship."

"What should I do?"

"Just keep an open mind, and don't rush anything."

Dr. Black switched the theme of our conversation and said he wanted to discuss my cat. I told him the same thing I'd told Dr. Pepper. I couldn't understand the sudden interest everyone was having in my cat. Just because he was diabetic was no reason to ignore *my* problems, and boy did I have plenty. Sometimes I wished I never took Anubis to the stupid vet. And you know what's funny? On the surface, there I was, a privileged white girl, while, in reality, I had a host of health issues that could not be seen by a naked eye. I realized then that everyone's reality is slightly different.

My reality is only real for me, while for others, it's distorted using their own lens through which they see the world.

THE FOLLOWING TUESDAY, I FOUND MYSELF IN MY cardiologist's office being lectured. Unlike the handsome Dr. Pepper, who was way out of everyone's league, Dr. Clemens was pushing seventy-three. On a *good* day. Liver spots covered most of his face, and he had thick pouches under each eye, kind of like bags, and not the designer kind. I mused that if he were at LaGuardia Airport, the TSA would make him check those in. His chin hung loose, kind of like a chicken's. When he was talking, I imagined him saying, "bok bok bok." I laughed, but he didn't know why. Dr. Clemens was board-certified and smelled of soap, two qualities I respected in a cardiologist.

While he was talking, I discreetly took a photo of him because it looked to me he'd been working out, and I wanted Mom's opinion.

"Chloe," he was saying, showing me his yellow teeth, "your cholesterol and triglycerides are way too high. If you keep taking Clozapine, I want you to understand how much danger you're putting yourself in."

"Doctor Clemens, Clozapine is the only way to avoid hallucinations."

"You're not far away from a heart attack."

"But Dr. Pepper said that if I stop taking it, I'll have another schizophrenic episode."

"So if Dr. Pepper jumps off the bridge, you'll jump too?"

I envisioned a bridge and cringed, saying, "No."

"Clozapine is interfering with your body and is the sole reason you've gained so much weight. Look at you—you're fat. Clozapine is the reason why your white cell count is so low. You must find another psychiatrist who can prescribe you something less lethal. In fact, I will speak to your mother, and we'll decide what's best for you."

After my appointment, I sent a text message to Mom.

Dr. Clemens wants me to find another psychiatrist. He thinks Dr. Pepper is unqualified.

Yes, I already talked to him.

We trusted Dr. Clemens because he'd been our friend and doctor long before Daddy passed away, for over twenty-five years. That day, I stopped Clozapine and ordered a chicken burrito for lunch.

While waiting on the burrito, I sent the picture of Dr. Clemens to Mom.

Look who's been working out.

Mom replied: *Working out, my ass. He sucks so much cock he's got biceps in his cheeks.*

Me: *He's gay?*

Mom: *In the closet. His closet is full of dildos, and one "source" told me he's into bestiality because he had a porn video of a horse screwing a guy, recorded on his TiVo.*

Me: *Are you freaking serious?*

Mom: *Yes, I was surprised too! Who's fucking got TiVo?*

Turns out, my boyfriend Kim also has TiVo. I went over to his place right after my appointment and was telling him what I'd learned about Dr. Clemens, which was when Kim showed me the black TiVo box. Kim lived with two other guys his age, and his apartment was across town, in Chelsea, on West Twenty-fourth Street and Ninth Avenue. When I walked in, I took notice of how much higher the dish pile was in the sink than the day before. I wondered if it was a competition to see how many dishes they had and whether they could keep using them indefinitely. I would hardly consider myself the cleanest person, meaning I don't clean because we have a cleaning lady, Siriporn—who's Vietnamese—and she comes once a week. Plus, I have an OCD mother who cleaned up after whatever Siriporn missed. But looking at the dishes in Kim's sink even I knew this was bad. While Kim was on the phone ordering pizza, I was hard at work on the dishes. Boxes from macaroni and cheese had filled up their recycling bin, and therefore many plates were soiled with yellow goo, which was hard to scrub off, so I let the dishes soak in hot water. Next to the recycling bin with paper, stood another one full of beer bottles, and next to them was the trash bin, also overflowing. The musty marijuana odor permanently lingered in the air, as all the three boys smoked dope regularly. Soaping a plate, I wondered why I was even there. Didn't I deserve better? A boyfriend who is a doctor, perhaps (someone like Dr. Pepper).

Kim was far from being a doctor: he was an actor, aka a server, and he was twenty-nine, two years younger—which is also a negative. Twenty-nine is a revolutionary moment in a person's life—right before turning thirty—and numerous articles advised against dating twenty-nine-year-olds. When the two of us met, I thought Kim was twenty-four with his baby face, and now, two months in, it was too late to back out. Kim was six feet and three inches tall, skinny beyond belief (precisely a hundred and fifty pounds), and pale like Cinderella, except he had no mouse- or bird-friends. Kim wears the same black skinny jeans and graphic tees, but I love his thick, beautiful jet-black hair and a massive (I wish I could say heart) penis. Even if Kim's apartment was disgusting, I couldn't help but envy he lived without his mother. That was *my* goal—to live "mom-free" later this year. I was also jealous of how Kim could eat anything he wanted without gaining weight. In fact, it seemed that anything he ate just ended up on my belly as fat rings. Like when they cut a tree to see how many years old it is, I have a theory that if the doctors cut me open, they'd find rings in a much similar manner. By counting a hundred and ninety rings, they'd quote Dr. Clemens and say, "You're fat."

We met at a bar, Kim and I, and I immediately liked him, not only because he had a woman's name, but he had an all-American look of a boy next door (who looked malnourished, with sucked-in cheeks). He later told me Kim was short for Kimball, as in the novel *Kim* by Kipling, but I thought his parents just wanted a girl.

As soon as Kim hung up the phone, I pulled him into his bedroom, closed the door, and jumped on top of him. I don't want to bore you with the details of what happened next, because I don't kiss and tell. But I do have sex and brag! We were humping doggy-style minutes later, and when we finished, the pizza arrived, or at least that's what we thought when we heard the buzzer. Kim pulled on a pair of shorts and a white wife-beater, pulled out some cash from his wallet, and went to let the delivery guy in. On the way out of the bedroom, Kim picked up my white underwear and threw it at me flirtatiously, and I ducked pretending it was a bomb and threw a pillow at him. We often played like that, and I loved the silliness.

As I picked up my underwear in my hands, I threw it back on the bed like a reflex. A brown spider was sitting on it. I jumped almost to the ceiling and shrieked like a little girl. I'm *terrified* of spiders to the point of insanity (ants and cockroaches are also a no-no). When the spider didn't move, I picked up another pillow and holding it in front of me like a shield I moved closer like a soldier in a battle. I poked the underwear with the corner of the pillow, but the spider didn't move. And that's when I noticed something absolutely humiliating: it was not a spider but a skid mark.

My embarrassment was beyond surreal. Had Kim seen it when he'd thrown it at me? I shoved the panties down the tote and had no choice but to go commando. I was so humiliated that I only ate one slice of pizza and flew out the door before Kim could protest.

TWO WEEKS LATER, THE GOOD NEWS CAME IN: ON MARCH 28, the police caught Sia's kidnapper! The kidnapper was disguising herself as a nun and was hiding in a monastery near a small Arkansas town called Pine Buff. Her real name was Ama Takayoza, and she was a thirty-year-old skinny Japanese woman from Michigan. She called herself Sister Mary. Sister Mary, my ass! The nuns who lived in the monastery, of course, had no idea Ama was the kidnapper because Ama had told the head nun, Sister Trinity, that she was a nun from a different monastery and she was looking after her friend's baby. The unsuspecting nuns let Ama stay with them for a couple of nights. How bizarre! The FBI, however, was on her tail all along and—bam—next thing you know, Ama's face is the only face shown all over the news. I finally took off the T-shirt with Sia's face on it and threw it in the laundry. I had been wearing it every day for the past few weeks, but it didn't smell at all.

Ama was a widower (or the husband-killer), had no kids of her own, and from what it sounded like had been planning to abduct a child for quite some time. That's why she came to New York. She stayed at a hotel on the Upper West Side for a week—near where my Aunt Josephine lives. Ama was casing the joint (aka Central Park) daily, getting her intel. Apparently, Hembadoon took Sia to the park every single day from nine in the morning until eleven. Talk about never changing a routine! The day Ama kidnapped Sia, she checked out early at 8:00 a.m., had free breakfast at the hotel, and was on her way to the park with extra baby clothing into which she changed Sia right away. That was incredibly mind-blowing, and for the next week, that's all I could talk about. Even Mom got tired of listening to me.

I was in bed reading when Mom messaged me.

I was looking up tickets to Cancun in April, and they're so cheap. Should we go for a couple weeks?

The fact that my mother was in the next room and was talking to me via text almost killed me. My cat, Anubis, jumped in bed next to me and assembled himself in his favorite nook near my ankles. In the meantime, I was replying to Mom.

I can't go for a month, Mom. I have doctor appointments every week.

When no reply came, I resumed reading my book to the sound of purring Anubis. I felt like I was a burden to her. Because of my mental problems, she was afraid to leave me alone and go on a vacation by herself. That was the reason why I wanted to move out to prove I *could* do it alone, and I *could* take care of my health, and I *could* be left unsupervised. I was not a child, after all, but thirty-one. Maybe Mom forgot that I grew up?.

Baby Sia was the star of the news for the next several weeks. Her parents profusely thanked the public and the FBI for doing such a great job and every volunteer who wore the T-shirt with Sia's face. I was glad then that I'd helped. On Wednesday, after watching another news piece about Ama Takayoza and Hembadoon Okeke (who now were both in custody), I checked out my horoscope. "Bring your 'A' game today, Pisces. When things go awry, don't panic and keep your cool. Today is a great day to squeeze in some shopping." Anubis jumped on my lap as I was sending a group text message to my girlfriends Calyssa, Natalia, and Lindsay.

Who wants to go shopping?

Anubis had just eaten, and with his filthy mouth, he wanted some lovin'. I scratched his belly but refused to give him a kiss, so he purred on my stomach while I continued reading my horoscope. "Helping others will help you keep your spirits high. Others may suspect your motives; give them no reason to doubt your strength. Focus on what's important and conserve your energy."

All three of my friends replied back, and we made plans to meet around five. To conserve my energy, as per horoscope, I took a bus instead of walking. When I exited the bus, I noticed how a frail lady with a walker was trying to cross Second Avenue, as the red light was about to change. I rushed to the middle of the street and stopped the traffic with my hand, waiting patiently for the grandma to cross. Some drivers honked, but I was reluctant. She turned around to nod at me and said, "Thank you." My horoscope was on point because it did feel nice helping the old lady, and my spirits were indeed high.

At Nordstrom, in such a great mood, I bought a beany and two sweaters. My friends bought some things for themselves, and overall we spend about two hours running around the store. I ignored Dr. Black's advice about telling the girls about my schizophrenia. What my friends didn't know wouldn't hurt them. We finished our day at McDonald's, where Calyssa ordered a Big Mac and a parfait, Lindsay opted for a side salad (because she's skinny), and Natalia got chicken nuggets. I went to town: one McChicken, large fries, Coke, and a strawberry shake for dessert.

Calyssa put a handful of my fries in her mouth and said, "I was almost mugged yesterday." All three of us gasped with our mouths full and held our breath while she continued. "Well, not really. I *thought* I was. The guy was following me, and I started panicking, but he just turned and jumped in a car. It was a good reality check, you know? To always be on the lookout. I'll never forget what happened to baby Sia." Calyssa unzipped her green bomber jacket as if to prove her point. Underneath, she was wearing the T-shirt with Sia's face on it. It made me smile. I loved it when she wore things I bought for her. Calyssa has beautiful black eyes and hair to match, which she braids to resemble Princess Jasmine. Other than that, we could be identical twins, because she is my age; minus two or so years. And she's my height; plus three or so inches. And she's my weight, minus forty or so pounds. "But it was a great reality check, you know?" Calyssa asked, and we all nodded. "So from this point on, I'm not carrying any cash on me—not that I have any. I may have a second job lined up. Fingers crossed."

"How do you have time for two jobs, a baby, and a boyfriend?" I asked. Calyssa lives with her cousin Christina who had recently given birth. I don't know how she juggles so many things. Calyssa shrugs for an answer.

"I'm glad nothing happened," Lindsay said while playing with her long, shiny blond hair. Lindsay is tall-ish, gorgeous-ish, and skinny-ish. In other words, she gets plenty of male attention. I'm secretly jealous of her thick spaghetti-ish strands; mine are short macaroni. "In my heels," Lindsay adds, "I would never outrun a mugger or a kidnapper. Or even be on time for a sale. And good point on not carrying cash."

Lindsay pulled out a wag of dead presidents, with Benjamin being the most prevalent.

"Why do you have so much money on you?" I asked.

"I need to deposit it to my account. Lucky pays me cash, and I have so much income but no bills—my rent is free."

"MILF," Calyssa said jokingly, and the two laughed. Lindsay couldn't be further from being a MILF at twenty-six (the youngest in the group). She's a live-in nanny; hence the rent and other bills are paid by the Knotts. It must be nice. I mean—wait—I don't pay any rent or any bills either. Yeah—it *is* lovely.

Natalia, our Russian transgender friend and she's the oldest also (so maybe wisest as well), put down her drink. She was wearing bright red lipstick that imprinted the plastic cup with the shape of her lips. She was wearing a gold necklace, the thickness of my ankle, and it looked massive. Gold bracelets covered her arms, gold rings on each finger. She was wearing a fur coat and a black Prada dress she had recently purchased.

"Fear has big eyes," she said.

The three of us turned in her direction, wondering what she meant by that. Natalia added, "It's a Russian proverb." She had told us before that Russians are superstitious and love proverbs. Black cats are supposed to bring us bad luck if one such cat happens to cross in front of you. My cat Anubis is black, so Natalia said I'm doomed.

"What does it mean?" I asked.

"It means when you're scared, you imagine things; your eyes supposedly get bigger when you're scared. It's from a folktale. It means fear makes us do crazy things."

Nobody said a word afterward, but I knew each of us was contemplating something in her mind, refusing to share. I met Lindsay and Natalia through Calyssa, whom I met at a bar in East Harlem last year. My ex-boyfriend used to live near East One Hundred Sixteenth Street and Second Avenue, and the bar was his usual hang out spot where he took me several times. After the breakup, he kept a pair of my underpants, and I kept the bar—that's the kind of property division you do when you don't have any kids. Calyssa introduced me to Natalia, the gambler, who took us both to Vegas for a weekend getaway where she works, while Calyssa and I enjoyed the outdoor drinking and the shows. Rich Natalia loved the company and didn't mind shelling out a hundred and fifty dollars for our tickets, the amount of money she'd make in under five minutes playing the roulette. It was our company that was priceless. It's hard to make friends after college, so I believed we all were grateful to have a connection, dysfunctional as it were. Calyssa and Natalia were definitely lushes, and I was not the one to complain while having my mental disorder. According to Dr. Black, I suffered a case of low self-esteem and was in a co-dependent relationship with the girls. It suited me well, to be honest. Let the past be the past.

When I got home, I immediately smelled trouble: Anubis was nowhere around. Without fail, he greeted me at the entrance with his tail up every time I entered my apartment. Not today. The apartment reeked of onions, which Mom adds to everything, and I hate that when she serves them, they're almost raw and inedible. You would assume after thirty-one years, Mom would notice that after I finish my meal, all that's left behind are the onions. But nope, she doesn't. Paula Deen was on TV, sautéing some butter in olive oil with a little bit of chicken. When I removed my boots and bypassed the kitchen, Mom waved a quick hello and continued her conversation with Aunt Josephine on the phone. Mom was suffering a severe case of camel toe, as her private parts were jammed in tight yoga pants she was unwilling to exchange. The fact Mom had never done yoga in her entire life was one thing, but also sincerely believed the tight pants were toning her thighs that (according to her) were out-of-control fat. She was shorter than me by a whole foot and weighed less than a hundred and ten pounds, but she never allowed me to see her actual weight when she stepped on the scale. One time while she weighed herself, I actually saw her lifting one leg up. Mom probably believed that would bring her fat percentage down. She can be such a drama queen. I slid into my Wonder Woman pajamas and wanted to cuddle with my cat. After looking under the bed and in Mom's room, I realized he was not in the apartment. I came to the kitchen. Chicken thighs were braising in a cast iron skillet while Mom was bent over the counter with a pen in her hand.

"Mom, where's Anubis?" I asked.

Mom shrugged her shoulders, flipped the phone to another ear, and resumed writing something down, presumably a recipe. Anger controlled me from that point on, and I ripped the phone off her hands.

"Mother!" I yelled. "Where's Anubis?"

"I don't know, Chloe. Give me back my phone."

"Mother, the cat's not in the apartment. Did you take the trash to the chute?"

"Yes!" she retorted, grabbing the phone back.

"Sorry, Jo, Chloe was being rude," she said to the phone.

She's done it again, I was thinking, annoyed.

Anubis would occasionally rush off when we took out the garbage, so it was important to watch him. But I knew mother was careless because she was probably gabbing on the phone with Aunt Josephine without paying any attention.

I stuck my head in the hallway but didn't see any cats. I stepped into the carpeted hallway floor barefoot and knocked on my neighbor's door. There lived a Japanese girl who was in "fashion," whatever that meant. Her name, she told me in her broken English once, was Chyna. That's just lousy geography on her parents' part. In front of her door, I saw a receipt from a recent takeout she must have ordered from a Japanese place across the street. As I was picking it up, Chyna opened the door with a piece of sushi sticking out of her mouth.

"Hi, Chyna," I said and gave her the receipt, which she took. "Did you see Anubis by any chance? He escaped again." Last time she was the one who found him.

Chyna seemed genuinely concerned, promising if she saw him, she'd let me know, and then she closed the door.

Mom thinks Chyna is a slut, which is Mom's slang for being promiscuous (which does not make you a slut, technically). I love being technical, by the way. Chyna invites a new guy every day. We know this because she asks her male guests to remove their shoes before entering her apartment, leaving the shoes outside the door. Today there was a pair of brown cowboy boots.

I continued along the corridor, knocking on every door. With ten apartments per floor, I knew right away, I was going to have a long night in the thirty-one-story building. Most tenants on my floor were home, but none saw Anubis. I checked the staircase and took the stairs down one level. Thank God, everybody knows me. I babysit several kids in the building and have an excellent reputation, so most people were helpful or felt bad for me. Mrs. Jenkins from 10-F offered me a cookie, and I ate it.

When I knocked on Agnes's door, 10-K, I knew I was in for a battle. Agnes, an elderly woman, lives right below our apartment and continually complains we're too loud by pounding on her ceiling with what sounds like a broom. With a cigarette in her mouth, Agnes opened the door as far as the burglarproof chain allowed, and her hairless Sphynx peeked from under her feet. Her yellowing gray hair hung loosely on her shoulders. Her azure eyes narrowed.

"What?" she spat out, flipping the cigarette ash on the carpet, which landed on her cat. The cat meowed and ran back inside. Her eyes were red, and she looked so frail in a white pajama gown that she always wore. Her hair stuck out in several spots as if she'd been asleep. I began breathing through my mouth because of the stench coming out of her apartment.

"Agnes, I'm sorry for bothering you, but did you see my cat Anubis? My York Chocolate? He ran away again."

"No!" She banged the door to close. The sudden meowing was then heard as other cats scrammed from such a loud bang.

I stood in front of her door, wondering if she'd forgotten to adjust her medication. Mom, a nurse, told me Agnes was suffering from depression and ended up in the hospital at least once a month, thinking she's having a heart attack, which would just be a panic attack in disguise, which, in turn, is merely a cry for attention. I would be depressed, too, if I were her. The murky cloud of cigarette smoke blocked out any evidence of light within her apartment; I was surprised it's not raining from such density. Mom spoke to Agnes's daughter, Antoinette, who traveled from New Jersey during the fake heart attacks. Antoinette said Agnes's apartment is filthy, which of course, I could smell, and also filled with junk because Agnes is a hoarder who's unwilling to get rid of her junk. She had over fifteen cats. According to Dr. Black, Agnes is mentally ill (just like me, but not quite), and was attached to her stuff because it made her feel secure in her home. When Dr. Black mentioned this to me, unwilling to end up like Agnes, I got rid of everything in my apartment that could potentially lead to hoarding.

I heard the lock wiggling, and Agnes exited with a hand-size piece of plaster in her hand.

"Dr. Phil is on full blast again!" she yelled. "My ceiling is falling down!"

"I'm sorry, my mother is watching TV, not me."

"Tell your mother to shove a remote up her snooty ass and turn the freaking volume down before I call the cops!" She propelled the piece of her fallen ceiling toward my face, and I had to back out, or she'd hit me. Once I regained my balance, I took the piece from her hands.

Agnes stepped back, yelling at her cat, "Get back in here, you dumb ass," and shut the door. I took the elevator one floor up and entered my apartment. Mom was watching TV on full blast, just like Agnes said. From below, we could hear Agnes banging on the ceiling—no wonder the plaster was falling down. I was so tired of their disagreements. For some reason, Mom liked pissing off Agnes and gradually turned the volume up more and more. I was livid about Mom losing my cat, but she was clearly unconcerned.

I'd had it! I turned the TV off to Mom's open mouth.

"Mother, get up and help me find Anubis," I said. "We need to check every apartment in our building."

"Don't be crazy and turn the TV back on."

"We need to find him."

"Chloe, he can't escape the building."

"What do you mean?"

"I mean, someone probably saw him and took him. They'll notify the building management."

I called the concierge down in the lobby. Mike was working tonight, and he's a funny guy. He said nobody called about the cat but mentioned that Mrs. Petit from upstairs turned in a gold earring and asked whether it was mine. It wasn't. But I told him it was and took it. No reason to waste good jewelry.

Since the cat hunt was going nowhere, I went to my room and decided to make a flyer. I found a good picture of Anubis on my phone, created a flyer in PowerPoint, and printed out a hundred copies until the printer was out of ink. I went online to a T-shirt making website and ordered ten T-shirts for my friends and myself with Anubis's face on it. I thought for a while and wrote: PUSS ON THE LOOSE in all CAPS. It looked great! It's as if I could be a T-shirt designer. I paid fifty dollars, plus forty-five for next-day shipping, and closed my laptop.

I posted the printed flyers all over my building, two per floor, and also posted one in lobbies of the adjacent to us buildings. I lost count by the tenth. I papered every bus stop and neighborhood businesses all the way from Twenty-eighth Street to Forty-Second Street—encouraging people to give me a call as soon as they saw a cat similar to mine. While having a burger at a diner after all the walking, I received two phone calls. The first caller was a telemarketer, and the second one was my mother telling me we'd be having short ribs for dinner tomorrow night. I texted my girlfriends, asking them to be on a lookout for Anubis. Even if Calyssa lives on Staten Island, Natalia is all the way in Brooklyn, and Lindsay is on the Upper East Side, they all said they would.

I barely slept that night, thinking about Ama Takayoza and the whole kidnapping ordeal. What if someone kidnapped Anubis the way she'd kidnapped Sia? What if a lonely lady saw a black catlet meowing on the street, took him home, and claimed him as hers?

I tossed and turned, wondering if I'd covered enough area with my "Missing Cat" flyers. Maybe I should have gone as far as Spanish Harlem and possibly Brooklyn, posting flyers relentlessly on bus stops and on subway entrances. Even though Brooklyn was across East River, the cat could have easily traveled that far on paw. Never underestimate cats or anything/anyone who plays with balls. I've watched many cartoons about animals and knew for a fact they liked walking.

There was a steady rise in cat crimes in my neighborhood. Anubis's face was third to hit printers this week, along with a Siamese albino beast named Ariel and a Scottish Fold, McFluffy. I feared someone was kidnapping them because if toddlers could be captured, so could be cats. Both species are domesticated and vulnerable, dependent, and light to carry; easy to snatch.

At some point, for a while, the heaving in my chest was so intense I thought I was having a heart attack, which of course, was a panic attack in disguise. However, in my case, a heart attack was hereditary from Daddy, and unfortunately, I was not watching my diet. You'd suspect with a mother for a nurse I'd be swathed with care, but the complete opposite was happening. Mom smoked a pack of cigarettes a day, had three glasses of red wine with dinner, and had an eating disorder, so she barely ate. She enjoyed cooking for me, and I never complained about what's on the plate, especially if it was something Southern. My love for fried food was passed along with Daddy's heritage as he was from Kentucky. Mom was from upstate New York—so she was skinny and/or just annoying.

The next morning, after Mom went to work, our landline rang. I jumped on the phone because I suspected it was about Anubis. It was my French neighbor, Bona Petit, from 13-K, asking me if I could babysit Noah ten to two. She informed me that she completely forgot she had to do something.

By "do something," she meant "do someone," whose name was Dr. Jose Grande, her OB-GYN she was having an affair with. I heard about the Grande-Petit affair from an inside source: my mother. Dr. Grande, Mom says, spits when he speaks—but where he spits when he speaks is a better question. I also heard he has a monster "devise," if you catch my drift, but again, it's most likely a rumor fueled by the sex-deprived nurses at my Mom's hospital.

Noah was only three and a half but smart and chubby beyond belief. Mrs. Petit told me to take the tyke to Central Park, which was a train ride away. The walk to the train was exhausting, but not for Noah, who sat in the stroller the entire way while I pushed the ninety-pound wonder.

Noah loved the swings, and that's precisely where he demanded to take him.

"Swings, swings! Let's go! Faster!" he was shouting from the stroller in the subway. I texted my friend Lindsay and told her I'd be in Central Park by ten-thirty, asking her if she wanted to meet me by the swings. She replied she would. Lindsay is my tall-ish/blond-ish/gorgeous-ish friend who's a live-in nanny on the Upper East Side, on Sixty-eighth Street and Park Avenue. We sometimes meet at Central Park when I babysit for extra cash, while Lindsay is sick and tired of the park being she's there every day.

What I hated about Noah, aside from his Bill Cosby nose, was how bossy he was, which was no surprise considering he was a spoiled brat. The other two kids I sometimes babysat on weekends, twins Lorenzo and Deluca, were petite and polite and liked to play tea parties. Not the beast Noah. He ate nothing but donuts and fatty breakfast sausages I microwaved for him, and just before leaving today, he drank a milkshake designed for a colt. I packed goldfish crackers along with three juice boxes, which he'd munched/sucked on while on the subway.

After exiting at the Fifty-seventh Street, I paused long enough to reach into my tote. I came prepared with flyers about the missing Anubis on the ready. I'd used the Petit's printer to print a hundred more copies as soon as Mrs. Petit left. Using a staple gun, I stapled eleven more flyers before we reached the playground.

I noticed Lindsay from afar, how she was flirtingly playing with her hair —a thin, tall rubber band with flyaway spaghetti strands. Lindsay's child was Charlotte, a beautiful blonde girl, who was four, and just as petit. Charlotte was shy, polite, and weirdly enough, bore a resemblance to Lindsay, as if she were her pet (which, they say, are supposed to resemble their owners). I just wonder how *I* resemble a black cat with my platinum pixie and purple highlights. Compared to Charlotte, Noah looked like a poor pup, drool dribbling out of his mouth, and his protruding belly was a reminder he'd eaten a rhinoceros for breakfast. He did look like my son, though, which was unfair.

Noah jumped out of the stroller before we reached the playground, and galloped forward with me closely behind. He hopped in a swing and yelled, "Push!"

"Oh my God, I'm so glad you're here," Lindsay said, extending her arms for a hug. She was wearing a tight striped sweater in navy blue and skinny black jeans. She looked in shape ad nauseam. Pink heels, as per usual. Charlotte was playing in a sandbox nearby.

"Why? What happened?" I asked as I began pushing Noah.

"Charlotte swallowed a crayon this morning and was choking," Lindsay whispered, but loud enough for me to hear. "I told her mother that crayons were dangerous, but did she listen? Charlotte scared me to death when she started suffocating, and if not for the maid, I'd have a dead child on my hands."

She was either shivering from the cold or from being scared.

"Did you not take a CPR class?"

"No. I lied to Lucky when she interviewed me. I really needed the job. But now I regret it. I should have kept working as a stripper. No suffocating children there."

"You should take a CPR class," I said. "It only lasts for three hours."

"I won't need to. I'm quitting and becoming a nutritionist."

"You're quitting because Charlotte swallowed a crayon?"

"Yes," she said and looked at Charlotte, who played calmly by herself. "You have no idea how scary it was. I don't want to be responsible for her life anymore. It's not worth my nerves. My hair is probably grey if I skip the salon visit next month."

Quarter-life crisis. What a yawner.

I've been there—done that. Lindsay has been talking about quitting this job ever since she started last year. Any little bump on the road and off she goes, unsure what she wants from her life. I envied her because I will never experience that again. When Charlotte swallowed the crayon, it gave Lindsay an excuse to quit. I was through this with Dr. Black six years ago, and I decided to give her big sister's advice.

"It just sounds to me," I said, "this incident was the catalyst that started this whole thing. Dr. Black says when we're scared of facing something, a negative event will prevent us from powering through. Basically, you're acting out of fear."

As soon as I realized I said Dr. Black's name, I shut up. I wasn't going to follow his advice and tell Lindsay I had a mental disorder, because she already seemed stressed enough.

"Who's Dr. Black?" she asked.

My palms got sweaty, and I could feel my cheeks heat. "Um, some doctor I saw on TV."

"Like Dr. Oz?"

"Yes, except Dr. Black is actually black. You know, he's sometimes late for his own show." As soon as I said it out loud, I realized how racist that sounded, and my cheeks got even hotter. I was embarrassed that it even crossed my mind.

"Oh," Lindsay said. "I've never heard of him. What channel is he on?"

"I'm not sure," I said, and from being nervous couldn't remember a single channel. "Um, MTV, I think."

"MTV?"

"Medical Television Network, I think," I lied.

"I see," she said matter of fact. "Anyway, yes, I'm applying to school to be a nutritionist. I've been thinking about this for a while—since this morning. Once I'm accepted, and my student loans go through, bye-bye, baby."

"I think you're overreacting," I said, giving Noah a harder push on the swing.

"No, I've been thinking about this for a while."

"Take a few days to think it over."

"I don't need to think this over. I always loved cooking, and I'd been talking about going to be a certified nutritionist for years. But then my friend said I could make five hundred bucks a night dancing on strip poles, and that's how I became a stripper. Easy cash was just that: easy cash. I didn't want to say goodbye to that until Lucky hired me. Not so lucky anymore, I guess, since I almost killed her daughter. But I want to learn nutrition. I mean, I'm mostly vegetarian anyway—and, did you know when you're hungry you're actually thirsty?"

"Really?" I said.

"Yes. Next time you're hungry, reach for a glass of water, and if you're hungry afterward, then eat. Saves you tons of calories and helps you lose weight."

"Okay, thanks."

"See?" she said. "I want to teach people about nutrition and post these tips on my blog."

"Maybe you *should* be a nutritionist then."

"I'll take some classes for sure. I definitely want to be a chef. Maybe even be on TV; who knows? I watch Food Network all the time. My friend Gretchen also introduced me to horse racing, so I've been putting bets on horses but didn't win anything yet. A psychic told me to bet on this horse, Rex, so fingers crossed."

"I didn't know you were a vegetarian," I said.

"Oh, sure. I even bought a rug shaped like tofu for my room."

"What do you mean by shaped like tofu?"

"It's off-white and rectangular."

"Aren't all rugs shaped like tofu?"

"No," she said and took a sip of water from a reusable bamboo water bottle. Lindsay is earth- and health-conscious and never uses plastic. It must feel nice to be so thin and healthy.

"Well," I said, "how are you sure that's who you're destined to be?"

"I'm not destined to be anything. How do people know they are who they are? Sometimes things just happen. Like, why have you applied to be a flight attendant?"

"Because that will let me travel the world—for free. And that's a career. I'll settle, get a husband, and have a daughter. My ultimate goal. I see myself as an old lady with gray hair—watching my grandkids. The future that resonates with me."

"How are you going to have time for anything if you're never home? Like, if you still had Anubis and moved in somewhere by yourself, how would you take care of him as a flight attendant?"

"Well, Mom can take care of him part-time."

"Don't get mad at me, Chloe, but maybe his disappearance is the sign you needed. Once you get your job, you can live your life for yourself. Without worrying about anything. Free to do whatever you wish. You're still young, no need to rush. It's not like you're mentally ill that you need to fast-forward your life. I mean, listen to you, you're already old, in grey, watching your grandkids."

"It was just an example."

"But that's what I mean by sometimes 'things just happen.' Planning is excellent, but I'm unsure what will happen after my nutritionist school. I could work for restaurants, the government, athletes, or maybe I'll get tired of it and be a stripper again. Who knows? Lucky, before being an oculist, was a florist. Although she has a terrible taste in flowers. Her favorites are marigolds."

"Marigolds?" I asked.

"I know, right? They're such ugly flowers. She has no taste whatsoever."

I was seriously contemplating whether I should tell her that I actually *was* mentally ill and could potentially die from a heart attack or see such hallucinations that could possibly be lethal. Then maybe she should agree that I must fast-forward my life after all.

Lindsay's phone rang then, and while saying "Hold on" to me, she picked up. "Oh my God," she said to whoever was on the other end of the line. "Thanks for calling." She pointed her finger in a way that suggested she needed to take the call and began her conversation.

Noah got tired after swinging for twenty minutes and demanded to go home. I told Lindsay about the T-shirts with Anubis on it, and she swore she'd wear it when hers came.

Mrs. Petit's apartment was similar to ours, with a master bedroom that comfortably fits a king bed, plus two nightstands on either side, a spacious living room, and one more bedroom designated for Noah.

It was past two, and Mrs. Petit was late.

Their apartment bore totems from every country on earth, as the Petits are avid travelers. The leaning shelf in the living room was filled to capacity with gift shop paraphernalia. Nesting dolls and lacquer boxes from Russia, lace napkins from Belgium, handcrafted Chinese teapots, porcelain beer steins from Germany, Venetian masks, Moroccan ceramic plates, and other miscellany. I enviously flipped through a photo album. Mrs. Petit had written an explanation on the back of each photograph with her perfect penmanship. There were places I'd never even heard of, including Tuvalu, Madeira, Comoros, Mauritius, São Tomé and Príncipe, and Vanuatu. The fridge was covered with magnets from pretty much every state in the U.S.

Then, straight out of jealousy, I started making fun of the Petits, imagining myself being on Ellen DeGeneres' show.

"Bona Petit went to Frankfurt," Ellen said.

"For all I know, she went to a bodega across the street and saw a giant frankfurter," I replied.

"The Petits hiked up to the Bitch Mountain in New York," Ellen said.

"Those bitches."

"They had soup in Accident, Maryland," Ellen said.

"The real accident here is Noah," I said.

Ellen laughed and said, "What about Missouri? They went to Mark Twain Nation Forest."

"Missouri is just a fancy word for 'Misery.'"

"What about that picture of the Turtle Tower in Hanoi?" Ellen said.

"How 'Hanoing,'" I replied and yawned.

"They were on Bora Bora."

"Um, boring boring."

At three, Mrs. Petit finally showed up being an hour late. She was glowing from the sex she'd had with Jose Grande. She paid me one-forty cash in seven crisp Jacksons. Without much chitchat, I took the stairs and let myself into my apartment. The package with my Anubis's T-shirts sat by my door. I quickly entered my apartment, cut open the box with a pair of scissors, and pulled out the T-shirts. They looked neat. White fabric with Anubis's black face in the center with PUSS ON THE LOOSE written underneath in pink. I put on the T-shirt that had XLL on the label and texted my friends, asking how soon they could start wearing them. I snapped a couple of photos of myself in the mirror wearing the tee and sent them to Kim. He texted back, saying I looked cute.

A couple hours later, I was reading my book when I received a text message from an unknown number. "Hi, I saw your flyer at the bus stop on Second Avenue, and I think I found your cat. His body is on Thirty-third Street and Second Avenue. I'm really sorry."

Attached was a frowny face emoji and a photo of a dead black cat.

Cat is dead. El gato esta muerto. When you start learning Spanish, you start with simple sentences that make zero sense, like, "This is a pencil." Who talks like that? We need to start with what's real because clearly, life is short. Todos moriremos—We will all die. Tu bebé es feo—Your baby is ugly. These are a handful of examples of sentences that resonate with just about everyone. I could no longer concentrate because of the chatter in my head. The voices had repeatedly been appearing when I was upset, and I should have seen it as a bad sign. They all belonged to different "people" without any faces, and they were screaming at me from different parts of the brain, confusing me further.

You're a cat killer!

Hasta la vista, baby.

Eres estúpido.

When will you finally die?

You're a danger to society, Chloe.

On and on and on.

I took two hits of marijuana to calm down, and the chatter dissipated. I knew the voices were not real, but it didn't matter what I knew—they were still *there*. However, each time it happened, it was getting worse, and I honestly thought I should start retaking Clozapine. Then Dr. Clemens's face would appear ahead, as if he was right in front of me, saying, "You'll die from a heart attack, you fat girl!"

"She will anyway!" a voice from the ether added.

When I opened my eyes, the voices were gone. Apparently, I had fallen asleep. I was feeling at odds, and for a minute, I sat on my couch, trying to remember what had just happened. That's the thing with weed—it helps you forget all your problems, but doesn't help with remembering. My body felt svelte and light, and I briefly closed my eyes, imagining myself all skinny and gorgeous like Lindsay. Would people actually stop and stare at me? Why does this society only care for thin people?

Since my phone was on my lap, I touched the screen to unlock it, and there it was, a picture of Anubis staring at me. He was my screen saver. And I suddenly knew the reason for the void I was feeling.

I opened my text messages and looked at the picture that was sent to me, unwilling to believe it. Anubis's ninth life was over on some dirty corner in Kips Bay. When my eyes began to water, I dialed Dr. Black from my home phone, my eyes glued to the screen of my cell. Dr. Black picked up on the third ring.

"Hi, Chloe, I only have five minutes. Is everything okay?"

"Someone found Anubis. He's dead."

"I'm sorry to hear that, Chloe. Who found him?"

"A stranger. I received a text message with a picture of a black cat who looks like Anubis."

"Did you confirm it's your cat?"

"No, I didn't go there. It's too real."

"Chloe, do not be afraid of reality."

"It's my fault."

"It's not your fault."

"He probably died from diabetes because nobody gave him insulin shots."

"That's the fact of life: people and animals die. Todos . . . morimos. It's a part of the agreement."

"I'm not okay with that agreement. I wish my sister were here—she'd know what to do."

"Matilda passed away sixteen years ago."

"She comes back."

"You're detaching yourself from reality, which could lead to another 'episode.'"

"What reality has given me? Nothing but heartaches, failures, and health problems."

"Chloe, are you taking Clozapine?"

"Yes," I lied and sniffled.

"Are you hearing any voices in your head?"

"No," I lied again.

"Are you sure?"

"I'm sure."

"When you start hearing the voices, the focal illusions will come next. There's so much on the line for you: a new job, independence, weight loss. You do not want to lose any of that, do you?"

I had no idea what I wanted. What I didn't want was to see my cat dead on some street corner.

"I have nobody to talk to about my issues, except you," I said. "*That's* what I want. I want friends who can pay attention and not friends who are always glued to their phones. I can't even talk about it with my own mother, who is also 'listening' while I try so hard to win her attention. But no, she's on the phone with Aunt Josephine."

"Have you tried talking to your friends about it?"

"Yes," I lied again.

"Chloe, detaching yourself from reality by not taking your medication will only make matters worse. Do you understand?"

"I do."

"I want you to contact your closest friends, Lindsay, Calyssa, and Natalia. Tell them you need to talk and tell them the absolute truth. After that, you will not feel alone. I really must get going, but I have an opening tomorrow at three. Would you want to take it?"

"Yes, please."

"I'll see you tomorrow at three."

When he hung up, I sent a group message to my friends. "Hi, guys, I need to talk. Really important. Anyone free to hang out?" I attached a cat emoji at the end of the message to hook them. People love mystery, and if you tell them your cat is dead, they won't come to console you but will say they're "sorry to hear" and you'll be still by yourself.

Calyssa replied right away, not in the group text. "Everything okay with the cat?"

I wrote, "Yes, and no. Can you meet me now?"

"If I take the four o'clock ferry, I can meet you at around five. Battery Park works for you?"

"Yes, that's fine."

"I'm babysitting Grace, so I'll bring her with me."

CALYSSA STEPPED OFF THE FERRY IN TIGHTS AND A WINTER coat. A dark green sheet was wrapped around her body, and inside of it sat baby Grace. Her feet in teensy boots and her head were the only two parts of the body sticking out, while the rest of her body was hidden under the sheet. I thought the sheet was smart, unlike strollers, car seats, or those large and unnecessarily expensive baby carriers. I've seen parents carry their toddlers in such a way but never had to do it myself. Calyssa had her favorite Michael Kors bag, in avocado green. I waved until she saw me. Her coal-black hair was in a bubble braid, and she had on Cleopatra makeup, something she'd recently started doing. She looked great. I envied all of my friends. They all had such beautiful figures, perfect makeup, elegant clothes. Maybe I should take Lindsay's advice and drink water when I'm hungry. Perhaps that would help!

"Hi," Calyssa said, approaching me. Grace made eye contact and smiled at me.

"Jesus, she's so cute. I love her monkey hat."

"Right? She's a little fussy today. She's been crying all day until we got on the ferry."

"Do people think you're her mother?"

"Not really. I mean Christina is Asian, for one. This older guy on the ferry with his wife said she looks exactly like me."

I looked at Grace, who was an exact copy of her mother, Christina.

"Really?" I asked.

"Yeah—really. So I told the guy, 'Thank you. And you, sir, look just like your sister.' I knew she was his wife. So he said, 'Oh, no, no, no. That's my wife.' And I said, 'Oh, okay. And this is my *niece*. And my cousin is Asian—but as you can see, I'm not. That's why the baby is Asian. And I'm middle Eastern because my father is from Turkey. So you don't have to say the baby looks like me.'"

I didn't know why she was so upset and worked up about a compliment but didn't want to push, and instead, I asked, "Did he reply?"

"Yes, he said, 'I was just trying to be polite, ma'am.' I told him, 'Polite by lying? Tell me I look twenty-five, give me a hundred bucks, or compliment my boots—that's polite.'"

"You really said that?"

"Ah-hum. Let's go to Battery Park."

We took the escalator down while Calyssa was saying, "I think that's what the problem with our society. We kiss ass way too often. Ask Natalia, she'll tell you. She's Russian, and she would never say I look like an Asian baby. She's not great with compliments either, but at least she's honest. You know?"

I knew. When I showed Natalia a picture of Kim, she said another Russian proverb: "Love is evil—you'd even fall in love with a goat." It's hyperbolic, meaning you never know whom you will fall for. But nobody really knows what she meant by that.

We exited the station, and I let Calyssa navigate the way, while I followed in her wake. "So you're saying," I said, "we should be more direct?"

"Not direct, but honest. I mean yes, I exaggerate sometimes, I admit that. But I never lie when it hurts others; only when it benefits me."

"And *that's* healthy?" I said.

"Of course. I mean, I tell you the truth. You tell me the truth, too, right?"

"Yes," I lied, trying to get the courage to tell her about my schizophrenia. It wasn't as easy as I first thought.

"I will happily lie to my boss," she said, "to my aunt, even to Christina, who always makes me babysit Grace. Not that I mind—I mean, I live with Aunt Sarah and Christina for free—but she still *uses* me. So I came up with lies. Last week I told Christina I had to work when in reality, I came over to Marcus, and we had mind-blowing had sex. A white lie—not bad—right?"

"Absolutely."

"But when it comes to strangers, why *lie* to be polite?" she asked, as if rhetorically. "You'll never see each other again. Might as well be honest. 'You need some Botox, sir,' I added at the end. He really needed it, though."

"I think there's a fine line between telling the truth and being a total bitch."

"I get it—totally get it. But if that's how *he* starts the conversation by lying, I'll be a total bitch. That's fair—right?"

"I guess." I have never seen her this hesitative, repeating "right?" after every sentence, wanting me to agree with her. What was bothering her, and why was she so insecure today?

Calyssa reached into her bag and produced a pouch of dried Turkish apricots. She offered me one, but I declined. Too much sugar. She tossed one in her mouth as if playing basketball and said, "Sorry for talking about myself for so long. I'm a hot mess today—don't ask why. Although if you ask, I don't mind telling you. So you have any news about your cat?"

"He's dead."

She stopped in her tracks, her eyes widening with sadness. When her mouth dropped, she said, "What?" and almost choked on an apricot. I kept banging on her back until she swallowed. "He's *dead*?" she asked.

I handed her my phone, so she could read the text that was sent to me.

"Oh, Chloe," she said and patted my forearm. "Are you sure it's him?"

"I'm pretty sure."

"Did you go over there to look?"

"I won't. I am not at fault here—right?" Now it was me who sounded like she needed reassurance. "Mom was the one who lost him, so *she* should go and take a look. I already forwarded her the text, but she didn't reply."

"Chloe, it's nobody's fault."

"It's Mom's fault. I just got him in October, but it feels like I've had him for longer because of that whole diabetes thing."

"Of course. Anubis was your baby. You even took him to Honolulu with you last year. I know how much he means to you."

"Thanks for seeing me. I really needed your company."

"That's what friends are for."

"Can we talk about something else?" I asked.

"You sure you don't want to ruminate about Anubis and let your emotions out?"

"I'd rather listen than talk right now."

Calyssa gave me a clothed-mouth smile, and her bizarrely huge eyes had sadness in them that told me she really cared. I thought then that she was my best friend. We were slowly walking by the water in Battery Park. A breeze swept the streets a couple of times, messing with Calyssa's braid. My short pixie cut couldn't be bothered by anything, especially with the amount of hairspray it deals with daily.

"Can I tell you about my weekend?" Calyssa asked, and I nodded.

"It was a disaster, let me tell you. So we ordered a new washer and dryer because the old ones broke, right? The new washer and dryer were supposed to come last week, but they didn't, right? So, of course, I ran out of clean underwear and had a sleepover at Marcus's place. I decided to use a coin Laundromat on our block, collected my junk in the bag, and guess what? They had just closed the door, and it wasn't even six. I banged on the door, got the attendant's attention, and yelled: 'I have a sleepover at my boyfriend's, and I need clean underwear. Let me in.' The attendant shook her head and pointed to her watch, like 'We're closed. I don't care about your clean underwear.' I banged on the door again and yelled, 'Big mistake. Big. Huge! Because I'll take my business somewhere else!' And she was like, 'Be my guest.'"

I smiled, envisioning the scene in my head, and said, "Did you take your business somewhere else?"

"No, I went commando. In fact, Marcus liked it better."

We assembled ourselves on a bench overlooking New Jersey, the famous Colgate Clock ahead of us showing it was five fifteen. Grace's eyes were now closed, her cheeks pink due to the fifty-degree weather.

"How's Christina?" I asked, referring to her cousin she lived with.

"She's stupid, as always. Last night we were discussing sex with celebrities and guess who she picked?"

"Who?"

"Spiderman."

"But he's not real," I said.

"Exactly. First of all, I told Christina, Spiderman doesn't like to have sex with Asian women. I heard it from a trustworthy source: The Invisible Man. But second, Spiderman spends too much time climbing buildings and that's a dangerous way to have intercourse. I'm all about safety: No having sex and climbing."

I laughed. "You're such a nerd."

Grace looked exactly like Sia Shirtley, the "no longer" kidnapped baby. Same button nose, rosy cheeks. I knew Sia had been returned, but my, my. Imagine if she hadn't. Calyssa would be arrested pronto. That reminded me of the Anubis's T-shirt I brought for her in a small size, but I decided there was no point in giving it to her anymore. He was dead.

Calyssa plowed on, "Remember I told you about how I was almost mugged?"

"You didn't get mugged."

"Well, *almost.* I mean, at the time, I thought I was going to get mugged."

"Right."

"I didn't tell you the whole story—that's why."

"It gets worse?" I said.

"Much worse. That day I borrowed another diamond ring from work. Don't freak out. It cost twenty thousand dollars." She paused to let that information sink in. Twenty-thousand-dollar ring, I thought to myself and imagined it. I'm pretty sure in a cartoon, my pupils would have become diamonds.

She continued, "It was platinum with the most precious diamond I've ever seen. I get off the ferry, in this unsafe Republican heaven called Staten ISIS, right? And so I see this guy following me. There was nothing valuable on me except the stupid ring. I see his shadow approaching me, but I'm too scared to turn to face him. I pick up my pace—so does he. I swear I could feel his breathing down my neck, and even the hair on my legs stood up from fear—I didn't shave that day. There were zero people around, which is just my dumb luck. Believe it or not, but that day I wished for peace and quiet—friggin' karma." She breathed in and out and pushed on. "So I'm walking, he's close behind. I take off the ring and down my throat in goes."

"What?"

"I swallow the ring. This way, he can't take it—right? I know then he is going to pull out a gun and be like, 'Money or I'll shoot you.' And what would I say? 'Here, take the twenty-thousand-dollar ring.'? Now the most expensive thing on me was my Gooseberry, but how would a guy know the value of a Michael Kors' bag? I had all the aces now."

"Jesus. You swallowed the twenty-thousand-dollar ring?"

"As soon as I swallowed it, the guy turned, like a soldier—bam—one hundred and eighty degrees—into a completely different direction. I stop and watch him as he approaches a black BMW and drives off. I stand there, dumbfounded, wondering what the heck did I just do."

"Oh, my God."

"Right? But wait. It gets worse." She loudly sighed.

"It can't get worse than that."

"Oh, much worse. To get the ring back, I need to poop it out."

She was staring at me for a while, while I contemplated what to say.

"Now I get your problem," I said. "You have to poop in a colander and wash it under running water? I've seen it in a movie somewhere."

"No, Chloe, pooping in a colander is not a problem. I mean, it is a problem on its own, but not currently. The real problem is, I've been constipated for three days."

"For three . . . whole . . . days?"

"Yes, for three . . . consecutive . . . days."

"In . . . a . . . row."

I didn't know what to think. Calyssa told me her dumb story without feeling ashamed to sound ridiculous. Why was I scared to tell her the truth about my mental disease? Her phone beeped, and she looked at the screen, saying, "Oh, shit."

"What?"

"It's my boss, Spit Ew."

"Spit Ew? What kind of name is that?" I asked.

"Well, his name is Andrew, which Jen and I diminished to Drew. But after all the spitting, we downgraded him to Ew. He's asking me if I saw the twenty-thousand-dollar ring." Her eyes doubled in size.

"He doesn't know you borrowed it?"

"Of course not. But it's not like I'm stealing them. I wear them for a day or two and return them."

"That's no good."

She stood up and readjusted her bag over the shoulder. "Chloe, I hate to break this short, but I better head on home and poop out that thing—if that's the last thing I do. Any suggestions?"

"Prune juice."

"Good call. I'm sorry about Anubis. Let's catch up next week."

"Sure."

I stood up, and she gave me a quick hug, saying, "Everything will be okay. Call me if you need me."

She hopped along the promenade toward the Staten Island ferry, while I turned in the opposite direction and went for a walk. While waiting in line for a hotdog, I received a text message from Mom.

This dumbass Indian chick, Alaknanda—hell knows what her name is—was at the hospital. She'd masturbated with a Chiquita, and it got squashed inside her anus. She couldn't get it out but finally used her daughter's miniature shovel. All she had to do was douche.

For some reason, I found it hilarious. I typed back: *Wow, people are stupid.*

Roger that. The pubic area is not for fresh produce.

Is she gonna be okay?

Sure, I was glad it wasn't a pineapple. But trust me, a white woman would never do a thing like that.

Mom was being racist again. Every time a person of color stepped foot in her hospital, Mom's first response was, "A white person would never do a thing like that." Dr. Black told me to talk to her about that, but again I was too chicken to bring up issues that mattered to me. He said I liked to sweep thing sunder my rug, and I jokingly told him it was our maid Siriporn who did the sweepin' in our house.

I decided not to fuel Mom's racist rage and didn't reply. She sent me a message anyway.

That's not why Alaknanda came to the hospital, though. She was scared she damaged her anus because her poop had been coming out red.

I was wondering why everyone wanted to tell me their poop stories today.

What happened to her? I wrote.

I asked her if she ate any beets. She said yes. I said: well, that's why your poop is red, you stupid Chiquita squasher.

I can't believe it.

Me neither; everybody knows you must use organic bananas. At least. Or a dildo. Anyway, Chloe, I saw your message about Anubis. I went to the corner to take a look. It's not him.

Attached was a picture of the same cat that was sent to me earlier, but the picture was now clear because Mom's phone has a high-quality camera. The cat in the photo was brown.

It's definitely not him! I wrote.

We'll find him. Don't worry.

That meant even if my catlet was still on the loose, at least he was alive. While walking toward the subway, I skipped like a little girl. I had the hotdog I purchased in one hand and a bottle of water in another, but I was not even hungry. I was beyond happy. When a homeless guy blocked my way, I did not feel like a fight.

"Can you give me some money?" he asked. "I'm hungry."

The smell coming from him was offensive, his skin smothered with white flakes, which could have been a rash. Mom would bathe me in iodine if she knew I even breathed in his direction. But I felt generous. I remembered what Lindsay told me about hunger and thought I'd use my new knowledge.

"Actually," I told him. "You're probably just thirsty." I handed him the water bottle, and he took it.

"No," he said. "Actually, I'm fucking hungry."

"You're thirsty. Trust me. Drink this bottle of water, and let's see if you're still hungry."

He rolled his eyes and downed the bottle in three seconds flat,

"Still hungry," he said.

Hm, I thought to myself. Maybe Lindsay's theory was wrong.

"Do you want my hotdog?"

He nodded. "Yes."

I handed him the hotdog wrapped in aluminum foil and to his "Thank you" I jumped down the stairs to the 6 train, suddenly hungry, and now also thirsty. But I was happy about Anubis being alive that I didn't mind the garbles of my stomach.

Mom messaged me when I got off the subway in Murray Hill.

Chloe, pick up some bananas. I think I'm low on potassium. I've been feeling really thirsty today. Just make sure they're organic and RIPE..

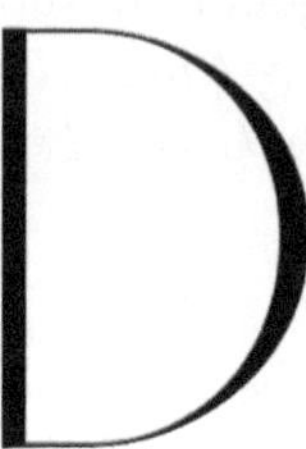

Devouring a red velvet cake I'd baked, I flipped through channels on the TV until I caught Paula Deen. I had just smoked a joint and drool instantly accumulated in my mouth at the sight of Paula Deen's fried chicken, perfectly golden and still sizzling hot. It was Friday morning, so Mom was at work. I *had* been craving fried chicken for a while; was that a sign? I made my way to the kitchen where we kept takeout menus from the local restaurants, and while leafing through them, the home telephone rang. When I looked at the caller ID on a headset that was lying on the kitchen counter, I didn't recognize the number, but it had a 212 area code indicating a New York City landline. I knew this because my home number also started with a 212. Who was that? With the headset still in hand, I returned to the living room, turned down the volume on the TV, and pressed the talk button.

"Hello?" I said.

"May I speak with Noe Tenderfoot, please?" The voice belonged to an older woman with a raspy voice resembling Marge Simpson.

"Noe?" I asked. "You mean Chloe?"

"Maybe. There's a huge drop of ink, and it looks like Noe."

"*Who* is this?"

“Barb Dwyer, with the Southern Wings.”

When she mentioned “wings,” at first, I thought she meant chicken wings, and my stomach produced an unpleasant sound. Barb Dwyer? Who was she? Then it suddenly hit me when I realized the dame was a hiring manager with the flight attendant job. We were supposed to have an interview a week from now, and I felt a jolt. Why was she calling a week earlier? To tell me some bad news? I straightened up my back anyway, and my heart began to pump harder. That was a dumb time to call just as I smoked some pot.

“Hello?” she said. “Noe, are you here?”

“Hi, sorry. How are you?” I cheerfully said. “It’s actually just Chloe, not Noe.”

She snorted. “Do you have a minute for our phone interview?”

“I do. I thought it was a week from now.”

“I went through the pile of applicants faster than I thought. None were qualified enough—imbecile doofuses. Your application was next. I’m in a little bit of a rush and want to jump in: Why do you think you’re a good addition to our team?”

My mind was relaxed after the pot, and I couldn’t concentrate. “I’ve worked in customer service before. Love it. Love people. I am goal-oriented, hardworking, and punctual. Love people—did I say that?”

“Yes.”

“Oh.”

“Where did you work in customer service?”

“I was a barista in high school.”

“I see that from your resume. Chloe, is it? This position requires a lot of movement, and of course, we couldn’t hire someone in a wheelchair.”

“I’m perfectly mobile.”

“What did you like about working in customer service?”

“I loved meeting new people, and my goal was to always have a satisfied customer.”

She snorted again. “Dealing with stressed-out passengers who want to be treated like royalty even if they buy the cheapest seats isn’t easy.”

“I understand.”

“You have to be tidy in appearance, and you cannot panic under any circumstances. There are many a passenger scared of flying. Can you think of a situation when you dealt with an angry customer?”

“Many times.”

“Just one is fine.”

I couldn't think of anything. While I indeed worked as a barista back in high school, more so because I liked the cute boys working alongside, remembering a story from years ago was not something I was capable of. Lindsay and Calyssa were both such good liars, and I envied how with such ease, they could unleash fibs as fast as their mouths opened.

"Chloe?" Barb said impatiently.

"Sorry, my cat is pulling on the cord." I start sweating when lying, and I felt heat coming to my face—thank God for a phone interview and not an in-person one. "When I was working a barista, there was this customer . . . good-looking young man . . . who swallowed a ring because he thought he was being mugged."

"And?" she said.

"The ring cost him twenty thousand dollars. My friend Calyssa says it's a real thing—they sell them at her store. Even more expensive ones. But the guy started complaining because he wanted to become a nutritionist. He was petrified. Just like my friend Lindsay. I had to calm him down." I was now extraordinarily sweaty. Also, I was shaking and felt cold, but my ears were burning, and according to the mirror ahead, red.

Barb sniffled, establishing her presence. "I'm not sure I understand. Was the customer angry?"

"Real angry. He left and went across the street, where there was another Starbucks."

Barb took the time with her reply. "I'm not sure I understand what you're trying to tell me. You will deal with such customers daily who are complete idiots. In any event, you sound fine. I'm reading over your application, and everything looks good. Except that you skipped a question about your weight."

"My weight?"

"Yes. How skinny are you?"

She was getting too personal, and I didn't like it one bit. "Is it vital to my employment?" I asked.

"Absolutely." Barb coughed so loudly into the phone without covering the mouthpiece. She said, "Sorry, Chloe. Yes, weight is the most crucial part."

"I don't believe I understand why."

"We are not allowed to discriminate based on gender, age, sexual orientation, or religion. Our aircraft fly domestically, as you know, and they are small. Requirements to be a flight attendant are strict. While we do not have a certain height restriction, you know for a fact people who are over six-foot-four are too tall. Same with the weight. There are no weight standards. However, you need to be able to fit comfortably into a jumpseat. Are you following me?"

"Not really."

"You're five-seven. For your height, you should be anywhere from a hundred and ten to a hundred and twenty pounds."

"Oh," was all I could say in response. At one hundred and ninety pounds, I was overweight, not just for health reasons or for aesthetic reasons, but for work reasons as well. I had to sit down on the couch as quite literally I felt like I was sinking into the ground, right down into the apartment below, where cranky Agnes was probably faking another heart attack.

"I'm one hundred and thirty pounds," I managed to say, lying, my mouth dry—man was I thirsty. I knew a hundred and thirty pounds was still higher than the requirement, but at least it wasn't ridiculously far off. One white lie to make me feel better. The way Calyssa does.

Barb coughed, but not as loud this time. "Darn it!" she said. "You're so close, Chloe, with just ten pounds to lose, though twenty-five would be ideal. Right now, you're too fat. You're definitely qualified for the position, but you need to lose those last ten pounds before your training begin, which could take a few months. We weigh in our flight attendants before their shifts. Every . . . single . . . time."

"Oh," I said, still in shock.

I felt a lump in my throat. What a feeling: within the course of the conversation, I experienced a jolt of excitement to only end up in a pool of disappointment. It's like being told, "You're an attractive . . . whore," or "Great legs . . . your mother has."

Barb said, "I'll keep your application handy. Call me back when you lose weight, okay?"

I nodded without replying and hung up.

I wasn't going to live alone, after all. I was too fat for a job; how ridiculous was that? I knew I was overweight, but that rejection just topped the cake. Lindsay was right about how to tame hunger. By the time I finished the conversation with Barb, my tummy was producing all sorts of hungry noises, but when I drank two glasses of water, the hunger went away. Maybe I'd found a way to lose weight. Now it was all about the timing. I envisioned that if I could lose a pound a week—the safest way to lose weight according to the medical research—I could get to a hundred and twenty pounds in seventy weeks, just a bit over a year. I was up for a challenge. To celebrate my newly-found health kick, I finished the red velvet cake, ordered a three-piece fried chicken from Papa Wing (no biscuit to save on the calories), and had two more glasses of water, which filled me up. I'm telling you—the water trick was working.

That same evening, I called Kim, and we made plans to watch a movie at his place, a universal code for humping. Kim's roommates were out of town, which meant sex on the kitchen counter, so long as there were no pizza crumbs like the last time. I'm all about stimulation during copulation, but that was literally a pain in the butt. After my unfortunate conversation with Barb Dwyer, I needed to see him. Funny how sadness makes you desperate for company, especially when you can forget about your misfortunes by smoking and having sex. I now felt terrible for telling Dr. Black that Kim wasn't husband material because as soon as I was upset, Kim was the only person there for me. Maybe he was husband material, after all. I could make an honest man out of him, as the saying goes, and he clearly enjoyed my curves, which I hoped wasn't a fetish of his, because I was determined—with all seriousness—on losing the damn weight. I stopped at his place on the way back from the Upper West Side, where I'd watered Aunt Josephine's plants since she and Analise were in Greece.

When Kim opened the door, I melted into his arms like butter in a hot pan. I could care less about the piles of dishes in the sink. We got stoned, ordered pizza, and then we did an adult thing with the lights off.

E

Every night for the past couple weeks, I had been hearing voices in my head—which I assumed was happening because I was not taking Clozapine. Some of the voices told me what to do, some shamed me for being fat or unemployed. Some voices shared the secrets of the Universe, but since it was all really scientific, I didn't understand anything. Same with when I watch anything with Neil deGrasse Tyson, the famous astrophysicist. I could listen to him all day on TV: weed, pizza, Neil—in that order—a perfect day. He has a soothing voice, and the images on the screen are fantastic, even if I understand less than 1 percent of it. The same with the voices. They appear out of nowhere and disappear just as fast, leaving me scared and wondering whether I should go back on Clozapine, which meant a road to an inevitable heart attack. I was so confused I wanted to cry. I'd stopped Clozapine three whole weeks ago but hadn't seen any hallucinations, just the voices, and wondered if maybe my schizophrenia was a thing of the past. Perhaps eventually, I could learn to live with the voices so long as I could distinguish between which are real and which are fake. Maybe a new medication would hit the market and it would work better than Clozapine without any side effects.

Dr. Black was right: I had been escaping reality. In the real world, nothing was working for me: my cat disappeared, my boyfriend was a skinny pothead who wasn't washing his dishes, and most importantly, I couldn't get my dream job as a flight attendant because I was overweight.

My new goal was to lose forty pounds to start. That night, after I left Kim's apartment, a voice in my head was telling me that I'm beautiful the way I am. Another voice was suggesting that I should apply for another job, where I would not be discriminated against because of my weight. A third voice told me I wouldn't get another job and that my dream of having a family of my own was ruined forever now that Kim was my "it's-not-going-anywhere-with-him" boyfriend.

I had no one to confide in about the voices, not even Dr. Black—because he believed I was taking my medication. I personally thought I was schizophrenia- and venereal disease-free, and it was only Clozapine that was making me sick, raising my triglycerides levels. I was also livid about the fact that I must rely on Clozapine for the rest of my life, and it wasn't cheap at over two hundred bucks per bottle per month. That was settled then: my new routine would be no more Clozapine, a better diet, and plenty of exercise.

Maybe, just like Lindsay, I should apply for school too, I mused, perhaps somewhere warm, or even in Europe. In the meantime, I'd be drastically losing weight and growing out my tresses, and by the time I graduated, I'd be svelte with Lindsay-like spaghetti strings. Perhaps opening my own business was not that far off. I could breed cats with an excellent pedigree and sell them. What do I need? I wondered and assumed a management degree.

As I was about to look up graduate schools, I caught myself on a thought that the conversation with Barb Dwyer was a catalyst for my desperation. I was acting based on fear rather than reason, which is precisely what happened to Lindsay when she decided to quit her job because Charlotte swallowed a crayon. Calyssa acted out of fear as well when she swallowed the ring. I was desperate for change. But at the same time, I was hoping someone would finally find Anubis, and things could go back to normal. A change was scary, because it was real. I was confused about what I was doing with my life. And even Mom was not home to hear the bad news. She was working an overnight shift and texted me at ten thirty at night.

Guess who I saw today at the hospital? Our neighbor from 11-F, the Asian one, Chyna, or whatever? She's being treated for syphilis (haw haw). Serves her right. If you happen to take an elevator with her, make sure you wash your hands right after. White girls would never let themselves go so low.

Okay, Mom.

Oh, and I checked her sodium intake. You won't believe the numbers. 160 mEq/L. It's all in the soy sauce. Yesterday, another delivery guy mistook our door for hers. Sushi again. Alaskan roll and avocado roll. She should just eat the rolls from her fat belly. Do we have any Advil? My back's been bothering me today.

Yes, we do, I typed back. Some things, like racist, hypochondriac mothers who like to gossip, never change. Could I, though, change? I dearly hoped so. I took a few hits of the weed, finished a potato gratin that Mom had made, and that helped me forget everything. No more voices.

The next day, I took a long walk around Manhattan. I needed time to myself to think and to sort things out. I figured if I started to lose weight, maybe I should go back on Clozapine because triglycerides wouldn't be a problem anymore. Earlier that morning, the voices in my head were so loud I could barely finish my bacon and eggs, four of each. The voices started to get on my nerves, and Clozapine could potentially stop them.

On the other hand, how would I ever know if I was getting better if I kept taking the medication? I had no idea what to do, and there was nobody to talk to about it. I felt lonely and alienated, and while bypassing Times Square full of people and families, I realized how ironic that was. The city that never slept had eight million people and not a single solitary soul to open up to. I saw a sign for *Wicked*, and I was so sick of myself I realized, while checking myself out in a glass building, I looked as green as Elphaba.

I was sitting on a bench near Chelsea Piers, when my friend Natalia texted me, saying, *I have some mews! Whatcha meowing?*

She thought it was cute when she made cat puns like *mews* instead of *news* or *right meow* instead of *right now*. It was cute when I had the cat, now it was annoying and more confusing than anything.

I texted back: *I'm in Chelsea by the Hudson.*

Let's mew up for dinner.

Where?

Mexican Restaurant called Sombrero at seven, mewyes?

See you there!

Even if I was annoyed at her for the cat puns, I still wanted to see her. I was wearing my PUSS ON THE LOOSE tee with Anubis's face on it and stopped by my apartment to pick up a medium one for Natalia. Kim and Mom already got theirs. Lindsay and Calyssa were next.

I was at Sombrero by six fifty-two since I always arrive early. And since Natalia was not on the premises, I told the host I'd wait by the bar, where I instantly ordered myself a margarita with salt on the rim. The bartender was not very attractive, rail-thin, and yellow in appearance, his back hunched. His fingers were long, like ten slender churros. He quickly shook the drink and brought the margarita, for which I paid cash.

I had never been to this restaurant before, and I really liked the interior, high ceilings, the tastefully decorated dining area in a Spanish motif. A perfect spot for a date. Kim had never taken me on a date because he's always broke, but I was hoping he would. I even offered to pay a few times, but he is stubborn as a cat.

Edison bulbs hung low from the ceiling throughout the restaurant. The wait staff was attired in black jeans with black tops, and I counted two male waiters and one waitress who was as heavy as me. I wondered if I could work as a waitress. The idea had never appealed to me, but clearly, the requirements were not as strict as being a flight attendant.

Something to think about.

I looked at my watch. It was 7:05 p.m., fifteen minutes since I arrived. Natalia is always late.

Mom sent me two text messages.

Pick up some eggs. I need to bake a cake tomorrow, and I forgot.

The second one was about our neighbor Steven.

That skank told me he was going to Disney World for a week. Let's plan our vacation tomorrow.

While replying to Mom, a shadow covered me.

"Sorry, I'm late," Natalia said as she plopped herself loudly on a chair next to mine. It was merely 7:07 p.m. We hugged to greet each other.

"That's okay," I lied, but it was not okay; I was royally annoyed.

The hostess showed us to our table, and I walked behind Natalia. Her brown hair was now collected into a ballerina bun, which was out of character for her. She usually wore it down in beautiful, shining ripples, making my platinum pixie with purple highlights resemble a teenager with anger issues. She was wearing pantyhose with leggings and boots. Black knee-length skirt, red off-shoulder blouse, and a red jacket. I wondered if Natalia ever looked down on me, being so—well—grown-up looking.

As soon as we sat down and our male server greeted us, we ordered guacamole. A different server brought chips and salsa. I dipped two chips into the salsa and what a delight they were.

But that was the extent of me having a good time. From that moment on, everything was about to change—absolutely everything. The image in front of me started resembling an old family video recording finished with blurry lines for a vintage effect. Natalia had divided in two, and her speech had become slurred. Her face got squished and then stretched.

Right away, I knew what it was: my first hallucination. Dr. Black had warned me about that. He said after the voices, the hallucinations would follow—and did they ever. I didn't want to scare Natalia or give her any indication that I was scared, so I downed an entire glass of water and focused on her lips.

"What is your *mews*?" I asked, mocking her puns. "You sounded excited."

Natalia was looking behind my shoulder, and I followed her gaze. She was staring at an attractive man in a suit sitting alone at the bar, looking back at her.

Flirtingly, she positioned one leg top of another, which would reveal more of her thigh for the man to see. Mom calls girls like her whores, and that's what word came to mind. She now looked at me when she said the weirdest thing to me, "I had the best of days, Chloe. The best. After hearing Calyssa's story where she almost got killed—"

"Mugged," I interjected. "Not killed."

"Same to me," she said. "I realized if I died on the alley—Staten Island of all places—eesh—my heritage would die with me. So I started shopping for some children online. And guess what now? I'm a mommy mew." As she said that, she flirtatiously dropped her shoulder, which glistened under the dim lights above, and lowered the red blouse. She tilted her head slightly toward the bar as if seeking our server. She sucked in her cheeks behaving like a—*WHORE*, I heard Mom's voice inside my head shout. *WHORE. WHORE. WHORE.*

I shook my head, which helped silence Mom's voice. The man, I noticed, was still staring at Natalia, and I was annoyed. In my Anubis's tee, I must have looked invisible to him, even if I, too, wanted male attention.

"Natalia, can you pay attention to me?" I asked. "You're a mommy—what do you mean?"

She turned her head back to me and said, "Sorry—I was looking for our waiter."

Yeah, right. Mom's voice again. *WHORE. WHORE. WHORE.*

"Mom, stop!" I said aloud to Natalia's confused face. I covered my mouth, and since my water was finished, I gulped from the margarita glass.

"I meant," I said. "Go on."

"Oh," she said, all nonchalant-like as if my screaming out was explained and forgiven. She picked up her phone from the table and turned the screen in my direction, saying, "I adopted these two African wonders today."

In front of me was a photograph of two black children who were five to seven years of age. I picked up the phone in my hands, mesmerized by the jungle on the background. The kids were boys, shirtless, hugging each other as if they were brothers. It was a good quality shot with the sun blazing on the background.

"You adopted them?" I asked, shocked. This was so out of the blue.

Whore.

Stop, Mom.

She's a whore. And so are you.

I closed my eyes and breathed out. The interruption of my thought process was beyond annoying.

I asked, "The kids will be living with you?"

"No, don't be silly," she said. "I'll send them twenty dollars a month, which pays for their food, clothes, and school. The first one is Akuchi, and the second one is Kwanza," she said, pointing at the screen as if I didn't know which one was first and which one was second. "Of course, I renamed them to Rich and Brown, respectively. I'm allowed to visit them anytime I wish—but in Africa—so probably not often—but first, I'm planning to adopt a whole village of Akuchis and Kwanzas and visit them all at once. How exciting is it? I'm a fucking parent, Chloe. A parent! You know what it means for me? Everything."

I was in a terrible mood by then. Natalia was making me mad by making fun of two underprivileged kids who were now "hers," as if money could buy everything. Money could not buy me the brain I wanted, nor would it help me lose weight. But the fact that Natalia was "buying" a whole village of kids made me tremble with rage.

"Why did you name them Rich and Brown?" I asked.

"I wanted to Americanize them. Then I'll teach them math."

"I had no idea you could adopt kids in such a way without having them living with you."

"Oh, there's all sorts of things you can do," she said and picked up the phone from my hands. I suddenly realized why I was so mad at her. She was living *my* dream. She'd found a way to have kids—and I—being a natural-born woman—have not. Being transgender disallowed her to have children of her own, so she went to adoption. I felt anger. That conversation with Barb Dwyer earlier was the catalyst for hostility.

"Chloe, are you okay?" she asked me.

"Yes, why?"

"You're so red—look."

The selfie camera on her phone was facing me, and I looked at the screen, noting that not only was I read but also puffy around the eyes with my ears sticking out. Ugh. I hated the way I looked.

"I'm fine," I lied. I feel like being silent. I was hot, and a drop of sweat was traveling down my back, dripping straight to the crack in my butt, which was uncomfortable.

The server approached us. "Would you like to order, or would you need another minute?"

"I'll have the chicken tacos," Natalia said. "Make sure the chicken is either fresh or organic, please. And no gluten in the tacos, correct?"

"I'll double-check."

"No cilantro, please, and no sour cream. I can't have dairy today."

There she goes again, I thought, becoming angrier. I seriously wanted to kick her shin like an angry kid at a playground.

"I'll have the shrimp tacos," I interrupted her. "And I don't care what it comes with. I'm not picky."

The waiter smiled—he was on my side. "Chicken and shrimp, coming right up. Any drinks?"

"Yes," Natalia said. "I'll have a frozen mango margarita, but please make sure the mango is fresh, preferably from Africa, now that I have kids from there. No salt or sugar on the rim. If you have tequila from Africa, that would be best."

"And for you?" the server asked.

I did not feel like talking anymore, annoyed at Natalia, and her "pickiness" and only realized after the fact how curt I was. (Did you ever notice that if you replace the letter "r" in curt with the letter "n," you'll get two different words with an exact same meaning?)

"Margarita," I said.

"Frozen or on the rocks?"

"Frozen."

"Sugar or salt on the rim?"

"Salt."

The server took our menus and disappeared, while I glanced in his wake, watching his cute tushie bouncing its way toward the kitchen.

"So, what do you think about my kids?" Natalia asked. "Aren't they cute? I love that they're black."

I put my leg on top of another, which kicked Natalia the way I wanted. I didn't even apologize, but I noticed movement under the table like she was moving her legs out of the way.

"Why?" I asked.

"We need some color in our lives."

I closed my eyes and opened them, trying to sound reasonable. "Mom, you're being racist."

"Thanks for calling me a mom. I know it was racist—it was intentional."

"Huh?"

"Racism is necessary."

"What are you gabbing about?"

"Look, racism is just like religion—it brings people closer."

"Racism is believing your race is superior to another race. How is that a good thing?" I said. I was flummoxed right now. I couldn't quite remember where we were located, as if I never knew.

"All I am saying is," Natalia said, "we use racism to our advantage when we need it. I'm not saying it's a good thing—it's just a tool in our toolbox. Just watch any documentary about prisons, and you'll see the segregation. If I adopt black children and then say a racist comment by mistake, nobody would question me because then I'd be like—sorry, my kids are black, so I'm not racist—get it now?"

"I *don't* get it," I said. "We are not in prison."

"We are. We are in a prison of our own minds. Trust me, I read a lot of self-help books, so I'm an expert."

With Sia Shirtley's current disappearance and reappearance, the topic of racism was gaining popularity at a rapid speed, and the last thing we needed was another civil war. And I'd have enough.

"Adopting is expensive," I said, changing the topic.

"It's not expensive. It costs ten bucks per child. Many of the kids look half in size, so I'm only planning to give those kids four-forty. I think I'll stop accumulating them when I adopt fifty-two, like a deck of cards. I ought to come up with a concept for how to recognize them and categorize them. Maybe I'll ask them to write their names in chalk on their foreheads. Maybe I'll categorize them by height, weight, or by how many rings each girl can put on her neck."

"What do you mean, rings?"

"You've never seen any documentary about Africa? The longer the neck, the prettier they're considered. They also stretch out their earlobes until they're long and resemble fettuccini—it's like a beauty thing. I plan to have at least ten fettuccini daughters."

"So you're adopting them why—to show how more superior you are to them?"

"Don't be silly. I need to start building my own family. If I die, so does my estate—my legacy—all the money I've earned. As you know, my mom's in Russia, and I have no other siblings. She stopped talking to me when I told her I was transgender, so I need to have kids of my own who will not discriminate against their own relative—their generous mother from New York. Once I cut my 'rooster,' I'll be a complete woman. By then, I may have several villages of Riches and Browns."

"What rooster are you cutting?" I asked. "Is that another proverb?"

"You don't know what a rooster means?" she asked in a condescending tone. "The pistol."

"What pistol? I don't understand what you mean."

"My cock!" she yelled loud enough for the man at the bar to hear. She covered her mouth and added, "I've never cut my penis—as you know. I was speaking metaphorically. We call it a rooster in Russian to make it sound less offensive."

"Oh."

"You Americans. Everything must be spelled out for you. You can't *think* metaphorically. Do you think the guy knows I'm transgender?"

"What guy?"

"At the *bar*," she whispered, annoyed like I was supposed to know.

"Yes," I said as a means to hurt her. I was being a "curt" with an "n," and I could care less.

Natalia was transitioning from a man to a woman in a most peculiar fashion. She'd found a pair of the most prominent boobs a credit card could buy but was in no rush to continue. She spent money left and right while working as a professional gambler. Profession gambler—in her own words—was someone who played poker for a living. She'd trained to lie flawlessly, to bluff like nobody's business, and to place bets with 99-percent accuracy. She was stalling the transitioning process, and instead, she was focused on "adopting" African kids. I was curious why she was waiting until the last minute to cut off her "rooster." Maybe the kids were her idea of distraction. Change, Dr. Black said, is scary, and that's why she wasn't ready to change. None of us are prepared to change because change comes with consequences—the foremost being a loss. We lose a part of ourselves, and Natalia would lose an actual physical piece of herself, which also ties to her emotionally.

Suddenly a question popped in my head. "Natalia, I get it why the Russian call it a rooster because here we call it a cock. But why the Russians call it a 'pistol'? I don't get it."

"I don't know," she said. "Maybe because a pistol shoots? Get it?"

"Oh," I said.

"Do you wanna see a vagina I'm buying?" she said, smiling from ear to ear.

Natalia found her phone and started swiping the screen, looking for a picture.

"Buy a vagina?" I asked, confused.

"Exactly. The vagina I'm buying costs twenty-five grand, and mine will resemble Jennifer Aniston's."

"What are you talking about?"

"My friend Oksana purchased a vagina just like Gwen Stefani's. The surgeon who did it is an artist, or more like a sculptor. Since I only have one chance to make it right—I want to make it *right*."

"It makes no sense that he could sculpt a vagina resembling Jennifer Aniston's."

"I have pictures to prove it."

"To me, all genitalia look alike."

"You have to treat your genitals with respect, Chloe. If you don't respect your vagina, you know what happens?"

"What?" I asked, curious where this conversation was going.

"Even your own pussy runs away from you," she said, snorting with laughter and pointing at my chest with a finger. I followed her gaze to the picture of Anubis on the T-shirt I was wearing.

"What?" I asked.

"Your cat—pussy—escaped. Get it now?"

"Well, that's rude. He's not a pussy."

"It was a joke, Chloe. Relax."

Our drinks arrived, and Natalia took a sip right away. Her jokes sometimes made zero sense, like today. Or was I imagining things?

"Speaking of your pussy," she said, "did you find Anubis yet?"

"No, and he's not a pussy," I repeated and took a long swing of my drink.

"Fine," she said, "it's not a pussy. But Anubis *was* your child, you know. Rich and Brown don't look dissimilar to your cat. If they decide not to write me letters, I won't make a fuss."

"Natalia, you're ridiculous. A cat and two African children have nothing in common."

"Not until you learn that Rich likes to climb trees and Brown likes taking naps during the day. They're fond of milk too."

Punch her in the face, a voice in my head said. *She's making fun of you. She's no friend of yours. She thinks your cat is a pussy.*

WHORE.

She is living your life.

She's now a mother, and you're just a fat failure.

"No, I'm not!" I yelled out.

"You're not what?" Natalia asked.

"I'm not a *failure*."

"I didn't say you were a failure."

"Yes, you did. You just said I was a failure. You are making fun of me because you're living my dream. You knew that I was supposed to be a mother and have kids."

"Chloe, what is going on? You're scaring me."

"I'll tell you what's going on. I'm leaving."

I stood up suddenly—and my chair dramatically fell on the floor, making noise. I found my wallet and pulled out sixty bucks from the cash I earned babysitting Noah. I threw the three Jacksons on the table, like, "Here, take the cash—you undeserving whore," and put on my coat.

"Chloe, our food isn't here yet," Natalia said.

"I'm on a fucking diet!"

"Are you drunk?"

"I *will* have a baby. You watch—you pistol-cutting whore!"

"Chloe—"

But then I was outside the restaurant. Cold—it was the end of April—and really dark for some reason. The sky without the moon was just like a bank account with insufficient funds: why even bother? I buttoned up, put on my hat and gloves, and raised my hand to hail a cab. Natalia's jokes were inappropriate, and I decided to cut her off for good for comparing two African kids to my cat.

Good, Mom's voice inside my head said. *Cut that whore off for good.*

I said I would—stop annoying me, Mom.

She stopped.

F

FUMBLING IN MY TOTE, I FOUND MY WALLET, PULLED OUT A MetroCard, and caught the approaching number 2 train. It was the next day, morning, and I was on my way to the Upper West Side to water Aunt Josephine's plants. After the fight last night, I received hundreds of messages from Natalia but read none of them—she was probably apologizing or sending one of those "Are you okay?" messages out of pity. I wondered whether she was angry. Frankly, I was feeling embarrassed for causing a scene at the restaurant and for leaving Natalia high and dry, with the wait staff perhaps wondering what the heck was that about. The voices in my head that night belonged to the bartender and the waitress as the two were chitchatting.

Explain to me something, the bartender was saying. *She's so fat, how did she get drunk in less than thirty minutes? She should have a high tolerance.*

She resembles the kind who pregames at home before she goes out—to save money.

That cheap low-life.

And she was high on marijuana.

Probably heroin too.

I was lying awake all night listening to their stupid conversation. Boy, did they have a lot to say about me. One waitress at the restaurant was also a plump girl so I couldn't imagine why they called me fat, but not her.

I was still unwilling to take Clozapine, because it was the sole reason why I'd gained the extra weight and why my cholesterol was through the roof. To be honest, the voices did not bother me at all, and I was having a blast listening to their confabulations. Like, yeah, as if I would *ever* do heroin! They're so dumb. As long as I didn't have hallucinations, the voices were now a regular part of my life, kind of like breathing.

As I got off on West Seventy-second Street, Mom sent me a picture of a scruffy guy asleep on a bench. Her caption was: *When the world is your living room.*

Thanks, Mom.

I think I'm getting sick, Chloe. Can you pick up some zinc?

Okay.

Aunt Josephine's apartment building was three blocks from the train on Central Park West and West Seventy-third Street and was an astonishing thirty-one floor high. Aunt Josephine lived on the seventeenth. The doorman greeted me upon opening the door, and the concierge at the front desk waved at me on my way to the elevators. I waved back, after which I stopped by the mailroom and picked up the accumulated mail and two packages.

I was waiting for the elevator when a momzie with a stroller joined me. Clearly fresh from Central Park. The tot inside was a toddler who was asleep, a boy by the way he was dressed in blue. His momzie's eyes were glued to her phone, while I couldn't help but notice her diamond ring the size of a quail egg.

"He's adorable," I told her. "How old is he?"

She looked up. "Thank you. This is Joshua, and he's nine months."

"Do you live in the building?"

"Yes," she said, "and yourself?"

"My aunt lives in 17-N, but she's on vacation. I came here to pick up her mail and water the plants. I'm Chloe."

It looked like she started thinking, but because of the Botox, her face did not move. "Is your aunt, Josephine?"

"Yes. You know each other?"

"I live in 15-F. Analise sometime babysits Joshua."

"Really," I said. "I babysit kids in my building in Murray Hill. Were you scared when that whole thing with Sia was going down?"

She melodramatically rolled her eyes. "You will not believe it. We had just about to hire an Au Pair from Africa, and then that whole thing happened. This is why we don't have a nanny now. I don't trust anyone black anymore. We are seeking someone full time with a lived-in situation."

The elevator finally came to the first floor, and it pinged as the doors opened. I entered first and stuck out my hand to prevent the doors from closing, while she pushed in the stroller. I pressed number fifteen for her and seventeen for me.

"I'm looking for a job," I said. "I was offered a nanny job nearby," I lied, "for this four-year-old . . . Charlotte. But I don't think I should take it. They only pay thirty dollars an hour. I was asking for thirty-five."

"*We* can pay thirty-five," she said. "Are you really looking for a job as a nanny?"

"Yes, ma'am."

She raised her hand. "Please. *Never* again call me ma'am. I'm Casey."

"Good to meet you, I'm Chloe. Would you like me to send you my resume with my references and stuff?"

"Sure!"

The elevator door opened on the fifteenth floor, and I exited with her. She fumbled in her purse until she found her wallet, while I kept staring at Joshua, dumbstruck by my luck. She pulled out a business card and offered it to me. We exchanged a few more words, after which I promised to email her later that afternoon.

And just like that—I no longer cared about the stupid flight attendant job. I was going to work full-time—live away from MOM—and getting paid big bucks for it. *And*—Casey didn't need to know how much I weighed—because she's already seen me and seemed satisfied with my size. Probably so that when we're seen together, I'll be the "smart" one. Working as a nanny was a humane and straightforward way to earn a living. And since I didn't know how to fit into a jumpseat on the plane, at least one thing I knew for sure: *kids* I knew. I texted Mom right away.

This woman in Aunt Josephine's building offered me a job as a live-in nanny for thirty-five dollars an hour, and she wants me to start right away.

When no reply came, I texted Lindsay, Calyssa, and even Natalia. When no response came from them, I took the steps up to the seventeenth floor and let myself into Aunt Josephine's flat. I was now in a fun, silly mood and started Britishize things in my mind—lift, mobile phone, trousers.

The flat was facing east, overlooking Central Park, and the sun was gushing through the windows. Even though it didn't seem that sunny downstairs, up here, the weather was different.

I took my shoes off and was skipping out of happiness. Babysitting Noah was one thing, but having a full-time job for almost 50 percent increase in pay from what Bona was paying me, which was twenty an hour, was another. I looked at my phone but still received no replies. My silliness was starting to melt—like—why nobody was replying to me? I texted Kim —crickets.

Aunt Josephine is too cheap (according to my Mom) for a cleaning lady, which is why it was a little dusty in the apartment. I wet a paper towel and swiped through the dusty areas until the paper towel turned grey. I completed four rounds. Satisfied with the results, I filled up the watering can—metal and painted white with a wooden handle (a present from Mom and I for Aunt Josephine's forty-ninth birthday), but—tsh—the guests thought it was thirty-sixth. I don't know whom she's trying to fool, but those crow's feet don't belong on a thirty-six-year-old—let me tell you that much. We actually meant it as a joke as if it was our only present. You should have seen the look on Aunt Josephine's face—full of disappointment—until we pulled out a blue Tiffany box with a white gold pendant necklace.

Mom gave me a look, like, *See? I told you she was a cheap whore.*

By the time I finished watering, it was barely 9:05 a.m. Before going back home, I decided to swing by the roof for a little photo session. The views on the roof were unmatched. Central Park sat in its glory on the palm of your hand. I loved the view of the new skyscrapers going up on the south side of the park.

It was windy up on the roof but not uncomfortable. New York, from up in the air, looks magnificent—no wonder all those rooftop bars are incredulously popular. The views alone justify the overpriced beer that cost a Jackson a pop. Sometimes we just take it for granted—everything—and being born in New York, I frequently forget how lucky I am to be living here. Grateful even while having my health problems. I'd wanted the stupid flight attendant job for months, and they turned me down because of my weight. Then in two minutes flat, down at the lobby, I found a much *better* job. I mean if that's not magic—New York City magic—I don't know what is.

A metal fence that came up to my waist surrounded the perimeter of the roof to help avoid falls. I approached the fence with my phone in hand, taking multiple pictures of the park. I flipped the phone and took several selfies. The light was perfect for photos, and I even liked the way I looked for once—my ears weren't sticking it out as much anymore.

Then, something unprecedented happened.

The most bizarre thing.

A pigeon landed on the fence near me out of nowhere. I wasn't prepared for it. The pigeon made a scary noise, and I shrieked. From that sudden jolt, I dropped my phone. It first landed on the ledge, and like in a movie, reality paused. Plop, plop, plop . . . slowly . . . my phone jumped toward the abyss. Plop, plop, plop. It stopped at the end to give me one last look, like saying, *Bye, Chloe, it was nice to meet you*, and then it vanished into the ether. The pigeon took off just as unexpectedly, and reality resumed.

I leaned over the fence and looked down, but, of course, it was pointless. How was looking down going to help? The wind unraveled my scarf, and I kept wrapping it around my neck. I was infuriated with myself. No, I was enraged with Aunt Josephine for making me come all the way up here to water her dying ficus, two dried-up Boston ferns, and overgrown ivy—and then dust like a damn fool!

I took the elevator down, exited the building, and was fruitlessly searching for the remnants of my phone on the sidewalk. I felt my anger meter going higher and higher. Everything seemed stupid now, even that damn job as a nanny. Perhaps it was my karma for saying how much I hated cell phones because they were ruining our lives and the way we communicated with each other. I quickly recalled there was over a grand in my bank account saved from babysitting the horse Noah and other munchkins in my building. I could afford to buy another six-hundred-dollar phone. It meant —to make up for the new phone—I'd have to work for Casey for like three full days. I was beyond annoyed.

I could not sit or stand still at that point. I decided to walk home for some forty-plus blocks to cool off and determine later whether I needed an expensive phone *that* badly. Mom would freak out if I didn't respond after an hour. Once home, I would hurry to call Mom from our landline to explain the situation. Once again, her daughter was a failure. Mom was doing a twelve-hour shift and wouldn't be home until after nine at night, and God knows how many texts she'd have sent by then.

I was in the middle of the park when I found myself bypassing the playground where I usually brought Noah and where Lindsay and I would occasionally meet—and maybe my new "office" if Casey hired me—it was still to be determined. I know Casey said she wanted me as a nanny, but sometimes you just never know. Her husband could come that night and be like, "Honey, we're moving to Peru." Even if Casey still wanted me after that, there's no way I'm moving to Peru for a job. I would not even move to New Jersey for a job.

Central Park play area was massive and could accommodate hundreds of kids. There were slides, swings, a castle, and a jungle gym. The little rascals were all over the equipment. For such an early morning, the number of kids at the playground surprised me, two or three dozens of them. Parents or babysitters weren't watching the kids, their heads down, their backs hunched, all occupied with their cell phones. The kids seemed to enjoy the lack of supervision. No wonder Ama Takayoza snatched herself a baby. The adults were l-i-t-e-r-a-l-l-y giving the kids away without so much as charging money. I was shocked—*shocked*—to see that the kidnapping story was less than inspiring, and nobody cared.

And then I heard *him*. His pleading meowing was somewhere nearby, and it sounded like crying. I stopped in my tracks, and, like a beacon light, I spun my head in circles. Despite the laughter and the city noise, the meowing was loud enough for me to hear—and it wasn't in my head like the dumb voices—it was real. I kept listening to the pleading sounds until I no longer heard it. Then the meowing resumed, so I followed it. The meowing was coming from behind a massive bush, separating the playground from the rest of the park. And I saw him, cold and shivering, skinny beyond reason.

My puss Anubis.

He was sitting on a bench near a stroller looking at me. He recognized me, but he was clearly too cold to move. I couldn't believe it. As if watching a Disney cartoon, the air around us illuminated, and birds were chirping. Everyone disappeared—it was just him and me on the whole planet. If I sang, in a cartoon I'd be singing a song. It seemed magical, surreal, something out of a fairytale.

As I came closer, I realized the cat had a white streak near his collar, which was Anubis' "scar," so to speak. When I picked him up, he was shivering and was cold to the touch. It makes sense; it was barely fifty degrees this morning. I gently placed my catso under the jacket, where he clung to me with his claws, his way of saying to never let him go. I peeked inside my coat. Wow, I missed him so much, and seeing him alive just proved how much I needed him in my life. I was wearing the tee with his face under the sweater, and now I was holding him. The feeling was unbelievable. All my problems were instantaneously gone. Ha—how a little perspective could change your mind, just one stroke from the higher power, and you're cured, almost like a miracle. And what a miracle that was! I could care less about the flight attendant job or high cholesterol, about being overweight or the pimple that appeared on my nose that morning. I wanted to sing with joy but was afraid mice and birds would join me like in the movie *Cinderella*, causing unnecessary stares. It felt as if my whole body came to an agreement, soul, and body aligned as one.

I wanted to text Mom and to all my friends, but since I'd dropped my phone from the rooftop, I was going to come home and call everyone from the landline like it was 1980. I wanted to *scream* from excitement. I was now almost running, skipping like a little girl, occasionally looking under my jacket to make sure Anubis was real. And he was.

Call it fate—the fact that I lost my phone—because otherwise, I would never walk through the park, choosing the subway instead. Another lucky point was Aunt Josephine's and Analise's vacation in Greece that forced me to water their plants and be near the park at the right time and place. There was a higher power, I realized. The pigeon that made me drop the phone out of my hands was a gift from grace, and I was going to remember that lesson forever.

GEE—I COULDN'T BELIEVE HOW LUCKY I WAS. I WAITED FOR several bicyclists to pass before I looked to my left and crossed the street. Central Park felt tranquil, and I no longer heard any noises or voices, just divine quietness, a pure and uninterrupted feeling of love. A horse was coming in my direction, and it was wearing a burlesque style feather headpiece that stuck out like Aunt Josephine's ficus. The horse was pulling a carriage with a couple of tourists inside, while the coachman pointed, perhaps reciting the history of Central Park.

The path opened a set of stairs, which took me toward a different road that curved ahead. A knee-length fence ran on both sides, and a sign "Do Not Feed Wildlife" sat behind it. I wondered what wildlife the sign was referring to unless it meant the guy sleeping under an elm. But he did not look "wild" at all. Cold maybe but not wild; wrapped in several blankets. The lampposts were turned on for whatever reasons, and all but one bench was empty. It was much darker down here. Maple, oak, and elm trees with lush verdancy grew alongside, kind of like tall soldiers, while azalea, yellowroot, and shadbush were their green feet. In fairytales, scary stuff happens when trees are involved, but I wasn't scared. In front of a European linden tree stood another sign: "Keep Off. Newly Seeded Lawn." I swear I'd seen that sign for the past five years. How much more "newly seeded" is it going to get?

As I walked, the sunshine occasionally penetrated the dark patch, and the light was whimsically seeping through the leaves. To my left, ran a small pond the length of a football field, curving ahead out of sight. Fully erect pines surrounding the pond reflected in it, giving the still waters a sick brown hue. A lone, leafless white mulberry, with thick, protruding roots, was hunched like an old crone, and its long, twisted branches almost touched the lake like fingers twisted from arthritis. In the middle of the pond, sat a white stork, and it was staring in my direction. Maybe the "Do Not Feed Wildlife" sign was referring to the bird. For some reason, mesmerized, I stopped to admire the stork, wondering why 1) it was alone and 2) why it hadn't migrated to Florida for the winter. I wasn't unneighborly; the stork was allowed to stay if it wanted to, but what did it eat in the winter, and wasn't it freezing? The wind swept through, pushing the stork toward me, turning it around as if on a carousel.

When I turned away from the stork, I saw Cleveland, I saw Seattle, I saw two people in a battle. They were arguing about something, moving their hands frantically as if words were not enough.

As I passed, the couple initiated eye contact with me and smiled; they were no more than five feet away, and they both waved to stop me. They were both Asian, but I couldn't tell whether they were men, women, or a combo. They were both bald, with identical red scarves around their necks, bright yellow jackets, and blue jeans. Both had mustaches and earrings, but one was taller and clearly in charge.

"Egguse me. We lose here," the head Asian said with a strong accent. He or she said something indecipherable, but since I was furrowing my brows, I heard, "Times Square. How do we get there?"

I pointed southeast, adding. "You can catch the yellow line to Forty-second Street from here."

"Sank you," they said in a duet, and both bowed their heads. I bent my head right back at them. They bowed again. Oh, Lord. I waved goodbye, thinking if we kept nodding, it would take all day. The duo turned and disappeared from sight, using one of the passageways hidden in the bushes.

For some reason, Anubis was bulkier than I'd remembered and was getting heavier by the second. I reasoned that I'd never carried him for longer than a minute, and five minutes had gone by since I'd found him.

I sat down on a bench to rest and slowly opened my jacket. My eyes were playing tricks on me because that Disney "happiness" filter diminished, and the bright, glitzy lights faded back to normal. I was back in New York. However, instead of Anubis, I was now holding a baby in a puffy black jumpsuit.

Wait—what?

I've told you before I was going to kidnap a baby—so that's how it happened. Not entirely my fault.

The baby, maybe four months old, had an Elmo hat on and a pacifier in its mouth. Its big blue eyes were watching me, and its nose, the size of a mailbox key, was bright pink.

I reasoned I must have been feverish. Dr. Pepper always reminded me the hallucinations could happen when I become stressed or excited. And I was both. So, was it my first hallucination after going off Clozapine? I believed so, because according to Dr. Pepper, after the voices, the illusions are next. Whatever my true desires, the mastermind helps me envision them, and lately, I'd been thinking a lot about babies, my biological clock ticking louder and louder. Of course, it makes sense my first hallucination was a baby.

Yes, fear was making my palms sweat, and my ears were like hot plates. I had to go home immediately and take Clozapine regardless of what Dr. Clemens had said. He could shove his lipids panel up his butt if he so desired. I was furious with him. Why didn't he weigh the cons and pros before basically "yelling" at me for my high triglycerides like it was my fault? In my current condition, I was dangerous, not just to myself, but to the society also.

My heart was beating faster and faster as I was getting more and more nervous. I was afraid to leave the bench, a woozy feeling settling in. I couldn't call Mom or my friends, and not like I could stick out a hand, and a taxi-horse would stroll nearby in the bushes of Central Park.

I felt terrified. I pulled out Anubis for some comfort, but he still resembled a baby in an Elmo hat. My imagination ran wilder than I thought because I saw the baby in such detail, it was scary. Its skin was luminescent, eyebrows blonde, and sparse. I remember when Noah was born, he looked much the same way. Mrs. Petit purchased him all these cutesy baby things, and I would be so jealous the baby was hers and not mine.

I brought "Anubis," aka his protégé—the baby—closer to my nose and touched his with mine like I always did, which made him smile, and he made a funny noise that resembled happiness. The baby's blue eyes blinked a few times at me. I blinked a few times back, while the plan was emerging. I reached into my tote and found a pot brownie I'd baked, and ate half. Once

I got a little high and calmed down, the common sense would return, and the baby would turn back into Anubis.

When the brownie kicked in, I was much calmer. But the baby was still a baby.

Which meant only one thing. It was real.

That's when I realized my first hallucination wasn't happening here and now—but it had occurred back at the playground when I thought I'd picked up my cat—while in reality, oh no!—while in fact, I'd snatched an unsupervised baby.

Just like Ama Takayoza.

No, no, no—this couldn't be happening. It was either a dream, and I would wake up soon, or this was a hallucination. There was no way I'd kidnapped a baby—at very least not consciously, because that meant life in prison. I'd been obsessed with Sia's case for weeks and knew the ins and outs of what kidnapping means to an abductor, and the future is as grim as you can imagine, man.

"Are you a cat or a baby?" I asked the baby.

He kept sucking his pacifier, so I removed it. If it was a hallucination, the baby would speak—and I would know it was just a phase that would go away. Last year, my dead sister Matilda spent an entire week with me, so I knew what I was dealing with.

I ate the second half of the brownie, but nothing was changing, and I sincerely regretted my life. How was it possible that nobody noticed me taking a toddler from a stroller? I remember seeing an adult nearby talking on her phone. I mean, did nobody seriously learned the lesson from Ama Takayoza? I couldn't believe it.

I could not return the baby—and be like what? "Oh, sorry, the wrong baby!" It's not like the baby was a broken appliance that I could deliver to the customer service counter and ask for a repair.

Besides, I had no receipt.

Although, not returning the baby also meant prison time. It was a lose-lose situation for Chloe.

No, it's not. That belonged to a voice in my head that interrupted my train of thought. *You've always wanted a baby, and now you have one.*

You should keep it. That was another voice.

You're a mother now.

No one saw you.

The voices prevented me from concentrating, and I didn't know which thoughts were mine and which belonged to them.

Leave the state.

Right now!

The last voice seemed to belong to me, but I couldn't be sure. I had to leave the state right away somehow. No one saw me taking the baby. Just like that, I was now a mother.

My heart was beating so loudly against my chest, it reminded me of the way Agnes banged on our ceiling, and even *that* now seemed dear to me. Bile climbed up my esophagus, causing me to vomit. The acid left my throat burning, while pulse prodded against my temples.

I instantly regretted kidnapping the baby. It's not like I got caught fishing when fishing was prohibited. My current situation was much worse. I think. I don't know how strict they are when it comes to fishing.

After thinking for what seemed like twenty hours while still sitting on the cold bench, I decided to return to the scene of the crime and tell the irresponsible parent I'd found the baby right here by the pond. There was nothing else I could do to escape life in prison.

They won't believe you.

Yet another voice. Suddenly, there was a whole forum happening as if my head were a chat room.

Someone must have seen you taking the baby.

Yes, you'll be recognized in seconds!

If you go back, you're doomed.

This is your new reality."

Don't try to escape it.

Disguise yourself.

Something took over my body, and I was no longer myself. I carelessly dotted freckles on my cheeks with eyeliner, after which I put on my hat, finishing the ensemble by pulling a hood over my head. I stood up and was on my way out of the park, tightly holding the baby under my coat.

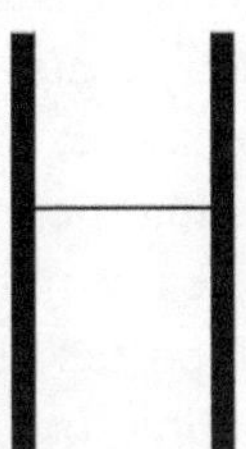

Heaving from a brief run, I paused to get my bearings at a traffic light ahead. Where was I going? The only plan I had involved New Jersey—the closest state, which I could reach in half an hour. What exactly was going through my head is impossible to explain, but I was not myself. I felt like a crowd-funding project, and multiple people were moving me like a marionette. It could have been a part of schizophrenia, but I was unsure. To get to New Jersey, the nearest PATH station was on 33rd Street, about twenty blocks away.

I exited the park, trying to look inconspicuous and busy, to indicate to the tourists I was not their girl when it came to directions. With one hand tightly holding the baby, I readjusted my tote on my shoulder and attempted to hail a cab. When one slowed in front of me, I jumped straight in.

"Herald Square, please," I said. The cabbie nodded, started the meter, and in seconds we were sailing along Fifth Avenue. When Sia Shirtley had been kidnapped, I became familiar with how the cops operated. They must determine first whether the circumstances meet the definition of a missing child and dispatch an officer to the scene. Afterward, when it's confirmed the child is indeed abducted, they work closely with the media, which is a crucial part of getting to the public fast. Not long after, they initiate an AMBER Alert. So far so good: nobody had been following me, I was in disguise with my freckles, and the baby was calm. With thousands of people roaming the streets, *anybody* could be the kidnapper, and I hoped the police didn't have enough force to check every pedestrian whether he or she was carrying a baby under those puffy coats.

Traffic along Fifth Avenue was scarce, which perhaps was the norm for a Saturday morning. We were passing the boutique stores: Tiffany & Co., Channel, and the other stores where I wasn't rich enough to shop. I noticed that the driver's name was Abdul, posted behind Plexiglas. He minded his own business, mostly concentrating on the road ahead, occasionally glancing at the GPS, which talked in a British accent and quite loudly at that. The cab ride seemed taking longer than it was supposed to be, and it left me with nothing but my thoughts.

I tried not to call myself a kidnapper—even if I *was* one. It felt strange. Nothing really changed, and yet everything had changed—if I'm making any sense. I felt scared and indifferent at the same time, a feeling I had never experienced before. It was unsettling. I thought of going home first to pack but realized by the time I packed and left, the cops would block every street in Manhattan. I was smarter than that, proved by my ability to give myself freckles as if I were Irish, radically changing my heritage. Mom had a twelve-hour work shift that started at nine in the morning and was already at the hospital. But I was not ready to face my doorman or any of my neighbors, especially the cranky hoarder Agnes.

Five stages of grief are denial, anger, bargaining, depression, and acceptance. While I understood the consequences of what I had done and was surprisingly unsympathetic, I knew that soon enough, things would get tense. And what grief that was! Thirty-one years I'd been a good girl—mostly—and then a second later the tables turned around, and I'm a criminal. Clearly, I was in grief because I was in denial.

We were approaching Herald Square, West Thirty-third Street, and Sixth Avenue. Macy's stretched an entire block, while other shopping outlets peekabooed from all directions. My apartment was several avenues east, and I quickly contemplated one last time whether I should go home, but promptly ditched the idea. Kidnapping is a time-sensitive matter.

Herald Square was busy with people, as always, which again worked to my advantage (more people; easier to hide among them). Cabs swooshed by, sharing the road with bicyclists. Abdul stopped the cab on the corner of West Thirty-third and Sixth Avenue. I paid him ten bucks with my debit card, tipping him a mandatory 20 percent. When I exited, the entrance to the PATH station was straight ahead, the train that would take me to New Jersey. I circumrotated my head, looking for the police, but luckily saw none.

And in I went. -into the unknown.

I reached the staircase and quickly descended underground. I was sure the station was teeming with security cameras, but I was too chicken to check and kept my head low. I decided to keep the baby under the coat until I was on the train—out of sight. I used my MetroCard to enter, and it still had thirty-five bucks leftover after I swiped myself through the turnstile.

Down at the platform, a train destined to Journal Square stood on the track. I was not familiar with the system except for knowing that Thirty-third Street station was a terminal. I referenced the oversized system map. The yellow line that stood on the tracks ended at Journal Square, where I could transfer to the red line toward Newark, the very last stop—as far away from New York as possible.

I kept walking down toward the end of the train, hoping for fewer passengers in the last car, and I was right. Several passengers had already distributed all around, maybe five in total. One of them gave me a dubious look but soon withdrew, while I assembled myself in a corner. I claimed the entire seat. I turned away from everyone, creating a nook so that other passengers saw nothing but my back. I unbuttoned my coat and looked at the wonder I'd kidnapped. It was sucking on the pacifier, unconcerned with the shenanigans. I removed the prominent Elmo hat and buried it deep in my tote. Under the hat, there was a baby blue bow, and I peeked under the black jumpsuit—there was a matching baby blue onesie. She was a beautiful baby girl and so calm she reminded me of Maggie from *The Simpsons*. Until I came up with a better name, I decided to call her Maggie. I removed the bow and hid it next to the Elmo hat.

The train departed shortly after a brief announcement from the conductor. Journal Square was seven stations away, four in Manhattan, three in New Jersey. Each stop supplemented a couple of passengers, but nobody was standing, with enough room for everyone to sit.

Once we crossed the Hudson, we emerged from the underground, and the entire way to Journal Square, the sun was shining through the windows. I needed glasses, I thought.

At Journal Square, I covered the baby with my coat and exited the train.

My transfer train to Newark was on a different track waiting for us with the doors open.

Inside the train, I claimed an empty seat and uncovered Maggie. Besides us, two more passengers were in the car, both African-American and both listening to music. I wondered whether Saturday mornings were never crowded like that. The workweek was over, and people were sleeping in at home, nursing hangovers from the night before, or making blueberry pancakes for breakfast. Thought of food reminded me that I shouldn't have skipped breakfast because, according to Lindsay, if you do, you're sabotaging yourself to eat more during lunch and dinner. Once I was in Newark, where it was safer, I could gobble on something.

An African-American lady, maybe forty years of age, jumped into the car as the doors were closing. Typically, on empty trains, passengers prefer to distribute themselves around the car, but she sat across from me, putting one unshaved leg on top of another. Bedazzled earphones were sticking out of her ears, and she was wearing all white despite the fact it was after Labor Day. It was hard to tell, but she was either talking on the phone or singing a tune. After a possible lice treatment, her hair was all gone. She'd penciled her brows and had painted her lips a shade of red my neighbor—who's a hooker according to Mom—wears.

We looked at each other. The woman in front of me was a perfect advertisement for don'ts of makeup. Her hoop earrings, like two car wheels, dangled around merrily, bedazzled with gems that sparkled in the sunlight. She was nipping at a drumstick. On her lap sat a to-go box full of fried chicken, and it looked freshly prepared. For ten o'clock in the morning, I considered her a lush. The rule of thumb is no fried chicken or alcohol until noon. But it was clearly five o'clock somewhere. The aroma that came from her direction was agonizing to my empty tub. I caught her staring at me. I averted my eyes, but it was too late because my curious look was the catalyst for a conversation.

She looked at me when she said, "Next time you in Journal Square, go to Mama's Fried Chicken."

"Too early for lunch," I said with an accent or what I wanted it to be, I wasn't quite sure what pronunciation I was going for, but Irish maybe. I couldn't just ignore the woman lest she assumed I was shady.

"I was just there for bidness," she said. "Sold three sticks."

"Dat nice," I copied her. "Three sticks of what?"

"I woke up at five dis mornin' from mornin' sickness."

"What's the matter?" I asked her.

"Hang on, Lila," she said. Then she looked at me, "Sorry, but I'm on the phone. Never mind, Lila, someone thought I was talking to her."

Great.

I felt stupid for assuming she was having a conversation with me. But just as well. I was not in a chatty mood, and if anything, she was a witness.

"Hello?" she was saying. "Can you hear—can you hear me, Lila? This is Glamazon."

Glamazon, I thought. No last name. She was sucking on the drumstick with such precision, working it like a lollipop.

"Them baby mamas be crazy," she was saying and laughed. "She should not give birth—no! That's how mama Tasheka died."

Glamazon put down a perfectly polished drumstick bone and reached for a thigh.

"No, Lila," she said, "I'm pregnant now. Yes. Jesus doesn't know. Well, now I can sell the positive test results to baby mamas. Do you need one to scare your boyfriend? You should. Just leave it in the trash and see what he says." She started laughing so hard the entire car was looking at her direction (which meant my direction as well).

"No," she was saying, "I don't sell my eggs anymore. This is so much easier—and I make so much money. That chicken I bought this morning? Eight bucks. You think I can afford this stuff without shakin' some booty on the side?"

I don't know about booty on the side, but I saw she had some fries on the side. The voice overhead announced we were approaching Harrison station. Glamazon stood up and put on sunglasses.

When the train halted, Glamazon exited without turning back. She kept talking to Lila. Glamazon seemed crazy to me, no doubt about it. Her business idea was smart, though—selling positive pregnancy test results—even if it helped me none at the moment.

A

s we were approaching the terminal in Newark, I wrapped my scarf around Maggie's head to serve as a hat and covered her from view with my coat. I exited the train and followed my fellow passengers who were walking toward the Newark Penn Station entrance. What struck me interesting was the percentage of white people versus black people. Noticeably, the black population dominated, and I was afraid to stand out. How could I quickly become part of the community without sounding racist? Should I ask questions about Michael Jordan?

Several momzies pushed their tots in strollers, others carried babies in bedsheets wrapped across their chests, the way Calyssa did with Grace. I'm a pro at making sheet carriers, having years of practice as soon as Noah was born.

It seemed risky keeping Maggie under my coat, and because of the other moms around, I wasn't nervous anymore and pulled her out. I was unprepared to carry the baby for so long, and my arms were tired. I needed to purchase a sheet for Maggie to keep her on my chest. Ahead, a vendor was selling all sorts of things: plastic cups, books, fabrics, magazines, souvenirs, and the miscellany, including a refrigerated section with drinks and sandwiches. Several customers leafed through magazines and books, while an African-American saleslady smoked an electric cigarette, her phone taking her undivided attention.

I priced the merchandise. A single queen size sheet in grey cost twelve bucks and was 100 percent cotton. Sold. I grabbed a bottle of water and a turkey sandwich from the refrigerator and proceeded toward the checkout. Then a strange thought came to mind. I turned and picked up a jar of Nutella off the shelf. I had no idea if it would work, but what if I smeared it all over my face? Would that make me resemble an African-American lady? I couldn't know unless I tried.

A customer in front of me was talking loudly on her phone, while the saleslady rang her up. Speaking on the phone was a smart idea. This way, the saleslady wouldn't ask any inappropriate questions. But I had no phone to fool her with. Instead, I pulled my scarf off Maggie's head and covered my head instead, covering my ears to have the saleslady think I had a Bluetooth speaker in my ear, the way Glamazon had. When the customer ahead checked out, I was next in line. I laid out the items on the counter while talking to myself. The saleslady scanned my items without making any comments about the baby, being mostly consumed by her phone—I could have stolen anything, and she would doubtfully notice. Babies are being kidnapped left and right—and all people care about is their phones.

I paid with my debit card, picked up the receipt, and collected my purchases, which the saleslady had bagged for me. I slid the debit card into my jeans' back pocket and pressed the plastic bag with my purchases into the tote.

I scanned the area for cops and whatnot and having found none relief washed over me. I found a sign for WC. The atmosphere in the station was lively, which calmed me down. I was glad to be the part of the commotion —the more people, the less visible you are. It's only scary when you're in an empty alley by yourself, which is usually a start to all horror stories. I wasn't afraid of witnesses because hundreds of people were roaming the perimeter. Besides, Maggie had been taken from Central Park—who would expect her to be in Newark so soon?

While I was picking the tote off the ground, someone bumped into me from behind. I turned to see who it was, but the hooligan scooted into a different direction—a young African-American boy—without so much as an apology. I couldn't blame him because of the number of people around, but "I'm sorry, ma'am" wouldn't hurt.

The bathroom smelled like a horse stall. While holding my breath, I opened a diaper-changing table and carefully placed Maggie on it. Several stalls were occupied. One lady was drying her hands. She gave me a casual look, but I turned around in time to hide my face.

A diaper dispenser sold diapers for a buck a pop, but money was accepted only in quarters. I, of course, had none. I wasn't sure whether it was time to change Maggie's diaper, but when I checked her, she was drier than the Sahara in the summer.

I shrugged out of my jacket, placing it on the table near the baby and got to work. I quickly tied the sheet that I'd purchased around my body and slid Maggie into the center pocket. I was smart calling her Maggie in my mind: the more I believed her name was Maggie, the more believable it would sound had someone asked, and I had to lie. While holding the baby with one hand, I brought one loose end of the sheet forward and slid it underneath her legs. I repeated with the other end and tightened both ends behind my back. I wondered if her mama had ever wrapped a sheet around her like that. My new carrying case seemed secure, and I tugged on it to make sure.

I entered an empty stall and put the tote by my legs. With Maggie hanging on my chest, I now had two operating hands. I twisted the lid on the Nutella jar and dug my fingers into the gooey chocolate goodness. There was plenty to work with, so first, I stuck a finger-full on my tongue, devouring the velvety texture. A little spasm occurred in my mouth from the sweetness. Next, I began smearing the paste all over my face, ears, and neck. Fortunately, Nutella was warm, therefore easily spreadable. When I assumed my entire face was well covered, I licked my fingers and exited the stall.

A dirty mirror by the sink showed me the worst nightmare—my face covered in Nutella—it looked exactly how you'd imagine. White streaks were all over the place as if a skin disease. That was the opposite of looking inconspicuous. The freckles that were on my face earlier were now invisible under the darkness of the chocolate. While nobody was around to watch, I quickly fixed the areas I'd missed and smoothed out the rough patches. There. Now my skin looked more or less natural. Even though I knew that getting out of town was a time-sensitive matter, I kept staring at my reflection in the mirror without moving. Red lips, orange sweater, yellow (platinum white) pixie, purple highlights, green eyes, blue jacket, pink scarf, white hands, blackface . . . It looked as if I'd been painted by a box of crayons, and I loved the effect. I tied the scarf around the baby's head like a turban and ditched the Elmo hat in the trash.

WHEN I EXITED THE STATION, I SQUINTED AT THE SUNLIGHT reflected in an office building ahead. There were several tall buildings in the distance suggesting that during the week this area was full of people in suits. The sky had mostly cleared, and only a few stray clouds were visible. The temperature was in low-fifties, and according to the weather report I'd read earlier in the morning, it would get to fifty-eight by two.

I shrugged out of my jacket and dumped it in a trash can by the entrance. My sweater was enough insulation to keep me warm, and Maggie was dressed in a black jumpsuit with my wool scarf around her head. I had to purchase a different jumpsuit for her later on, and I had enough money in my checking account. If her parent had seen me taking Maggie out of the stroller, and even if Glamazon somehow figured out I was the kidnapper and she blabbed to the cops, now my navy blue jacket was gone and so was the Elmo hat. Plus, my face was now covered in Nutella.

A convenience store was visible across the street with a name on the awning that read CONVENIENCE STORE. I had to purchase some sort of concealment, and formula for Maggie. Too bad it was not Halloween, because disguising then would have been as easy as pie. When I heard the word pie, my tummy gave a kick. That finger full of Nutella was insufficient, and I made a deal with myself: next time I kidnap a baby, I should eat a big breakfast. Two other stores stood on either side, their windows broken, awnings burned, with only signs TOBACCO and LIQUOR discernible. I guessed tobacco and liquor were now hard to get, with both stores out of business. I crossed the street.

I opened the door to the convenience store, while an old-fashioned bell ding-ding-dinged, announcing my ingress. Nine aisles were marked by oversized numbers from one to nine but without any further aisle description. I picked up a basket by the door and noticed how the store clerk—an Indian guy in a brown cardigan—studied me carefully, nodding oddly to acknowledge me. To avoid being asked questions, I pretended I was talking on the phone via Bluetooth to my boyfriend, Kim. "Yes, yes," I was saying, "Uh-hum, yes." The clerk got the hint. Belatedly I realized there was nothing in my ear that could serve as a Bluetooth device, but there was nothing to do now about that mistake.

I disappeared in the first aisle and studied its contents. There were paper cups and plates, dinnerware, tools, padlocks, light bulbs, and the second aisle was full of party goodies, along with books, postcards, and other miscellaneous stationery. A purple party wig was seven, and I snatched it off the shelf together with a face-painting kit that cost five. I skipped the next aisle, full, in most part, of home-cleaning supplies. Aisle four was where I found the baby formula, a new cute baby hat (with a face of a monkey on it), and diapers priced at ten. Good thing I had about a grand stored up in my checking account from all the babysitting.

School supplies were in the next aisle, and I picked up a large backpack with the print of Princess Tiana from *The Princess and the Frog*. It was a good idea to hide my tote bag in it because my tote bore a stitched Anubis' face on its front and was a pretty good identifier to the cops. In the grocery section, my choice of food was soda, chips, and a milk chocolate bar. The very last aisle was a haphazard collection of items unsuitable for any other category. I grabbed a thick self-adhesive mustache from the array and stuck it in my jeans' back pocket when I was sure to be out of sight.

Uh-oh, I was shoplifting already.

I was the only customer, and the clerk eyed me every time I turned from one aisle to the next, watching me in a large convex mirror positioned in the corner. The clerk was skinny, with balding gray hair, and his nose was an inch apart from his jaw as if he had no teeth, an odd expression on his face.

That was the extent of my shopping.

At the checkout counter, I was loudly saying to the imaginary Kim, "Yes, Kim, Sheila has to go to school. I'm at the store now—hang on."

I placed the basket with my stuff in front of the clerk and read his nametag that said Harshit. To my right, the sunshine beamed through the unwashed window, and I saw Harshit so clearly I counted five whole zits near his nose. He said something indecipherable and made a funny face expression for Maggie, while I visibly tapped my ear to indicate I had on a Bluetooth earpiece.

While Harshit was scanning my items, a phone rang somewhere in the back of the store. He lifted his finger like he'd be back and fled the checkout area. Nobody was looking after the store—and I looked around to double-check for cameras but noticed none. I threw the baby formula in my tote, burying it deep on the very bottom. It must have been the law of the criminal world: the more you steal, proportionally, your lifting habits grow as well.

I waited for about a minute or two, while a sneaky suspicion had popped into my head. Where was Harshit? What was he up to? Suddenly the light from the window to my right diminished as someone was bypassing the store outside, blocking the sunlight. A cop.

I

It took me half a second to react, which is how I ended up scrunched up like a cinnamon roll in the last aisle. Harshit had called the cops and had hidden in the back as a result. The bell above the door dinged when the cop entered. There are three reactions to danger: fight, flight, or freeze. I was the last one, Elsa from *Frozen*. I couldn't see the cop, but his boots stuck to the linoleum, producing kissing sounds as he walked.

"Harshit, where are you?" the cop said with a Jersey shore accent.

I hoped I was out of sight.

With knees bent, I bobbed my body up and down to relax and to prevent Maggie from making any noise—rocking keeps babies composed and quiet.

The cop kept calling for Harshit without any apparent urgency. Maybe he was skeptical that Harshit had caught an outlaw and therefore wasn't in a hurry. But soon, my knees started to give in under pressure, and I briefly wondered how long before I collapsed.

Ship, ship, ship! Holy ship! I was doomed regardless! My tote, with Anubis' face stitched on the front, was still on the counter! There was no way to fetch it as the cop stood beside it. My ID, wallet, stolen goods were all in the tote. Inside, the police would also find a Judy Blume paperback I was reading, a turkey sandwich, and my fingerprints. My face was so hot that it warmed up the Nutella and, mixed with sweat, it was trickling down my cheek, drop by drop along my neck and into the boobs. If I were killed somewhere in the wild, I was basically an ant-magnet right now. I dotted the sweat/Nutella mixture with my sleeve.

From my vantage point, I was able to observe the cop in the convex mirror without him seeing me. The smudges on my face looked ridiculous, but I couldn't care less about that now. The cop was rocking back and forth on his boots, calling for Harshit. He was clearly in no rush. What if catching a kidnapper was the last thing on his mind?

Maggie moved her hands, clinging to me like a monkey to a palm tree. I prayed she wouldn't give me away by crying. The mirror assured me I looked ridiculous with a baby on my chest, but looking ridiculous was better than being arrested, being a Republican, and/or being dead.

"Harshit? Where are you?" he kept asked over and over.

Apparently, he had no armory on him: no gun, radio, or handcuffs—nothing. A cop would also drive a car, I surmised, but none were visible ahead through the store windows.

Suddenly he did a one-eighty and entered the first aisle. I lost sight of him in the mirror, thinking he should be getting closer toward the center. It was my only chance to escape. I sprinted forward.

As I was about to pull the door to open, I realized the tote was still on the counter. Ship! I raced back to the counter, lifted the tote, and had to drop it when I heard "Freeze!" with the same (Italian) Jersey shore accent.

The cop jumped in front of me, pointing a finger pistol in my face.

"I'll be a monkey's uncle," he said. "I knew it was you, lady. Hands up."

A weird feeling enveloped me. It felt like I was submerged in water: the picture in front of me had slowed, and I was holding my breath. I read somewhere that flies see the world in slow motion, which is why it's hard to kill them since they're faster than you in that regard. That's how the cop appeared to me, like a human trying to kill me, but he was moving slowly, languidly. The adrenaline that was pumping in my blood made me feel like a superhero (or at least a fly). My mind worked a hundred times faster, like a computer (or at least a tablet). It seemed I had paused life! It was unclear how long that would last, but I turned around and back, while the cop stood still like a statue. His frozen face muscles made him appear friendlier, but the finger pistol threw me off. Why was there a finger pistol? I concentrated on his fingers, and just as suddenly, the underwater veil got lifted, and I deeply breathed in.

The cop had a severe nasal discharge happening. He tried to suck it back in through the nose, but fruitlessly, which is why he stuck out his tongue and licked his upper lip, which looked quite chapped.

I raised my hands, thinking whether I could take the five-foot cop in a fight. Yes, he looked weird, and he had no weapon, but he was at the authority to arrest me. The handlebar mustache and a mullet was a silly look on anyone, let alone on a man in New Jersey circa 2017. He was now laughing, choking on hiccups.

"Did you see Harshit?" he asked me, the finger pistol pointed straight to my face.

The happiness on his face was one of those honest expressions a cat makes upon seeing his owner. Drool, like a mountain creek, dribbled from the side of his mouth, and his eyes, though aimed at me, wondered around his eye-sockets like two antennae controlled by the weather channel.

I cleared my throat and asked as if I didn't know, "Who's Harshit?"

"The owner of the store." He put his finger pistol away, blowing its tip as if it were on fire, and put the invisible gun into a nonexistent holster. Half his teeth were yellow; the other half had immigrated to China. "Scared you granny-slapping good, didn't I? Relax, I'm no cop."

"You're not?"

"I fooled you too, didn't I? Harshit gave me this costume for Halloween last year. Looks real, doesn't it?"

"Yes."

"Did you see Harshit?"

"He's out back talking on the phone."

"I scared you gussied up high cotton, didn't I? This costume looks real, doesn't it?"

He picked his nose with a finger and placed the same finger in his mouth, gleam in his eye, suggesting a delicious taste, though I decided to pass on doing the same. I wondered why he kept repeating sentences over and over.

Harshit reappeared, limping on his left leg. I was glad the cop was not here to arrest me, and it felt like I lost two hundred pounds—light like a feather, and happy beyond belief. I dug into my tote, retrieving my wallet, but when I opened it, my debit card was not in its usual spot at the top. I opened the flap, looked, but it was definitely gone. I rewound the cassette of my brain, trying to recall using the card last. I remembered putting it in my back pocket after paying for the sheet and the turkey sandwich. I checked the pocket, but it wasn't there. And then the last puzzle piece fell into place. A kid bumped into me from behind as I was bending over my tote. He must have stolen it.

Ship!

I didn't have any credit cards, nor did I carry any dead presidents.

I said, "I forgot my debit card at home. I'll be right back. Please keep my stuff on the counter for me. It'll be half an hour or so."

"Okay," Harshit said, and started chatting with "the cop."

I picked up my tote and walked toward the exit without turning back.

It was now ten fifteen in the morning. Outside, the cloudless sky indicated a beautiful day ahead. I remembered how, in my childhood, we used to watch nature for weather patterns. When birds flew low, it meant it'd rain. If the grass had dew on it, it meant the day would stay dry. If you watched an erotic movie, like Caligula, expect your fingers to get frisky.

The branch of my bank was located around the corner, across the exit from the Newark Penn Station. I had misplaced my debit card once before, after a wild night out with the girls. The very next day, I called my bank to report the card as lost and requested a new one. A representative said a replacement card would arrive in a week. That very same night, there was another party Calyssa had invited me to, but I had no cash or card. I went to the bank, and the guy who greeted me by the door told me I could withdraw money by using my driver's license. Which was my only hope now.

Back at the Penn Station I washed off the Nutella from my face to avoid any questions about my identity. I'd have chosen a cleaner bathroom—say, at a restaurant—but many such restaurants had started a trend where you must purchase food first before using the facilities. Now that I resembled the picture from my driver's license, I entered the bank. Like a seasoned criminal, I instantly noticed a security camera and averted my face in the opposite direction. I say "seasoned" like I'm a crouton.

Maggie was not giving me any trouble, and I was surprised at how calm I was myself. I knew panicking would not help. Maggie made me resemble a heifer, adding bulk to my previously bulky exterior. If you're skinny like Lindsay and you gain ten pounds, people will notice, and whispers will be exchanged because ten pounds on skinny is like adding a bun to a hotdog. When you pass way over a hundred and eighty pounds, any ten pounds added to it is like adding more sand to the beach: No one will notice the excess, and at this point, the game is over. You might as well finish the last muffin at the party while everyone is watching. I know I should love my body—and the yoga gurus say to be grateful to be alive—well now what? I'm thankful, but my body was still a hundred and ninety real pounds.

A man in a polished gray suit waved at me at the end of the lobby, his gesticulations robotic. He introduced himself as Rusty Brown, and after I told him what I needed, he sent me to the teller's window—where I withdrew five Benjamins.

I spotted a bus stop as I exited the bank. Boston, Washington, Baltimore, Montreal. That's what I should take, I realized—a bus. I obviously couldn't fly or hitchhike—and on buses, they don't check your ID. I noticed a bus leaving for Washington at eleven thirty, in less than an hour. I bought a one-way ticket to D.C., which cost me twenty-two fifty. I placed the leftover dead presidents in my wallet, together with my driver's license. I stuck the paper ticket in my jean's back pocket and hugged Maggie, thinking about what I should be doing next.

Seeing other momzies with babies at the station made me feel safer. It was clear by now the cops had no idea I was in New Jersey. Usually, you can sense the commotion when something is wrong. People are suddenly on a lookout, sirens wail, helicopters chop around in circles in the sky. It was nothing like that. It was peaceful instead.

Now that I had about an hour to kill, I returned to the Penn Station to change Maggie's diaper. In the bathroom (the third time), I bought a diaper from the dispenser and placed Maggie on the changing table, after which I removed the jumpsuit. Underneath, she was wearing two more layers: a pastel blue crochet cardigan with two stitched yellow baby chicks on the bottom, and a polka dot bodysuit tucked into blue cotton pants. I giggled, thinking Maggie was like a head of cabbage, and I was removing the leaves, trying to reach the core. Maggie wiggled her feet when I slid the pants down and unclasped the bodysuit from the bottom. The diaper gave a crunchy sound when I unfastened the tabs. I folded the dirty diaper and found wet wipes that I always carry with me in my tote. I used four wipes in total to clean Maggie's bum. While holding her with one arm, I placed a new diaper on the changing table, lay Maggie on it, and fastened the tabs. I quickly dressed my little cabbage, layer after layer, in exact order the way she had come from the factory. I looked in the mirror before exiting the restroom, and Maggie and I locked eyes. She smiled, and I smiled. Her eyes were huge compared to her head. I always thought babies were incredibly cute and would always secretly one of my own. Now she was on my chest. I wanted to cry from how good it felt—but first, I needed to get out of town. My bus would depart in just a little over thirty minutes. I had to pay for the stuff at Harshit's convenience store, and that was the extent of my nightmares.

I was across the street from the store. I had been so relaxed thinking I was safe that when I heard a police siren, my psyche went into overdrive. Panicking, I sprinted toward an alley that was created ahead between two brick buildings, both about five stories tall and covered in colorful graffiti. I hid behind an oversized trash can that stood to the side and waited. Behind me was a solid concrete wall, perhaps ten feet high, ending the alley. Three more metal garbage cans stood there. No windows, no doors, no other passageways visible in sight. If the cops had entered the alley, I was entirely at their mercy with nowhere to hide. Of course, if I were physically in shape, I could jump on a trash can, reach the top of the wall, climb over it, and once on the other side start running. But, alas, with my . . . um, full figure . . . I doubted I could do it.

A black-and-white appeared in sight for half a second and disappeared, its sirens diffusing into the cold air. I was holding my hands over Maggie's ears to prevent her from going deaf. As the car moved farther away, the siren dissipated completely. I didn't realize I'd been holding my breath, so I gasped for air. The cops weren't hunting for some fresh kidnapper meat, it seemed, but I was trembling nevertheless. I wondered if from this moment on, I would always shake in fear every time I heard a siren—but maybe that's how most criminals get caught—because of their own paranoia.

On the other hand, don't take precautions, you end up in jail. I guess it's better to hide every—single—time. Like they say, it's better safe than sorry.

I closed my eyes, listening to my heartbeat like a jackhammer drilling sidewalk—loud, obnoxious, and destructive. *This* what was going to give me a heart attack, not greasy food. I stood up, holding on to the trash bin for support and started toward the convenience store when a silhouette entered the alley. I stopped in my tracks. It was impossible to discern whether it was a man or a woman, a civilian or a cop, but I assumed the worst—it was an alley, after all. The silhouette moved fast like a queen piece on the chessboard, and the next thing I knew, there was a blunderbuss staring at me.

"Money or I'll shoot" was the next thing I heard.

J

Jesus, I thought to myself. Behind the gun, stood a young black man with a shaggy Afro that resembled a chia pet. I protected Maggie by tightening my arms around her.

"You're deaf?" he said. "I said money, or I'll shoot."

"But I have a baby."

"I said money, or I'll shoot you—and *sell* your baby."

"It's not mine to sell," I said and shut up.

My hands were trembling as I was going through several different scenarios of how this interaction might go. Either he takes the money and lets me go or takes the money and shoots me anyway. Without the money, I'm as good as dead. I reached into the tote and handed him my wallet. I couldn't believe I was being mugged in broad daylight, especially with a baby on my chest. I was sure if I were pregnant, the mugger wouldn't give up his seat on the subway. He opened the wallet, partially satisfied with what he saw, proved by a grin on the side of his lip.

"What else you got in the bag?"

"There are four dead Franklins in the wallet. Take them all. Just please give me my driver's license back."

"I said, give me the damn bag." His tone suggested he was losing his patience. Maybe because nobody else had ever negotiated with him before. I took one step back, leaving him to search the tote all he wanted.

"I need to feed the baby," I said, "and I don't have any more money on me. I'm running away from a very abusive husband. Please . . . man . . . don't be so heartless."

Pointing the gun at me, he reached into the tote and threw the items out of it.

He mumbled, "Shut up," as he kept his search.

"I met Michael Jordan during Black History Month," I lied, but he ignored me anyhow. I mean, if those two topics—Michael Jordan and Black History Month—meant nothing to him, what would?

He pulled out the jar of Nutella, baby formula that I stole from Harshit, and a paperback I was reading, *Iggie's House* by Judy Blume. The book was about interracial friendship, and I wondered whether I could break into this guy, telling him white people are not his enemy. He was wearing an unmarked gray hoody with sweatpants, and running shoes, while a massive gold chain dangled in front. His skin color was coffee with milk, but really heavy on the milk. No sugar in that coffee—that's for sure.

He flipped the tote upside down but found nothing of interest. I could've *told* him that much, had he asked if I had anything valuable. For somebody who looked seventeen, the assailant stood tall at about six foot seven, a good enough height for playing basketball rather than conducting illegal activities. Still, I was not about to go ahead and suggest that. And then what? At the peak of his career he's asked how he decided to become a professional player, he'd be like, "So I was in this alleyway in Newark, mugging this woman with a baby . . ."

He picked up the orange pill bottle with my medication for cholesterol. Even though I wasn't taking Clozapine, I had it on me too, but it was deeper inside the bag, and I guess he failed to find it. He shook the bottle in front of me as if it were a baby rattle.

"Is this oxycodone?" he said.

"It's a prescription. Please, don't take it."

"Don't lie to me. I bet it's oxycodone."

"It's not—" I said. I wanted to scream, *Read the motherfucking label you fucking piece of shit!* Although there was no point in going all HBO on him.

"I love Diana Ross," I said instead. "Don't shoot me. And I think Jesus was black. I'm *your* friend."

He apparently was above a reply.

He stood up and glanced at me. His eyes were like two sharp blades reflecting a sliver of sunlight that was able to sneak in between the two buildings. *Fatal, bled to death, morbidly obese*: the kind of words that kept appearing in my mind, the words a mortician would use to describe my injuries to a fellow mortician. I cringed. The assailant retrieved a bill from my wallet, crumbled it in one hand, and tossed it at me. The ball hit my forehead, right between my eyes, and fell on the ground.

"Money for food, for baby. Now run, and nobody gets hurt."

What just happened?

Did the mugger—seriously—had just given me my—own—money?

I was beyond humiliated by that fact. If the mugger meant to kill me, he would have done it already, right after realizing that aside from the four hundred dollars, I was a deadbeat.

Then something came over me.

I leaped forward.

I managed to get a hold of the gun, pushing his hand up so the muzzle would face the sky. I roared like a lioness and kicked the skank in the shin. Surprisingly, he let go of the gun, his eyes popped open in surprise. With a free arm, I punched his face. I was in a rage I'd never experienced before. I was what Shakira called a "she-wolf," and I had a newly found respect for the Colombians. Now that I was on the other side of the gun, I felt authority, aggression, and adrenaline mixing in. I was going to humiliate him. I was going to make him my bitch. I would put him on a leash and walk him like a dog to the convenience store—all the way on his knees until they bled. I would buy a pair of scissors and watch Harshit harvest his chia pet.

"Hasta la vista, you dumb little fuck-fuck," I said as I pointed the gun at him.

"Big bully!" he yelled.

He sprinted toward the end of the alley, holding my wallet and my medication in his hands. He jumped on an aluminum trash can and reached the top of the wall using both hands. I looked at the gun with curiosity, wondering how people operate it. I hadn't planned on shooting him, but he left me no choice. I took a deep breath, closed my eyes, and pulled the trigger.

Nothing came out. Just a soft click.

The gun was empty.

Meanwhile, my former bushwhacker disappeared from sight, jumping to the opposite side of the wall. I inspected the gun closer and my mouth opened in disbelief as soon as I realized I had just been mugged by a plastic toy gun from Muggers R Us.

So many emotions. The mugger had taken the entire wallet that had all my money *and* my driver's license in it. I couldn't call the police—obviously—which is when it finally hit me—that I could *never* call the cops—ever—or even go to a hospital—while I had a kidnapped baby with me. I pulled out Maggie from the sheet and looked at her cute face. She blinked, and I blinked back. Somehow, I got calm.

But I was still an outlaw.

In a way, now I was not dissimilar to the chia pet assailant—or Ama Takayoza.

I dashed toward the trash can after the guy but stopped midway, thinking I couldn't climb that high. Not with Maggie on my chest anyway. Since it was already past eleven, I reminded myself the bus would leave in less than thirty minutes. If I continued pursuing him, I'd miss my bus to D.C., and then what? I didn't have enough money for another bus fare.

I could return to the bank probably, but what if Rusty was at lunch or gone for the day? No self-respecting bank teller would help me withdraw any money without my ID. Chances I got caught right here in New Jersey had risen immensely. Thank god the bus ticket was in my jeans' back pocket and not in the wallet. Sometimes muggers are so silly. He didn't check any of my pockets, but I could've had a diamond ring worth a million dollars in them, which of course, I didn't, but since he'd failed to check, the joke was on him anyway.

After placing Maggie back in the sheet, I knelt before the tote to collect my stuff off the ground, haphazardly shoving them inside. My eyes were watery with tears. My ego underwent a reality treatment about the fact that life can be cruel, and there was no justice to be served. The crumbled bill lying on the ground by the flipped tote was a Jackson, which I'd received in change at the bus stop. For whatever it was worth, the Jackson could buy some food for Maggie. A turkey sandwich wrapped in Saran was still intact, which meant I'd be fed as well.

I stood up and, while drying my eyes, I wondered whether this is how it felt to be a minority. You can be 100 percent right, but it doesn't matter because your voice doesn't count. You can cry all you want. You can feel sorry for yourself. In the end, if you're still a minority, it either makes you or breaks you. I was *definitely* a minority now, no doubt about it. I mean, how many kidnappers can you name offhand?

I dumped the toy gun on the ground, and it bounced, while its echo publicized once again how stupid I was to be mugged by a teenager with fake weaponry. Once I reached D.C., I mused, I'd figure something out. I'd figure out how to cash in, feed Maggie, and find a place to stay. For now, my goal was to flee New Jersey and deal with questions later.

To stay on the up and up, I had to disguise myself. And—whish—a light bulb went off. I patted my butt and exhaled with satisfaction. Because I was liberated. Because the self-adhesive mustache I'd stolen from Harshit was still there.

I unwrapped the package, removing the protective strip from the underside and adjusted the handlebar mustache above my lip. It was itchy, and I sneezed. No wonder scruffy men perpetually scratch their faces and balls. Do men, I wondered, shampoo their mustache or let it stay dirty? What if they have a runny nose? Does it all end up in the bush? My father wore a thick, bushy mustache, partially white and partially yellow from all the cigarettes he smoked, the color combination of Lassie. To be honest, I was not a fan of seeing that. Mostly because I hate dogs.

When I approached the bus terminal and found my bus, I positioned myself in line behind an Indian lady in a turquoise sari. She was gabbing on the phone with an Indian accent, an ebony suitcase by her leg like a good doggy. About twenty by twenty inches, her bag was the replica of a suitcase of the passenger who was next in line, but hers had a purple ribbon tied to the handle on top. "Hi, this is Nefertiti," she was saying. "No, Nefertiti. You can call me Titi."

At eleven twenty, the doors to the bus opened. Big and bulky at the sides, a white guy in uniform wobbled out and opened a compartment door by the front wheel, revealing a hollow space for luggage. He was our driver. His jet-black hair was thick and unruly, so animalistic and "safariesque," that I had an unexplained desire to watch *the Lion King*. He helped passengers haul their luggage inside, checking tickets at the same time. Being tenth in line, I entered, partially covering Maggie with the tote, and claimed the very last seat near the bathroom. Other passengers distributed themselves around the bus without looking or talking to one another. Due to the lack of passengers to fill the entire bus, some seats remained empty, and most people sat by themselves unless they were a couple. I felt like a pimp after getting a whole row.

The bus driver walked in last, arranged himself behind the wheel, and closed the door, which released a gentle sigh as if it was relieved for some reason. The driver put on sunglasses and readjusted the side mirrors.

I yawned, checking the view in my window, waving goodbye to New

Jersey with an imaginary hand. I'd made this far already; could it be much more difficult in the future? I dotted my i's and crossed my t's when it came to covering my tracks and disguising myself. But as soon as I let my mind relax, the voices inside my head reappeared.

You're like the monkeys from The Jungle Book.

Yes, because they kidnapped Mowgli, and you kidnapped a baby.

You're a monkey!

Whenever great deeds are remembered in this jungle, one name will stand above all others: our friend, Baloo, the bear.

They were laughing and teasing for the next two hours, quoting Bagheera, King Louie, and Mowgli. But then, near the City of Brotherly Love, it came to a halt when Maggie became fussy. I mixed the formula with bottled water, and that was precisely what the doctor ordered. I was famished by then too and munched on the turkey sandwich I'd purchased at the Newark Penn Station. After lunch, Maggie fell asleep.

We arrived at 6:25 p.m., two and a half hours late due to heavy traffic near Baltimore. Our driver parked the bus downtown in a large uncovered field across the street from the gates to Chinatown. He stepped off the bus and started removing suitcases from the underneath compartment. It was getting lively inside after hours of silence. Maggie had been asleep in my arms, as I'd removed her from the sheet near Philadelphia. But now she woke up and started crying. Babies *love* doing that. I tried to calm her down by rocking her, which didn't help. I tried the formula, and she had some. I must change her diaper again, but that had to wait. After the formula "supper," I offered her the pacifier, which she gladly took.

By now, I'd gotten used to the thick mustache above my lips. Nobody had given me a suspicious stare, meaning the mustache had fooled them. The cops were searching for a lady, and I could prance by their noses with a superior smile. I was no law enforcement, but while stuck in traffic, I had put myself in their shoes. They couldn't possibly check *every* baby in *every* stroller around *every* city. They don't have enough troops for that. Even if indeed they checked *every* baby in *every* stroller in *every* town, I was not in New York anymore.

Besides, I'd also considered the fact that there were *actual* criminals in this world: seventeen-year-old muggers, murderers, child molesters, skinny girls, and even Calyssa who stole rings from work. Compared to them, I couldn't possibly be the *worst* of the bunch. Lindsay almost killed her baby by lying about taking a CPR class. *Killed*. I didn't steal anything or *kill* anyone. Yes, I'd kidnapped a baby—so what? Natalia was kidnapping African children left and right.

Satisfied with my thought process—in which I was not a hardcore criminal—I stood up and moved toward the front. Ahead, people were in the process of getting up, and that created mild congestion. In the meantime, I looked back to make sure I didn't leave anything behind, and my eyes found Titi, who was blabbing on the phone two rows behind. Her turquoise sari was decorated with a light-brown floral pattern, and she wore the sari with blue jeans. For a final touch, there was a red bindi in the middle of her forehead. Her hair looked silky and dark, and it contrasted with her skin color, a cross between honey and peanut butter. Not a zit in sight. Her hair sat on her head in thick clusters, kind of like long brown turds that were pooped out and attached to her head, dreadlock-style.

I exited the bus and gave the area a circumvolution, learning swiftly I was at the corner of Eleventh and H Street. The sky was sketched in vibrant pink and purple. In an hour, it would probably get dark. The smell of beef with broccoli was whiffed from Chinatown, and that's when I realized something: I was homeless. For whatever reason, it hadn't occurred to me before. In April, it's brutally cold at night. With zero money to spend, I was at the mercy of providence.

I decided to just go. I readjusted my tote, and off I wandered. Soon I stumbled upon a metro station called McPherson Square, and it was the sign I needed. I took the steps until I saw a row of kiosks in view, an oversized system map above. I knew I could figure out where to go. If I could figure out the New York City subway map, I could figure out just about anything.

I referenced the map. Unlike the tangled subway in the city, in Washington, the metro seemed to consist of only six lines denoted by color. In New York, trains bear alphabet letters, numbers, and further grouped by color. McPherson Square Station was in the middle of the blue/orange/silver track. Coincidentally, they are my three most favorite colors. On the map, the city of Washington was shaped like a diamond and then further outlined by an octagon, connecting parts of Maryland and Virginia into a metropolis. Several lines crisscrossed, later disappearing on their own outside the diamond, and then out of the octagon.

I picked the last stop on the silver line, as far away from the city center as possible. The price for a one-way ticket was a whopping four dollars and thirty cents. I bought my ticket with the leftover twenty that the mugger had generously provided, and took the escalator down to the platform.

The silver train arrived five minutes later. I claimed a window seat and placed the tote on the seat next to mine to ensure no one sat there. I removed Maggie from the sheet and turned her. She was watching me with her big, beautiful eyes while sucking on the pacifier, and I exaggeratedly stretched my mouth. Then I removed her pacifier and opened my eyes as wide as I could muster. She giggled when I made that funny face. I tickled her a bit, and her entire body shook in delight, like, *"Stop it, Mommy, but don't really stop it, just keep doing it."* I used to do the same with Noah when he was a toddler. Little kids like when adults loosen up and do silly stuff like that. The train soon exited from the underground, and the track appeared to be running above a highway the rest of the way. The baby kept touching the glass window with her teeny hands, leaving prints all over the window. I followed suit and left a greasy impression of my palm next to hers. Mumbling, she hit my palm with hers. It felt real, and surprisingly liberating. Whatever was the God's plan, clearly it was unfolding now, as the two of us were bonding over handprints on the subway's window.

A plan on how to snatch us some housing popped in my head, but it sounded imperfect, and some would say even stupid, but here it is regardless: I'd knock on a random door and ask to use the telephone. I'd then talk loudly on the phone and say something like, "Linda, you're stuck in New York because of a hurricane? I was supposed to stay with you tonight. Where am I supposed to stay? Listen, I don't have any cash on me, and the banks won't open until tomorrow. Where will I sleep?"

If I were the hostess and saw a woman with a baby (which means trustworthy), I'd be like, "Oh, why don't you stay here?"

The plan worried me. I looked at Maggie for confirmation, trying to see what she thought. I turned her toward me, took off her pacifier, and whispered, "Blink twice in a row if there's any verisimilitude to this plan." Believe it or not, she blinked. Twice in a row. She understood me.

Do you understand me, Maggie? I asked her in my head while looking directly in her eyes.

Yes, Mommy, she answered.

You do? Why didn't you speak before?

You put the pacifier in my mouth. You can't talk with a pacifier in your mouth, either, Mommy.

Oh!

She made so much sense. I couldn't believe it. *Of course*, babies can talk.

Our genes are responsible for communication, and we're born with an operating system in place, kind of like my Apple laptop. I hugged her so tight for calling me Mommy as it was the best validation.

Do you know my name?

It's Mommy.

That's right. And what's your name?

Maggie.

Good girl. Wish us luck as we try to stay over someplace tonight.

Good luck, Mommy.

Soon the train huffed to its last stop—Wiehle-Reston. The dusk had consumed half the sky, and I tied the scarf over Maggie's head for warmth and put her inside the sheet. I gave her the pacifier, which she seemed to crave.

Sit tight now, okay, Maggie?

With only fifteen dollars and seventy cents left, Maggie and I needed all sorts of things, starting with food and diapers. It had dawned on me to never kidnap a baby unless I was loaded. With my driver's license gone, there was no way to withdraw any money from the bank. Tonight I was focusing on getting a place to stay, somewhere nearby, and tomorrow I'd start worrying about coinage.

Upon exiting the train station, I noticed trees and bushes growing on either side of the road, street lamps emitting a bright yellow light. I was not used to such quietness. The few passengers who exited with me minded their own business, and I followed them toward the exit with my tote at the tow. Most passengers disappeared in their parked cars, leaving me all alone. I could see a couple of houses peekaboo from behind the tall trees. On one lamppost, there was a "Missing Cat" flyer, as was on a lamppost next to it.

More cat crimes. I guess missing Anubis was not enough.

I turned and ended up on Sunrise Valley Drive. Cars zoomed by with a swishing sound to my left, while I contemplated which way to go. I needed some sort of a sign—and when Maggie kicked me hard with her foot, I saw it—bright and clear: CANDY'S CORNER in pink neon—a convenience store.

Thank you, baby.

My instinct was telling me the store would have formula and diapers for Maggie, and a sandwich or something for me, because my tummy was growling. Another "Missing Cat" flyer was posted against the glass door, asking if anyone had seen a pudgy orange catzilla with enough fur for two sweaters. The reward had not been offered, so I assumed nobody would be searching for the runaway (or kidnapped) kitty.

The lady behind the counter smiled as I entered. I stretched a smile in return and hid in the first aisle. Little bottles with baby faces were on the shelf in front of me, and I snatched several bottles of ready-to-drink baby formula, the only kind I knew. That's the kind Noah grew up eating, as did Calyssa's niece, Grace. Diapers for two bucks a pop were on the shelf below, and I grabbed four. In the next aisle, I retrieved a donut and an old hot dog, which looked brown and unhealthy.

"Well, what's her name?" the cashier, whose name was Martina written on her chest, asked me.

"It's Maggie," I said. I assumed calling her Maggie was safe in front of strangers since it wasn't her real name. I actually wondered what her real name was, but thought once I watched the news, a story about her would come up.

"You're cute, Maggie," she told the baby. After Martina scanned all my items, she added, "twelve ninety-five." Belatedly, I realized the mustache was still above my lip, and I was not speaking in baritone. Holy ship. I hope she didn't notice. I handed Martina the leftover cash, and she counted my change, after which she bagged the items. I thanked her and exited the store.

I crossed Sunrise Valley Drive, shivering from the wind that was only accelerating. The smaller boats on Potomac River had probably been issued a gale warning, as strong waves tend to be dangerous.

The street ahead was called Great Meadow Drive. The dusk was intensifying quickly, due to the lack of street lamps in this neighborhood. Final orange bits of sunset had been eaten and replaced by thick clouds to assure me the night, at last, had fallen on Virginia, dim and cold—like my neighbor Agnes—and even the moon could not be seen as it had apparently gone fishing.

I was trying to find the courage to execute my plan, and as I was passing a house after a house, the more terrified I was becoming.

But then something clicked.

There stood a house illuminated by a weak, unsteady porch light, which flickered with a hum. The house was hidden behind a tree with thick leafage, but I could see how it was old and sagging, a broken fence surrounding it—almost as if abandoned. I unglued the mustache from my face, and I took a deep breath, thinking this is it. A thin layer of snow crinkled underneath my feet as I walked. My ass was damp from fear.

Kicking the snow off my boots, I now stood in front of the house, and even in the darkness, I saw its viridescent moldy color, paint peeling off in big chunks revealing wooden planks underneath. The light above the front door was on, while up the steps to the right, in the shade, sat a silhouette in a rocking chair, moving back and forth in complete quietness. The chair screeched with a high pitch tone, while the person's visage was hidden in the darkness of the porch. Creepy a bit. In front of me, I saw the beginning of a scary movie (or a documentary about a missing kidnapper named Chloe Tenderfoot), which involved a haunted house full of unsettled souls. Frightening? To say the least. But I had no choice. When you're an outlaw, nitpicking about a place to stay is imprudent. Placing my tote on the ground, I stopped by the first step and cleared my throat to warm up the pipes, which for some reason, were dry.

"Excuse me. May I use your phone?" I asked the silhouette that I assumed belonged to the house potentate.

A dog woofed somewhere in the distance once, but its echo made it sound like it was a whole pack of them. Dogs scare me because they seem happy all the time. Are they all on Prozac? With all the cats missing in the neighborhood, I expected at least a meowing or two.

The rocking chair on the porch stopped moving. The person stood up, bones audibly creaking, and I noticed that the stranger—a woman—was wearing a dress and was using a cane for support as she made her way toward the light. Her old-fashioned dress was way too outdated, with a lace collar that belonged to Cinderella. The woman removed glasses from the top of her head and placed them on her nose. Those were some thick freaking lenses. Now that I could see her clearly, I assumed she was a septuagenarian or about the same age as Agnes.

"Cece, is that you?" she asked in a voice that you could only describe as the "hopeful" voice.

Unhurriedly, like a centipede, she proceeded toward the staircase, shadows slowly replaced by colors. Her hair and skin tone were pale honeydew with sunk-in cheeks in a tinted green. Her hair was collected on top into a perfect cinnamon bun. Her dress, with large shoulder pads, was blue. She grabbed the guardrail and descended the five steps down. Belatedly, I noticed that a few balusters were missing, and those intact were covered in mold.

"Feels good," she said apropos of nothing, as she reached the ground. She looked me over and smiled. "Gives me the needed exercise—that's what, Cece. What did you say, dear? I couldn't hear you." Her voice was high pitched and a little shaky, no accent of any sort—just a good old American dame.

"May I use your telephone?" I said. For reasons unknown, I found myself shouting, foolishly presuming the madam was hard of hearing. "I was supposed to meet my friend, but she didn't show up. I don't have a cell phone."

"You don't have a what now? You have to speak up, dear." She noticed Maggie, who was moving her hands and feet up and down as if saying, *"Hi, grandma. Take me!"* Babies and their grandmas—I'm telling you—inseparable, like H2 and O. Oh wait. That's separable.

The woman perked up. "Is that Bertha?"

"No, I asked whether I could use your phone," I said.

"I can't believe my eyes. That's Bertha."

She seemed genuinely happy. She kept limping toward me with the support of her cane. Print daisies on her dress were yellow or torn. When she stood a foot away from me, way past my personal bubble, I noticed her malnourished face. She was underweight and no higher than five-two. But her belly was sticking out. Up close, her glass lenses were thicker than an inch.

"What's that, dear?" she said. When she pushed her glasses in, her eyes appeared the size of a bicycle wheel. "Is that little Bertha?"

"Her name is Maggie."

"Charity. What a lovely name. I'm Miriam." She cleared her throat. "Turtle. And you are, dear?"

"Um . . . Ball." I lowered my head in embarrassment because I was lying to an old woman. "Crystal, my first name."

She slowly breathed in the cold night air. "You have to speak up, dear. I'm not twenty anymore."

"Crystal Ball," I yelled, almost too lurid.

"Crystal Ball, how nice. She's a good friend of mine. How is she?"

"She's . . . okay," I said slowly, and my face cringed automatically—like, what? I was unsure if we were talking the same language anymore. "May I use your phone?"

"Sure, Cece, it should be in the house someplace. You need help with your bag?"

"No, thanks, I'm cool."

"Oh, I wasn't offering to lift them, dear. I'm in no position to lift heavy weights, as you can see. I was just trying to be nice. Okay, dear, follow me. The room is all set up for you."

Astonished, I pulled back. My *what*—room? Was my plan too obvious, or was she plain crazy? I mean, the conversation was slowly sinking in—she thought I was someone named Cece who had a baby named Bertha—who had a room in her house—her daughter?

What on earth?

Limping, Miriam began climbing up the steps, holding the cane with one hand and the guardrail with the other. I picked up my junk and followed in quiet. The steps squeaked and deepened under my weight, and I wondered whether a raccoon was living under the house. I heard people with homes have raccoons—that's all. A dead plant sat by the steps in a large terracotta pot, a dirty welcome mat by the door.

Was it really happening, I wondered. I turned back. The dark ether behind me resembled the Atlantic Ocean, stretching for miles on end without a single lighthouse in sight. This was the time of the night when hungry sharks came out, and if my plan failed, "Charity" and I would be eaten by morning if left out in the marina. When Miriam opened the front door, she got swallowed by the darkness, and I heard, "Come in, come in, dear."

It was like stepping into a black hole, and I momentarily hesitated as fear caused an uncomfortable cramp in my stomach. I left the tote on the porch and walked into the void, swaying hands in front of me to avoid whatever danger could be lurking ahead that I couldn't see.

Doesn't smell all that bad, I thought. Mold, mildew, musty sock smell. You'd expect *at least* that from an old woman whose muffin top orbits around her body like the rings around Saturn. Agnes's apartment, whenever she opened her door, smelled not dissimilar—and I always felt bad, wanting to help without knowing how, and that's how I felt now.

Miriam, in the meantime, quickly dissolved in the blackness as would a chameleon, leaving me to the smell, which somehow decided to organize a party of two gag reflexes. From that moment on, I was breathing through my mouth. Don't underestimate an old woman so quickly. Even without using my nose, I tasted mud on my tongue. Ahead, a TV set was flickering like a little star out in the sky.

Lights went off.

Words "holy ship" bounced around my brain like a ball in a pinball machine—and were an understatement. I was relieved to learn the smell made perfect sense. Where *was* the damn house? I knew where: hidden under the piles of junk I saw in front of me.

It was overwhelming. As if in a movie, my eyes zoomed in and out from one place to the next—haphazardly. I saw boxes, chairs, tables, old TV sets with antler antennas, and bicycles with no wheels. Newspapers, clothes, takeout containers. Flies. I wondered if I was having another hallucination, and I looked at Maggie, waiting for her to turn into a cat, but she didn't—which meant this was real. Green eyes were watching me from every possible corner that belonged to an endless array of kitties. My eyes tictocked from one to the next, while the cats jumped around, playing hide-and-go-seek.

I had to close my eyes as if to recalibrate my vision, and I breathed through pursed lips to avoid hyperventilating.

Under no circumstances would Maggie and I stay at Miriam's house. Was there an alternative, however? I'd never been to a hoarder's house before—this one belonged to one for sure—but I'd heard they were mentally ill. I decided I'd rather spend the night outside than stay overnight in that dump. I swiftly turned and exited, briskly sucking in the fresh air.

A police beacon blinked far in the distance, its siren bringing me back to reality. The cops *were* searching for me, after all. They finally realized I'd left New York and traveled all the way to D.C. Shoaling around in the darkness was asking for trouble, to get arrested, and/or to get mugged. Taking a deep breath of clean air one last time for the road, I stepped back into the house with the tote at the tow and shut the door shut behind me. I left it by the door, paused, and started the inspection.

The floor was trick-or-treating as a trash bag, and I could not discern whether it was wood or carpet underneath. Maggie didn't seem to mind the stench at all, but she kind of gobbled like a turkey and hit me with her legs.

Now, easy baby girl.

Holding her legs with my hand, I wondered whether little tots could tell the difference between aroma and the smell of death that whiffed from every possible item I laid my eyes on. A staircase ahead provided access to the second floor of the house, where Miriam's bedroom was probably located. If her bedroom was anything like the dump sight in front of me, I hardly expected a clean mattress. Where did she want me to sleep again?

Miriam reappeared with a confused expression as if she'd forgotten what she was doing.

"What do you need again, dear?" she asked me.

"A telephone."

"Oh! The phone must be here someplace," she said in a tone as if it's reasonable to search for a telephone under piles of crap. Miriam threw aside pillows, lampshades, and books. I giggled, thinking we were underwater in *the Little Mermaid's world*, treasure-hunting for human objects.

"There it is," she said. Miriam offered me a phone without a cord. Of course, it could have work wirelessly—in some other parallel world—but to be polite to the crazy expression on her face, I retrieved the handset and dialed a number.

"No dial tone," I said reassuringly.

"Oh, boy. Try this one."

The next phone she offered came with a cord, unplugged—obviously—but without a dial tone either. On an episode of *Hoarders*, this one lady purchased so much junk, she couldn't afford to pay her telephone bill. Maybe Miriam was the same way. I had to play Make Believe since she was apparently clueless about her cutoff telephone service.

"This one's legit," I lied.

Her face attained a genuine smile. "Good, good. Make your call, dear."

The phone was vintage, with a rotary dial plate, perhaps stolen from a museum of antiques. Its white base was sprinkled with pink roses, which gave it a defined character—and I instantly guessed its value on the black market, but since I knew nothing about *that* kind of market, I gave up. I dialed Calyssa's number, which I knew by heart, rotating the dial ten times back and forth.

I cleared my throat, ready for shouting, and sang loudly, "Hi, Calyssa! It's Chloe!"

And it hit me—I needed to lie. To erase my mistake, I coughed and started over. "I mean, Crystal. Hi, Chloe, it's Crystal. Where are you? I'm here in Virginia by the train stop where we were supposed to meet, but you're not here. What? Because of the bad weather, all the flights are canceled? Are you *sure*?" I was enunciating every word so Miriam could eavesdrop on the conversation. "But, Chloe, I have nowhere to stay and have no money for a hotel. What am I supposed to do?" I paused to give the imaginary Chloe time to respond. "Okay, thanks, bye."

I hung up, grimacing.

I handed Miriam back the phone with a phony expression of sadness on my face—I imagined I was eating onions that Mom adds in everything—and said, "Thank you, Miriam."

"What's wrong, dear?"

"My friend is trapped in New York because of a hurricane. All flights have been canceled. She was going to pay for the hotel—and without her money, I'm absolutely broke."

"You say bad weather in New York?"

Nodding, I locked eyes with a furless cat. "I know. I'll return to the train station and sleep there."

"With Bertha? At the train station? I wouldn't hear none of it. Your room is ready, dear. I haven't touched it ever since you left."

Her eyes were so enormous behind the thick lenses, almost cartoonish, and were as blue as a cloudless sky. Or like a lake, inviting me to undress and jump into them, a thought of which provoked a giggle. Miriam was confusing me with someone else for sure, but a smile was already flexed on my lips. I hid it, of course, ashamed of taking advantage of the little old lady. I kept breathing through my mouth, lest not to vomit, and fanned my palm in front of Maggie for whatever it was worth.

"Are you sure I'm no trouble?" I asked.

"Absolutely, Cece. Come upstairs. Bring your bag with you."

Miriam paused near a staircase in the middle of the room. I followed her through the impenetrable path, kicking at items and shaking my head in disbelief. A broken guitar with no strings attached appeared in view, together with a piano that was now only good for timber. Entirely out of character for this house, the wallpaper had a chinoiserie pattern with peacocks and flowers of all types and sizes. Miriam was all over the place with her decorating skills. Modern plastic chairs in white were visible underneath a contemporary grey futon, which together resembled a fort where her kitties played. A grand dramatic chandelier with clear faceted crystals—in seven or more tiers, like an upside-down wedding cake—was hanging in the middle of the room, sparkling, with the bronze body underneath. Edison-style bulbs were visible in the kitchen to my right. I was scared of what I would find in the next room (a den, perhaps?) that appeared ahead but was dark with only a measly light coming from a TV set and, ironically, for a woman who was hard of hearing, there was no sound.

After a successful attempt to cross the room, I paused briefly near the staircase. The balustrade that once used to be white was now scratched from the cats' claws. Ornate spindles, all intact, resembled hourglasses, each one just adding more and more time for whatever (or whomever?) Miriam was waiting for. Some woman named Cece? A man, perhaps?

It seems everyone is waiting for a man these days—and I briefly saw Kim, but not long enough to think of him any further.

Miriam was mumbling a song under her nose, and while holding the railing and her cane, she managed up the carpeted steps, which were brown in color. To the naked eye, it was clearly not the original color the carpet had come in when it had been installed. The cats watched us ascend, but none followed. I know cats. They're like kids, and they don't care about the adult business. All they want to do is nap and play and go potty in a sandbox. When Miriam reached the last step, she tugged on a string hanging above her, and a low wattage bulb flickered promptly above her head.

I looked behind me to check out the house from this vantage point, wondering how in the hell I ended up in a hoarder's home.

My karma was really down.

Miriam proceeded toward the end of the hallway, where she stopped long enough to unlock a door with a key. She flipped on the light in the room and entered it. When I stepped in after her, my eyes popped open from the view.

The room—unlike the death trap downstairs—was immaculate. A rustic white chest of drawers stood by the door, an off-white rug under a wooden crib, an antique twin bed with big, puffy pillows to the left. An off-white shelving unit sat between two windows straight ahead. Translucent curtains were drawn, underneath which blackout shades peekabooed.

"I haven't touched a thing ever since you left, Cece."

At first, I surmised it was a hallucination after having smelled enough garbage. But when I pinched myself, nothing changed. The room felt like stepping into the past, which, while physically impossible, was achieved through preservation. Even though I was not Cece, I appreciated the notion of having my own room that someone had been saving for all these years. The bedroom was a time capsule to the simpler times. The past, immaterial, whether yesterday or five thousand years ago, feels like the simpler times. Because it's done and over with, and, therefore, that made those times simpler.

"I'll fix you supper while you unpack. Welcome back home, dear."

She kissed me on the cheek, Maggie on the lips, and quickly withdrew. I saw nothing but emptiness in her blue eyes, kind of like those of a psychopath's—a bland and almost sick—void expression. My grandpa had the same face branded with a solid look of hatred and sorrow after the Vietnam War. His aura felt unfriendly and was almost feasible. Even though he lived with us until he died fifteen years ago, mentally, he seemed to be living alone in his own world. As was Miriam. At first, I wrote her off as cuckoo, but on second thought, she resembled someone from a psych ward, not a serial killer. Hoarders—and Miriam, by definition, was one according to what I saw downstairs—have mental disorders, and compulsive hoarding is a form of OCD. I learned from Agnes's daughter, Antoinette, that her mother was suffering from syllogomania or a fetish for trash. Most hoarders live in isolation, and once that isolation starts, they start building a relationship with things rather than people. Miriam acted as if I was her relative, a close friend, or someone dear to her, whoever that Cece was. As of now, I was in no position to question her motives. She was eager to help, and if I had to be Cece for the night, then Cece I was.

The room for sure had been designated as a nursery. The walls were wallpapered in pastel green, with white asterisks of different sizes splattered throughout. A small lamp with an eggshell lampshade sat on top of the chest of drawers. It barely smelled up there.

I carefully removed Maggie, now sleeping, from my chest, and gently placed her in the crib. I untied the sheet, wondering whether the FBI might have offered a reward for catching me. Miriam had trapped me in her parlor, providing room and board and supper, as she put it. On the other hand, maybe she was seeking company. Living solo must get lonesome, whether you're alone inside your head—like those hallucinations I sometimes experience—or outside of your head. I felt such loneliness many times when I was unable to tell my friends about my mental disorder.

Secrets can definitely make you suffer.

For what seemed like an unnatural amount of time, I was staring at Maggie, unwilling to leave her alone. Had I only had her for one day? It already felt like a century. Unlike us, guilty adults, babies are pure and carefree and loving. A baby is like a blank canvas, and I wondered if I could raise her like a perfect daughter using only the best crayons. Skinny like Lindsay, beautiful like Calyssa, and rich like Natalia. Or would Maggie grow up resembling an insecure Lindsay, lying Calyssa, and insensitive Natalia?

Maybe none of us are that pure, after all.

As soon as I stepped away from the crib, I started missing her, and there was another thing I missed. My phone. In the past, I was critical of my friends when they pulled out their phones during our get-togethers. Now, I would be one of them, messaging my friends. Being addicted to math, I was so good with numbers I knew everyone's phone number by heart. So technically, I could call them, but I knew it could lead to danger. The FBI taps your friends' and family's phone lines because nine out of ten, you'll contact them soon. My mother was probably going berserk when she realized I was not at home for the brisket dinner that she'd put in a slow cooker earlier this morning before leaving for work.

So wait.

Did that mean I could *never* see my friends and family again?

Ever ever ever?

Just that one thought gave me a jolt.

You know what?—I told myself—I'm ready to deal with reality. And I promptly locked any thoughts away with a mental padlock.

BY THE TIME I DESCENDED DOWNSTAIRS, AN OLD GRANDPA clock stroke ten. The clock was located somewhere in the living room, but it failed to reveal itself, being hidden somewhere under the piles of trash. The cats watched my entry, clearly afraid. Of all the cats missing in the neighborhood, I wondered were any of them here?

I locked eyes with a fluffy cat and imagined how he got here. "Hi, I'm Fluffy," he was saying to Miriam upon knocking on the door. "My friend was stuck in New York because of a hurricane."

"Come in, Cece," she told the cat. "I have a room for you."

"I'm Fluffy—not Cece."

I snickered while visualizing the fantasy, but when I came back to reality the fluffy cat was gone, and a big orange cat was in its place, licking his . . . um, let's, for now, say it was his paws.

The sound of running water accompanied the sizzling of meat in butter ahead in the kitchen. The smell overpowered the stench and was making me hungry. I proceeded toward the aroma, stepping on something crunchy, then on something sticky—then something crunchy stuck to something sticky, and the crunchy sound was now escorting me.

The kitchen was located near the entrance, illuminated by a weak but warm Edison-style light bulb. A stove and a refrigerator were the only kitchen appliances visible, no microwave in sight (broken ones, however, were tossed around the living room like cars in a junkyard). Miriam hustled over a frying pan, from which thick smoke puffed out into the air, dissolving the morbid hoarder smell. There was no fire detector in the vicinity, or it would be going off already. (There was no carbon monoxide detector either, which kind of scared me because I was unwilling to die so young and pretty). Plus, I thought, by law, those two detectors must be installed in a house. Then again, how would I know which laws were applicable in Virginia, especially to someone like me with such a cantankerous track record?

I watched Miriam cooking for two minutes as she flipped down the raw side of the steak, revealing the opposite side, the most perfect shade of brown, almost black, the same hue as Kim's hair. Steak for sure has made its way to my top-ten list of favorite things to eat. I didn't have high cholesterol for nothing! The steak kept sizzling as Miriam opened the refrigerator door. By the sink, I saw a chipped plate with sautéed spinach that looked as appetizing as would polished malachite. Yuck. Whoever invented spinach hated humanity. (Was it *you*, God?) I looked up at the ceiling and giggled at my silliness. Miriam was speaking to herself or humming a tune, but it sounded like a bunch of gobbledygook. Her ankles were thick "cankles"—as they were called—calves turned into feet without any apparent ankles. She turned off the stove, moved the pan to a trivet, and while holding the frying pan in one hand, she grabbed an oversized fork. She stabbed the steak with it and transferred it to the plate with the spinach. Maybe Miriam thought I was Popeye. My rambunctious stomach told me it couldn't take it any longer and needed some food in it, like yesterday.

For the first time in minutes, our eyes met, a soothing smile on her lips, a hungry expression on mine.

"Let's sit out in the dining room, Cece. What would you like to drink? I have milk and apple juice."

"Apple juice, if no trouble."

"Oh, no trouble at all. Grapefruits are really cheap, so I'll squeeze them myself."

Grapefruits?

Miriam reached into the fridge and retrieved three grapefruits. When was it okay to tell her I'd ordered apple juice? Such customer service wouldn't fly at McDonald's—I thought to myself and giggled again. From a drawer by the sink, she found a juicer with a thick reamer going up like a dome. She cut the fruit in half straight on the counter without using a cutting board. Miriam took each half and twisted them against the dome until the juice dribbled into a cup underneath. From above the sink, in one of the cabinets, she found a tall glass and poured the freshly squeezed juice into it. The pungent smell of citrus almost overpowered the steak. I was not sure why she was squeezing the grapefruit—did she misunderstand me? I was glad I hadn't asked for milk, or she might've produced a cow from the pantry and started squeezing milk from an udder.

I wouldn't even be surprised.

"Go to the dining room, Cece. Take the plate, and I'll bring in the rest."

Swiftly, she pulled a drawer by the sink, where she picked up a steak knife and a smaller fork. She placed them on my plate and offered the plate to me.

She held salt and pepper shakers in one hand, juice in the other. I followed her toward the dining room, hungry like never before. It was a small alcove at the end of the living room, and it could potentially be closed off with French doors that stood open to either side of the wall, with junk preventing them from moving. Dust and grime seemed to have permanently settled on the panes together with spider's web. Two windows were hidden by more junk, with visible scratches on the wood left by Miriam's loyal feline companions.

The "dining room"—I must address it in quotes—consisted of a couch, or an apparatus resembling one. It must have been purchased at a 25 percent sale during the Mesolithic period (or anywhere in the Stone Age range). The brown leather-looking cushions perhaps once belonged to a mammoth, whose fate was to end up as furniture. I know that thousands of years ago, mammoth molars were used to make weapons, so other parts were clearly used as well. One black kitty with spiky ears was shamelessly clawing one side of the couch, and I could see a wooden plank underneath the shredded fabric. I briefly—and purely hypothetically—wondered if my mom would go berserk if Anubis had ever done that. Upon seeing me, the cat ran toward the living room.

The TV set was straight across, while a round dining table stood next to the only window with its curtain drawn. A pale khaki table runner ran the length of the table with fake white lilies in a crystal vase in the middle.

The dining room appeared in a somewhat better state than the living room or the kitchen. However, the fresh cat poop was smeared all over everything like butter on bread, some of it dry and crumbly like goat cheese. Boy, was I hungry! Miriam reached the table and placed salt and pepper shakers with my juice on a lazy Susan. The beige carpet reeked of cat urine and Agnes. Under the TV set, there was an old mahogany TV stand, purchased right after WWII. A china cabinet leaned on one side, ready to collapse.

"Dig in, Cece, while it's still hot," Miriam said to me.

The cats meowed in the living room, but only one was fearless enough to investigate the new stranger invading their home. She was an ebony Bombay cat with yellow eyes, and she looked deprived of food. She meowed in short intervals, knowing perfectly well about my steak that was out of her view, all the way up on the table. Her tail, long and serpentine, twisted around my left ankle in a loving but fake burst of affection. Cats know how to kiss ass. After taking care of Anubis, I was used to saying no to needy cats who could beg for hours until they get what they want—and then, suddenly, you no longer exist for them. As I petted her, she unwound her tail, and it went up to my arm like poison ivy, but plush and silky to the touch.

Miriam turned up the volume on the TV by rotating a dial on the set and returned to sit with me. Even though the TV set was antique—its free-standing carcass lifted by four tall legs—the picture was in color. I would never guess anybody still had one of those.

A news anchor, Skip Jones, came in view. If only he could see himself being squished into the small frame like that. The spinach was now cold and was beyond overcooked, but I wasn't about to complain to my gracious hostess about the free food she selflessly offered. The steak looked good, but as I cut a slice, I learned it wasn't. Dry and rubbery. Even though Miriam squeezed the juice from the grapefruit in front of me, for some reason, it had a particular "past due" taste, and just like with prune juice, I knew I'd be blowing up Miriam's bathroom later that evening. But beggars, as the cliché goes, can't be choosers.

"Breaking news," Skip was saying. "Lykke Fawcett—a five-month toddler—is reported missing in New York City. Lykke was kidnapped from Central Park earlier this morning, but it wasn't reported until an hour ago."

A shot of a young woman in handcuffs came into view, and something squeezed in my stomach. I turned toward Miriam, whose eyes were closed and mouth open. Was she asleep already?

"Lykke is five months old," Skip continued, "and she was under the supervision of her babysitter, Selma Karr, her nineteen-year-old Swedish nanny. Selma was looking for Lykke around the park all day without reporting it to the authorities. The FBI has just begun the investigation, and as of right now, no suspect has been identified. The Fawcett family refused to comment, but the reward of thirty-five thousand dollars has been issued. If you've seen the baby or have any information, please call."

Maggie's picture appeared on the screen with her name underneath: Lykke Fawcett.

"This is Lykke's most recent picture, taken this morning," Skip said. "This morning, she was wearing a red Elmo hat, a blue cardigan with two yellow chickens near the hem, a polka dot bodysuit, blue cotton pants, and a black jumpsuit."

When the footage ended, Skip Jones was back in the studio together with a co-anchor, Will Miller. They started discussing the topic, while I was thinking: Lykke Fawcett was my Maggie. I loved her real name much better, wondering its origin and meaning. I carefully looked at Miriam one more time, whose eyes were still closed and who was now snoring. A black puss with hunched back purred on her lap absentmindedly. Selma Karr, therefore, was not the parent who was sitting by the tree playing with her phone as I'd initially thought. She was Lykke's irresponsible nanny/spy. The news also meant that while I had been en route to D.C. scared of every shadow, nobody had been after me, and therefore there had been no witnesses.

I could not believe my luck.

Voices filled my head with congratulations.

The authorities have no leads.

You've made it. What a relief.

Congratulations, Chloe!

They were on my side today. Usually, they intimidated, repressed, or laughed at me. While they chatted, I tried to focus on Lykke. I now knew she was five months old. Or as my dead sister Matilda would say, five months young.

Maybe she's six.

Did they actually say five?

Maybe you're wrong.

You're always wrong, Chloe.

Maybe you're not even Chloe.

Is your name Matilda?

The chatter was getting so loud, and out of control, I was getting confused and could not concentrate. What did the voices mean telling me I was not Chloe? Then who? How could I ever be my dead sister Matilda?

Maybe you're the one who died.

And she's the one who is alive.

She was prettier than you.

And skinny.

I rushed upstairs, locked the door, and jumped on the bed, covering my ears with a pillow. I quickly realized the voices were inside my head and not outside, which meant the pillow helped naught.

"What do you want?" I asked them aloud.

To die!

You're a worthless fool.

You don't deserve a baby.

You're just a baby yourself!

Yeah! Maybe you're the one who is five months old.

And then it hit me! The only way Lykke could speak is when a pacifier is removed from her mouth. If my mouth had a pacifier, the voices would stop. I wasn't about to take Lykke's, so I stuck a thumb in my mouth.

And immediately it came—peace.

With the thumb in my mouth, somehow, I fell asleep.

L

Lazily, I rolled around the bed. An awful dream, in which I kidnap a baby, lingered in my mind with such great detail that it sent a chill down my spine. Thank God it was just a dream, I thought, shivering. My bedroom was dark due to the blackout shades, but not pitch black. For reasons unknown, I lay right on top and not underneath the sheets like I usually do. My clothes and boots were still on, my head spinning. I sat up on the edge of the bed, rubbed my eyes, and studied the surroundings. Even in the darkness, a shiny chest of drawers was visible against the wall like an iceberg out in the ocean, suggesting imminent danger. The bedspread and pillows I was sleeping on smelled of mildew, sewage, and unwashed genitalia, which could be mine, I quickly realized. I knew right away that the room I was in was not the room I grew up in. I was elsewhere.

Was I at Kim's place? Or was I getting long in the tooth and had dementia already? To process, I let a full minute pass, giving the pieces of the puzzle time to come together. Then, rather suddenly, the events of the previous night flashed in my mind like a bright neon sign, and my heart accelerated upon realizing that *nothing* that had happened last night was a dream. The mental reel spun inside my mind, showing me the Asian couple in Central Park, Glamazon, Harshit, the chia pet mugger, the bus driver, and Miriam. I *was* that criminal I was afraid of being. After watching the news, I had gone upstairs, kissed Lykke goodnight, and rather quickly passed out without so much as taking my boots off.

As my eyes adjusted to the darkness, a crib lurked in view.

I cringed because my fears were now confirmed. Without any money to spend, I instead spent the night with Miriam, the hoarder. Meanwhile, the FBI was on my tail, regardless of whether they knew I was hiding out or not. Just a few seconds ago, even believing it was all a dream helped me cheer me—until I realized the grim truth of it. Growing up in the upper class, I was used to getting what I desired. I clapped my hands or rubbed a metaphorical lamp, and Daddy was there for every demand of mine like a personal genie. It lasted way into the "adulthood"—I'll say that in quotes—

when he'd passed the torch to Mom. Now I was annoyed my money was inaccessible as if I were ten. I wished for a pleasing-smelling apartment, like the time right after Siriporn leaves. I wanted to hop to McDonald's across the street for a tasty breakfast. None of which could happen any time soon.

The crib caught my attention again. I was reluctant to look inside, afraid to confirm my fears. The baby was quiet, which meant she was asleep.

I was yet to figure out how to contact Mom and tell her I was okay. I was gone for only a day so, hopefully, she hadn't reported me missing like she did last October when I was in Hawaii with Calyssa, Lindsay, and Natalia—another time when I was suffering through a schizophrenic "episode" without knowing it. My dead sister Matilda was with me the entire time together with Anubis. Now they both were gone.

I heard a knock inside me. *Knock, knock.*

Who's there? I answered.

It's your bladder.

It's your bladder who?

Crickets.

I knew what was happening—I needed to use the restroom, like yesterday. It took an effort to get up, with my left leg numb. I waddled toward the bathroom and paused by the crib just enough to assure myself Lykke was asleep. The crib stood empty. Wait, a minute, I thought. So was it a dream or wasn't it?

Or was it—oh my God—Miriam's plan all along?

Heat rushed to my face. Where was the baby? Did Miriam call the cops for the reward? She'd known I was the kidnapper from the moment she saw me!

I unlocked the door and sprinted downstairs, instantly gagging on the smell of garbage. Spending the night in a clean room helped me forget about the hoard kingdom that was Miriam's hacienda. I was breathing through my mouth and found the old grandpa clock I'd heard last night, which showed it was seven in the morning. The curtains were drawn, and it was dark, but the sunshine was peeking through the cracks in the head jambs. Miriam was sitting on her ratty couch with Lykke on her lap and several cats by her feet. No cops.

I loudly cleared my throat for Miriam to hear. "What are you doing with her?" I said, which sounded more like a bark by a hungry bloodhound.

Miriam smiled until dimples pierced her cadaverous cheeks. Her thick glasses sparkled, reflecting the light from above, while her stark, cerulean eyes with generous lashes were watching me. "Finally, you're up, Cece. Look, Bertha, your mommy's up."

Lykke—dressed in cerise coveralls with a bunny print—laughed when Miriam picked her up high in the air and handed her over as if she were an aircraft preparing for landing. I extended my arm, and Miriam surrendered the baby, who sneezed as I picked her up. Lykke's eyes toddled between us two, as if unsure which one she liked best, me for kidnapping her from the park, or Miriam for kidnapping her from upstairs. Miriam, in the meantime, without losing momentum, picked up a calico cat with heterochromia—a condition when the eyes have two different colors—and I knew the term because I had a cat like that. This calico had one blue eye and one green. Miriam began playing the airplane game with it. I had no idea Miriam was flexible enough when just yesterday she was using a cane. Had she healed overnight?

Lykke extended her arms, and I hugged her closer, trying to get a sense of what Miriam was up to.

Are you okay, baby?

I'm fine, Mommy.

Did she plan to take you away from me?

No, Mommy.

Did she hurt you in any way?

No, Mommy.

But I wasn't sure Lykke was telling the truth.

"What were you doing with her?" I asked Miriam instead.

Miriam dropped the calico cat on the floor, and it landed on another calico playing nearby. "Bertha and I just came back from the grocery store."

I was skeptical. "How come a grocery store is open this early?"

"Cece, did you forget about the Hogsmeade's grocery store on Wiehle? It's open twenty-four hours."

"Of course I remember," I lied.

"Bertha was a good girl. She liked riding with me in an electric cart." Now she was talking to Lykke. "Yes, you did, sweetheart."

"How did you get into my bedroom? The door was locked last night."

"I have a key, dear. You were sleeping, dead like a corpse, and Bertha was fussy." She spoke to the baby again. "Yes, you were, now. We've already taken our nap and had our lunch." Miriam spoke in baby-voice, which was cute.

My anger was slowly subsiding because I realized I couldn't get mad at this woman. It was unfair she'd snooped around my bedroom, but I couldn't demand privacy while being a guest/criminal. The important thing she was telling the truth, and even Lykke confirmed the accuracy of the story by shaking her head when I looked in her eyes and asked her telepathically whether Miriam had lied.

"I was exhausted," I murmured, somewhat embarrassed for snapping at her. Miriam didn't seem to mean harm.

"Nonsense. Attention to the baby is fundamental. Excuses are just lies you tell yourself, Cece. Bertha wants to see the pond and the frogs. Let's get her ready."

"Frogs? Isn't it too cold for frogs?"

"Cece, geese are always here at this time of the year."

Miriam offered her arms, and I returned the baby, who I'd had in my arms for less than a minute. Miriam asked me to hold a hooded ivory bunting, into which she slid the munchkin. Lykke seemed cooperative. Miriam added the tiniest mittens I'd ever seen, a fleece hat, and adjusted the hood on top. I wondered whether she had just purchased the clothes along with the groceries, or whether she'd kept the stuff all along, saved up for her granddaughter Bertha, or whoever Bertha was. My first instinct was to protest against taking Lykke outside in broad daylight. But since the FBI was behind on the investigation, it was okay for now. Plus, if Miriam's neighbors saw her with the baby, they'd assume Lykke is her granddaughter, and even if they confronted the old woman, Miriam would be like, "This is Bertha," and none would be the wiser.

While Miriam was dressing Lykke, I let my eyes wander around. The house was what I assumed a dumpster in Chinatown looked like. On a good day. Except without a screaming Asian man trying to sell me fake Dior sunglasses. When a dirty, toothless man offers you a "genuine" Hermes leather bag for one hundred bucks, two questions come to mind. First, when was the last time he took a shower? And two, do you think he knows a cheap Chinese restaurant around here that serves a mean chicken lo mein?

My eyes wandered more.

Swarms of cats were all over, a sight I'd only before seen on TV. Not only was it illegal to keep dozens of pets in such proximity, but it was also unsanitary, a recipe for a host of diseases. The reeking smell of rotting foodstuffs and feces could probably insult Amou Haji, the world's dirtiest man who hasn't showered in sixty years. I needed to figure out how to get some money and get out of there as soon as possible.

"Are you ready, you cute little thing, you?" Miriam asked Lykke.

The baby laughed in response, perhaps amused by Miriam's bonnet.

Mommy, look, Nana is wearing a lampshade.

I laughed. *Now, baby, be nice.*

In her marigold peasant outfit, Miriam was not dissimilar to a slave, and I wondered why she was wearing an ensemble so ancient. Not like she didn't have any money as there were thousands of dollars' worth of appliances all over the place and (expensive, as it adds up) cat food. Perhaps Miriam just had terrible taste.

Miriam proceeded toward the front door but stopped halfway. "Are you coming, Cece?" she asked me.

"Maybe later."

Miriam put on a fur coat, and I could swear a family of moths jumped out of it as if parachute-jumping. If I had to describe the coat by using an emoji on my phone, it would be the monkey with eyes closed—Mizaru. I frequently used that emoji when I meant that whatever was sent to me was painful to look at it. The coat had been given a haircut in prison with nail clippers. Upon seeing Miriam wearing it, homeless people came to mind, those who sit near off-ramps with cardboard signs and/or by Whole Foods.

I felt sorry for her.

Her daughter Cece (I assumed that's who Cece was—and perhaps dead?) was not around to tell Miriam that such a coat was the ugliest thing. Over my dead body would I ever let my mom go out of the apartment in such an outfit.

I followed Miriam to the door and watched what she'd do. When she opened the door, the incoming sunlight made me squint. A red pickup truck stopped by the STOP sign to let Miriam cross the road, after which she reached the pond with tall bare trees surrounding it. Heaps of snow sat in clusters on the lawn like little silvery bunnies, ready to melt in the next few days if the weather would hold. Meanwhile, I wondered why it had snowed here but not in New York or New Jersey. The breeze swooshed in through the open door bringing in crisp April air, almost like a miracle that helped cover the sour smell of trash. Some things, like clean air that has no odor, we take for granted.

I left the door ajar to let the house aerate and then opened the shades to let in the sunshine. The cats had been living in the dark dungeon long enough, and hopefully, none turned into vampires. The light seeping through the windows was like a spotlight at a Broadway show, but in my case, the main actor on stage was soot.

My, my.

Miriam's army of cats was all over the house, in nooks and crannies, on top of microwaves, or sitting on the carpeted staircase aimlessly watching each other. I shook my head in disbelief. It'd probably taken Miriam a decade to hoard such massive mounds of paraphernalia. And no doubt Miriam was stealing all the "lost" neighborhood cats. "Stealing" may not be the right word. If she saw a homeless cat and took it, that's not stealing. It's not like she was breaking into houses while people were asleep, hunting for their kitties. But with all the posters I'd seen last night, finding a missing cat and then not returning it, while not criminal, is lousy. Nobody wants to be friends with a lousy person. Another calico cat approached me, and she looked horrible with her whiskers wholly gone. She was just an inquisitive cat, I thought to myself while picking her up.

Watching Miriam in the distance, petting the cat, I couldn't help feeling stupid for my paranoia. I'd falsely accused her of calling the cops on me when I'd discovered the baby was missing from the crib. As a first-time criminal, I was wondering whether I would experience the jitters until the time I die or if the fear eventually wears off. The good news was Miriam believed I was her daughter Cece, or at least *some* close relative. However, since we both were unhinged, a teensy fear bug crawled in my stomach and stayed there. Some call them butterflies; for me, they're only centipedes. Miriam was a sweet little old lady on the outside, but who knew what dark secrets she bore within? Never, as the cliché goes, judge a book by its cover. Miriam also made me think of Mom. Both had daughters gone, no husbands, and if not for our cleaning lady Siriporn and me relentlessly throwing things out, Mom would be a hoarder as well.

I turned on the TV, hoping for no new developments in my case. On the dining room table, there was a cold breakfast plate with eggs, bacon, and a buttered toast. While the TV was warming up, I treated myself with a piece of bacon. I can eat bacon all day, or anything made out of a pig for that matter. I carefully bit into the bacon, enjoying the salty, smoky, crunchy feel of it. The TV was tuned to the news channel because it was the last channel watched. Caption "Breaking News" sat in bold red letters underneath the anchor Will Miller.

Will was saying, "Selma Karr, Lykke's nanny, was a spy. She helped to meddle with the United States elections. On her laptop, the FBI found secret documents and communication with people of Russian descent—but what she was getting in return remains unclear. Miss Karr has lived with the Fawcett family for only three weeks, and according to her background check, had no previous records with the police. She was gathering Intel during the daytime hours, while the Fawcetts were at work. If Lykke's hadn't been kidnapped, Karr's cover would remain undiscovered."

I was now eating the toast, which was rye, dry, cold, and old. What I was hearing about Lykke's nanny, Selma Karr was a shock to me. Selma reminded me of Hembadoon Okeke, who was an African Au Pair during Sia's case. Both are clearly irresponsible nutcases. Had Selma been paying attention to Lykke rather than playing on her phone, she'd have noticed me approaching and would've prevented the crime, thus allowing me to stay home in bed with Kim.

The footage ended, and a new one began, with Will Miller narrating, "More development in the Fawcett case. The FBI found two witnesses who believe they'd seen the kidnapper in Central Park yesterday. Our reporter, Erin Wilson, is live with Hung and Jessica Chao."

I stared at the screen, paralyzed, watching the Asian couple that had asked me for directions early morning yesterday. They saw me not five minutes after I'd taken Lykke out from the stroller. The centipede in my stomach kicked me hard. My throat was tense, and I almost choked on the food. It was only a matter of hours before the FBI completed the puzzle. The male looked directly at the camera, description reading: *Hung Chao III, Witness.* Behind them, a police station was visible.

"Me and my wife were looking for . . . um." He was speaking loudly in Chinese, while English subtitles appeared underneath. "What were we looking for, wife?"

His wife appeared on the screen. "For our friends from the Republic of China, who were looking for us," she said, also in Chinese. *Jessica, the Wife,* was added underneath.

"When we saw the picture of the kidnapped baby, we knew it was her," Hung said. "Besides, we could use the reward offered by the FBI." He laughed creepily, the way a child molester would upon entering a playground. He rubbed his palms, and the only item missing was a sickle in his hands.

"They will offer the reward," Erin Wilson was now speaking to the camera, "to somebody who can lead toward the suspect. So far, the Chaos got nothing. This case vaguely reminds of one that happened about a decade ago, when a man kidnapped a baby, who then later turned her in for the reward. The FBI will have to check the Chaos' story for consistency, Will." In the background, a Chinese translator was heard.

"We are consistent," Hung said and laughed.

"And?" Erin pressed on. "You said you saw a man with a belly."

"Not a man," Hung said, lifting his finger in the air. "Bearded woman. My wife used to work for a circus in Italy. She's very flexible, my wife. She did a number where they cut her in half." He started laughing hysterically, and almost suffocated. Confused, I touched the area above my upper lip—like did I really look like I have a mustache?

Jessica's close-up appeared on the screen. "I told my husband, 'Hung, I think this woman is the one I worked with in Italy.'"

Erin said, "How did she look?"

"She looked disturbed," Hung said, raising his finger, "like a baby chimpanzee after losing his mama."

"No," Erin interrupted, "I didn't mean how she looked emotionally. Could you provide any physical attributes?"

"She was Bia Biatchi," Jessica said, "the Italian bearded woman. I'll recognize her from any place, from any angle, in any tights. We spied on her for several minutes until we lost her in the bushes. She moved like Bia, in slow motions like a fat elephant."

"Clothes, accessories, anything that can help move the investigation further?" Erin asked.

"She was obese," Hung said, his finger still up in the air. "Like a bloated balloonfish."

"She wore a dirty blue winter jacket that looked like it was stolen," Jessica added. "Her hair resembled the hair of a gorilla, just like Bia's, and her nose was shaped like a . . . like a . . . What was it shaped like, Hung?"

"Like a chainsaw, wife. With nostrils big enough for a fist to fit into each."

Involuntarily, I touched my nose, feeling insecure. Did I look like a bloated balloonfish with nostrils that could take fisting? If you ever want to feel bad about yourself, kidnap a baby and let two strangers named Hung and Jessica describe you.

"This is her picture," Hung said and produced a picture of a bearded woman, which he tilted toward the screen. The cameraman zoomed in. I could now see the resemblance between a chainsaw and her nose, the gorilla hair, the puffiness of a balloonfish.

But she did *not* look like me! I'd be damned if she did.

Erin was now in view. "The circus Hung has referred to is touring the country and is called 'Clowns Who Weigh Zero Pounds.' Most of their performers are kids or young-and-freakishly-looking people. They are teeny-tiny. That's their thing. They perform numbers such as being locked up into small objects where a cat could barely fit. The circus is currently in Atlantic City, New Jersey, which means the Italian woman, Bia Biatchi, could have easily come to the city to kidnap Lykke Fawcett. Back to you, Will."

"Erin, you think Bia planned to kidnap a baby all along?"

"Hard to tell, Will," Erin said. "Bia knew she was in disguise. Her obvious alibi is Atlantic City, two and a half hours away by car. A source tells us that the circus employs a huge selection of European children, mostly homeless or parentless."

"So she had a motive—they need kids in their circus—right?"

"Correct."

"Is it even legal to employ kids in a circus?"

"Yes, Will. Their circus is basically a huge Italian family. The performers mate with each other, and when those children grow up, they repeat the cycle, and in most cases, we're talking incest. As far as we know, there are quite a few toddlers with severe congenital disabilities. If Lykke Fawcett lives in that bedlam, we may never find her among the other hundreds of toddlers."

I turned the TV off while finishing the last crumbs of the toast. I was giggling, my spirits uplifted because it was apparent the FBI was playing a losing game. By the time Bia Biatchi was named innocent, I'd be long gone across the rainbow and forgotten about. I even saw a quick daydream where I purchased Lykke's first brassiere when she turned twelve, and that meant my future didn't involve prison. With Hung and Jessica as my witnesses (who talked nonsense), I stood a chance of pulling this off, mainly since Bia's mug shot was now the face the FBI was after. And she did have a motive to have Lykke working for her circus. Did *she* kidnap the baby?

Oh, wait—I'm such a dope. I had literally forgotten that *I* was one who kidnapped Lykke, and my brain started wandering. When Sia's case had been developing, I much the same way would sit in front of the TV, eating cannoli chips, trying to figure out whodunit. Only today, it was me.

I let my mind take a walk, and this is what I was thinking. If I stayed with Miriam for a month, say, my trace might be eliminated for good. Miriam believed I was her relative, so if I played my cards right, I was allowed to stay in the empty room upstairs. Even if Cece showed up, whoever she was, she probably couldn't care less about Lykke and/or wouldn't connect the dots. I would tell her Lykke was my daughter. Why would Cece even care who I was? What was it to her? Lykke would eventually grow up and become unrecognizable, and I'd tell my friends I'd adopted a baby or gave birth. As time passed, I'd come up with an explanation for my momzilla, and later to my closest friends. I could tell them I followed a guy of my dreams, but he was controlling and overprotective and prohibited contacting my relatives. So I ran.

Or—I could also tell Mom that I got back with my ex Sam (who was a girl) and didn't want to bother her because Sam and Mom did not get along. I don't want to go into this whole "lesbian affair" thing, but I must add Sam had a military-style haircut and acted manlier than the feminine Kim. When I first met her, I thought she was a guy until we started making out. Her penis did not grow like it usually does with guys during heavy petting.

Mom hated Sam, ever since right after our second date last year. Sam was complaining to Mom how bad she wanted a bidet, and unlike a Brita water pitcher, Sam had no filter.

"Dora," Sam was saying, "every ass deserves a touch of love. A bidet doesn't just make your ass or your pussy cleaner; it brings you pleasure as well. I almost passed out at Linda's last night. Better than a fucking vibrator."

Unfortunately, Sam was dead serious. Mom didn't say a word all evening, behaving passive-aggressively—although I heard plenty as she was complaining to Aunt Josephine over the phone later that night. The very next day, Mom took me to Dr. Pepper because she thought I was having another "episode" by dating a woman, and my medication dosage was adjusted. Since then, any time I wanted to manipulate my mother and get her to stop bothering me for whatever reason, I brought up Sam. It worked like a charm every time.

So I had several lying avenues to pursue.

I opened the back door, and, since the front door had been open, a cross-breeze swept in, making some cats jump and hide in available crevices.

"Yes, that's what clean air smells like," I mussitated under my nose to no one in particular.

Crisp morning air—first of all, shouldn't be called crisp. It's not *bacon,* for God's sake. Let's say, refreshing air. What I was trying to say, after only two minutes of the cross-breeze, the house smelled less foul. I breathed in the fresh April air, blew out the stale CO2, glad I was making my new living quarters more appealing to my taste. My high school physics teacher, Iona Schwartz, used to scare us about CO2 poisoning—symptoms of which included hallucinations—which wasn't as scary compared to Miss Schwartz's baldness associated with lung cancer, a deformed ear, and Adam's apple coming out of her shoulder. I always wanted to ask: "And hallucinations—*that's* what scares you?"

Thirsty after eating the dry toast, I decided to have some juice. I opened the fridge and slammed it shut.

Inside, lay a dead, rotting pussycat.

My blood pressure was rapidly rising, causing a nosebleed. The following hour or so seemed like a mere hallucination, almost dream-like. I was sure had I measured my blood pressure with a monitor, it would read hypertensive crisis or anywhere near a hundred eighty over a hundred and ten. I was ready to call 9-1-1, fearing a heart attack, but somehow was able to hold my horses. An unhealthy breakfast plus a dead cat in the fridge were enough to unleash the breakfast from my stomach. All of it, straight into the kitchen sink. The mugger in Newark took my beta-blockers, so there was no medication I could take to lower my blood pressure.

When the heat inside my throat subsided, I reached the dining room. I needed to sit down. Miriam's ratty old couch was as comfortable as a wooden bench, but I didn't care. I was unprepared to see corpses so early on, and I was pretty shaken up. I vomited the second time, this time on the floor, adding to the shit-stained carpet. An ugly cat with one eye began eating the urped bacon, and I closed my eyes, slowly breathing in and out. Thirty minutes of sitting motionless helped bring the blood pressure down.

I remembered how, at some point, I looked up pet hoarding because of Agnes and her puss collection. One site I'd come across said, "Animal hoarding is a mental disorder. Usually, animal hoarders aren't aware they're hurting their pets by failing to provide proper care. Seeing dead animals on the premises are not uncommon, due to the hoarders' inability to part with their pets. Animal hoarding is related to senility (any number of brain diseases) and even focal delusion."

Feeling somewhat better, I approached the window and watched Miriam play with Lykke by the pond. She served me that steak with fresh grapefruit juice, which she kept in the fridge with the dead cat. What a nutjob! I hated her right now, but at the same time, I understood her better. Dementia, loneliness, and focal delusion (hallucinations) explained why Miriam believed she was with Cece and Bertha. Even thinking about deserting Miriam to her lonesome felt heartbreaking. I imagined reaching her age and ending up alone like that, with nobody to talk to—when the only thing to look forward to was death, cats taking over my home. Miriam's tabbies kept her company, true, but animals can't substitute for genuine, human connection. My chest became heavy with pain once again. I returned upstairs, splashed some water on my face, and lay down.

I WOKE UP WHEN MIRIAM KNOCKED ON MY DOOR. THE LOUD grandpa clock downstairs made it clear it was noon.

"We need to bathe Bertha now," she told me and went straight to the bathroom in my bedroom. I could no longer see her, but she continued, "The tub up here is clean because I didn't touch it ever since you left, Cece."

Several pussies were peeking through the door, but I didn't let them enter by closing the door. They were meowing in a tone suggesting hunger and boredom. I'm not a vet, but some of the cats seemed sick to me. I didn't know with what exactly. The cat flu? Adolescent benign focal crisis?

Lykke was sitting in a high chair, watching Miriam scrub the double-slipper tub with a rag. The tub feet were lion paws, hammered copper exterior, polished copper interior. I picked up the baby, who looked at me with her beautiful blue eyes filled with love. I removed the pacifier from her mouth, which allowed her to speak to me.

Did you have fun by the pond?

Yes, Mommy.

Did you see the geese?

Nana said they were frogs.

If I let Miriam raise Lykke, she'd grow up confused between frogs, grapefruit, and cats. I was excited to spend time with Lykke. I wanted to bathe her, sing to her, bond with her. But now in between us stood "Nana." Miriam turned on the water, after which she added two squirts of shampoo under the stream. Suddenly, foam started bubbling up, creating luscious, creamy clouds.

The tub was not perfectly polished but clean enough, and it stuck out of the wall in the spacious bathroom, long and cavernous with a curtain that could wrap around the entire length. The downspout faucet was mounted to the wall, and it looked antique, made out of brass with white porcelain lever handles, a hand shower sitting in a crate above.

When the tub had been filled halfway through, Miriam checked the water temperature by deepening her elbow, and her face underwent a weird transformation as if she were a thermometer calculating degrees. Her eyes kind of shifted from left to right, her tongue was sticking out from the side of her mouth and kneeling, she was halfway submerged into the tub. With her crinkling bones, I was afraid for her life. Miriam, satisfied with the result, attempted to stand upright, but something clicked in her back, leaving her wailing.

"Are you okay?" I asked. "Can I help?"

"Lower back pain always comes back in the winter like clockwork."

I wondered briefly whether I should mention it was spring—and it's been spring for over a month now. Decided against it. What was the point? Miriam stood up using the side of the tub for support, half her left hand covered in bubbles. She used her peasant-looking outfit to wipe it clean.

"Thank you for drawing the tub," I said. "I can handle bathing the baby on my own."

"*I* wanted to bathe her, Cece."

"But you've had her all morning. For what, like five hours?"

"Cece!" she snapped. "You were not even paying attention to her! I went to the pond to show her the frogs, and you wouldn't even come along."

"I had just woken up!"

"Excuses, excuses."

"I'm serious, Miriam. I want to bathe her."

"Nonsense. Take a nap, Cece. You look flushed."

"*You* take a nap. I've just woken up from one."

"Well, mine is in two hours!"

It was like arguing with Mom, another mule. Both did whatever they wished without ever consulting me or listening to me. Suddenly, no more words were needed because, to my surprise, impudent Miriam grabbed the baby from my hands with force, thus ending the argument. She placed Lykke on top of the washer that stood by the medicine cabinet, after which she started undressing her. Miriam wouldn't even let me bathe my own baby—who did she think she was?

I was fuming. That, coupled with an earlier incident of elevated blood pressure, could wreak havoc on my system. I took a step back before I did something stupid like kicked her in the shin. I observed from behind the threshold as if there was a transparent screen ahead, and I was prohibited from entering. I was present in the room, but I felt unwelcome because Miriam was adamant, the ruler of her own universe—her trashy house—where I was still a guest. Subconsciously, I knew what was happening in front of me, but the surroundings appeared foggy, or like an illusion.

Dozens of minutes passed, and I watched, unmoved, frozen in place as if by black magic. Was Miriam a witch?

A witch who killed cats!

When the smoke cleared, Miriam brushed by me, with Lykke wrapped in an oversized white towel, and the transparent screen was no longer there. Wherever I'd been the past thirty minutes, flying in my own world was no longer valid, because the reality returned.

"Time for a nap, Bertha," Miriam whispered as she arranged herself by the crib and placed Lykke inside of it.

"Miriam, I can put her down for a nap," I said, but again got ignored.

"Let me read you a book, little darling," she said and picked up a children's book off the shelf in the corner.

"Miriam, do you hear me?" I asked.

She didn't. Lykke mesmerized her as if *Miriam* was now spellbound, and there was nothing I could do except make a scene, and perhaps a fatal mistake.

"Fine!" I shouted. "Then *I'm* going to take a shower."

I felt a sudden rush of heat on my forehead that went straight down to my nose, mouth, and then neck. Like a spotlight, it kept moving down. Through the chest, the tummy, and finally, it settled in my crotch. Well, that was awkward. Was this argument turning me on?

I closed the bathroom door and turned on the hot water. Regarding body cleansing supplies, there was a bar of soap I wouldn't even wash my floors with, but a bottle of shampoo stood on a shelf nearby. My breath smelled foul after vomiting, but there was no floss or a toothbrush in the vicinity. I opened and closed the medicine cabinet door and caught my reflection in the mirror. My hair desperately needed brushing with no brush in sight. My ears stuck out, and the only difference between Dumbo and me was, he has a trunk and no problems with blood pressure. I hate my ears. I hate them more than I hate my thighs, poached chicken breast, or kale—sometimes, all three end up at the table together. One of these days, I thought, I'd have to consider otoplasty. To prevent bringing further attention to my useless cactus paddles, I'd never pierced my ears. Yes, I was thirty-one without a piercing. Right now, I regretted not having a single piece of jewelry, not so much to show off, but to pawn it if the times got rough, which they did.

I encircled the curtain around the tub and stepped in through the middle where the tub caved in. The interior was still warm after Lykke's bath. I turned both levers halfway, which made the water dribble from under the faucet on my feet. The middle lever, I hoped, was the switch that turned on the shower overhead. After I turned it, a stream of hot water spewed from above. I picked up the hand shower off the hook and held it with my hands like a dear relic: like a diary or a basket of fried chicken. I was slowly warming up after the shiver attack a couple of minutes ago.

While the water was rushing over my body, so was panic rushing over my body much the same way. Even though I'd only had Lykke for one day (plus change), I was exhausted already and wanted to give up. I couldn't even handle *an old lady Miriam*—let alone a child and soon-to-be toddler. How was I supposed to handle the FBI? I longed for home, bed, weed. In that order. I craved a bubble bath and a shower with my expensive body wash. I had no identification on me and no money. I couldn't shave my legs, and little bristles that had come to the surface were prickly to the touch. My life had been disrupted, and I doubted my ability to continue the journey, living the life of a girl with a Pieces tattoo. That's all I had on me that nobody could take away. They can have my ears, though, if they wish.

What if I just leave Lykke with Miriam and decamp? Will Miriam report Lykke to the authorities? Should I, instead, leave Lykke in front of someone's doorstep like they do in movies?

Today, on day one of the FBI chase, I was tested, and, apparently, I disliked to be challenged.

I wanted to disappear like a cloud of smoke—poof—straight into Kim's arms; right under his blanket where it was nice and cozy, and where I belonged;

with the TV playing on the background, but us not paying attention to it, while we're in the middle of our make-out marathons. Upon thinking of Kim, a sensation—that same heat—passed through me like a lightening, my finger automatically following it down toward my engorged "vagin," as the French call it. I lowered the hand shower, turning the stream toward my girl who was begging for attention. Just last week, Kim and I were kissing on his bed until he hardened, his hand rubbing my thighs, his other one on my neck giving me a massage. His scruff brushed against my cheek, which I liked—and we were high, so the pleasure was double. His tongue was now caressing my ear, his hands on my breasts, fingers squeezing my nipples. I breathed heavily, unable to open my eyes from such pleasure. When the eyes are open, the sensation is not the same, similar to when the lights are on. There's no need to see his hairy body. Even though I liked some body hair, naked Kim looked more like a fuzzy tarantula, but white and not poisonous—and the darkness of having eyes closed erased the weird contrast. Plus, while I knew he loved my curvy body, I still felt insecure about being on display like a diamond ring in Tiffany's window.

Kim usually took his time with foreplay, his tongue all over my body, me whimpering until I had to beg him to fuck me—but today he seemed in a rush, like an animal who just wanted to get off and offload his offspring. I didn't mind a bit. I mean, someone wanted my body so desperately he couldn't wait to be inside me, show me his love, his loyalty, his passion.

Some girlfriends of mine have said in the past that a man will fuck anything (I guess they meant "anyone"?)—but with this special bond Kim and I had, plus the fantastic sex, it was impossible to imagine him enjoying another girl. Maybe I was selfish when it came to Kim. I was unique to that boy, and I felt it through the language of affection.

Quickly Kim's hand was moving downward and found my panties, which were as promptly down to my knees. One of his fingers was now inside me, sending a shiver down my back, goosebumps rising on my arms. I wanted to stroke his enormous penis, imagining it inside me, but it was far away from my hands. Now two fingers were pleasuring me. Kim was now looking straight into my eyes with such eagerness that it was beyond passion. It was something else. He pulled my hair back, which exposed my neck, and he kissed it, like a vampire ready for a snack.

He pushed me down on the bed and stood up, his dick dangling, wet with precum. He grabbed my panties with one hand and pulled them off, after which he spread my legs wide apart, his head buried in my girl. Soon his tongue joined the party. I was on my back, eyes closed, while he was downtown for close to ten minutes, licking, sucking, enjoying his time. For some reason, I thought he was eager to fuck me, but maybe he just wanted a taste, a preview. He loved going down on me. His tongue artfully, almost artisanal, went in and out and around, then while holding my lips apart, he was teasing my clit with the tip of his tongue. At first, I wanted to return the favor, but when I opened my eyes to let my intentions known, he spit on his dick and—suddenly—he slipped his schlung inside me, slowly at first, inch by inch, until he was deep inside.

He felt hot against my body, each thrust making me wetter and warmer —and I started to sweat. Gentle at the beginning, he soon was thrusting his pecker so deep that in a cartoon, it would be coming out of my mouth. His hand was dominantly gripping my neck. It really turned me on, knowing that while he may be feminine outside of the bedroom, he showed me who was in charge when the lights go out.

Kim slowed down, put both hands on the bed around me, and started sucking on my nipples, ferociously slurping like a beast. It was the first time I wondered whether it was how a breast pump felt. He had no idea what he was doing, but by then, I was too turned on to complain. Selfish to get off, I wanted him to thrust even harder, but I didn't want to say it, so I pressed his body against mine and trapped his head between the sisters. I then squeezed my hands on his lower back, pressing it hard against my pelvis. He got the clue, flipped me around, and fucked me doggy style until I heard him moan, slow down, and finally pull out.

I opened my eyes. The steamy bathroom was like showering outdoors during fog, something I experienced during camping. The water was splashing against my curves while two fingers were deep inside me, the sensation of climax lingering. I felt like I hopped on top of an airy meringue, with a hundred-and-ten-volt electricity shooting through my fingers, leaving them to pulsate from the orgasm. But the feeling didn't last long. When I pulled out my fingers, I felt disgrace about shamelessly masturbating, while there was a kidnapped baby on the other side of the wall. Have you ever lost one sock after doing laundry? That's how I felt: angry and confused.

I turned off the water and wrapped a towel around myself, trying to contain the sudden shivering. I sat on the edge of the tub—trying to divert my thoughts from Lykke—and only sex-related topics were on my mind—after masturbating, mind you, so not wholly inappropriate. Like why do they call it "doggy style"? That position is only suitable for when a guy wants to slap your booty. Have you ever seen a dog slapping another dog's ass? Plus, calling sex after animals is bestiality.

Before I met Kim at the bar, I was quite active on dating websites. One guy with gold teeth messaged me, "Come suck daddy off." First off, the worst—opening—line—*ever*. Second, calling yourself a daddy is such a turn-off. If you're fat, have a hairy body, and a red ass, call yourself a monkey. If you're overweight, hairless, and want to hump, call yourself a dolphin. But never a daddy. In his profile, he said he was well-seasoned, and his hair was salt and pepper. Was he a crouton? He looked like he shopped for his clothes at FedEx, and in another photo, he was surrounded by four dogs. Please never say you have four dogs. Three, or three and a half maximum, but never four. Three proves you love animals, which is cute, four shows you're just a hoarder. Just like Miriam.

Then I started wondering something else. The last time Kim and I had sex, did we even use a condom? Did it even matter? In my condition, it was dangerous to carry, and I'd have to abort it. The only thing I should really be worrying about was not getting an STD.

After having crabs in college, you know what's truly important.

You whore.

Kim thinks you're a pathetic loser.

Who's bad in bed.

"Enough!" I said out loud and, scared, stuck a thumb in my mouth. The voices stopped.

I stood up and tried to look at myself in the foggy mirror, but couldn't. Even the mirror didn't want *me* to see myself—I felt so much shame for what I did. I was like a child with a pacifier in my mouth, and it was probably the most embarrassing I'd ever felt.

I exited the bathroom and eased under a blanket on the bed, away from Miriam, who sat by the crib, watching me. The shivering wasn't stopping any time soon, as if I had the flu or hypothermia. I no longer cared about the consequences. I had to confess to her. The voices were getting stronger, louder, and more frequent than usual. Let me get arrested, I thought. I deserved it. Maybe I would end up in a psych ward and not in prison. Well, is there really a difference? I didn't care. I was already in the prison of my own mind. I could learn the truth by taking Clozapine, a bottle of which was still in my tote. Screw high cholesterol, mental health seemed more

critical. I reached for the bottle but got interrupted by crinkling bones. Miriam was hovering above me like a helicopter searching for a suspect. She nested beside me on the bed, a worried expression on her face.

"What's wrong?" she asked and touched my cheek with her palm. "You're like an ice cube and pale."

"I've got something to tell you, and you're not going to like it."

"What is it? Are you hungry?"

I smiled. Miriam was too cute, a total Mom-move on her part. "No, Miriam. The truth is, I wasn't supposed to meet my friend last night. I lied because I needed a place to stay."

Miriam sounded like dice against a board game when she twisted her body, her bones crinkling so loudly against the quietness of the room. Several kitties meowed behind the bedroom door, and one was trying to get in by sticking her paws underneath. Scratchy, scratchy.

Miriam took my hands in hers. Her warmth felt nice. Sometimes I forget how much I long for a human touch—we all do, I opine, in an isolated by the smartphone society of our generation. Miriam hadn't touched anyone in years, and I wondered if she felt it too, the connection, the thing that unites us all—that energy of light.

"I know that much, Crystal," she said. "Your friend couldn't possibly be stuck in New York. My mind was playing tricks on me when I met you last night. I thought you were Cecelia."

The sanity in her voice alarmed me. No more baby-talk, no more Cece, no more craziness. She seemed normal, which was frightening, and she even remembered my fake name, which was Crystal. Serial killers in movies behave much the same way, calm and sane, on the verge of being psychopathic. There's no reasoning with them. Actually they like when you try to negotiate with them, trying to use your feelings to exhort theirs. While *they* have *none*. Miriam, however, looked so miserable there was no way she was a murderess.

"I'm aware of everything," she added sadly as if she wished she hadn't known the truth.

I swallowed, clearing my throat. "You know about me? You know what I did?"

"Of course, I know. A woman on the run. Trust me, by now, I figured you out."

Miriam knew I was a criminal all along, and she hadn't called the cops. She'd made me dinner, babysat for an immoral soul, and played with a kidnapped baby. What is wrong with people these days? No wonder there was a dead cat in her fridge—and who knew where else? In her basement? Had she had one for breakfast?

She was brain-damaged.

Miriam removed the thick glasses, and her eyes appeared scarlet, swollen from tears. I straightened up on the bed but was afraid to meet her eye.

"Tell me the whole story, dear," she said.

I waited with a reply. I was unsure about how to proceed. The voices had quieted down, and they sat there waiting for my response, waiting to jump out like predators any second and ruin it for me.

"I don't know why I did this," I said after ten forevers of silence. "I just took the baby and ran as far as my eyes could see, which was far because I have perfect vision."

Miriam nodded in response.

"I'm sorry I lied," I said. "Are you going to call the cops?"

"No, dear. I will protect you," she said with solace in her kind eyes. Why did she want to keep a criminal in her house? For the company? She was putting herself in danger to save me—us—Lykke and me.

"You will?" I asked. "Are you sure? What if they find me?"

"So what? Men can do whatever they want, but we girls must be brave and help one another."

"What do you mean?"

"He must have been a repressive man."

I nodded without thinking. Then stopped nodding. "Wait. What man?"

"Your husband, dear," she said. "Who else? I figured you were in danger and needed a place to stay. Secretly, of course, I was waiting for Cecelia to come home much the same way. But I'll probably never see her again. I hate her misogynist husband."

I moved my tongue above my chapped lips, tasting the salt from my own tears—perhaps a good enough indication to cut down on my sodium intake and also a good enough reason for finding a Chapstick.

Again, the sanity in Miriam's voice was frightening. She thought I was running from a husband and not the FBI. In her defense, her story had more ground than mine. Not every day you see a woman kidnapping a baby, and yet you see stories about how all these celebrities are filing restraining orders from their abusive husbands (or wives—yes, that happened too).

Wow.

I felt stupid for almost 'fessing up to a crime. Sure, I'd committed it, but what Miriam didn't know couldn't hurt her.

I was relieved I hadn't spilled the beans, because, suddenly—as I was looking into her kind eyes—the truth seemed like lying, and lying seemed like the truth.

"Yes, he was a monster," I said. "Once he left for the bar, I knew he'd return ready to beat me. I grabbed the baby and fled New York."

I watched Miriam's eyes, a shade of baby blue, multiplied by the thickness of her lenses to the size of a hen's eyes when a hen is laying an egg. Ouch. Her left eyelid covered half of the left eye like a lid on a pot. I thought if she were British, the droopy eye would drive on the opposite side of the face, and be lighter in kilograms.

I giggled at my stupidity—since joking is a defense mechanism against serious matters, like this one—but when Miriam didn't offer a reply, I said, "How did you figure me out?"

"Well, easy, dear. You said your friend was stuck in New York because of a hurricane. There are no hurricanes this time of year. You see, I write down the weather every day. That's what I do. I keep a journal, and it says it was bright and sunny in New York all week. I try to document as much weather as they show on the forecast. Occasionally, when they talk about Europe, Africa, and other states, I write that down too."

Miriam produced a journal from the depths of her attire and offered it to me for inspection. I took the decaying journal and started from the beginning, flipping pages that were filled with doodles of sun, moon, raindrops. The sheets were colorful and interactive, and so meticulous as if she was thriving for a bestseller.

Miriam watched me excitedly, like a cat before you throw it a ball of yarn. The familiar kindheartedness of my grandparents was something that drew me closer to Miriam from the beginning. I wondered, suddenly, if Agnes would ever let me stay overnight like that had I needed help, and whether she'd also open up about her own hobbies like Miriam just had. I found it amusing, however, that I'd thought I was deceiving everyone, while in reality, I got caught because of a simple lie—a hurricane. What was I thinking? If Miriam was intelligent enough to uncover my dark secrets, could the FBI be searching my apartment in the city already? Or had I tricked them? Miriam took her glasses and started cleaning them with the hem of her peasant attire.

"Miriam, who is Cecelia?" I asked matter-of-factly while leafing through the journal.

She made a face. "My daughter. She never steps her foot in this house because she's ashamed of me. You've seen the house; Shakespeare should write such tragedies."

"It's not half bad."

"Save it, Crystal, it's bad. I've accumulated stuff over the years, and I just can't say goodbye to my kitties. Cecelia won't understand it. They're my family. They're my everything."

"Miriam, some of the cats are sick. We better have them checked by a professional."

"They're fine."

"They may look fine on the outside, but they are hurting on the inside. With real pain. I had a cat too, who's recently passed away because he was diabetic. Or at least I think he's dead. He ran away. I knew about his condition because I took him to the vet to assure he wasn't sick or hurt—and apparently, he was—with diabetes. It's a real thing for cats. Unsanitary environments bring disease. Wouldn't you be better off knowing they're happy and healthy?"

She considered a response with eyes closed. "You're right. I've thought about it before, but no vet will step a foot inside this house. You know that."

"I'll help you clean up."

"What do you mean, 'clean up'?"

"Throw away all the junk from downstairs."

"You won't do any such thing!" she said sternly.

"But why? I thought you just said you wanted my help."

"You don't have to throw anything away. You can help me organize things. Maybe dust a little."

"Dust?" I said with exasperation. "That dust is now soot, Miriam. You know who you remind me of?"

"Who?"

"My mother."

"Your mother?"

"Yes, my mother. She's been wanting to go on vacation but can't because I'm—" I shut my trap before I said, "schizophrenic."

"Because you what?" Miriam said and cupped a hand over her ear.

"Because I'm sick."

"Because you're quick?"

Oh my god, I thought, trying not to lose my temper. "Sick, sick. I am *sick*! I have high blood pressure and elevated cholesterol. Mom can't leave me alone because she's frightened I'll die once she's absent. But she wants to visit Europe, and she deserves to go. She's confused. You have the same dilemma with your cats."

"You have some lemon what?" she screamed.

"No, not lemon. Dilemma."

She opened her eyes wider. "I guess."

"You guess what?" I asked.

"When life gives you lemons, make lemonade. Right? Is that what you're saying?"

"No, not quite, Miriam."

"Exactly," she said.

"Exactly what?"

"I lost my sight."

"No, Miriam, that's not what I'm saying," I said.

"You're absolutely on point, Crystal. I *was* straying. From my daughter and from myself. But I have an idea. What if we cleaned the house and threw out some stuff?"

"That's exactly what I was trying to tell you all along!" I couldn't believe she took my idea and made it her own. "It was *my* idea."

"Yes," she said, "starting tonight will be ideal. You *are* a godsend."

I was lost. Why would she take my idea and make it hers? At least she agreed. I could help her clean and make the house livable to my taste.

"I can start cleaning today, sure," I said. We also must give back the cats that don't belong to you. Yesterday I noticed several flyers by the train station, and I distinctly remember a big orange cat Garfield was missing, and I saw a similar one earlier this morning in your house."

Miriam said, "Cecelia gave me an ultimatum: I either give away most of my cats or no visits until then. I know that some cats are missing from the neighborhood, but I wasn't ready to say goodbye to them. I'm ready now. I wish to see my daughter more than saving cats. We should return them to their respective owners. What do you think? There are flyers all over the neighborhood. We can match those to the missing ones."

I was on the verge of calling the whole thing off. Not only did Miriam steal Lykke from me, but she was now taking all my ideas! My anger subsided as fast as it came when Miriam started sniffling. She reached into a pocket, where she found a white lace handkerchief. With it, a small, perhaps four by four inches photograph fell out, and while Miriam was blowing her nose and drying her eyes, I picked up the photo in my hands. A woman and a man were sitting in front of a Christmas tree. I wondered if the woman was Cecelia or not.

"Miriam, who is this?"

Miriam looked at the photo I was holding. "Cecelia and Jack."

"She looks just like you."

"Thank you, Crystal," Miriam sniffled. "She was adopted, though."

"Oh. Where does Cecelia live?"

"Right here in town."

"Right here in town? And they don't come to visit?"

"Why, yes. And Jack prohibits *my* visits, too. Jack says, I'm stinky."

"What an ass!" I said, knowing perfectly well he's right.

"Yes," Miriam said. "He has no class."

Cecelia was wearing a Christmas-looking sweater; next to her, Jack wearing a red plaid shirt, holding a cat in his hands.

"They have a cat?" I asked, surprised. For some reason, I had an impression Cecelia hated cats, but I guessed I'd been wrong.

"Yes, Betty. She was my present to them a few years back."

Betty was a Siamese cat. Not that it's any of my business, but calling cats after humans is what I consider cat abuse, especially if it's Betty. Regardless of what Miriam said about Cecelia being adopted, Cecilia and her mom were like the Russian nesting dolls, absolutely identical, and their facial features differed only by the amount of time age had drawn on their faces. Maybe it's another mirage. You say it's your child, and people automatically see the resemblance. (The way Calyssa looked similar to her niece grace to other strangers.) You say you're from Russia, and people think you're an alcoholic. (The way Natalia said she'd been called.) You say you're vegetarian, people think you're annoying. (A guy on a date told that to Lindsay.) You say you're from Midtown East, and people believe you are rich. Which I was, I guess. (With my family's money, that is.)

When Miriam took the photo from my hands, our conversation ended. She was deep in her thoughts, and I was deep in mine.

Miriam, lovely as she seemed, needed a psychiatrist to check on her. I would know. I was with Dr. Pepper and Dr. Black for some time, but they were nothing new. In my childhood, there was also Dr. Norma Lass. It was right about the time when I was twelve, a bedwetter with no breasts, just two middle fingers in their place. My period, though, had come one year earlier with acne and hair in areas Mom hadn't warned me about, like above my lip. Daddy was happy to shell out a Benjamin an hour to have a doctor write an explanation for my immature behavior and a strong need for breast implants, which I finally installed seven years ago; perfectly round, triple D-cups. For some reason, both my parents alleged bedwetting was unacceptable, but it stopped that same year when my eight-year-old sister Matilda suddenly died from sepsis, or rather a septic shock. That was a blood infection with extremely low blood pressure. When we realized what was going on, it was too late. Matilda had been taking antibiotics for a lung infection, and bacteria were now resistant to treatment. At the time, I'd had nothing to do with my baby sister because I still considered her a baby, and she annoyed me no end. She wanted to play children's games where I was now a grownup missus with my very own Cabbage Patch Kids doll. Now I would gladly cut my arm just to see Matilda again. Funny how time changes priorities. Or, perhaps, it's one of those "you want what you can't have" scenarios. Either way, the irony was not lost on me.

Months passed by, and I gained ten pounds as if on a whim. It was only going downhill since then. I was literally eating my sorrows, which was what made my parents have me see Dr. Lass in the first place.

"See," Dr. Lass said one time to my parents while I was in the other room listening from behind the door, "I have noticed a link between children who are born on February 29, and the way they mature. Somehow, *unexplainably*, because they only have 'real' birthdays every four years, they stay in the mindset of their leap-year age. It's strange, I know, maybe even out there, but it may be the only explanation. Hence at twelve, Chloe is only three. For a twelve-year-old, she should be engaging in social activities, but she keeps mostly to herself."

I wondered if Dr. Norma Lass had a point. It kind of made sense. Since I only had a "real" birthday once every four years, I was developing four times slower than my peers. Which could explain my maniac "episodes," when my brain could not catch up with my immature behavior. In eleven months, next February, I'd be turning thirty-two, and according to Dr. Lass, I would only be turning eight, in which case Lykke Fawcett was merely a doll I was playing with. But I was determined to prove Norma wrong. I could feel the voices were starting again, so I stuck the thumb in my mouth to shush them. I'd found a way to tame them. *Now,* who was an eight-year-old baby who didn't know how to take care of herself?

Minutes later, Miriam was asleep on my bed, while I quietly descended downstairs to see what I was running up against. It was now two in the afternoon, and the kitties greeted me by giving me their usual nonchalance. A fight was happening near the kitchen between an orange catzilla and a black cat so big it resembled a walrus. When they saw me, they paused like—*Sup?*—and took the fight to the dining room where they were out of sight. In such close proximity, battles were inevitable, just like with relatives who live together for prolonged bouts of time (read between the lines: me and my mom). The cross-breeze from earlier had been a terrific idea because the house only partially smelled, nothing more than, say, a turkey sandwich left in a backpack over three months. Don't ask me how I know.

According to Miriam, the trash pickup days were Wednesdays (in three days) and Saturdays. First, I was planning on collecting lots of trash—at least bones, cat poop, and rotting foodstuffs—anything that smells; broken appliances, boxes of newspapers, and other "unsmelly" stuff would go next. Under the kitchen sink, I found rubber gloves but no trash bags, but why would Miriam even have any? As trash bags were concerned, the *house* was a trash bag. But I couldn't haul *that* to the curb by myself, I thought to myself and giggled. Ugh—I had to go to the store. With no money, that is. At first, I considered bothering Miriam, it was her trash after all, but then I decided against it. It was my "thank you" card to her for letting me stay. You don't come to a birthday party and demand a birthday cake and a present from the host.

I scanned the perimeter, casually wondering if I could pawn a valuable appliance from the array of junk in front of me. Would Miriam notice? Or would that be a lousy thing for me to do? I was doing Miriam a favor by cleaning the house and needed the money for the cleaning supplies. I was sure she'd understand. Just in case, though, I decided to keep my pawning secret between the litter of cats and me. Natalia came to mind, the wealthiest person I knew. I got upset I couldn't just borrow money from her, which I'd done earlier in January to purchase my cell phone. I found a pawn shop in yellow pages and referenced the black-and-white map provided in the back. I didn't know Miriam's exact address, but I remembered I bypassed Great Meadow Drive, a thickish line on the map. Candy's Corner store was, well, on the corner of Great Meadow Drive and Preston. I estimated where Miriam's house might be, next to the pond, a black oval on the map. The pawnshop sat in a small plaza-looking area along with McDonald's, a Starbucks, an antique store, a liquor store, a gun shop. Yikes! Great—now what to pawn?

My eyes glided across the living room like two lasers, pew-pew, pew-pew, and settled on one of the vintage telephones Miriam had. The one that caught my attention had a copper base. Everything here seemed to be copper, and if you had a deficiency in copper, you could basically lick anything. I picked up the phone, estimating its weight like a body scale jumping between numbers three and four; like my mother, it had no body fat. There were a swivel plate and an old-fashioned handle set on the cradle on top, ornamental flourishes resembling something old and European, like a façade of an Italian cathedral, finishing the design. I emptied my tote bag off its content and put the phone inside. Its value probably wasn't much, but when you're broke, anything that is not *nothing* is worth *something*, or words to that extent. I climbed to the second floor to tell Miriam I was leaving, but when I opened the door to the bedroom, she was still asleep. If Lykke became fussy, Miriam would wake up and take care of the munchkin. Taking Lykke along was like asking for trouble. I checked on her anyway. She was asleep, just like Miriam, my little angel, all swaddled and peaceful. Later, I had to tell Miriam Lykke was five months old, and there was no need to wrap her anymore.

. . .

T

he pawnshop, Alimony Pawny, sat between a Starbucks and an antique store, where I could see vintage junk through a large but unwashed window. I entered the pawnshop as a friendly "ding-dong," announced my entry. The woman clerk was chatting up a customer with a ponytail who'd brought in an electric guitar. His tattoos ran all the way to his neck and probably started somewhere down the leg, which was covered by khaki pants. The wall behind them was full of guitars. The clerk spoke loudly in a baritone, her voice suggesting ninety years of smoking I love smoked-out, drugged-out, alcoholic women—hence I was friends with Natalia. They have the best life stories. Peripherally, I was studying her. Her shoulder-length brunette mop sprouted several inches of gray roots, signifying three months' worth of skipped salon appointments. Her shoulders leaned forward, leaving her with a hunched back. Wrinkles around her lips resembled a tutu. Other than her face, she was kind of pretty. But it was her demeanor that reminded me of Natalia, the same facial expression, the same roughness to the voice.

When she noticed me, she said, "I'll be right with you, hun." She spoke deeply, from her lungs, and I was also wondering whether she was adopting African children online.

The vitrine running across the length of the store displayed gems, watches, and guns ready to shoot the minorities. In this part of the country, you are lucky if you're white and straight (and all three of us in the store were). I was not about to tell them I'd slept with a woman in the past—Sam, the girl who wanted a bidet—so if anybody asked, I was straight, married, and Catholic.

As it happened, I'd never needed to pawn anything, and I was unfamiliar with the protocol. I knew the pawn people gave cash, which was precisely why I was here appraising Miriam's phone. But would she need proof it was mine? I wasn't sure. I'd been raised in the upper-class family, with a nurse mother and a banker father, and money was never an issue. Even to this day. Daddy splurged on high-quality Japanese steaks and blew one Cuban cigar after another. That, coupled with salt and love for fine wines, gave him a heart attack at the age of forty. I was still a teenager, thinking a heart attack was not an epidemic disease it is now. Only when older do you realize lifespan proportionally diminishes as your unhealthy choices multiply. With all the investments, Mom was sitting on a goldmine, and when she passed, the jackpot was all mine. Granted, I was not in prison by then.

With the clerk idly chatting in the background, I browsed around the shop. Video games, gadgets, TV and computer screens, printers, DVD players, even rifles. Mostly electronics, which is precisely what people buy and sell these days to make extra cash. Electronics depreciate slower than clothes. A bunch of movies in a box was sold three for three. A plain gold ring, two hundred.

The clerk hid the guitar in the backroom and returned, while I kept gazing at what she would do. She opened the cash register and pulled out a bunch of bills, mostly dead Washingtons, from the look of things. I wondered whether the guy would drink the money and never return for his possession unless it was stolen, so why would he care? When he left, I was the only customer in the store, and I approached the counter.

"How can I help you, hun?" she asked. "I'm Sally." Her name tag read "Sally Maye. Owner."

"I'm Crystal—nice to meet you, Sally. Could you please appraise my family heirloom?" I asked, took the phone out of the tote, and placed it in front of her.

Sally lit up a cigarette. "Let me see, hun." From the depth of her apron, she retrieved a loupe the size of a clock face. She stuck the loupe in her left eye and held it in place with facial muscles between the cheekbone and the brow. In such a position, with the cigarette at the side of her mouth, she was multitasking, smoking, and appraising. "Not bad, hun. I haven't seen such elaborate European-style flourishes on the housing in a while."

"It was a present."

"What is it, copper?"

"I think so."

Sally removed the loupe and inhaled some smoke. "It's not stolen, is it, hun?"

I mean, define stolen? Did I break into an old lady's house and robbed her?

"Nope," I said. "Totally mine—well, my grandmother's—but she doesn't need it—I bought her a cellphone."

"I see," she said, blowing the smoke out. She flipped the ash into an ashtray and took another drag, the end eliminating bright amber. Her skin was yellowing at the fingertips, nails about an inch long, fire-truck-red nail polish chipped. Her neck, understandably, was crepey and sagging toward the décolleté, where her boobs were dotted with pigmentation. I wondered whether she was from a sunny state like Florida. Every woman, just like Sally, with fried chicken skin, seems to be from the south.

"I'll take it for fifty," Sally said.

I was surprised by the low offer. My face failed to hide the disbelief, and my eyes widened, head tilted slightly forward, nostrils twitching uncontrollably. I was expecting at least three hundred. What a dupe I'd been. Sally's eyes widened to mimic me, letting me know I owed her a reply.

"Fifty, as in *dollars*?" I finally said after a long pause.

"No, Crystal, fifty fucking Rupees."

"How much is it in dollars?"

"I'm joking," she said and laughed/coughed—it was like two in one shampoo, done at exactly the same time to save money/water.

"You're joking about the price?" I said. Honestly, Sally was an intimidating woman, and I was confused.

"I'm joking about the Rupees, Crystal, not about the price, which still stays the same."

"Wait—price as in I'm selling it or pawning it?"

"You don't know how this works, do you?" she said as a statement. "Love me a newbie—welcome to the intriguing world of pawning business. Once you pawn—the game is on—you never go back, Crystal. It's as addicting as gambling."

"Oh," I said and paused to think, wondering what other treasures of Miriam were pawnable. Guitars? I didn't want to get Sally's hopes up, so I said, "No, it's just this once."

Sally pursed her lips, perhaps thinking, *Yeah, right.* She exhaled the smoke through her nose like car exhaust, while I was thinking how many Rupees she was giving for guitars without any strings.

"Hun, I can either buy your phone or loan you the money for thirty days—pick one—and do it carefully."

"Oh."

"Yeah, *oh*, hun. What do you prefer?"

"Sell," I confessed. Miriam didn't need several nonworking phones in her house, so why would I want to get it back thirty days later?

"I mean, I don't *want* to buy your phone," Sally said, "but if you're in a pickle, I could offer fifty clams for it."

"Only fifty?"

"*Only*?" she said and laughed/coughed again, this time, the fit lasting longer than expected until she tapped her chest with a fist. "Fifty is plenty to sell. If I loan you the money, I can only give you thirty-five."

"Seriously?"

"You'll have a month to pay it back, hun, pawnshop standard."

"But *fifty*? It costs at least twelve times more."

"Don't kid yourself, hun. I gather it's from the fifties. Nobody uses the rotary dial anymore—just inconvenient. Why *I'm* interested is because a production company had recently called inquiring about a phone similar to yours. You and I could both benefit from such a proposition. But if fifty is not enough for you, take the phone someplace else. I'm not here to rip you off."

"Sorry, Sally, I didn't mean you were unfair. I've just never pawned anything before."

"Look, hun, this is how it works. Unload it for fifty, and it's a done deal." Sally wiped her palms against each other as if to prove she was telling the truth. After she exhaled, she added, "Leave it as loan security, then forty-five max, and come back within thirty days to repurchase it."

"What about the film production guys?" I asked.

"What about them?"

"You have a buyer already."

"The film people are persnickety—all about the little details. Say, they need a harp guitar from the nineteen twelve, but I only have a Gibson mandolin. It looks similar to an untrained eye, but they aren't. Same with Les Paul line—much different between Standard and Junior."

"I understand. Sally—I *am* in a pickle—so any way we could negotiate? I mean, look at the flourishes. I doubt you could find anything like it in all of Virginia. I'm sure the film company will buy it at a higher price."

"They don't buy; they rent, hun."

"Then rent it to them for a hundred and fifty and give me seventy-five."

Her look was dismay, and I wondered if I went too far. "I can give ya a hundred clams if you can verify your identity with a photo ID and a social security card. I need that information in case it ends up being stolen. These are the shop rules and non-negotiable."

"I'd rather just pawn without a track record."

"Don't say 'pawn.' Say 'left as loan security.' That's how bankers talk."

"Fine. Would you give me more than fifty?"

She blew the smoke in my face and blessed me with a round of her ratchet laughter, looking askance. "I'm impressed. Most women who come here do as told. Not you. You know the problem with women, Crystal? They're afraid to ask for a raise, afraid to leave their husbands, afraid to negotiate. You're hard-nosed. Where are you from?"

"New—" I said and shut up, my mind working overtime. "Orleans," I added. "New Orleans."

"No fucking kidding. So am *I*! Where in New Orleans?"

My cheeks heated slightly from frustration and embarrassment. "Um . . . Bourbon Street?"

"Get out."

"Trust me, I want to," I mumbled under my nose. With the money—that is.

"I had a shop on Bourbon, off Ursulines Avenue. Same name. Alimony Pawny."

"Oh, I believe I'd passed your store before," I lied, but was now curious what made her move from the deep South. "What are you doing in Virginia?"

"I moved to Arlington last year to take care of my mother. It's a big transition for me. But you know, I love helping folks like you to get back on their feet—imagining you all like my children. I like it here, although to tell you the truth, it's difficult to meet new men out there. In New Orleans, I dated like nobody's business. Here? Nada in twelve months."

I snickered because Sally awfully reminded me of Natalia. The two shared the same loud voice, piercing eyes outlined with thick eyeliner, and even a body to match, even if Natalia's hunch was only starting. They'd both been trying to transition to a new life: Natalia from a man to woman, and Sally from the busy streets of Louisiana to the quiet streetlets of Virginia. Both women clearly sought distractions. Where Natalia was helping the starving African children, Sally was lending a hand to various Southern deadbeats. From that point on, I felt such a strong connection to her, even her face features softened, and I saw Natalia's perfect porcelain complexion.

"I passed a bar down the street," I told her, "and you know a bar is the best way to meet people. That's how I met all my friends, including, um, Latalia." I don't know why I was still lying and making up names as if Sally was going to pick up the phone and call the cops on me. But, once you become a criminal, lying is fundamental, kind of like when it's fundamental to eat junk food while inebriated.

"I used to *love* drinking," she said, her eyes lit up with excitement. "These days, I get awful headaches the next day. Nobody can run the shop other than me."

"Close it on weekends."

"I can't do that—weekends are the most profitable."

"Then hire help." Miriam popped in my head—and I started imagining her working here with Sally. A junk house and a junk store—they were a perfect match. Hey, why not pimp the nonworking lady out? "I may even have somebody who needs a job if you're hiring help."

"Who?"

It felt out of the blue—but fitting . . . you know? Like a missing shoe on Cinderella. The plan was unrolling as fast as I could open my mouth, saying it. "Her name is Miriam. She's retired but spry like a dozen cats. Boredom is making her depressed and delusional. She even confiscated my baby from me to occupy her time with something—*anything*. If she works here with you, I could clean her house freely without her bugging me."

Sally was contemplating. I stood in front of her and genuinely believed it could work unless I completely misread Miriam. Who was I to know whether a job offer could spring her back to life? My *heart* felt so, that's all.

"You know what?" Sally finally said. "You may be right. Does the help have to be black?"

"*What?*" I said.

"Don't pretend you don't know!" Natalia, in front of me, said. "Like in the movie about the help who were black. Is Miriam black?"

"No, Natalia, it's really inappropriate to say such things in our century. I know we're in the South, but that doesn't give you the right to say racial slurs. Just because they're two African children, you can't call them Rich and Brown and pretend they're your servers. Even if you're only joking, racism is for real. You should be ashamed of yourself."

This time it was Sally's turn to say, "*What?*"

I realized what I'd just said, the word vomit of the past, the response I'd never given to Natalia back at the Mexican restaurant. Here I thought I was Jack from "Jack and the Beanstalk," and that I was going to climb it up and snatch my pot of gold. And there I was standing, with all my beans spilled. It's as if the giant was saying, "Be he alive, or be he dead, I'll grind his bones to make my bread."

My ears, or rather the tennis rackets they are, were hot from embarrassment. I had forgotten entirely about Sally, my mind ruminating in the past, pretending there was Natalia in front of me. My mind was playing another trick on me. Slowly, Natalia's face was pixelating as if blurred out in a television show for privacy reasons. When Sally came into focus, she was awaiting an explanation, proved by a discombobulated look in her eye.

"Don't worry about it," I said, trying to come up with a lie. "I'm rehearsing a line from a play."

"Gotcha. Well, here's an idea, Crystal. I've decided to hire some help. Do you know anybody who needs a job, hun?"

"I just told you, Miriam—" I said and shut up. There was no need to get upset. Miriam and Sally, for whatever reason, wanted to take all the credit for *my* ideas. Fine by me—for now—but I'd reap my rewards later when the time was right. "Yes, Sally, I know someone—her name is Miriam. I'll ask her if she wants a job. If not, post an ad in the local newspaper. Also, let's sell this beast," I said impatiently, pointing toward the phone.

"Hun, max is sixty-five clams, but that's my final offer."

"Sold."

Sally stubbed out her cigarette, winked, and took the phone in the back.

Sixty-five dollars was naught, but I looked at it the following way: One, I no longer needed to seek a "pawnstress" to buy the phone from me. Two, Miriam didn't need several non-working phones in her house. And three, I needed the money *now*, not only for myself but to also help Miriam clean up by buying the trash bags. If Miriam agreed to work for Sally, I could start pimping the cats away, cleaning the house meanwhile, and be hidden from the FBI with a place to stay. In a way, I was like the Genie from *Aladdin*, granting everyone a wish.

Sally returned and handed me three dead presidents: a Grant, a Hamilton, and a Lincoln, making me sign a waiver that the phone now belonged to her. I promised Sally Miriam would call if she was interested.

Afterward, I stopped at McDonald's and had a QP with cheese, fries, and a large Coke, wondering if other kidnappers celebrated similarly. And what a celebration that was! I'd turned trash into cash—call me Jesus if you will. At Rite Aid, I picked up two boxes of industrial-strength trash bags, thirty per box, thirty gallons each. Also, I added two plug-in oil burners, scented lavender and rose, respectively, along with some baby formula for Lykke.

T

he snow was steadily melting, creating puddles by the side of the road. On the way to the house, I was splattered twice by careless drivers until I reached Miriam's quiet neighborhood. I took note of the street Miriam's house was on, which was Silentwood Drive. It was always a curiously of mine trying to figure out why certain streets had certain names. In New York City, it's obvious why there was a Thirty-third Street after Thirty-second. But in rural places like Virginia, you deal with a completely different system. Silentwood sounded like words "silent" and "wood." Is wood ever loud?—I giggled. The air was scented with pine, rich and fresh, and white globs of snow were still sitting on Miriam's overgrown front lawn. I was suddenly coming up with business ideas to mow people's gardens for extra cash. Why frigging not? I could pawn enough stuff to buy a lawn mover in nothing flat. When Lykke turned seven, I'd put her to work too. As I was checking out a perfectly mowed lawn that belonged to the house across from Miriam's, a woman with a blond bouffant looked on with curiosity through a round window. Living in such close proximity, she knew who Miriam was—no doubt—wondering why there was a stranger all of a sudden. I felt chilly as if someone dragged an ice cube down my back. I swiftly hid my face by doing a one-eighty until I faced Miriam's front door. I turned the nob, and after tugging on the door, which was unlocked, I entered, my heart pounding. Miriam's cats scattered all over, hiding in broken appliances and empty pizza boxes. Cats are so silly sometimes, kind of like men's balls. I looked through the peephole, but the woman had abandoned her window view. That was worrisome. In movies, neighbors in such small towns call the police for the silliest reasons. Usually, a 9-1-1 operator is the family member of the person who's calling because everyone in that town is related and knows each other. One of those conversations was happening in my head.

9-1-1, what's your emergency?

A woman is staying next door with a boarder, but I've never seen her before. She looks dangerous.

I asked whether there was an emergency.

Charles, I'm serious! She looks like a criminal.

Dorothy, don't be silly. I'll see you later tonight.

Fine. I'm making fried chicken for dinner.

Don't invite your mother!

I won't!

Miriam was watching the weather channel with Lykke on her lap. The baby noticed me and waved her tiny hands. I waved back, but first thing first. I plugged in the oil burners, one in the living room, one by the entrance. When the oil warms up, it releases the fragrance and fingers crossed, I hoped it would diminish the deadly smell in mere hours.

As I joined Miriam on the "couch"/peace of wood, she passed me the baby without much chitchat. She was eating sunflower seeds, spitting the shells straight on the floor where a tawny cat was sitting by feet. Lykke seemed happy to see me as she banged my breasts with her fists. A family of cockroaches was crossing the wall, slowly and unafraid. One of them waved.

Did you have a god nap, Lykke?

Yes, Mommy.

Good girl. I love you.

I love you too.

While I was feeding her the formula, I pointlessly tried talking to Miriam. I told her about the pawnshop where she could work if she wanted to (but only if she took a shower). Miriam mooed she was interested, and that concluded our conversation. I reminded her I was going to start cleaning tonight, meaning at some point, sooner rather than later, we need to begin returning the cats—one by one. She mumbled in response, which concluded that discussion. Okay, I thought, so she wasn't in a talkative mood.

The three of us watched *Sister Act* with Whoopi Goldberg, and I laughed nonstop the entire time, thinking that, in a way, I was Deloris. Instead of witnessing a mob scene, I *was* the mob scene, and Miriam's house was the convent in which I was hiding. My life was literally just a bunch of movies interlaced with one another, so in a way, I was Hollywood!

I had forgotten I was a criminal, so at seven, when the news came on titled BREAKING NEWS, the reality hit me hard.

"Miriam, could you take the baby upstairs and put her to sleep?"

"Cece—" Oh, by the way, I returned to being Cece again, which meant she became stubborn. "You told me you wanted to spend more time with her."

You just couldn't please that woman. "Yes, true, but I am a little tired."

"Nonsense! Go upstairs and put her to sleep."

I moaned. "Mom, please," I said and had to literally shush my mouth with my palm. Our bickering reminded me so much of my bickering with Mom, I slipped. But what happened next was mesmerizing to watch.

When she heard me calling her Mom, Miriam perked up. Nobody had been calling her the word "mom" up until today. Her facial muscles relaxed, her eyes smiled, and she looked like she was levitating.

"Of course, sweetheart," she said and offered her hands. I passed on the baby, a little unsettled. Partially frightened, partially relieved. I was half-and-half—just add me into your coffee. I kissed Lykke on the cheek and said aloud, "I'll join you upstairs in a couple hours, my sweet girl, right after I clean a bit, okay? Be good now." Lykke nodded, but since there was a pacifier in her mouth, she couldn't answer.

When Miriam disappeared upstairs, I hurried toward the TV and turned up the volume.

Will Miller and Skip Jones were sitting in the studio, dressed to impress; the former in a blue navy suit and red tie, and the latter in a similar outfit but with a polka dot tie. News anchors, in general, are handsome, even if today Skip wore too much makeup. Will was narrating: "New facts in Lykke Fawcett's case. Yesterday, two witnesses confessed they'd seen Bia Biatchi—an Italian bearded woman—who is part of the traveling circus currently having shows in Atlantic City."

A portly lady with flushed cheeks appeared on the screen, and she took up most of the red leather couch across from Will and Skip. "Bia Biatchi" was written under her. Her eyes were ginormous, outlined with thick eyeliner as if we couldn't notice them the first time, and they were puffy, suggesting too much sodium. Salt helps retain water and plumps you up. (I would know.) Her once coarse black hair was speckled with white and was sparse and limp, scalp visible in several spots, and she let the hair fall down to her shoulders in streaks, vaguely resembling Cruella de Vil. She was wearing a white cami with black horizontal stripes that looked unflattering no end. Her neck was tied with a bright red ribbon. (Like a present, but to whom?)

The interview had been going on for some time, and I wasn't sure where I cut in. I remembered from yesterday how the Asian couple was accusing Bia, comparing her to me. I was offended, of course. There was no way I looked three hundred pounds, with pouches of water balloons on my face, and even a mustache—all visible on Miriam's teeny screen, meaning in real life the features stood out twice as much. Don't forget the camera adds ten pounds, and Bia must have had at least four cameras pointed at her.

"Let me repeat," Will was saying toward the camera," Bia Biatchi has an alibi. At the time of Lykke's kidnapping, Miss Biatchi was spending time with her boyfriend, Ugo Farro, in a hotel in Williamsburg. Saturday morning, the two were intoxicated, as reported by the FBI medical examiner. The security cameras proved the couple had never left their hotel room."

Belatedly I realized my palms were sweaty, and a fuzzy white cat I've seen before was lying on my feet. Miriam called him Pongo, and he was fat with spots of black near his rear. *He* looked more like Bia Biatchi than I did.

Skip joined Bia on the red couch, and the two shook hands. While his petit arm was hidden under the suit, with a glimpse of a tattoo peekabooing from underneath, Bia's arm jiggled excessively. Skip said, "Miss Biatchi, now that you're in the clear, why do you suspect the Chaos said you were the kidnapper?"

And Italian translator was heard on the background, and Bia answered back in Italian, with subtitles appearing as fast as the stenographer could type.

"Jessica Chao and I go a long way. When we worked for the circus together, she could never get dates with that eel face of hers. While every man wanted me—because of how sexy I look. Jessica had to settle for Hung, but he is unattractive."

She didn't say, "unattractive." I heard she said "stronzo" in Italian, and I remembered from my Italian class it meant "asshole."

"The Chaos claim you are married in Italy, and your husband lives back there," Skip said. "They say you practice polygamy, and Ugo Farro is your husband number two."

If Bia was embarrassed, she showed no sign of it. "Jessica is a liar, and my private life is none of her business."

"One more question, Miss Biatchi."

"Call me Bia," she said flirtingly.

"You work as a stewardess?"

"Yes, but we call it a flight attendant."

"Of course—my apologies. Why then the Chaos said you worked for the circus?"

"Clowns Who Weigh Zero Pounds? Do I look like a clown? Jessica looks more like a clown than I do. Jessica is still mad at me for the time I humiliated her, which turned into a three-ring circus. We were friends back then, and we even went puppy-shopping together like the way girlfriends do. We set our eyes on a beautiful Boston terrier, and both wanted it. The store attendant suggested we let the puppy choose whom he liked more. Jessica stood in one corner of the store, and I in another. The puppy started in the middle, but right away, he sprinted toward me and jumped in my lap. I don't blame him. I am more attractive than Jessica."

Skip waited for the translator to finish and said, nodding, "That explains a lot. Thank you for your time, Bia."

"You're welcome," she said in English with a strong accent and batted her lashes.

The fuzzy white cat Pongo was chirping in my lap for some reason, and I petted him, gliding my hand over the fur back and forth, which he seemed to enjoy. How was it possible that I was overweight for a job as a flight attendant, but Bia wasn't? Two of me could fit inside her with some room to spare.

On the other hand, I'd only applied for a job to one airline—which didn't mean all airlines hired skinny girls. Oh, my God. Was it all my fault at jumping the gun? What a dufus I'd been! This whole thing might have been avoided by not taking that first interview personally. That interview with Barb Dwyer had been the catalyst that multiplied my misfortunes with a snowball effect. Going off at Natalia, losing my phone, having that first hallucination at the playground. It's only gone downhill since. Kidnapped a baby, been mugged by a fake gun, and now living with a hoarder with forty-odd cats.

Suddenly Pongo caterwauled so loudly and dashed forward I didn't realize what had happened until he was gone. Apparently, I'd clawed so deeply into him there were balls of white fuzz in my hands as if I'd been plucking him like a chicken.

I was beyond mad, and the voices inside my head were babbling cheerfully, and, this time, actually, I wanted to listen. I wanted to see what they were saying about the whole situation and whether they were on my side—because sometimes you never know. Was it my fault, or was it circumstantial? Since the news segment was not yet over, I had no time to listen to the gossip, so I stuck a thumb in my mouth and continued watching.

Skip was now facing the camera. "The Chaos are currently held in jail. Turns out, they were caught dealing drugs and are facing prosecution. The pair had a brilliant scheme, and they mostly targeted men visiting New York City for business. Hung Chao was a sushi chef in a sketchy restaurant in midtown Manhattan. Not only are immigrants prohibited from working in the U.S.—unless they have a DHS authorization, which a source told us is hard to obtain—but Hung put various drugs into the food, one of them being a love-inducing MDMA. The drugs made the patrons vulnerable to theft by the escorts that the Chaos would provide—at 'no cost.'"

Skip continued, "The scheme was bizarre but straightforward. The 'no cost' ladies would escort the drugged businessmen to their hotel rooms, and not only would they rob them, but they would also film such encounters on camera to later blackmail them. But thanks to Lykke Fawcett's kidnapper, whoever he or she is, the police finally got a chance to look into the Chaos union. More details to follow."

The camera shifted to Will, who smiled and said, "More development on the Fawcett case. We have another witness. Our reporter, Erin Wilson, from Newark. Tell us what happened."

A black woman appeared on the screen, sitting in what I surmised was her house, Erin across from her. I smelled my armpit, a bit disgusted by myself for running around without deodorant. The hag on the screen was the same lady who took the PATH train with me who was talking on the phone and had a bucket of fried chicken on her lap. She was now sucking on a lollipop, sticking it back and forth in her mouth, which, if I were a man, would sexually distract me. She was dressed for Halloween, despite it being April: bright pink hoodie jacket with white oval-print throughout, and cropped cheetah-print leggings.

"Glamazon. Egg Business Owner" description read under her. I remember how she shut me up when I thought she was talking to me, but she was on the phone via Bluetooth. Today she was wearing a gold chain outlining her name—Glamazon—plus matching earrings. Her hair was a combination of a Halloween costume and a weave, a Halloweave if you wish, her mop assembled the way a crown on a pineapple would. Glamazon and Erin were sitting on brown leather recliners facing each other. Erin was wearing her signature white blouse with a red coat, red whore lipstick, straight blond hair, layered, and styled to perfection. Ugh—she looks like such a lady. Thinking I hated her, I farted.

"How are you doing?" Erin said.

"I'm fine."

"Could you tell us how you encountered the kidnapper?"

Glamazon removed the lollipop out of her mouth with a slurping sound. "We took same PATH train. Uh-hum. Was Journal Square. I'm, uh, headed for some bidness in Harrison."

"What kind of business?"

"I sell eggs." She turned toward the screen and lifted her pointer finger, nails log, and pink. "Miss Fine . . . Miss Glamazon . . . Fine." She was speaking slowly as if to let people write down her name. "Eggs . . . and positive . . . pregnancy . . . results. That's Fine . . . Miss Glamazon . . . Fine."

I couldn't believe it. She was shamelessly advertising her illegal business on national television in broad—well, nightfall—daylight. Even though her last name was Fine, there was nothing *fine* about her from my perspective. I was shaking because Glamazon seemed like a blabbermouth—and those talk.

Erin said, "Please describe the kidnapper for me, Miss Fine."

Glamazon propelled the lollipop back in her mouth. "She chubby—or pregnant, but like month nine, you know? Look like Pippi Longstocking.

She have them freckles. Uh-hum. Her ears were huge, stuck out like them parachutes."

"You're sure she was a woman? The Chaos swore she was really manly or at least a bearded woman."

"No beard where I'm concerned. She say she babysitter. She have blue coat. She say her name . . . let me see now. Promise. Broken. Yeah, uh hum. Broken Promise. Or, she say she from Brooklyn, maybe?" Glamazon shrugged. I couldn't believe she was making stuff up. I mean . . . I should talk. But still.

"Broken Promise from Brooklyn?" Erin asked.

"Yeah, uh hum. That what she say. And then I say *my* name: Miss Fine . . . Miss Glamazon . . . *Fine*. I need no reward, Erin, you know? But my fiancé, Jesus? Want to have them childrens, and I know a million dollars work just fine for dat."

"The reward is only thirty-five thousand."

"That's fine—that's fine!"

"Thank you, Miss Fine."

The camera found Erin's confused face, and she was looking directly at the camera, fiddling with her earpiece. "Skip, Will, as you can see, the suspect turned from being a white male with a mustache to a woman with freckles who resembles Pippi Longstocking. It's possible, in my opinion, there are two kidnappers involved. Maybe husband and wife, brother and sister, or two unrelated friends."

"From what the police told us, it is uncommon for kidnappers to work in pairs," Will said.

"Kidnappers—as one police officer explained—are commonly known to work alone," Skip said. "As of now, we know the kidnapper escaped from New York City and was in New Jersey that same morning, meaning he or she, or even *they* have some sort of plan. We're going to keep a closer look on the case, while we ask you to look closer at this face." Lykke's picture appeared on the screen. "Remember her face. As the kidnapper is concerned, if you see somebody who looks suspicious or just fat, or if you see a baby that looks like Lykke Fawcett, notify the authorities immediately."

I couldn't listen to them anymore and turned off the TV. As long as people like Glamazon Fine kept identifying me, there was a chance of pulling this off. Of course, it bothered me people saw me as this disgusting, overweight woman with big ears, a mustache, a disproportional nose. Maybe it was done for the show. If the kidnapper had been described as a pretty white girl who was petit with blond hair, basically an Erin. Who would believe them? I remember watching a documentary about our prisons and how the prison population was chiefly black, while outside of the prison, the black population was only 12 percent to 64 percent being white. White supremacist gave racial and discriminatory speeches that would make you want to question the Thirteenth Amendment. Racism, sexism, and homophobia still exist. But being a straight white feminist, there was no way for me to experience the life of an undocumented immigrant. You have no rights, and police brutality is no joke.

This was the second time in twenty-four hours I felt like a minority—with the only difference being, for me, it was a choice, while for the rest, it was not. Regardless of my opinion, in people's eyes I was a criminal. I could argue until I bled from my ears it was my doctor's fault—doctor Clemens —who prohibited me from taking Clozapine. I mean, there was no point in taking it now because the hallucination already had happened. But who will listen to a criminal? Was I actually a criminal, though? I was a mentally ill woman. I would scream to only net laughs from other privileged people who would look down on me as if I were a beast. Wow—our country was sad.

You got away!

Those who end up in prison are not your problem.

You are free.

Enjoy your freedom, and be careful.

You're a petit blond girl.

Your ears are small and beautiful.

And your nose makes everyone envious.

The voices were back, and they were on my side—and boy was I happy they interrupted my hateful thoughts that were spiraling out of control. They even called me petit! A big smile stretched across my face, and I stood up, my mood uplifting more and more as various voices saluted and congratulated me. It was like listening to upbeat music. I started cleaning the house by picking up items off the floor while compliments flooded. I started with leftover foodstuffs, paper receipts, disposable plates, avoiding the fridge with the dead cat inside at all costs. The McDonald's Quarter Pounder with Cheese I had for lunch would have to suffice as dinner, too. Until the desiccated cat was removed from the refrigerator, there was no way I was eating Miriam's cooking.

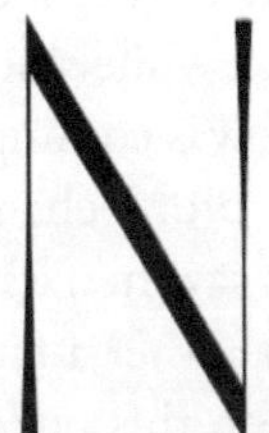

Noisy Lykke woke me up sometime in the morning, wailing as if she'd been given a tetanus shot on a Monday before work. The remnants of my dream, in which a crane held me by my foot upside down, cleared, and I quickly forgot the details, rubbing my eyes. I hovered over the crib to establish my presence and peed in the bathroom at rocket-speed. How much water had I drunk the day before? The stream was nonstop. I returned to the room, lifted the baby, and once I had her in my arms, I opened the sheers to let in the morning light.

A park with evergreen trees stretched ahead with a pond in the middle, which reflected the stark blue sky. The pond took two-thirds of the park and was in the shape of a perfect oval. The combination of beryl and cobalt was mesmerizing. Yesterday, while trying to locate a pawn shop, I'd found a map of the area in the yellow pages and tore off that page, which was still in my back pocket. I retrieved the map and unfolded the paper, studying it. The park was called the Emerald Park, perhaps named after Emerald City, Virginia, a small township located on the opposite side of the lake.

I opened one bottle of the ready-to-drink formula I'd purchased yesterday and secured a silicone nipple at the top. I warmed the bottle under hot water until it felt warm enough for my munchkin. While Lykke was sucking on her food, I was wondering why the food for babies is called "formula." Did the mathematicians create it? And if it is indeed a formula, like one plus one equals two, then why are there so many other formulas? It had taken me ten whole tedious minutes to pick this one bearing the cutest baby on the case. Babies on other bottles looked like their formulas didn't add up on the math. It had been a while since I babysat a baby or a toddler —not since Noah—and it slowly was coming back to me. In the upcoming weeks with Lykke, I'd become a pro. I changed her diaper and exited my bedroom. A rat stopped when it saw me, its whiskers still moving at rapid speeds. It was not even a rat, but rather a fat and brown piece of meat the size of an animal balloon. I've seen this rat/giant baby in the movie *Ratatouille*, where he was a chef, and his name was Remy. Remy smirked and continued its journey, while I continued mine. Seeing animals and vermin had become so routine, I barely acknowledged them. If Siriporn had lived in Miriam's house, I wonder how long it would take her before a heart attack. Probably not as long as Remy's tail.

Downstairs, I realized the oil burners purchased yesterday were helping, disguising the cats' odor by a third if speaking in strictly mathematical terms. Now that the rotting foodstuff was gone, thanks to my cleaning debut last night, it barely stank—unless I was getting used to the smell, in which case all my efforts were for nothing. Miriam wasn't on the lower level. I opened the sheers. An overcast day ahead was promised by the gloomy skies. Clouds, like continuous sea ripples, stretched for as far as horizon allowed suggesting an upcoming rain. I unlatched a window facing the front porch, moving the top partition upwards. Cold air swooshed in through the screen, and it was of particular freshness only available during snowfalls.

In the morning light, the house appeared scarier, definitely a nine on a scale of ten. Like in a sweatshop, itsy bitsy spiders were knitting their silky webs, and their knitwear decorated most visible surfaces. Miriam must have made a deal with them: they can stay over for the winter as long as they provide her with sweaters and socks. Cockroaches marched all over the place in a shameless funfair, conquering new "neighborhoods." The head roach, like Genghis Khan, was riding a horse with a sword in his hands, giving orders to his army on how to combat the Jin dynasty. I shuddered with disgust. Several cats were rigorously scratching themselves—a sign of lice I'd learned from Anubis. Soon, soon enough, they'd be taken to the vet.

Black trash bags fully filled up and tied rested by the door in a heap. I'd filled them up last night, fifteen in total, but decided to take them out in the morning. Miriam wouldn't believe her eyes how much the place had changed. I'd need to take a broom and sweep off the webs and then purchase boric acid powder for the roaches and mousetraps because I'd seen a few mice as well.

Now then, how much money would that cost me?

When the grandpa clock announced it was seven, the cats began meowing as if on cue, demanding food. Holding the railing, Miriam yawned while descending downstairs. Under her pajamas, I saw London, I saw France, I saw yellow underpants. She was wearing the Sun-Maid Girl's red bonnet. After saying good morning, she opened several cans of wet cat food and emptied their contents on paper plates. She talked to the cats, calling each by an individual name. There was Fluffy, and there was Coco, Mitten, and Zoe, Precious, Bella, Smokey, and Muffin. There was a tabby named Lucky, but from the way she looked—with a tail resembling a dried-up flower stem—there was nothing lucky about her. Another one, Ester, had enough fur to ignite in flames if, by accident, she bypassed an operating stove. Just as swiftly, Miriam kissed Lykke on her forehead and proceeded toward the kitchen, where she pulled out a carton of eggs.

"Cece, want some eggs?"

"No, thank you," I said. I was hungry but was going to take my chances. Even if the eggs were not contaminated with the rotting cat inside the fridge, I wasn't going to offer my fate to God. Just one thought of it was going to make me sick.

"Please?" she said. "Pretty please? With sugar on top?"

My growling stomach couldn't resist, and I meowed a noncommittal, "Sure." I could just pretend to start eating and empty the plate on the floor, and none would be the wiser.

Happy that I said yes, Miriam turned toward the stove. She sounded just like my mom—both such babies who got offended easily if you didn't eat their food. When would they finally grow up?

It was fun to watch her cook. Miriam would crack an egg, then would say to each, "I apologize, Chicken Little, but you'll be eaten." She apologized to six eggs. I had no idea how to comment on that, except that her apologized eggs looked edible. Hm, maybe I could try them after all? On the side were refried black beans and steamed broccoli, both dreadful looking. Miriam's big blue eyes were watching me in admiration as she placed the food in front of me.

"Come on, Cece, all gone," she sang. "All gone."

With clench teeth, I swallowed one forkful and said, "Do you have ketchup?"

Everything tastes better with ketchup.

She scratched her head. "I believe so." She stood up and checked inside one cupboard, where she found an almost empty bottle. "I have to buy some more. Here, Cece."

I squeezed the rest of it all over my plate and—while thinking of the consequences of eating all that fiber in the beans and broccoli—I somehow finished everything. I told my butt: "I apologize, Butt Little, but I see some flapping, bursting, and squeezing in your future."

I heard laughter in my head, and the voice that I assumed belonged to my Butt replied, "You got me at 'Little.'"

After breakfast, I went to work. By nine in the morning, having filled up eight more trash bags, I decided to take a break. I'd straightened out the living room, organizing junk as I went along. The reeking fumes were at tolerable levels now. All Miriam was left to do was to call the vet to treat the sick cats. Sometime soon, the carpet had to be replaced.

I hauled the heavy bags outside, one by one, to a designated area in the corner that served as a public dumpsite for several houses. A tall white wooden structure surrounded the area to hide the unpleasant view of trash. Thankfully nobody else was taking out the garbage, but the two recycling bins were already full. A sonic sound of an airplane made me aware of one flying low above me. There must have been an airport nearby because the plane was landing. Vaguely I heard the hum of the freeway. Other than that, Miriam's neighborhood bore an unsettling quietness. In movies, bad stuff happens in exactly the places I was in, people bored to death ready to explore new things, like giving you a lobotomy with a pair of chopsticks. I clearly missed New York and wished to find a homeless person sleeping by the pond. Apparently, everyone was housed in this town. I know I bitched about loneliness in the past, how with eight million people around, I felt insignificant in a big metropolis. This town, which, according to the map, was called Springfield, was giving me the creeps.

The trash bags created quite a sight, and I dearly hoped it wouldn't attract tourists the way the Great Pyramid of Giza does. I could still clean the house and fill up bags, but I decided to wait hauling them until the Department of Sanitation picked up the first batch before dumping more. I didn't want to overflow the area, thus attracting unwanted attention from the neighbors. My plan was to continue cleaning later today after feeding my growling stomach for lunch. I was craving McDonald's, and no one was going to stop me.

On my last trip—after pulling twenty-some-odd bags, I accidentally spotted Miriam's nosy neighbor. The blond was watching me from inside her house using binoculars. She withdrew from her window in seconds upon realizing I'd spotted her, the honeycomb shades falling in a place she'd stood. Intuition was telling me she continued watching from another window. I dearly hoped she was no trouble and had to ask Miriam about the sneaky brat. I rushed back in and locked the door behind me.

Miriam appeared to be on edge because, as soon as I entered, she almost threw Lykke at me like a toy.

"Is everything okay," I asked her, checking on the baby, who seemed fine.

"I'm out of cat food, dear. I am going to the supermarket in a bit."

"Could you take Bertha with you? I need to some errands for an hour."

"I can't, Cece."

"Why not?"

"You need to spend time with her."

"Look, I gave birth to her," I said. "The least you can do, Mom, is to watch her while I go buy more air freshener." I didn't want to tell her I was going for a burger, but what she didn't know wouldn't hurt her.

"I am not your mom," she said. "So don't play me."

I took a step back. Miriam was still calling me Cece, and yet I was not her daughter? I was afraid she was cracking down on who I was.

"Then, who am I?" I asked her.

"You're Crystal—my cleaning lady."

"Excuse me?" I said, offended.

"I am giving you room and board for your services."

I audibly growled.

"Miriam, what's going on? Why can't you take Lykke with you? Where are you *really* going to? Are you going to the police? I don't want my husband to find out I am hiding in your house."

Her eyes were as reflective as a mirror. "To tell you the truth, Crystal, I am taking Zoe and Precious to their owners."

Miriam handed me two "Missing Cat" flyers with pictures of a Siamese cat and a skinny Ragdoll. The street addresses told me nothing because I didn't know the area.

"I am so proud of you!" I said. "What made you change your mind so quickly?"

Miriam looked embarrassed. "I know the kitties were not mine to take in the first place. Thank you for helping me understand that."

"No worries. If not for me, my mom would be swimming in the trash. Did you notice how much cleaner it is already?"

"Yes." Miriam gave a look around and started crying.

"Don't cry," I said. "Instead, please call the vet. The house will only look better by the day, so we want the kitties to feel right at home."

"I will call a vet after the supermarket, and after I return the cats."

Miriam picked at her tears with an old-school handkerchief. "I wish you were my daughter," she said. "This is the nicest thing that's happened to me since menopause—when I accidentally discovered gold in my backyard."

"Gold?" I asked. "You found gold in your backyard?" I know she just had said that but I couldn't believe it.

"I just have said that," she said as if reading my thoughts.

"I know. How much gold are we talking about?"

"Enough for a world tour. I sold it, of course, got a big chunk of change. I sent most of the money to Cecelia. Jack doesn't work, you know. I don't have a will and may not be around for long."

"I'm sure you will be," I said. A picture of swimming in gold like Scrooge McDuck popped in my head. "By the way, please don't tell your friends or anyone I'm staying with you. Okay? I'm afraid my husband might pick up scuttlebutt and find me here."

"Unequivocally."

"Miriam, do you think there's more gold in your backyard?"

"Maybe, why?"

"We need money for the vet and for Bertha. Can I try digging? We'll split the profits."

"You can try, Crystal, but the ground is solid as a rock in April. Maybe in the summer?"

"Sure," I said sarcastically. For gold, solid rocks were no match for me, and the digging would start in the afternoon. Forget cleaning. Money was more important.

WHEN MIRIAM LEFT FOR THE SUPERMARKET AND TO RETURN the two cats, I peeled a grapefruit I found on the counter and turned on the TV. I was going to wait until she returned to go for lunch. I was skittish, taking Lykke with me, especially since a neighbor was lurking around.

Belatedly I realized I'd forgotten to ask Miriam about her and rolled my eyes at myself.

The TV warmed up, and I turned on the sound by twisting the knob. Skip Jones was narrating, "Broken Promise is officially a ghost. She could be in any state. Nobody understands how she managed to pull it off. If you have any information, please call the number on the screen. *Anyone* suspicious is a suspect. Does your neighbor suddenly have a houseguest? Is there a new baby at the playground? Call the FBI immediately. Better to be safe than sorry. The reward of thirty-five thousand has been bumped up to fifty thousand. By the way, please be careful and don't interfere with the kidnapper. He or she may be dangerous."

When a portrait of the kidnapper emerged on the screen, sketched in pencil, I knew I was safe. The sketch artist had turned me into a fat and ugly lady, with big pudgy lips, face smudged in chocolate, nostrils big as if I shoot cannonballs out of them, eyes of a small dirty rat.

She looked like me in no way.

I could walk out with Lykke right now, go to a police station, and tell an officer I'd seen a kidnapper yesterday in Tennessee—to throw them off my scent, and nobody would suspect I was the kidnapper.

I turned off the TV and hopped upstairs with Lykke in tow, thinking I was going to McDonald's to have a congratulatory breakfast. It was safe to leave the house with the baby. I finally made it, and there was no way it was dangerous right now.

But disguising would still help. I went back down again, giddy like a little girl. I raided the closet by the front door where Miriam kept her outwear, and my eyes fell on an orange Indian sari, which reminded me of Titi from the bus. The sari gave me a brilliant idea for a bindi, which I quickly created with a red Sharpie that I found in a kitchen drawer by the stove. Judging from the portrait of the kidnapper kindly drawn by the unreliable witnesses, the cops were searching for Broken Promise, not Chicken Masala. Therefore, why would anybody pay attention to an Indian lady? I stepped into my jeans and noticed how well they fit, no more grunting or sucking in the stomach. Maybe I'd lost some weight!

In the bedroom, I found a pink hat and a pink fleece onesie in the dresser, into which I slid Lykke. I tied the gray sheet around myself and set the baby in the middle. The baby was so chill, enjoying her mommy, who was in a great mood. I made funny faces, sang, and otherwise acted goofy. How could I not?

For outwear, I borrowed Miriam's coat from the downstairs closet—a knee-length pastel pink tweed with plump round buttons. When I looked in the mirror, the mirror gasped in disgust and closed its eyes. What I saw was beyond stupid. First, what stood out was the contrast of trying to look Indian to my platinum blond pixie cut with dark roots and hazel eyes. My pale skin and a bindi together was not a flattering combination. An Indian sari, good ole American dungarees, a sheet with a baby inside could be described in two words: fashion kill. The pink tweed coat added insult to injury. But I had no choice. It was thirty-two degrees outside and cloudy. On the second inspection, I didn't look half as bad. I never followed fashion anyhow, so what's it to me what others thought? I looked "different" for the lack of a better word. Exotic, even. In my eyes, I saw poise, I saw a tease, I saw a woman who craved a burger with cheese. I referenced the map of the area and found the McDonald's where I'd had a meal just yesterday after pawning the ring, trying to come up with the fastest route. I felt safe with that ridiculous drawing in the circulation, but I didn't want to take any chances. In and out of McDonald's in ten minutes flat—back to the house, right in time for Lykke's nap.

I pulled on my mittens, picked up my tote, and opened the front door, peeking outside. Quiet, no nosy parkers. I checked the blond neighbor's windows—the blinds were drawn. Good. I slowly closed the door behind me, leaving it unlocked. If I returned before Miriam, I didn't want to wait in the cold.

A row of identical stucco houses Barbto my right, where a heavy woman (heavy, according to my eye-scale) was walking a pooch the size of a miniature golf ball. There's a saying that all pets resemble their owners. Not all owners resemble their pets, it turns out, I mused, unless the woman was into putt-putt. But that would also mean Miriam looks like forty cats. There's a picture to haunt you for months.

At the STOP sign, I turned right and kept going until I reached Sunrise Valley Drive, the main road from what I could tell. When no more cars appeared in either direction, I crossed the street and continued down Wiehle Avenue. On Wiehle, traffic was lively, due to the working class being gingerly on their way to their respective enslavements.

A runner bypassed me, and just as fast, he was out of sight. Running in this cold weather? He was crazy. But he didn't even look in my direction, and I felt confident in this Indian attire: I saw Boston, I saw Oklahoma City, but nobody I passed seemed as pretty. I caught myself on how giddy I felt about the fact that the police had made a composite drawing of an alien. I was singing a song from the Wonderful Wizard of Oz. "Because, because, because, because, because—of the wonderful things he does."

Mommy, you're silly.

I know, Lykke. You want me to sing you another song?

Nothing too scary!

Okay, maybe from a different book.

I reached the Fairfax County Fire Department, while the McDonald's peekabooed from the bushes across the street. I waited patiently for cars to halt so I could cross when a police siren indicated an approaching police vehicle. I hurried toward the savanna in the opposite direction. The siren was nearing, beacon lights reflected in the windows of the Fire Department. Several black-and-whites zoomed by down Wiehle. I couldn't see how many because I was afraid to turn around, eyes closed, pretending I was invisible. Must have been at least seven cars! What in the world was going on?

Next, an ambulance swished by, but oddly in the opposite direction. Cars slowed down and moved to the berm when another ambulance appeared in sight. The first ambulance disappeared ahead, while the second lost speed, turned right, and entered the McDonald's lot. Following it was a black-and-white.

Crap.

I watched as the ambulance parked near the entrance, while the cops got into the drive-thru lane. Two paramedics exited the ambulance with a gurney in tow. The driver jumped out and entered the restaurant, holding the door for his colleagues, who brought in the stretcher. Someone had decided to die so early, it didn't seem fair. Shouldn't take long, I hoped, unless the paramedics were going to stay for some fries. At the thought of hot, salty, most delicious fries, my stomach produced a tune somewhere in Christina Aguilera's voice range, singing "What a Girl Wants." And this girl wanted something greasy. We were sitting in the bushes for close to five minutes, and Lykke started getting impatient. She twiddled, kicking me with her arms and legs.

Don't worry, Lykke, you'll soon be old enough for fast food.

Why is it called fast food?

Because it's fast.

Then why is it taking so long?

You're a smart girl—you figure it out.

Finally, the paramedics rolled out the unlucky customer. I couldn't see the age, but it was a man who'd perhaps gone wild on the apple pies until his heart shook its head and said, "I don't think so." The driver helped haul the customer into the vehicle. The ambulance reached the road with beacon lights on but no siren. It disappeared from sight, and at the same time, the cops left the area too.

When I saw no cars from any direction, I crossed the road. Several automobiles were waiting in the drive-thru line. Another black-and-white materialized almost out of nowhere, and I jump behind a receptacle that stood to the left. My heart started racing so fast I lost my balance and fell on my butt, but was lucky enough not to make Lykke cry. The cops turned into the McDonald's lot, parked out front, and exited: one fat, one lean. Well, that's just unfair, I thought. I watched from behind the dumpster, scared as hell. If the cops caught a whiff of me, that's it, brother. It is true, the kidnapper looked nothing like me, but I was acting sketchy by hiding behind a dumpster. In the end, it's better to be safe than sorry.

Minutes dragged while I did everything in my power not to vomit from the horrific rotting smell, which reminded me of Miriam's house on day one. I looked on. The cops were still inside, visible through the tall windows that hugged most of the freestanding structure. I couldn't tell what they were having, but one was definitely eating a burger sandwich. I wondered at this hour whether they served breakfast or a regular menu or both. With some restaurants, you never know. Rules change per zip code.

I was growing impatient, as were the voices in my head. I quickly put Lykke's pacifier in my mouth to shush them. I can't believe the actual baby had no intention to cry, and the pacifier was really just for me.

After ten minutes I realized nothing was going to get accomplished by sitting there behind the receptacle looking pretty. I turned in the opposite direction and made a big loop, listening with both ears for sirens. It was safe in Miriam's house, and it was safe to leave the house to pawn the telephone without carrying Lykke. But with the baby, I felt frightened and completely lost my appetite. On the bright side, I felt lighter and lighter and perhaps even lost an extra ounce or two.

Once in a quiet street behind McDonald's, I reached for the map. There was a way to reach Miriam's house without taking Wiehle, which appeared to be crawling with cops today. There was an alternate route, which took longer but was safer and was through Emerald Park.

I saw a black-and-white going down Wiehle. I hightailed to the restaurant, and sure enough, the cops were gone! My appetite returned. I decided to grab a meal to go and rush back to the safety of Miriam's house. I entered to see a small line of two waiting to order, a short older Indian clerk behind the counter. The fact I looked Indian as well was quite a coincidence.

A TV in the corner was showing BREAKING NEWS written on the bottom in oversized red letters as if to declare danger and catch your attention. A person was narrating the story, but somehow I'd gone deaf after seeing Miriam's slightly off-balance and sagging house on the footage. Police cars had meticulously fenced the area to prevent a potential criminal from escaping. Two officers with rubicund faces in military green helmets were guarding the area, while others were probably hustling inside with guns and dogs. My mouth opened because I quickly realized where all those pesky police vehicles had been going when I was across the street. The cops had finally found me.

OH, CRAP, WAS MY FIRST THOUGHT. WHAT HAPPENED NEXT WAS purely instinctual and mostly out of my control. As if tapping the heels of my ruby red slippers three times, my heart released a similar tap for extra adrenalin. Somehow, I left the premises and found myself in Emerald Park, hiding underneath a sycamore tree. In Africa, I'd be a gazelle with a coalition of lions after me. My body was in survival mode. My body and mind operated at two different levels, and one could not keep up with the other and vice versa. I was heaving from the run, unprepared, my gazelle thighs burning with heat, my hooves aching.

The wheels in my head were spinning. I forced myself to focus on the intent of laying out the facts. First, I was wearing Indian attire, which even Miriam knew nothing about. Second, my ID had been put to rest in Newark, which meant the cops wouldn't immediately know who I was. Unlike other witnesses, however, Miriam could describe me with precision, because I was not in disguise while staying upstairs. ID or no ID, my composite portrait would be posted all over the Internet in nothing flat. No wonder Miriam acted sketchy when I asked her to babysit Lykke. Yeah, right—like she was going to give Zoe and Precious away. What was I thinking? My brain pushed the panic button, and the ringing in my ears was unbearable. I had to run, but was it even worth bothering with at that point? My fingerprints were all over the house.

I had to give it a shot. Even though I was royally screwed, I wasn't making an appointment to get arrested right away. It was the FBI's job to find me, so let them do it. I wasn't planning on walking back to the house and be like, "Here I am, folks, on a gold platter." Well, quite literally, as Miriam's house stood on a goldmine. Since I was getting a life sentence in prison, I should enjoy as much of my life outside as possible—until caught. Like they say in our justice system, you're guilty until proven otherwise. For me, however, I was free until proven "otherwise."

Besides, even if Miriam ratted you out, the police must verify the authenticity of her claim. They will look at the threads, and if it connects, then they will proceed.

The voices were back.

That means you have plenty of time before it's confirmed they're on your tail.

What are you saying?

We're saying the police can't just announce they've found the kidnapper. Miriam is a delusional hoarder. She's an unreliable witness as far as we're concerned.

But I just saw her house on TV! They're on to me.

You know how desperate reporters can get trying to hit pay dirt. Half the time, they assume their news is worth something.

In this case, the piece is worth something.

True.

That's not helpful! So what do I do now?

Think.

Well, waiting for nightfall is not an option. The cops will start blocking every road in town as soon as Miriam gives them my description.

That's true also. So what's the plan?

The plan? I wondered. The voices helped navigate my train of thoughts that seemed to be out of whack otherwise.

Are you gonna try to leave the state?

Yes, I should leave the state! Plenty of states are conveniently nearby: Maryland, West Virginia, North Carolina.

Check the map, dummy—hurry!

A helicopter was chopping the air above, and it swooshed back and forth. I referenced the map, taking a note that Dulles International Airport was in the vicinity. Nearby stretched I-66, and I-495 crossed it near Vienna.

Taking I-495 would be the ideal scenario because it connected the north and the south, and if I could get to Richmond, I could consider myself safe(r).

It was only ten thirty and gloomy, daylight as my worst enemy. Darkness, therefore, is always better for criminal activities, I realized. No wonder the nighttime is scarier.

So what are we doing?

First, I need to leave this area. Then I need to reach Tysons Corner, which sits right off I-495. Should I try hitchhiking a ride to Richmond?

I waited for an answer.

Hello, I said and tapped my temple. Anyone home?

Do it.

Thank you!

I checked on Lykke, who seemed fine. I offered her the pacifier, which she took without saying a word. She hadn't cried or wet herself because she understood the situation perfectly, that Mommy was in danger.

I exited the park on the opposite side and was on South Lake Drive, a quiet neighborhood street.

Try to get a ride.

A stingy light appeared to my right, which was a motorcycle with a biker on it who resembled Gru from *Despicable Me*. He had a massive upper body with a scarf, skinny legs, and no hair. Gru didn't even look at me once as he roared past me into the Everglades. Other than him, the road appeared empty.

I tried focusing again, but my mind kept wondering how much information the cops had collected about me already. The investigation had only been going on for two days, and voila, the police stood in front of me just mere seconds ago. They knew more than I thought they did.

First thing first!

Clearly, first thing first! I personally hate that expression because it makes no sense. It's idiotic.

You—personally? As opposed to your other twenty-five personalities?

Stop mocking me.

It is what it is.

And stop saying that! I know it is what it is.

Suddenly I knew what to do. It is what it is until it is what it is *not*. I needed to pretend I was someone else! What would Lindsay do, I wondered? She would perhaps turn on the charm and act all glam—

though, in my coat, the nicest thing anyone could give me was the middle finger.

None of which helped.

However, I looked Indian, just a perfect ground for an accent and a story. Abused by a husband again? Didn't feel right.

No gas money and need to take the baby to a day center so you could go to work.

Makes sense!

I heard a screeching of wheels. Ahead, a Mazda reached the STOP sign at the intersection, and without counting the mandatory three Mississippis, the driver proceeded forward with screeching of wheels. I raised a thumb, but the driver, instead of stopping, hooted the horn and bypassing me, he rolled out the window, a white younger male who was yelling out expletives. Cigarette smoke and music were temporarily smelled and heard until he rolled back the window.

Racist asshole.

Was he a racist because I was Indian?

Of course. Don't be stupid.

That's so annoying. Had I been without disguise, he'd stop and help me.

This hitchhiking business won't be easy.

I swallowed and turned around, wondering if there was an alternative. Public transportation was a strict no for sure, and neither was returning to Sunrise Valley Drive, which was full of cops.

A lady on a bicycle crossed a tiny wooden bridge ahead and disappeared in the park, following a brick road ahead. A vehicle rumbled somewhere close by, transporting chickens, or at least what I could tell from crowing and squawking. I hated standing there helplessly, waiting for a car to pass. Nothing gets accomplished by an act of waiting.

A white limousine reached the STOP sign ahead and remained there for some extra time. Oh great. Rich people never pick up hitchhikers or give petty dimes to pretty dames.

Try anyway.

That's stupid.

Try.

I haven't even seen a mansion big enough to accommodate someone wealthy enough for a limousine.

If you're not gonna try, you'll die. Nothing gets accomplished by an act of waiting.

I closed my eyes to breathe out. I was ready to take Lykke's pacifier again because the voices were getting on my nerves, using my own words to make fun of me. When I opened my eyes, however, my thumb was stuck out, and the limousine stood next to me.

They not only controlled my head, now they controlled my body as well. I knew how to make them stop talking, but how would I prevent them from using my body? Tie myself up? That was the opposite of what I was trying to accomplish in the first place!

A tinted window on the passenger's side disappeared inside the door, revealing a white tootsie in a fur coat who was chilling with a flute of Champagne in hands. The doxy looked filthy rich, elegantly posing as if someone was watching. Her tight skin contour suggested a relatively recent plastic surgery with a surgeon who'd apparently majored in gums. Concubines fascinate me because they're feminists, and in front of her was a woman who needed help.

Use the story about not having enough gas money.

"Excuse me," the woman said flirtingly and batted her lashes. "You resemble someone who speaks Indian." Her voice was soft, with a Southern accent and a drunken twang.

"I do speak Indian," I said with Harshit's accent. I do, that is, considering they speak English in India.

"Honey, my driver is lost, and I'm late for a luncheon at the Colchester Golf Club. Vijay doesn't know left from right in this . . . strange neighborhood. His GPS has died, and with my long nails, I can't type the address on my phone."

"Why don't you let him type in the address?"

"He doesn't know my passcode. Anyway, sweetheart, can you tell him which way to go?"

Name Colchester Golf Club sounded familiar. I'd seen it on the map, located near the airport.

"Do you want to give me a lift?" I said. "I'm headed that way. I need to get to the airport."

"Sweetie darling, I hate them babies, and we don't own a car seat for one. Pointing your brown finger for Vijay will suffice."

"The baby doesn't need a seat. By law, Indian babies must be transported on their mothers' chests."

"Is that true? I'm sorry, but babies are not my thing."

Neither is grace.

I automatically looked up. I don't know why I kept doing that every time the voices spoke. "I don't have to sit next to you," I said. "I'll sit next to Harshit."

"It's Vijay."

"Even better!" I said, opening the door, which was locked. "I'm sure I'll be more helpful than not since I've lived in this area for twelve years and know the ins and outs of every street—except for the creepy street on your left."

The rich floozy pouted. "I don't know."

"Well, I do, baby, since I ain't lost." I turned around and waited. I totally just copied Vivian from *Pretty Woman* when she meets Edward. I'd already hooked her, it seemed, so while she was contemplating, I decided to avoid eye contact. I retrieved the map and quickly found her destination, which was not at all far. But far enough away from the police.

Listening to the dowager, one would assume she hardly spent a day in school.

"Shh," I said aloud, and then to her, unrecognizing my own voice and brazenness, "You can go ahead; it's right around the corner. I am so mad at my husband, who took the car when he knew I needed to take the baby to the daycare. If I don't get to my work on time, they will fire me."

"Didn't you say you were headed for the airport?"

"Um, yes, yes, but that's where I work, you see."

"I see."

"By the way, I love your coat."

She coughed up a laugh, as a means to acknowledge she enjoyed the compliment. "I like you, sweetie. Okay. You can sit with us—just don't let your samosa breathe on me. I'm Regina."

"Nefertiti," I said, remembering the way Titi had said it. "But you call me Titi."

"Good to meet you, Titi. You can call me Regina."

"I know. I know."

As I reached for the handle, Vijay jumped out of the driver's side and stormed off in my direction, yelling something difficult to understand. Maybe he thought I was his relative; otherwise, why else would he be yelling at a stranger? He was tall and handsome but looked rude and vigilant. Vijay opened the door for me, and I slid inside across from the missus.

See? That's how it's done.

"Okay," Regina said. "Titi, how far is the club from here?" She offered me her flute of Champagne, but I politely refused. I was not in the mood to taste her saliva splattered on the rim. What was I, a DNA testing service?

"We'll be there in ten minutes," I said.

Geometry was my favorite subject in school. I loved angles and vectors, so getting lost wasn't going to be my business, especially when a map is involved. I approximated the travel time for fifteen minutes. Vijay rolled down the partition that divided us.

"Vijay," I said, making my accent stronger, "turn right at the next intersection. Take that to Lawyers Road, where you turn left. When we reach Bride, take a right. Then proceed three miles straight. See how easy? Right, Lawyer, left, Bride, then a right. Should be a song."

Vijay replied, took the map off my hands, and speaking whatever his native language he closed the partition.

Finally, we were moving, and I took a breath of liberation.

Regina is Lady, and you're the Tramp.

Oh, totally.

They need spaghetti so they could kiss.

She's not a lesbian.

But she kissed a girl.

And she liked it!

Several voices were now speaking, and I wish there was a way to shush them without putting a thumb in my mouth. But somehow the description fit perfectly because by looking at the two of us, that's how we would be described, a lady and a tramp—and I assumed the voices were referring to the movie. Regina vaguely resembled Lindsay with her shining blond hair and slim body.

"What's the name of your . . . thing?" Regina asked with a raised eyebrow. I kept rocking Lykke, wondering what Indian name sounded legitimate enough. Madhukar? Her continuous stare scared me, and out of nervousness, I said Caesar.

"Hm," she said and pouted.

"Regina, do you live around here?" I asked, trying to get attention away from me.

Her laugh came out as evil as it gets. "In Reston? No way. No offense to you, though, or other, um, people? I live in Chevy Chase, of course. My cousin Karen recently got engaged, and she has the biggest ring you've ever seen—except mine."

Regina offered her perfectly manicured hand for inspection, where I noticed a princess cut diamond ring. It looked lifeless in the darkness of the limo, but I assumed in daylight Regina was always the center of attention, a focus for rumors, the best dressed.

"That is so fetch!" I said.

"Titi, don't try to make fetch happen. It's not going to happen."

She withdrew her hand and said, "Anyway, Karen asked me to luncheon at the Colchester Golf Club, where they plan to have their engagement party a week from Saturday. Why they couldn't find anything closer beats me. Karen needs help with decorations and ideas, as I clearly have an exquisite taste. And of course, the menu is vegetarian—which is what I am."

"You look like a vegetarian," I said.

"Thanks, darling. And you . . . You said you were late for work. What do you do?"

"Just housekeeping." Which wasn't entirely untrue, considering I was doing exactly that for the past two days.

"Housekeeping at the airport?"

She remembers everything!

Sly.

"Yes," I said. "Housekeeping at the airport."

"Titi, I need a live-in housekeeper to work full time. Would you be interested in a position?"

"Really? Why me?"

"Well, you're . . . Indian . . . and stuff."

What a racist bitch!

Well, her driver is Indian.

Maybe she has a fetish.

What's wrong with the word fetch?

"Shh," I said under the disguise of clearing my throat. And asked, "What are the responsibilities?" I wasn't looking for a job, clearly, but I wanted to keep the conversation afloat. Regina more and more resembled Lindsay that I started warming up to her and even wanted to reach out for a hug.

Regina emptied her flute. "Responsibilities? Nothing extraordinary: cooking, cleaning, massage."

"Massage?"

"Yes, I like a massage at noon with my glass of chardonnay. Our current housekeeper is an old maid—Meekleen—who can't even remember what I drink for breakfast. I order a mimosa, and there she goes planting marigolds."

"Marigolds?"

"I know! Thank you. They're such ugly flowers."

"You're going to fire her?" I said.

"Of course. Once your old gelding is washed up, time to replace her with a fresh colt."

"Even if I worked for you, you said you don't like babies."

"Sweetheart, you can put your little curry on a wet towel, and he'll crawl around the house and help you clean. As long as you keep it away from Trusty."

"Who's Trusty?"

"My bloodhound."

Vijay pressed on the breaks so suddenly, I almost flew into her. I couldn't see much through the tinted windows, and the gloominess of the sky helped none. I assumed we were at an intersection.

Working for a wealthy floozy sounded convenient but foolish. She wanted me to wash her panties, give her a massage at noon, have Lykke crawl around her house on a mop. That woman was all sorts of insane. Plus, if I was hired, Meekleen was let go, whoever she is. Unlike Miriam, I doubted Meekleen had gold in her backyard or a gold tooth, which is why she worked to keep her ends meet. I didn't know how old she was, but judging from Regina's story, Meekleen was anywhere in the geriatric range.

What if she cleans for pleasure?

Yeah. Like that's a thing.

You wanted Miriam to go working at the pawnshop.

Because she's lonely and needs something to do. Look how she was monopolizing the baby!

"Did you say something?" Regina asked.

I brought a fist to my mouth and fake-coughed, my face slightly hot. I wasn't sure if I was speaking to the voices aloud or inside my head, and I was afraid Regina would find out.

"No," I said, "just dry throat."

Regina opened the minibar and retrieved a Coke, offering it to me, which was so sweet. The offer, not the soda. I reached forward to grab the can, and while opening the tab, I noticed a cuff gold bracelet on the floor next to her cream pumps. She'd probably dropped it a while ago, and being rich and all had forgotten all about it. That bracelet might be worth hundreds of dollars, I thought.

Snatch it, or we will.

Ugh, the voices were getting annoying—and criminal!

I looked up from the floor, studying Regina. Connected, her both knees were tilted to one side, a conservative way to hide her beaver. She was wearing a hot pink peplum bustier maxi dress underneath the coat. Her blonde hair had been recently blown out at a place where they don't also offer manicure and occasional takeout Chinese.

She noticed me staring at her dress and said, "On Mondays, we wear pink."

"Totally. Me too." This was true because Miriam's coat was pink—washed out and dirty, but pink nonetheless. She gave an apologetic smile and pretended to notice, but in reality, her mind probably blurred me out lest she'd go blind from the unpleasant sight.

A phone rang so loudly, I jumped and hit my head on the ceiling of the limo. It was hers. Regina picked up and turned, facing the window. I aimed for the gold bracelet with my foot while Regina was occupied with her conversation.

"I am *not* giving you back the ring," she said to whoever was on the other line. She listened to some yelling that I could hear from my seat.

"I don't care if I broke off the engagement," she said calmly.

"That's the rule!" was heard from the other side, followed by something indecipherable.

Like a reflex, Regina moved the phone away and spoke to the bottom piece where the microphone was located. "Aaron, stop yelling."

"Boo, you whore," I heard him say, and I involuntarily cringed.

I turned away in an attempt to attain an innocent face. My foot, however, had completely covered the bracelet. While she was listening, face averted, I slowly moved my foot toward me, wondering whether rich people install cameras in limousines. But then again, what for?

"Aaron, I'm in the middle of something. Let me call you back in an hour."

Regina hung up. I was able to drag the bracelet all the way, but she'd hung up too soon before I could snatch it off the floor.

"Wrong number?" I said, hoping a joke would uplift her mood. Clearly, it was not a pleasant conversation. She mentioned breaking off her engagement—that's some pretty severe emotional stuff.

"I wish it were the wrong number," she said.

"I'm sorry you're going through whatever you're going through."

"That's why I'm drinking."

"Wanna talk bout it?"

"Not really."

"Oh, come on, Regina. You can tell me. Whatever is in your heart, just go ahead and spit it out. Besides, if I become your maid, I need to know all the truths and lies; otherwise, I wouldn't be able to protect your secrets—if you have any, that is."

"You're right. You're smarter than I thought, Titis."

"It's singular, Titi."

"Well, Titi, I don't see any harm telling you. I'm leaving my husband of two months—Aaron. He just wasn't working out for me."

"Kind of like a dress that is a wrong color?"

"Exactly that. And now he wants the ring back."

"So give it back."

"But I love it so much."

"You have to give it back. That's the rule."

"I know. But what if I told him that my niece played with it and swallowed it."

I audibly groaned and took a sip of Coke. "Why does everyone swallow things?" I thought of Lindsay's Charlotte, who swallowed a crayon.

"Who swallowed what?"

"I don't know," I lied, making stuff up. "Just a saying. Like, 'Why don't you swallow a ring?'"

"It's not a saying."

"It is in India . . . Nah! Indiana! Yes, Indiana—that's where I'm from," I added.

"Is that why you're white?"

"Regina, you can't ask people race questions like that. Why is everyone so passionate about where the other person is from?"

"It helps you connect," she said. "Curiosity?"

"Forget it, Regina. Tell me about Aaron instead." I finished the Coke and squeezed the bottle, a trick Lindsay taught me how to save space in a recycling can. Yeah, like that helped me get far in life.

Regina played with the ring, adjusting it on her finger. "I just fell out of love with him, you know? Nobody understands that. Before the proposal when, three months ago, I wanted to break up with him, but everyone kept saying, 'You can work it out. Just give it time.' I gave it time, plenty of time—two extra months! And what? We got married, and nothing changed. I just need a change. Why is it so difficult to understand?"

"I understand. Not like, 'I understand what you're saying,' but I also understand what you're saying. I meant, like, you said why is it so difficult to understand . . . and I definitely find it easy to understand . . ." I had no idea what I was saying, so I paused.

She was not even listening to me and plowed on. "I'm just sick of it.

There wasn't a day I enjoyed my life being single, you know? In elementary school, Damon was our neighbor, the most handsome boy in my class—my first kiss. We dated until high school, where I met Michael, who I dated through college. After that—well—after that, I kind of played the field a bit until I found the first real love of my life, Hans Anderson. He was a German entrepreneur whom I met through the charity I volunteer with. Two years later—dead. Left me all his money."

I thought she was going to cry, but she didn't. "I'm sorry, Regina," I said. "What happened?"

"Heart attack."

"Heart attack," I repeated right after, nodding.

"Only forty-seven."

"Only forty-seven."

"He was so handsome, so generous."

"So handsome, so generous," I was saying. I was now shaking my head in what I belatedly realized was an attempt to mimic her gestures. I'd found myself doing on several occasions before, and I'd read about in a magazine. We imitate each other when we think it's needed the most. To comfort or to console. Or even to gain an advantage. I snapped myself out of it.

"Regina, what happened afterward?"

"I remarried again," she said matter-of-factly as if to prove her point how in her life there was a nonstop relationship marathon. "To another German businessman, Helmut, whom I met through a deal Hans had made. We were married for three years until I realized he wanted kids." Regina was now sobbing. "I can't have kids."

"I stood up as far as the limo ceiling allowed and sat next to her, taking her hand in mine. "Calm, calm. You don't have to continue. I understand. I now completely understand."

Regina wiped her tears, and her voice was back to normal.

"I just need some change," she said.

A picture of coins quickly appeared in my mind, but I shook that away. "Then change."

"I'm trying. I told everyone Aaron was a cheater—to save face. And guess what my mom said? That it doesn't matter! She then told me that her father cheated throughout their marriage, and she let it slide because she said that's what women should do."

"Some people do cheat," I supplied, unsure what to say. Her problems seemed so different from mine that I couldn't relate whatsoever. It appeared, however, she was on the right path anyway.

"See?" she said. "You understand. So it's all settled then! Come with me to the club, and you can start working tomorrow."

My reply "no" was interrupted by a phone call—saved by the bell, as they say. Regina was back to her rich self, no apparent problems visible from the outside, no feelings, no pain. I was glad she opened up, and my initial perception of her had changed, from rich floozy to poor woman. Appearances are just that: our way to disguise our problems. There are perhaps only a handful of people who have no problems (good for them if they can do it), but for most of us, life is hard, regardless of what form it takes. I returned to my seat. From eavesdropping on Regina's conversation, I learned she was talking to Karen, the bride, because of the things she said about the band booked for the engagement, the Armani dress she needs to try on, blah-blah-blah.

We entered the golf club through a set of iron gates, where a security guard in a booth nodded and let us through. The two-lane road we were taking was long and sneaking around as if we were in a labyrinth of some kind, either side set in dramatic topiary. A gardener was clipping a bush with oversized pruners, creating geometric shapes out of otherwise dull shrubs. He was working on a spiral design that looked as delicate as a medical procedure for breast augmentation.

Vijay slowed the limo, and ahead I saw a Victorian building with arched windows and a rising clock tower. I felt relief. Now that I was somewhat far away from Miriam's house, I was safer. I wondered how soon the composite portrait would be released to the public. I estimated that it took no longer than rolling a joint, but I was willing to take my chances. I bent to scratch my leg, picked up the gold bracelet off the floor, and sat up, wondering whether Regina's maid robbed her as well.

I checked the time: a little past eleven. The limo came to a stop under a porte-cochere that had ornamental columns on either side. Vijay opened the door and grimaced when he saw me. I acknowledged the odd expression and protecting Lykke with one hand and clutching my tote with the other exited first, followed by Regina, who was still on the phone. She proceeded toward the entrance, motioning me to follow by wiggling her fingers. A young, suave doorman greeted her. He was wearing a blue uniform with gold buttons and gold soutache, white gloves, and a matching hat. When Regina passed him, he opened the door and glanced at her booty. Unlike her overly inflated breasts, her flat ass had been assembled from the pancake mix. By a cook who attempted to make a steak. I guess not even the filthy rich could change their body to the disproportional standards of a Barbie doll. Regina disappeared in the building, swallowed by a hungry beast, and I knew I'd never see her again as if she were nothing but a mirage. I tightly held the gold bracelet to prove otherwise. I had to leave the state, to a magical place where there were no TV's, where people wouldn't rat me out. That *was* a kicker.

Vijay smashed the door to close, gave the baby and me a scowl, and jumped behind the wheel. He exited the porte-cochere and quickly marked his territory by stretching the limo across several empty parking lots behind us. No other cars were visible in the vicinity. Maybe men golfers only played in the summer, while the winter was devoted solemnly to the women's club activities, like weddings and such.

The doorman kept the door open for me. "Are you coming, miss?" he asked me.

"In a few," I lied, for some reason speaking with a British accent as if that was making me sound classier (in that embarrassing coat). "Tell Regina, I'll be right back."

As I was about to take off in the opposite direction, I noticed a fawn-colored wallet on the spot where seconds ago stood the limo. Lykke began to fuss, perhaps sick from riding in such lavish cars. She, too, was tired of the rich. I picked up the wallet and opened the trifold. Vijay's Maryland driver's license rested under the transparent plastic window in the middle, credit cards tucked in pockets on either side, several dollar bills visible alongside. His last name was Parkvankar. Based on his birthday, he was a Gemini, a sign that was least compatible with us, Pisces. Inside the wallet, next to the money, was a key to a Honda with its easy-to-recognize capital H. The Honda was perhaps Vijay's own car he drove whenever he was off duty. I couldn't believe how irresponsible he was, losing stuff around like nobody's business.

I decided to return the wallet to its owner, but I paused long enough to slide the stolen bracelet on my wrist first. After covering the bracelet with the coat sleeve, I approached the limo and knocked on the window. Lykke kept moving around in the sheet, so I wobbled slightly to keep her occupied.

The window slid down, revealing Vijay, who was in the middle of counting money, mostly one-dollar bills. On his way to a strip club, I surmised. The radio was broadcasting local news, something about an accident near Tyson's Corner.

"What?" Vijay snapped angrily, and I instantly took offense. Why was he angry with me?

I cleared my throat, preparing to release my Indian diva accent. "You lost your wallet, Vijay, and I have it. I'll give it back to you if you apologize for your tone."

He folded the cash and hid it in his suit pocket. He was wearing white gloves and a white shirt, while the rest of his suit was black, black cap with a reflective plastic visor Vijay scowled like an animal and double-checked each pocket unwilling to take my word for it. Failing to find his wallet, Vijay opened the door, which forced me to jump back and exited. Next to me, he was a foot taller, eyes burning with hate in a fiery rage.

"You stole my wallet?" he said. "You stole my wallet, and now you want to steal our jobs."

I had no idea what kind of hanky-panky was happening in his mouth, so I took a step back to avoid the smell. "What are you talking about? I found the wallet on the ground by the entrance."

"Give it to me!"

An evil laugh escaped my mouth. "Apologize, and maybe I will."

"I heard everything you said to Regina. You are going to replace my mother, Meekleen, and from this point on, you're on my watch list."

Get in line, I thought.

"She's your mother?" I asked.

"Yes, she's my mother. Didn't I *just* tell you that, bitch?"

"Hey!" I said, covering Lykke's ears. "Babies are present. I had no idea she was your mother, Vijay."

"My son works there too, Shupaleesh."

"I thought Regina hated babies."

"He's not a baby, he's eleven."

"So, you're mad because Regina offered me a job?" I asked.

"Yes." He reached for the wallet, but I hid it behind my back. I assumed he wouldn't dare to smack me with the baby and all. It all made sense now, but there was no way he was allowed to call me a bitch. So I wasn't going to tell him I wasn't taking it until he apologized.

"I'm sorry, Vijay, but the job is mine," I said. "And again, never call a woman a bitch, especially when she has your wallet."

"I've worked really hard to get this job, *bitch*," he said with emphasis.

"You're not the one who immigrated here forty years ago, started your life from scratch. You can't just waltz in here and ruin this for me."

I had no time to listen to that. What was the point? Did he assume I was his shrink or what? He clearly wanted to hurt me by calling me a bitch, but I decided not to take it personally because it clearly wasn't. At the same time, I shouldn't apologize for something I didn't do. What suddenly hit me was something absolutely euphoric that I couldn't believe I hadn't realized it sooner. Vijay's car keys that I had behind my back in his wallet gave me an idea. There was no way I'd hitchhike a ride this early in the afternoon without some cop spotting me. I had no car and no money to rent one, plus my driver's license was in some dumpster in New Jersey. But if I had keys to a car—any car—I'd have wheels.

I wondered how I could get my hands on keys to a car. Steal one from someone. Perhaps at a bar. Patrons get wasted and become easy targets for seasoned criminals like myself.

"Listen, Vijay," I said, offering him the wallet. "I'm not taking your job —I promise. I have a job of my own. Just because Regina offered me to be her masseuse—slash cook—slash champagne runner, doesn't mean I'll take it. She can't order me around just because she's got the dough and a mimosa in her hand. If you personally feel unappreciated, maybe you need to find yourself another job. You are in charge of your fate, and I understand your anger, but it has nothing to do with me. Talk to Regina. What's *really* bothering you?"

He took the wallet without replying, and that was enough answer.

"Take care," I said and turned. I'd have to ask that gardener how to get out of this place.

I took the pacifier out of Lykke's mouth so she could speak to me.

Are you okay, baby? Why are you fiddling?

Mommy, I'm hungry. And I need a nap.

I know, sweetie, but we're in a bit of a pickle. Soon, I promise.

Where's grandma?

She's back at the house.

I know what you did—you kidnapped me.

Lykke burst wailing while cold perspiration trickled down my back. It couldn't be happening. The one person who should care for me was against me.

Baby, nobody kidnapped you. I saved you.

I want to go home to my real Mommy!

I put the pacifier in her mouth, unable to believe this. If Lykke was against me, there was no reason to even continue.

Tell her it's a game of hide-and-go-seek.

Tell her if she's a good girl, her Mommy would find her.

Kids are dumb—they'll believe anything.

The voices were on my side again. That's when I noticed the trend that when the voices were against me, Lykke was on my side and vice versa. But what did it mean?

Lykke, we are playing hide-and-ho-seek. If you're a good girl, Mommy will find you.

Like magic, Lykke stopped crying. The voices were right. I didn't want to question their intent, I was just happy they knew what to do. I removed the pacifier.

Are you going to be a good girl, then?

Yes!

Okay. I promise I'll change you and feed you soon.

"Wait." I heard Vijay's voice behind me. "Please, forgive me."

I turned, surprised. His hands were behind his back, and his facial features had softened. I could see that back in the day, he was handsome. Not to say he was old, maybe in his late forties, but he was not as well manicures as the gardens surrounding us. Stress does that to people, and he was clearly suffering for reasons I had no desire to learn.

It seemed exhausting listening to Miriam and Regina and now Vijay, and I realized I had more compassion for Dr. Black, who listens to people daily.

"Thanks," I said.

"Maybe I can give you a lift as a thank you?"

"What about Regina?"

"What about her?" he asked.

"Wouldn't she need you?"

"Not for hours, probably. I didn't mean to Florida or anything, but I heard you were headed to the airport?"

I barely hesitated when I said, "Take me to a bar." The plan had unfolded as immediately. I could snatch car keys in a bar after making someone really drunk.

Vijay was clearly taken aback. "At eleven o'clock in the morning? No bar I know is open."

"Good point. Do you know a shopping plaza nearby? Something small, where I can have Chinese food for ten bucks and then go to a bar across the street whenever one opens." I had change in my pocket from selling Miriam's phone, which I assumed was enough.

Vijay scratched his head. "Oh, yes!" He raised his finger and made a gesture with his hand, like "Follow me."

Vijay turned right upon exiting the golf club. On the radio, there was a song by Britney Spears, something about a womanizer. Britney had been raping the radio for years, and I wondered when the states would become obsessed with someone new and exciting, perhaps from Canada or the UK. New Spice Girls, perhaps? I used to love them. Since the partition between us was open, I asked if Vijay could switch the station. He was now cooperative and did what I asked. I recognized the voices of Skip Jones and Erin Wilson.

"What I don't understand," Erin was saying, "is how the kidnapper could travel from New York to Virginia without being caught. It makes no sense."

"She obviously knows what she's doing," Skip said. "Perhaps she's done it before, stealing something that doesn't belong to her. Now what?"

"The FBI is investigating the house," she said. "They're looking for prints, but the situation does not look promising. According to the medical examiner, the lady of the house, Miriam Turtle, has dementia and doesn't remember what she did this morning, let alone having a kidnapper staying her. She's mentally ill."

"Who called the cops?"

"Her neighbor, who's a stay-at-home mom."

My ears went up like antennas. Miriam's neighbor! The one who had been watching me. I couldn't believe it.

Erin was saying, "She called the authorities this morning and said there was a stranger with a baby staying at her neighbor's house. When the police arrived, there was no trace of the kidnapper—so we really don't know all the details—the neighbor could be lying. Without checking, she negligently assumed."

"How did the kidnapper manage to leave without a trace, and then vanish?"

"The neighbor saw her taking out the garbage, which might have been her clothes. Miriam Turtle is a hoarder. There are over forty cats in that house."

"Wow. Is it even legal?"

"What, to have a kidnapper in your house?"

"No, the cats."

"Oh," Erin said. "It's no on both accounts. The house is unsanitary. Our reporter was unable to get any closer, but he talked to the neighbor, who wishes to remain anonymous. She told us she had been reporting Miriam to the Department of Sanitation for years, but the authorities looked the other way. She claimed the stench was unbearable even from her own house. Our investigation disagrees with that statement. It didn't smell all that bad."

"The hoarder and the kidnapper may be in cahoots. Is that right?"

"We believe so. But don't hold thy breath. The neighbor who called also has dementia. When we asked her how long ago she'd spotted the baby, she thanked us for the cookies and closed the door."

Perhaps I was off the grid again? From what I'd just heard, there was a possibility the police would dismiss Miriam's neighbor's claim. Especially since she suffered dementia, which can't be a comfortable condition to live with in the first place. Imagine having breakfast and then five minutes later wondering if you ate or not. The anchors said Miriam had dementia as well, but I was doubtful. Any person could claim that, and it's not easily proved. Was Miriam . . . covering for me by saying she had memory problems? Why would she cover for a kidnapper? That made no sense whatsoever. She had so much to lose, her freedom, her daughter, and, most importantly, the cats—her real family. Miriam definitely suffered through something, but it was not dementia. Loneliness, yes. Focal illusions, double yes. All that confusion, however, bought me some extra time.

I was so caught up in my thoughts that next thing I knew, Vijay was standing to my left with the limo door open. Mere seconds later, after I exited and thanked him, the limo vanished as if never existed.

Ahead of me was a Walmart. The parking lot was filled to its almost full capacity with cars, shoppers with empty carts entering, full carts exiting. One car would leave, another would take its place. Perfect. I just had to figure out how to execute my plan involving motor vehicle theft.

I bivouacked in a quiet, shady corner, watching shoppers. Lykke was now calm, thank God. Common sense reminded me I should be feeling terrified and stupid, but I didn't. I felt fine. Uplifted even. Some of my muscles, including the sphincter of my anus, had stiffened, though for which reason left me unnerved. I mean, it's not like in the time of danger the first thing your body should do is assume you'll be raped in the butt and immediately proceed to tighten all possible entrances. Like the holes on a sinking ship.

Yawning, I watched the inflowing and outflowing traffic of cars, contemplating a plan of action. I needed an inconspicuous vehicle to avoid drawing attention to myself. I intended to unearth my quarry, watch where they put their car keys and follow them like a predator into the giant supermarket. I envisioned bumping into them from behind to distract—unassumingly—"Oops, I'm sorry," I'd say, and while they were disoriented, I'd snatch the car keys. I'd seen it done in movies before, so it must be a thing criminals do. Stealing terrified me, but somehow I was creepily overexcited about it, primarily since my freedom depended on it. Again, a primal instinct. For the past two days, my body was solely running on adrenalin and cortisol, the hormone of stress, and I wondered if the biochemistry of my brain was changing to prevent me from easily freaking out.

I waited. Being in a car with Vijay reminded me once again how much I missed testosterone. During the ride, Vijay's natural scent was being whiffed off of him, permeating the air and getting into the leather seats, kind of like when a dog marks its territory. Kim's room smelled like him, accentuating notes of masculinity and something woody. Special. Different? Like *him*. I wondered if Kim missed my scent too.

A blue Volkswagen van entered the parking lot, a car so striking I stared at it like it might be a mirage. The van had to be circa 1960, still in mint condition, and I wondered what kind of magic—big black magic perhaps? —had kept it together. I recalled seeing a similar van my hippy parents used to borrow from their friend Daydream Sativa. As a child, I understood why the van was decorated with flowers but didn't understand why Daydream couldn't use deodorant. Nostalgia was almost palpable. I reached in my coat pocket to text Mom, and withdrew, annoyed at myself. I *had* no phone.

I watched the van zigzag in search of a vacant lot. The driver found it in the back of the overflowing lot and carefully backed into the space to make his exit less of a hustle. Daydream Sativa used to park head-on, after which she'd spend ten minutes backing out, a much harder task, apparently, especially if your van is full of painted daisies and people think you're sweet, while you have a filthy mouth with the windows closed. "Freaking skank!" she'd yell at someone while smiling at them in the safety of the car. "Hurry the hell up, bitch!" she would say to a pedestrian. While I would wonder to myself on the back seat while playing with Mr. Potato Head: "Can that lady in front of us really hurry up in that wheelchair?"

I envied the driver of the van, wishing for a time machine. I'd totally rent a similar van for a weekend getaway with my girlfriends—had such a thought crossed my mind before. I was having a euphoric feeling of regret. Living in New York my entire life, I'd managed to avoid driving, even if at sixteen, I received my driver's license. I was excited about seeing the official document with my picture on it describing my age, sex, name, and other credentials that made me feel legit like I was ready for the big gal world.

The driver, a white guy wearing sunglasses, exited the van, a baseball cap on his head with black hair sticking out from underneath. He looked young, in his late twenties/early thirties. He was wearing tight-fitting clothes in black: a jacket, skinny jeans, and sneakers. He slightly resembled a homeless guy. He didn't have a dog with him, though. A set of keys was hooked on a long metal chain and attached to his belt. Perfect! Even if his van was not exactly inconspicuous, the guy seemed like easy prey, petite and lightweight, such an ideal opponent to pick a fight with.

You should run over him with a cart.

And while he's disoriented, you snatch those car keys, girlfriend.

I followed him into the Walmart, discreetly sucking on my thumb.

I grabbed a shopping cart upon entering. I immediately placed a six-pack of cinnamon rolls inside the cart to appear unassuming, your typical pretty plump girl shopping for her pastries. No one would have believed had I grabbed a salad. Lykke kicked me so hard and spit out her pacifier on the floor.

Baby, be careful with this!

It's for you, Mommy.

I don't need it. I have a thumb.

I bent over to pick it up, and my mittens fell out of my pockets. Annoyed, I dropped them in the cart and wiped off the pacifier first, blowing on it. I stuck it in my mouth to disinfect and hid it in my pocket.

Be a good girl now. If you cry, you will have to suck on that dirty pacifier.

The guy snatched a shopping cart that seemed to belong to an older woman who was slowly picking out tomatoes, her hands trembling, cane for support. I couldn't believe he did that. She looked so frail. He started pawing through the prepared foods section of hot entrées and cold antipasti. He was indolent to cook, considering he was lazy enough to obtain his own cart. Now I felt better about my plan, but unlike what the voices had suggested, I wasn't going to run him over with my cart. I seized a large pouch of chips, threw it in the shopping cart, and noticed its flavor: Rock Hot Chili Squid. Do people actually eat crap like that? Yes, I do!

The store seemed to stretch forever, with groceries to the left, clothes and merchandise to the right, Customer Service and bathrooms lurking behind. A box full of DVDs with a sign "Five or Under" was inviting. An Indian lady in a colorful sari was pushing a shopping cart while speaking on the phone, three munchkins hopping in her wake. All three gave me a strange look of what resembled surprise. Was that the bindi on my forehead? A worker with severe acne was stacking soy sauce in an ethnic section full of noodles, soy sauces, peanut sauces, other items high in sodium and sugar, and pouches of what resembled dried cockroaches—basically divine foodstuffs for those who speak Mandarin. But I didn't, so I politely declined. I know I wasn't shopping for "real," just pretend-shopping while I was gathering intel on the van driver. Even so, shopping smart was vital.

The guy reached the next aisle, where he sketchily browsed the surroundings as if casing the joint. I averted my eyes, but kept watching him in my peripheral vision and grabbed another pouch of chips to cover my face with. Holy crap! A hundred and sixty calories per twenty-eight-ounce serving. I lowered the chips below my eyes just in time to notice him pocketing a chocolate bar into his coat while nobody was watching. Excellent—the first man I'd laid my eyes on was a criminal who cared none about the "Buy one, get one free" sign above him. "Steal one and it's free" was the sign he saw.

He avoided the freezer aisle, which meant he needed no ice cream, which meant he was not depressed, which meant . . . Oops, he was in the next aisle already—that's what it meant.

I followed, occasionally sweeping through shelves to make it appear like I was actually shopping. So far, my cart was full of nothing but chips, sweets, and a two-liter bottle of Pepsi. What only people must be thinking! I replaced the regular Pepsi with a diet one immediately.

A strategy about how to snatch his keys had materialized. All that masturbating in the shower was going to pay off because I was planning to use my secret weapon: my sexuality.

I was going to flirt. Yup, just like that. The night I met Kim, he was showing me magic tricks trying to impress me without noticing my cleavage was more and more open as the night went along. I was hooking *him* while he foolishly thought the opposite.

Uncertainty held me back. I asked myself to count to three, go over there, and let my newly found spunk take over. I needed a push. Somehow, a strange sensation passed through me, and when it came out, it smelled terrible.

Someone touched me from behind, and I jumped, doing a one-eighty. A tall Latino man was staring at me, holding a mitten.

"Excuse me, mademoiselle," said he with a heavy accent.

He was the most handsome man I'd seen in real life, with dimples and a demeanor of a boy next door. I was clutching the cart behind me with both hands, shaking from a sudden crush and embarrassed that I had just farted like a total loser. No one had ever called me a mademoiselle before, which is French for "miss." Sometimes I forget I *am* actually a miss. I'd been called sexy, curvaceous, but never a mademoiselle. His perfectly tan skin was even and smooth as if he lived on the beach, and bulging pecs and biceps as if he slept at the gym. He was wearing a white V-neck underneath a puffer jacket, a gold pendant visible together with two large nipples poking through the almost translucent white fabric. His coarse hair was combed back with a slick.

I knew he expected a reply or *anything* coming out of my mouth, but my tongue was in a spasm. My nose started picking up on the smell of what had just oozed out of my butt.

"I didn't fart!" I yelled.

"Farht?" he repeated in the same heavy accent, but loudly for everyone to hear. I had no idea how he took such a disgusting word and made it sexy. "Farght." I saw doves, the reality slowing down as my heartbeat was accelerating.

"I *said* I didn't do it! Don't *look* at me!" I said defensively, really embarrassed. I knew my face was now red, but there was no preventing that. I looked like a walking piece of trash with a red marker on my forehead, farting, and there he was, a man of my dreams.

"Sorhy, mademoiselle. My English. She's no prhetty goot."

"How's your credit?" I blurted out.

"Parhdoh?" he asked. "Yorh okay?"

"It was a joke," I said, covering the shopping cart with my body completely. I was hyperventilating, so I fanned my face with my hand. He'd seen my groceries, which were the items of a lonely, miserable cat lady. My face ignited in flames, and I heard the fire alarm going off, mostly due to the gas. We were clearly miscommunicating, so I began waving my hand in front of my face and clipped my nose with another. He stretched a smile that should be illegal in this country, a beautiful, bleached smile with teeth that were perfectly aligned and could chomp on a steak like a pro.

"Yoo loose yourh glof, mademoiselle," he said, offering the mitten to me.

Sofia Vergara, her equivalent, or some other beautiful mujer—hooked her arm into his. Of course, his girlfriend. She pointed at Lykke and muttered something in Spanish, a big smile on her face. Her shining hair was from the Pantene Pro-V commercial. It smelled delicious, had no split ends, and each strand was as thick as a fishing line. I would know. Daddy was a big fisherman.

"Gracias, muchachos," I said, squeezed the mitten off his hand, and turned, knowing perfectly well my face was the shade of red chef Gordon Ramsay would call a perfect medium-rare.

I deeply breathed out, realizing I'd survived. Thirty seconds or so later, I turned back, watching them going through an aisle with chocolate. They were in their early twenties, never having to worry about eating junk food because their metabolism was working overtime. They probably don't even yet know words like sodium, metabolism, and/or overweight. Her thighs were the size of my wrists, and she was wearing skinny jeans that showed her skinny butt. Had I known her better, I'd assume she was strutting and posing, as if there were cameras all around. Which they were. I was suddenly feeling so insecure and angry. I've heard it all before: we should love ourselves regardless of our looks, blah blah blah. Fine, if *you* could master it. But how could *I* stop this feeling of worthlessness from ruining my life?

My eyes crossed. Why did I remove my mittens, to begin with? I returned the lost one back into the coat's pocket, where I'd kept the money from pawning the phone, but the money was gone. I paused, checking the second pocket. Ditto. The money probably fell out with the mitten. I looked back but saw no cash lying on the ground. Someone had either found it and took it or returned to customer service. I had no time to check. My face heated up to a perfect well-done.

Ping. Your roast is ready.

Actually, that was precisely what I needed. Somehow, irrational anger makes you do unpredictable things. I was no longer skittish.

Those Volkswagen keys are mine, boy!

I reached the aisle where the guy was comparing two brands of beer as if to decide which to pick. Beauty secrets I may not know, but *the beer* I do. I entered the aisle, parked the cart near margarita mixers, and approached him, pretending to search for something to drink. He smelled woody, masculine. Different. The keys were hooked to a chain, among which the van key was hanging denoted by a massive W. Ten to fifteen different keys were there as well like he doubled as a realtor or a superintendent.

"Hi," I said in what I surmised was my sexy voice, losing the Indian accent in the process. The guy turned around. Up close, he was somewhat cute. He was the type of cute Mom calls: "He's cute if he's rich."

"Hey," he said noncommittally. He was still wearing sunglasses as if he was hiding from the cops. If I could have a kidnapped baby on my chest, the least he could do was take them off. He did a double-take, taking in Lykke.

"You should get this IPA," I said, tapping a six-pack of beer I knew.

"I've never tried this brand. Is it hoppy?" he said with a Southern twang.

"Oh, my God. Are you Donny? Donny Gold?" I said.

He paused. "I can be. What's your name?"

"Titi. Or better yet, Tater Tits," I said, winking. A mademoiselle would never fart, but Tater Tits would. The guy was so much like Kim that I felt playful and aroused.

"Buck Mooney. Your parents named you Tater Tits? Isn't that child abuse?"

I prayed to the voices: Please take over. There was no way to handle the situation without them.

"I was just kidding," I said, and vomit of words followed. "My name is Nefertiti Parkvankar. Tater Tits is my nickname. This is not my baby, see? I wet-nurse her because I overproduce milk, and babies eat mine like they're tater tots. Only they're tater tits."

"Oh."

"You remind me of someone," I said, trying to remember a guy I hooked up with ions ago. "His name was George, and he was just as handsome too. Sorry if I interrupted you." I imagined being a flight attendant right now: flirty and amatory. Belatedly I realized he'd been inching closer.

"No worries, Taters. Who's he anyway?"

"An ex-boyfriend of mine. He broke up with me."

"Why?"

"He hated blowjobs."

"Seriously?"

"Yup. He was the only guy I knew who had no libido and who wasn't turned on by a girl going down on him. I took it personally, of course, right after he told me to use less teeth."

From the corner of my eye, I noticed a bulge growing in Buck's pants.

I added, "I would tell you more, but it's a very . . . *long* . . . story."

The men get turned on by dirty talk, and Buck was no exception. I decided to fill him in on more details, but first I did a quick surveillance of the aisle to make sure nobody was listening. Besides us two, the aisle was empty. Buck kept holding two beer cans, patiently waiting for more filth out of my mouth.

"Have you heard of this new sexual position called Fresh from Bangladesh?" I whispered, and he shook his head for a no. "It's when a dude blindfolds a chick and does anything he wants."

"Anything?"

"Anything," I whispered and leaned closer. "Including anal." If I were a flight attendant, I imagined this was the amount of sensuality I'd offer to each male customer of legal drinking age. My lips almost touched Buck's earlobe while my fingers touched the keys, and I tugged on the belt. "I'm sensing you haven't had much lately—and I'm quite open if you know what I mean."

Buck appeared mesmerized for a moment, cleared his throat, and returned both beer cans to the shelf. Sweat droplets emerged on his face, and who knew where else.

"So IPA, huh?" he quickly said, withdrawn. He picked up two six-packs off the shelf and held them in front of him like a shield, a cloud of discomfort hanging over him.

"Thanks," he said. "I'll be seeing ya."

Buck wiggled his way out of the aisle and disappeared from sight in the clothing section, while I stared at my perspiring hand with the chain of Buck's van keys in it.

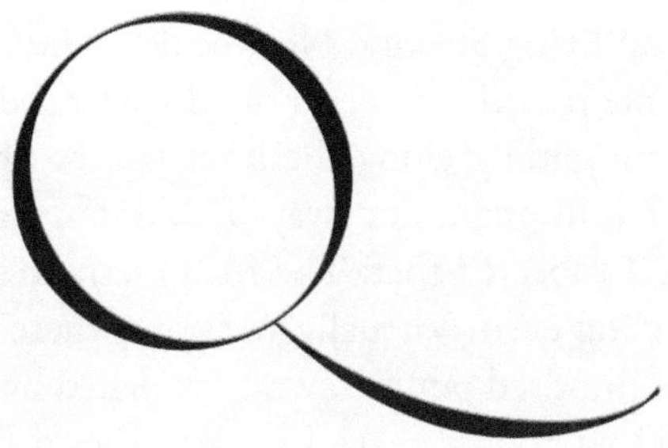

QUICKLY, WHEN THE COAST WAS CLEAR, I ABANDONED THE cart in the booze aisle and skedaddled out of the store in suspended animation to the congratulating chatter of the voices. Most people know about the fight-or-flight response, but there's the third, the freeze response. That's how I felt, still back at the store, frozen, watching Buck's slim tushie wiggle away from me. He hadn't been prepared for what seemed like a perverted woman helping him pick the best beer. I certainly hadn't been prepared to act that way. I found myself outside. Buck's van stood where he'd left it, toward the end of the lot, which was now receding for some reason. I recovered the keys and found the one with W on it that slid right in.

I jumped behind the wheel, inserted the key into the ignition, and the engine roared to life. I brought the belt underneath Lykke and clicked it in place. When I hugged the wheel, I realized driving wouldn't be comfortable with the baby, especially since the van was a stick. In the rearview mirror, I swept through the back of the van, which was littered with beer bottles, carton pizza boxes, heaps of clothes. Belatedly I picked on the smell of ramen and something else laden with MSG. Great. Like a dime piece, I jumped from one hoarder to the next, per the law of losers, evidently. Yeah, yeah, complain more, Chloe.

I eased out of the parking space and turned left toward the exit, watching the Walmart entrance for. I didn't know what I would do if he jumped out of the store and started running frantically in my direction. Thankfully, that didn't happen.

I exited the lot and turned on the radio, where a foreigner was singing, who ended up being Shakira. No wonder I didn't understand a word that came out of her mouth whenever or wherever she was opening it.

I was soon gliding along the interstate at fifty miles per hour toward Richmond, a hundred miles away. The traffic was sparse, but at this hour, barely noon, I expected that. The road mesmerized me, so enchanting and freeing. Puzzling even. Virtually weapons, these heavy machines weighing three to four hundred pounds, were propelled by physical forces like galleys out at sea. How cool is that? In math, they'd be vectors with their own trajectories—all with purpose and accordance. Nobody was driving purely out of peradventure. Life is hard as is—why take a chance out on the road? My bedroom in New York was overlooking the FDR drive, which is essentially a highway. Sometimes, after smoking some dope, I'd sit out on the balcony, staring down at the never-ending speeding lights—life, in its pure form. Humanity was always on the run, whether hunting prey, escaping predators, or metaphorically from our feelings. That's why out butts, the most prominent muscle, evolved to grow to support us upright. I wondered if, in another few million years, our butts would grow bigger due to overeating, or smaller, due to dereliction. No doubt, I'd prefer smaller, but inactivity, in theory (and practice), leads to more obesity, so there goes nothing.

As a New Yorker, I frequently forget about the world outside of Manhattan. Kind of like I oftentimes forget about others by being trapped in my own head. In front of me was the life I never knew I'd have—this road of uncertainty, a new daughter. I was confused about whether I wanted that life or not, and some thinking was in prompt order.

First, I fiddled with the radio, searching for the news. Certainly, by now, more developments had been made. The radio itself had an LCD screen where the current frequency was displayed. I scanned, letting the frequency numbers go up, listening to everything from pop to rock to country. No news. Lykke kicked me when a station with a kid's song came on, a duet, man, and woman. The male voice was telling us to put our hands in the air, and he sounded like in a cartoon, he could be a beaver with two oversized front teeth protruding excessively. The woman sang in falsetto to the sound of cheering kids, including Lykke. From watching hundreds of cartoons during my hours of babysitting, I learned that if the kid likes the current selection, let them watch it. Or, in my case, hear it.

You like this, baby?

Yes, Mommy.

Good girl.

The van felt intimate. It's strange how a van the size of a giant's shoebox made me feel safe, sane, and at home. I watched other drivers, wondering if they had a similar experience. As we were going downhill, the grey road ahead blended into the silver sky, making cars disappear like in a magic trick. A mountain range in the distance, speckled with snow, appeared shimmering from atmospheric refraction. This natural "mirage" is caused by the velocity of light through air or turbulence. I wondered if my hallucinations were due to the same effect but inside my brain. Staring at the distance mesmerized me so much, my senses switched off. I was on autopilot.

I really shouldn't have been left alone in a car like this. With just my thoughts. The voices lay dormant, the quietness deafening. The radio was playing, but the sound didn't register. I cranked open the window, hoping the fresh air would bring me back, but the state of cryptobiosis couldn't be overturned.

I knew what it was.

The same state had happened to me before in the past during an "episode." They are visions or micro-dreams. The mind takes naps. They occur when the brain is too tired and needs a breather. During the nap, the reality pauses, letting your mind disconnect, and have you wonder in the endless labyrinth of your subconscious mind, seeking the answers you're unable to answer when awake. This void I was in seemed cool. I could bend the rules of space-time, engineering my own reality. With my hand, I pushed Lykke out of the car, rotating her suspended body in the 3-D vacuum my mind had created. It's as if I now stood in front of the van, watching straight at us, me Chloe and her Lykke. Behind them, the road stretched for miles with cars, and with my hand, I could move the picture in front of me left or right, up/down, back and forth, faster/slow. I pushed it away, items in front of me fading into darkness. With my right hand, I brought my fingers together, condensing the earth to such a size that it could fit in my other hand. Now I could zoom in and out anywhere in the world, the same way as I could do on my phone.

I spun the earth until North and South Americas were in the middle, tapping the general area of North East to drop a pin. With two fingers, I zoomed out, and the picture in front of me plummeted like a crashing airplane. It was fun to watch. When the map stopped moving, a portion of the Atlantic Ocean was still visible to the right, while the eastern states were bunched up together like penguins in Antarctica.

I kept zooming in and moving the map until I saw Long Island that ran perpendicular to the tiny, by comparison, Manhattan. More and more. And then I saw who I wanted to see, my friend Natalia. It was entertaining to watch her in a frozen state like a mammoth that died in Ice Age, preserving itself fully intact. She had placed her hands behind her head to ruffle her hair, boobs out, stomach in. I cracked open her in half like we did with the frog in the seventh grade. I saw no heart. In front of Natalia, there was a picture of two African boys she was "adopting." I realized, she had too much time on her hands. Paying someone ten bucks a month is not adoption any way you slice it. I went deeper into her brain and saw what she was thinking. A vagina, resembling Jennifer Aniston's. I started laughing so hard I almost suffocated. My problems, *real* problems, like my ears being too big, didn't seem even remotely as stupid.

Why I blew up at her at the Mexican restaurant was clear. Natalia never sugarcoats anything and names things as they are. That hurts. Before I met Kim, she'd say something like, "Chloe, you're fat. Lose weight, or you'll never find a boyfriend. Men not attracted to the jelly in your belly." She was wrong in the sense that I later found Kim, but that's not the point. The point is, we Americans are not used to being told the truth. Natalia, vain, and probably narcissistic, keeps her body in shape. But as far as I know, she was single herself, so, for real, should I even listen to her? Calyssa would instead say, "You're not fat! Fat is an ugly word. You don't have a boyfriend because you're busy." It would make me feel better, but I'm *not* busy. It's not the truth.

In the end, I would be unhappy nevertheless. Natalia was always seeking for new ways to dispose of or as she called it "invest" her money. She often picked up the tab, and in the past, she paid for extravagant meals, drinks, and trips. I believe Natalia was trying to "buy" our friendship because of severe low self-esteem issues. Whenever I needed to purchase something out of my reach, she'd offer to lend me the money, over and over. For her, it's easier to pay out than to deal with the problem. What did Natalia really want? I tried to dig deeper, but her pixelated brain showed nothing.

I was beyond confused about what approach to self-care was more appropriate, Calyssa's flattery one, or Natalia's (if/when I was ready for the truth).

Excited, I quickly zoomed out and went to Staten Island. I saw Calyssa in the john, phone in her hand, a picture of a teacup Pomeranian on the screen. Like I did with Natalia, I dissected her and saw the diamond ring that was passing through her colon. It seemed days from emerging, and I wished I could warn her. She was all over the place, that girl, a proverbial "hot mess." Her pattern was clear.

Last year she'd attempted to blackmail her boss into keeping her job—which kind of worked as far as I remember, but that story was so convoluted I still am not sure what happened. I mean, she's nonstop trouble. The stories she tells often have discrepancies in them as if she lacks a brain, and I take whatever she says with a grain of salt. Not only does she exaggerate, but she is also unbelievably partial. The only reason we clicked, I believe, was because I love listening to her voice, her stories. She leaves it up to me to decide which are real and which are imaginary. Calyssa makes a boring story about a trip to a grocery store interesting. More often than not, I escape reality in her company, dissolving like French vanilla ice cream on the tongue. Sure, Calyssa is a biased fibber—but she got her stuff done one way or another. Natalia, for instance, went to casinos to play poker to make her fortune. She would sit at a table, and you could never read the expression on her face. That's called bluffing, which is different from fibbing. I was interested in finding out what story Calyssa had cooked up for her boss about the missing ring. I tried to zoom in deeper, but her brain looked foggy. Well, so, in a way, was her entire life. It's as if she had just been born, being two-days old in a thirty-year-old body, excited about everything, too smart for a toddler, a bit doltish for a grown woman.

I dragged the picture through the Upper Bay, and toward the Upper East Side. Lindsay was sitting on the sofa watching Charlotte coloring. Lindsay looked scared. More crayons for Charlotte meant a possibility of choking. What a liability babysitting could be. I would know. Unlike Calyssa and Natalia, Lindsay never lies, unafraid to voice her fears. While the other two would never admit they're scared of anything, Lindsay is the Cowardly Lion of the group.

But she also isn't honest, either, I believe. She had her own technique of how to push agenda—by example. She was all skinny as proof that whatever she was doing worked. She wouldn't tell me that *I* was unhealthy or fat, but I could read that between the lines. When she told me to drink water before each meal, she wasn't saying I should be doing it. Because if I confronted her, she'd be like, "Oh, no, I didn't mean for you. I meant, in general." That phrase, "in general." In general, it pisses me off. Lindsay was a passive-aggressive observer, offering unsolicited advice, which nobody seemed to take. As soon as she told me the story about Charlotte swallowing a crayon, I knew she was over her job and was bored to death.

Lindsay craved more attention than any woman I knew, but the attention was not up for grabs. She didn't quite understand she was standing on an empty street, screaming for help without opening her mouth. When I met Lindsay last year, I instantaneously hated her. You know, like the first time I ate tofu with her, and it was gross, but she'd make these munching noises like she was enjoying the taste of that over-processed mature edamame. She wanted us to notice how skinny she was by eating the tofu that contained no hormones or antibiotics, MSG (whatever that is; a TV studio?), or GMOs (whatever that is; another TV studio?). Well, maybe I freaking love hormones and antibiotics. What's it to her?

In the new era, we have become so obsessed with ourselves that we care less and less about other people. Everything is in abundance, and we like to supersize everything. Superficially, we're all about fixing the "system," without understanding what the "system" stands for. Tons of articles have been emerging recently about people being "too busy" for everything, a new universal code for showing the others you have a "life." When they say, "Get a life," what they truly mean is "Start saying you're busy." The busier we are, the higher our social status supposedly is, because the more we work, the more money we make, the less we're needy. We also struggle with what is commonly known as FOMO, an acronym for Fear of Missing Out. The Millennials sought knowledge, which arrived in the form of a smartphone. We quickly became addicted, less available for friends and family, and now we are "busy" with stuff. Many young people I know, including Calyssa and me, live with our parents, unable to afford our own housing. Are we less ambitious than our parents, the Baby Boomers? There is indeed a gap, but it was quickly filling up with misinformation, miscommunication, and misfortune.

New machinery came with programmed text messaging for hands-free communication. How about actually *watching* the road and texting when you get home? Not an option anymore. Mom was always on her phone, even when watching TV or talking to me. How could that be considered communication? I'd once brought it up, to which she defended her phone and yelled at me, her daughter.

When I was spending time with Mom, she was on the phone messaging her friends asking what they were doing; when I was not spending time with her, she was on the phone messaging *me* asking where I was. She had the FOMO and wanted to know what everyone was doing. The world was racing toward faster communication and mobile applications as substitutes for real books, real friends, and real life. I felt I could barely keep up. I felt lonely every day.

Babies were different. Regardless of whether there's a new technology that was set to blow your mind, babies were the same. For millions of years, we've been giving birth, and we've mastered it to such precision that doctors can predict a person's delivery day several months in advance. Same as when launching a rocket—to a second. And yes, every single time a new parent gives birth, she acts as if she's discovered plutonium. I don't know why I said that, but I thought it would be cool to discover plutonium. Something to brag about, for sure.

Someone cared for my precious Lykke because otherwise, the cops wouldn't be turning Miriam's house upside down. Babies are the future, regardless of how awful that future will be. Young people are the most important to our survival as a species. They are fascinated with climate change, while the old folk believes it's a hoax, and there's a difference right there. Nobody would lift two fingers to save me, an old heathen if I were kidnapped, but when it came to Lykke, the whole world was attempting to rescue her, especially since a prize was involved.

I zoomed out and swiped up, having the map go down to Virginia, where I found Buck's van. I stood on the highway, the van in front of me, and looked at Lykke behind the windshield. Unsettling feeling. I didn't look like myself. My eyes bugged out like I was pushing a ring out of my colon in the john. I saw fear in her eyes, that woman who I saw in front of me. She looked possessed by a demon that made her take that little baby and become a heartless criminal with a Sharpie bindi on her forehead.

Who was she, that girl? Was she me? I was unable to tell.

Lykke's face was starting to get animated. That happiness babies produce, just by being—is incredulous. They're loved for nothing rather than opening their mouths, gargling a string of words that made no sense, that mystery child. Who will she grow up like, we wonder. She's fat anyway —another doughnut wouldn't hurt. Well, Mrs. Tenderfoot, your daughter needs to get on cholesterol-lowering medication.

What a disappointment.

And just like that, I was back on the road, gliding on the shimmering highway at fifty miles per hour. Lykke was crying, and I assumed she had to be changed and soothed. A sign ahead promised Richmond was seventy miles away. I was now far away, and therefore safe. I took the next off-ramp upon spotting a sign for a rest stop.

Rambling flamboyantly, the van shook and swayed from side to side. I exited the interstate taking a narrow road until I reached the rest stop area, where a diner of sorts stood in the middle with a Confederate flag above it, sandwiched between a gas station with a mini-mart inside, and a Starbucks. Behind the plaza, several wooden pavilions were perched on a hill and served as a temporary refuge for the cranky drivers. The Confederate flag drew attention to itself, but only because I hadn't seen one since middle school when we were studying the Civil War.

The parking lot was full of cars and pickup trucks, while eighteen-wheelers chilled in a separate adjacent lot, kind of like segregation. Good, because I didn't want to maneuver around, competing for a parking spot against those giants. Circling row after row, I realized the lot was fuller than I'd at first imagined, and I entered the last row, noticing an empty space. I approached the spot, but so did a white, beat-up Cherokee, a grandpa behind the wheel with a handicapped sign attached to his rearview mirror. We both attempted entering the spot at the same time, but I paused, offering the space to him as a courtesy. I do the same when providing a seat on the subway to a pregnant woman or an elderly person. I had noticed all the handicapped spaces were taken in the front, so grandpa had no choice but to roam the lot searching for a regular civilian spot.

A car honked behind me. I slowly exited the last row, letting a few pedestrians pass, and entered the next row, which I finished without any luck. One spot possessed a "Do Not Park Here" sign, underneath which read in a smaller font: "Or your car will be towed and impounded." Lord, I wished to be towed and pounded myself. By Kim. I guess I was still horny —probably from the nerves, which I never knew was a thing. I snaked loop after loop until I saw a car backing out of a spot. I halted behind and turned on my blinkers. When the car left, I took its place and killed the engine.

"Okay, Lykke," I said out loud. "We've made it. I hope you're ready for whatever's next."

"Meh," she replied.

"Meh is right."

I opened the glove compartment, trying to find a map, but what I saw was a tablet. I clicked on the home button, and it woke up, sixty percent charged, and no passcode to get in. Buck was more stupid than I thought for allowing strangers to his darkest secrets from recent porn searches to STI symptoms. Just to prove my theory, I opened the Internet browser and scrolled through his browsing history, which was full of finance articles and no porn.

I typed, "Where am I?" and a map of Virginia popped up. I clicked and zoomed in. A little arrow showed I was in Nottingham, near Richmond, and I "woo-hooed" myself. I'd driven for close to two hours without noticing how time progressed because it was now two-thirty in the afternoon, and I was far away from D.C. However, whether I was safe in Nottingham was the real question. I knew I'd be safer after crossing the border with North Carolina, so I quickly looked up directions to Charlotte. The map suggested it'd take four and a half hours to get there by car, with a distance of two hundred and seventy miles in between. I let that sink in: I could be in Charlotte before seven. Logically, however, it would be best if I proceeded after the sun went down. Twilight in April starts closer to six, so if I remained in the parking lot for the next couple hours, I would drive in the dark.

So what was I supposed to do? The diner lurked in the distance, and my tummy produced a hungry song. If you ever wondered what that sounds like, it's a cross between Madonna's "Frozen" and the *Titanic* score when the ship sinks. I thought I could do a cheap burger at the diner and maybe even a slice of apple pie. First, purchasing new clothes was essentials for disguise, but there was one teensy problem: I had no dead presidents on me. Hm. I spent the next ten minutes, spitting on my fingers and rubbing my forehead until the red bindi was gone. Step one was complete.

I checked out the rearview mirror and eyed the back of the van, which was full of stuff, thinking I should paw through some of Buck's paraphernalia. Perhaps he'd stashed some cash in a safe place—who knows? If all went to hell, I could always go back and sell the tablet to Sally.

Before I exited the van, I watched for copzillas, witnesses, or anyone who looked suspicious. Aside from a weird guy who was talking to himself, nobody seemed sketchy. I hid Lykke from view with the coat and held her in place with one hand.

I exited with my tote at the tow and eased into the van through the middle door, sliding it shut. Empty bottles of beer partially covered the floor, and some of them worked part-time as ashtrays. Belatedly I realized that was the smell I was wondering about since the beginning. A standard-size white pillow and a shaggy blue blanket on the seat resembled a bed made. The corners of the pillows were tucked in and resembled dumplings, and if there was any soy sauce, I'd sure shoved them in my mouth. The blanket was like a bed of lettuce. I realized I was freaking starving.

So it appeared Buck slept there. Had I stolen his entire home? I covered my mouth and giggled because it reminded me of the time when I was in Tennessee, and some folks I met there believed that African-Americans had taken their home too. Hence, the Confederate flags.

I looked around the van some more, wondering at several things at once, like why Buck had kept a paper trimmer around—what was he cutting? Its teal board was square with an alignment grid and dual scale ruler, both in inches and centimeters, a guillotine blade at the end.

A small radio sat on the "nightstand," which in reality was just an upside-down wastebasket by the make-up "bed." An issue of *Playboy* magazine sat wide open to a page where a naked lady also sat wide open. Tissue paper was scattered throughout scrunched into paper balls, but what Buck used them for was none of my business. Some of the "none of my business" stuff had been sprayed on the naked *Playboy* lady. Ugh, sometimes I forget how disgusting guys can be, and I wondered if Kim was just as gross. (Hint: he was.)

A mini-fridge stood in one corner, at the sight of which my tummy loudly growled. Lykke's eyes popped open from such a terrifying sound, and I soothed her by gently tapping on her back. I found diapers in the tote and quickly changed her on the seat, all the time praying the blanket was clean.

Afterward, I fed her lunch, wondering how I could purchase more formula with no money. My protective instincts were kicking in, and unlike cats, birds, and other animals do in the wild, I couldn't just leave her alone in the van while I roamed the streets of Nottingham, searching for scraps. While she ate, I knew I wouldn't last long on just the fat storage in my body, that soon enough I'd need carbs, protein, and a healthy dose of fat, basically a burger, a perfect product to hit all the macronutrients at once, with a small but beneficial boost of vitamins and minerals found in lettuce and tomato.

The fridge was filled with two shoeboxes, and I open the first one.

Inside, dead presidents were buried. Packs of Benjamins followed by Grants, all neatly tied with rubber bands. Same story in the second box. Smart. Buck kept the money in shoeboxes since he had no safe and assumed it was . . . well, safe. Screw the Madison Avenue boutiques; *these* are the kind of shoes I liked.

How was it possible, though, that someone resembling a vagrant had such a massive amount of loot—estimated at fifty to a hundred grand? And he shopped at Walmart? Driving this clunker? Something wasn't adding up, and my heart was starting to pound.

Was Buck a mobster? Running away from the police was one thing, but I didn't want to run away from the mob—or at least I wouldn't be able to run far.

I swallowed, put the boxes back, and closed the fridge. There was a suitcase by the refrigerator, so I unzipped it to find nothing valuable, skinny black jeans, black tees, eyeliner. Was he wearing eyeliner? I went back down the memory lane, and Buck's face appeared in view. That's why memories are unreliable because now he resembled Jack Sparrow, the pirate, with eyes outlined in thick black. I didn't know whether that was the truth, and I could beat myself to death but wouldn't be able to recollect. So that was the truth as far as I was concerned. Anything before that was also a blur, memories obstructed by adrenalin and the survival mode. When you're in survival mode, the last thing your body needs is to remember unessential details. It literally felt like a hard drive in my brain was erased—but I had no time to think any more of it.

None of Buck's clothes would fit this beautiful curvy girl, who was me. Same as with Kim. When I dated Sam, the lesbian who liked to wear plaid and/or walk braless, we borrowed each other's outfits often. Well, she borrowed mine more than I borrowed hers. I'm usually not the leather girl, and she had plenty of that in her closet. Buck was skin-and-bone, and I was sure his clothes wouldn't even fit my dyslexic cousin Analise, who is a vegan and who used to like torturing animals. She's so annoying too and eats only organic stuff. She'd ask, "Is this cucumber organic?"

"Who cares?" I always want to tell her. "It's not like you're using it for a salad, stupid."

Next to the "bed," there was a printer wrapped in a case, an Ethernet cable sticking out from underneath. Buck hardly struck me as the type who knew the basics of a computer, let alone being knowledgeable enough to operate a device that I had problems setting up myself. I removed the cover, and stared at the device with an open jaw, blinked, closed my eyes in disbelief, opened them again. This was when Lykke nudged me, and I returned to reality. The printer was no regular printer I'd seen. In the paper feeder, sat a sheet of paper, letter-size, with Benjamin Franklin printed all over it. Buck printed his own money and used the paper trimmer to cut the bills off the sheet.

I removed my mittens and opened the fridge. I got one of the shoeboxes and retrieved a bundle of Benjamins. They appeared decent. (I mean, *I* appeared decent too, and I was a criminal—so decent attributed nothing.) I undid the rubber band from the stack, taking one banknote to explore it closer. It was made so well I doubt I could tell the difference between Buck's money and the real money. Buck resembled someone who ate nothing but ramen noodles, plus he was slender like one, but he produced extraordinary results in the cash subdivision. Perhaps, he once worked for the Department of the Treasury, and upon having been fired, Buck decided to print his own currency and stop paying taxes.

I was starting to realize this "birds of a feather" thing was not entirely untrue. So far, I'd only met other criminals along the way.

There was no way I could use the counterfeit currency, even if my life depended on it—which it did. One thing was to be caught with Lykke, but who would recognize *her* face? All babies look the same, cute, fat, and dribbling from the mouth. On the other hand, *everyone* would recognize Benjamin Franklin's face. They all look different to me, each new bill more handsome than the next. If the cops found the van, they would automatically dust for prints. Since I'd only touched one bundle, I quickly stuck it in my coat's pocket, put my mittens on, closed the shoebox, wiped it with tissue paper, and returned it to the fridge.

Now what?

It was time to disguise again. I removed my jeans, searching Buck's "apartment" for a plastic bag into which I could hide the pair, and I quickly found one under the seat. I dumped the jeans into the bag, thinking the sari was enough insulation against the cold.

In that exact order: I hid the printer under its original cover, rolled my eyes, exited the van.

While reasonably sure I was safe in Nottingham, I doubted I was safe being seen in the vicinity of this counterfeiting vehicle. Before exiting, I made sure the parking lot was clear of suspicious people, which it was. I spotted a trash can on the other side of the lot, where a black cat was salvaging food. My heart literally skipped a beat. I mean, I knew it wasn't Anubis, but it hurt anyway. When I approached the trash can, the cat scrammed in the opposite direction toward the woods without doing a double-take.

I dumped the plastic bag with my jeans into the trash can when the following thought slapped me hard: I lost the pawn money at Walmart, and the only way I could gobble at the diner was by using Buck's spurious currency. Unless I pawned Regina's bracelet or Bucks's tablet somewhere. Buck was such an idiot too. Why print Benjamins when they are the most conspicuous to begin with? He had fifties in the shoeboxes, but they were just as conspicuous. No Jacksons or Washingtons.

My growling stomach sent a text message to the brain: "The money looks fine; let's eat. You can leave a counterfeit bill on the table and scram before they realize it's fake. Just handle the cash with your mittens and keep Lykke away from being seen." I completely agreed with my stomach's text message, and I messaged back: "You're right. Thanks!" It was almost like texting Mom!

I returned to the van, retrieved Buck's blanket to hide Lykke as per my stomach's wise request, and checked myself in the rearview mirror. If I looked ridiculous in the sari with a bump on my chest covered in a blanket, the mirror didn't say a word. But I knew it was wondering who was the fairest of them all. (Hint: me.)

S

Soon I was inside the Merfolk Diner. It was set up a way I imagined a diner to be with booths distributed along the perimeter, tables for four scattered throughout, with the counter and a lady in a fishnet working the register straight across from the exit. There was something fishy going on—no, literally—with fake seafood hanging from the ceiling, starfish stickers glued to the oval windows, and coral reefs and beaches painted on the walls. Even one customer resembled a jellyfish with his enormous head. Protecting Lykke from view, I waited to be seated, while the smell of bacon was being whiffed from the kitchen. The wait staff was wearing white bottoms and red tops with their first and last name handwritten with a Sharpie on "Hello My Name Is" tags. Several bypassed me with food on their trays, and by now, I was drooling uncontrollably. It looked as if I was the only Indian woman here, well—Indian in quotes since I was wearing a sari—while everyone else was white, with no quotes. Instead, they had bellies, and I fit right in.

A waitress approached me with a friendly smile and freckles. Her name tag read Anita Chill.

"Hi," she said with a smile. "Just the two y'all?"

I stood there dumbfounded, watching Anita, who resembled my friend

Calyssa, coal-black hair and all. Was I having another psychotic episode, aka hallucination? In schizophrenics, hallucinations come when the brain is unable to deal with reality and needs a comfort buffer, creating an entire experience right inside the mind. It was disturbing how real Anita seemed, so perhaps it wasn't a hallucination. I had no idea. She was probably sixteen if not younger, and worry was written all over her face. I assumed the many acne dots on her face were inherited from her mother, Connect DiDots—and I wanted to take a pencil and draw the lines from one dot to the next.

"Ma'am?" Anita said. I looked up, realizing I'd been staring at her for a while. "Just the two y'all?"

"Yes," I said.

"I got yer table over here, Shug."

The temperature on the premises was hot and humid, which had awarded Anita with a frizzy Afro, while the plump hips had been most likely awarded by the fried food. She halted by an empty booth and waited until I sat down before putting a menu in front of me.

"How y'all doin'?"

"Good," I said.

"The special today is catfish. It comes with a side of mashed taters, greens, and a biscuit."

"What makes it special?" I said.

"It's eight bucks."

"I like that." I couldn't get over how much Anita reminded me of Calyssa, and I wanted to keep listening to her voice. "What else, Anita?"

"Oh, wait, we've replaced the greens with okra—I forgot. The freezer where we'd kept the greens lost power after the cook, lazy Susan—who, by the way, ma'am, looks just like Paula Deen—I mean, ya can't make a silk purse outofa sow's ear—plugged in her hairdryer, which tore up the outlet. We couldn't fix the darn thing until earlier this morning."

I had not the faintest idea what she was talking about, guessing Anita had always been this talkative, just like Calyssa, but nevertheless, I marveled in her company. I just wanted to keep listening to her voice, the Southern drawl.

"Why is your cook called lazy Susan? Is she lazy?" I asked.

She looked around in an attempt to make sure nobody was listening.

"Well, she hasn't got the sense God gave a goose," she said quieter. "She sleeps with 'bout every guy in town. Rumor has it, one time she spent the night with, like, eight guys, and they spun her 'round like a lazy Susan. But her name *is* really Susan. Coincidence? I don't think so." She whispered the last sentence as if sharing a secret.

"No, of course not," I agreed, nodding.

Anita smiled and winked. I had earned her trust. "Anything to drink, ma'am?"

"Diet Coke, please."

"It's flat, ma'am."

"Well, anything else to drink, Anita?"

"We have water, ma'am, but it's tap. Nooooo, thank you—right?"

"Why? Tap is fine."

"Why, ma'am. Haven't you heard a rumor about Allen Ranch, who contaminated the public water system with his semen?"

"No, I have not," I said. "I'm not local."

"It may not be true, ma'am, just a rumor. Draw your own conclusions."

"How do you know he contaminated the water?"

"Why, ma'am, Mary White got knocked up! She is married to the sheriff. The baby came out . . . black, just like Allen Ranch. Same teeth, the dentist said. After a long investigation, the sheriff's department concluded it was Mr. Ranch's semen in the water that got Mary knocked up, and they put Mr. Ranch in jail."

"Why nobody else got pregnant?" I asked.

"I don't know, ma'am. I've been on birth control since I was thirteen."

"Really? Is it safe?"

"Relatively safe, ma'am. I mean, the pill's not that big, and I've only choked on it once."

Anita swept her eyes across the room, and I followed them to a wall clock in the shape of a sea urchin. I realized I'd been hogging her time asking all these questions. I must have been impolitely staring at her because she self-consciously covered her face with a napkin, pretending to blow her nose.

"Gotcha—so no water," I said quickly. "Anything else to drink?"

"Orange juice."

"OJ is fine, Anita."

"Be right back."

Now alone, I checked out the menu and set my tooth on shrimp and grits. My booth was equipped with a jukebox, a novelty you'll see nowhere else. There were songs by Jackson Five, the Beatles, Janis Joplin, and The Troggs. There were ten songs per page, and ten pages in total denoted from letters A through K. To pick a song, I had to press a letter, a number of the song (from zero to nine), and insert a quarter, which I didn't have. Does Buck Mooney (or other counterfeit-production guys) make his own quarters? I wondered. Did it even cross his mind? A patron in the booth behind me was playing "On the Radio" by Donna Summer.

Anita reappeared with a tall glass of what seemed like iced tea, unnaturally yellow and overly effervescent.

"Here's your sweet tea, ma'am," she said, offering me the glass.

"Anita, I ordered orange juice."

"Oh, I'm so sorry, ma'am." She put her hands on her hips, slapping them hard first. "I've been as busy as a one-legged cat in a sandbox. This news on the radio about that monster in the lake brought us all kinds of tourists. It's mega-jammed here today."

"A monster in a lake?"

"You heard nothin' 'bout that? Oh, right. You're not local. According to the news, it resembles the Loch Ness Monster, and everyone's trying to catch it. I saw some scary posts on social media, and someone even took a selfie with the monster lurking behind. A Richmond tobacco factory is offering a prize of one million dollars to those who can catch it."

"Sounds like a good advertising scheme to me."

She dismissed my comment and continued, "We're the only diner in the area, so today we're busier than Walmart on the first of the month."

"Really, that's okay, Anita, I understand. You're overwhelmed—and it's hot here anyway. Sweet tea will suffice. But, really, a million dollars. I wish I had a net. And a boat, huh?"

"Who knows. My entire family is at the lake right now. Fingers crossed."

She crossed her fingers, as did I. We both laughed awkwardly until we heard crickets.

She cleared her throat. "I'll give you two minutes to look over the menu."

"No, Anita, I'm ready to order. Shrimp and grits."

Anita turned her head slowly, left then right, making sure nobody was listening to her, like the last time, and turned to me, pursing her lips. She said, "Not my business, ma'am, okay? But there's been a rumor about this perverted supplier who uses horse poo to grow corn, which he feeds to his cows. He sold the milk to the cheese shop, which is where our Swiss cheese comes from for the grits, and the cheese is not even Swiss. He imports it from Switzerland. I didn't even know where that state is."

"Isn't horse poo called manure, a natural fertilizer?" I asked.

"Exactly. Who wants to eat that?"

"Not me," I lied so as not to lose her trust, and glanced at the menu again, annoyed, scanning past the entrées, afraid to order something involving a prerequisite and an explanation.

"So, what's safe to order, Anita?"

"The special: catfish."

"Oh," I said. "*That's* why it's special."

The special was the only item on the menu that hadn't been either fertilized with horse poo or had semen it in, and I was sold.

"I'll get the special, then."

"You won't regret it, ma'am."

"Let's hope not."

During the moment of silence, Anita acknowledged the baby on my chest, wrapped like a burrito in Buck's blanket with only face and arms visible.

Anita said, "Aw, she's just as cute as a button! What's her name?"

"Um," I said, thinking, but nothing was coming to mind! It was tedious. Why did everyone want to know what her name was? It's like in New York the first thing people ask you what you do for a living. At a party it's always like, Hi, I'm Chloe. And them saying: What do you do? It's like "do" is the most essential part of my life. In New York, not only must you be beautiful and skinny, you must make an equal amount of money just to get laid. In case you make a baby. Now it's a 50/50 mutual fund. Ever since leaving New York, nobody had asked me what I did, and it wasn't a coincidence.

"Ma'am?" Anita asked, patiently.

"Agnes!" I blurted out.

Her eyes popped open as if *I* were the Loch Ness Monster. "Agnes?" she said with such repulsion that spit came to the side of her mouth, which she wiped with her tongue. "That's an ugly name," she added.

For some reason, I took offense and wondered whether it was because of my neighbor Agnes. "It's not ugly, Anita. It's just different."

"But it's an old-lady name."

"Why, yes . . . it sure is. But it doesn't make it ugly just because it's an old-fashioned name. It's not like it's Barb, you know?"

She smiles. "Be right back with your special, ma'am."

When she left, I wiped the sweat off my forehead, and checked on Lykke, thinking in the interim how dangerous that whole encounter could have been. I should be more careful in the future, no arguing. Why did it bother me about Agnes? I felt peculiar, frightened even. Now that I was hundreds of miles away, I suddenly—what?—missed her banging on the ceiling trying to get some peace? It wasn't our fault, mine and Mom's, for her hearing aid being turned all the way up while we watched *Dr. Phil.* Lykke was reaching for the table with her clumsy hands that were of similar size to a cat's paw. And those paws, mind you, cause enough damage to make you cry. Miriam's couch was example one. Lykke almost spilled the lemonade, and I slid it toward the jukebox away from her reach.

Anita returned a few minutes later with a plate full of fried chicken, French fries on the side.

"Here's your order, ma'am," she said.

"But I ordered the special," I said as she placed the chicken in front of me.

"Dang it. I'm so sorry, ma'am. I forgot. I'll get your special right away." Anita scooped the plate off the table.

"Anita, what's the matter with you? You look like something's bothering you. Tell me what happened—maybe I can help. I'm a therapist," I lied, pretending I was Dr. Black. "You can trust me. I'm on your side."

Anita sat across from me, put the plate on the table, and wiped her tears with a sleeve. I claimed the plate and stuck a handful of fries in my mouth. I couldn't wait for the amendment.

"I'm fixin' to lose it," Anita said. "One disaster after another. This morning, the commode got clogged. I wanted to call the plumber, but I'm not speaking to my brother. Then, I was supposed to deliver a bunch of nuns' habits to Richmond this morning. I wash clothes part-time."

"You're very ambitious, Anita," I said with my mouth full.

"You know, we're paid nothin' here, and when the gov'ment knocks on my door, they take most of the bread out of my mouth."

"It's probably contaminated with something anyway."

She chuckled. "Today, Ursula quit. Claimed she'd been harassed by the boss. He called me this morning and told me I had to take her shift. I told him it was my day off and had to deliver the habits by seven tonight. He said I can either come in or be fired. He thinks the sun comes up just to hear him crow. I called Mama to see if she could take the habits to Richmond, but she can't. She's busy workin' too."

"Where does she work?" I asked.

"Nail salon in Ashland. Mama's, like, the best nail technician ever. Just look at my nails." Anita offered me both hands, and I mumbled something in response, like, oh, how pretty. "She'd do better if she put the bottle down. She and her man BJ rarely work, especially if they're on a bender. Mama makes her own hours whenever she's got appointments with clients, but BJ is a bad influence and about as useless as a screen door on a submarine."

"So you're the only one—like—who takes care of the family?" I said, copying her manner of speech.

"Pretty much. I'm as poor as a church mouse. Pretty much three months behind on the rent, which is why I wash clothes for the nuns at night. The rent's so high 'cuz we live in a two-bedroom apartment with my Uncle BS, my cousins Scuttle and Grimsby, Grandma, Grandpa, Skinny the dog, and three cats, Lucky, Unlucky, and the third, which we call Uterus. We could have easily gotten a studio for less than five hundred."

"That's a lot of people for a studio, Anita."

"What can you do when you work for tips?"

"I guess nothing if you like to eat. Wait a minute, your Uncle who?"

"BS."

"BS? As in what?"

"Blake Senior."

Isn't calling your child after bullshit (BS) or blowjob (BJ) called child abuse? I just shook my head, baffled.

"That's why no one else can get them habits to Richmond," Anita said. "Sister Trinity already called to remind me twice that if I don't get them to her today, she'll never use my services ever again. That's ten bucks a week!"

"Sister Trinity doesn't sound nice."

"I reckon she's nice. I see where she's coming from. They're going to some kooky nun-only baking contest tomorrow, and they need clean habits to look good for Jesus. I promised to deliver the habits on time, but I'm working this double for Ursula, and I won't finish 'till midnight. Sister Trinity said she and the sisters go to bed by seven, and they need the habits before then. I brought them to work with me, hoping Ursula would show up, and I could race them up to Richmond."

Anita had been sniffling throughout her story. She started weeping, and I took her hand to pat it. Sometimes, I realize how unfair life is for the kids who support their parents. Anita was just a teenager who should be spending time with teens her age. I was fortunate enough to have had a childhood where working was not an option, which carried on into my adulthood as well. Anita, for sure, had no childhood to speak of. Girls need to spend time with other girls their age—gossip, write in their diaries, fall in love with boys—not serve contaminated water and grits made with horse poo. The poor girl, I was thinking, will become a serial killer by the time she turns twenty. I knew this because there would be no other way to shoot off steam, unless she signed up for kickboxing, which, I was sure, she couldn't afford anyhow.

Then I did something I'm not sure I still understand. I decided to help Anita. In front of me, I saw my best friend Calyssa and no longer the sixteen-year-old girl who was in a bind. I had to help her out. My stomach squeezed uneasily while my heart began racing.

"Anita, I'm headed for Richmond. I can deliver them habits for you if it's on the way."

"You would?"

"Sure!"

"Well, butter my butt and call me a biscuit!"

"I'm a nun myself, Anita."

"Didn't you say you were a ther'pist?"

"Why, yes, so you do listen, Anita. Coincidentally, I'm a nun therapist, which means I work with nuns exclusively. But I'm still considered a nun. I majored in the . . . missionary."

"No kiddin'? Where's your habit?"

"You don't need one when you're devoted."

"With all due respect, ma'am . . . May I ask, what's your name? I don't believe I asked."

"Sister Titi—and that's called a bindi on my forehead—a sign of royalty and devotion to Him."

"Ain't that a pretty name—Titi! But you don't have anything on your forehead."

Oops, my bad. I'd forgotten I'd wiped the bindi back in the car.

"Thank you, Anita. Titi is short for Nefertiti. But friends and family called me Titi. Since you're my God-sister, you call me Titi."

"Titi, why would you want to do a favor for a stranger?"

"You're no stranger, you're my friend now. What's more, you remind me of my friend, Caly . . ." I was saying the name "Calyssa," but thankfully shut up on time. I swallowed and continued. "Debra. She looks exactly like you, but she passed away when she was . . . twenty."

"Good Lord, I'm sorry 'bout that."

"Thanks, Anita. She swallowed a ring with a two-karat gold diamond! What a lesson. I realize if Debra were alive and had to go through what you're going through, I would want someone to help her."

I sounded grown-up saying things like that in a steady voice, kind of like a real nun or at least a therapist.

Anita instantly cheered up, wiping the running mascara with a napkin.

"Since you're helping me, Titi," Anita said, "the lunch is on me."

Anita disappeared and returned, two totes in hands. The habits were neatly folded and came out to the top, like extra foam on a latte. Anita wrote down the address for me, which I'd have to look up later using Buck's tablet. I had no idea how else I could travel except utilizing the counterfeiting van. At this point, hitchhiking was dangerous and went on par with something stupid, like eating steak, which was a road for a heart attack. Anita's spirit was clearly uplifted, though, which made me happy as well. Her face showed no more tension because now she could serve food assured her habits would be delivered on time. Anita reminded the meal was on her, which was great because I wouldn't dare to pay that poor girl with the fake money.

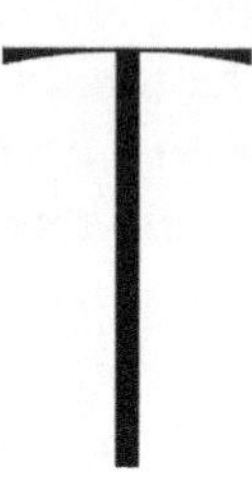

Thinking how to execute the "habit" delivery, I had a perfect disguise plan! I was going to use the diner restroom and change into one of the habits—there were dozens, and I was sure the nuns wouldn't miss one. What kind of a cop would stop a nun, I was thinking—what a perfect cover. I took one habit from the very top and entered the bathroom alcove. I pulled on the bathroom door only to find it locked. I banged until a customer inside shouted something vulgar and indecipherable, and I hoped he would wash his hands and his mouth with soap. The bathroom could only host one patron at a time, which was ridiculous, considering everything else in Nottingham was either contaminated, or there was a Loch Ness Monster on the loose.

To my right, a set of double doors led into the kitchen, a nautical round window in each. The cook in a white uniform who resembled Paula Deen—lazy Susan—was chopping onions. I love Paula Deen, even if sometimes her recipes are too southern for my palate, meaning if I don't stop myself, I'll eat whatever's placed in front of me. Several other men and women hustled around the kitchen, but none of them resembled celebrities.

When the patron exited the bathroom, I slid through the doors and locked up.

Lykke was performing karate with her hands, a type of martial arts I thought you're prohibited from practicing unless you're at least eight and/or Asian. My judo teacher was Wan Tu, named after each tooth he got. I learned how to efficiently disarm a mugger with a knife by grabbing his wrist and twist. Not that it ever helped me, except one time when I disabled a kid who was holding cotton candy—because I desperately craved candy. Judo lessons didn't really help in that situation, but being ten years older did.

I set up the diaper changing table in three seconds and lay Lykke on it.

I quickly put the habit over myself, and it fit like a glove. By the time I saw my reflection in the round mirror, I'd fully transformed from Titi to Sister Mary full of grace. Turns out, I looked hideous as a nun. My platinum hair had grown into a disaster that should have been set on fire, bleached, and then shaved. I noticed near the top left near my breasts, there was a name embroidered on my habit, and since the reflection in the mirror showed it backward, I couldn't tell what it said right away, but then I learned it said my name was Mary. Might as well. I felt like a Mary anyway.

Without wasting any more time, I left the diner.

Back in the van, I sat behind the wheel and stretched my legs, wondering what I was doing with my life. I picked up Lykke and pressed her close to my heart. Just rubbing my hand against her back brought me comfort. That first day when I met her, her beautiful button nose, clear skin, pinkish undertones. Her blue eyes were huge, covering half of her face as if she were a Japanese anime. Too bad she and I spent very little time together, but I knew once the manhunt was over, we would have so much mother-daughter fun.

The following was nagging at me: Was it selfish of me to help Anita deliver the habits, so I was forced to go to church and perhaps make a confession? I had to tell someone, *anyone*, about Lykke, or I was going to explode, much the same way as would skinny jeans on me. Was I literally trying to cover the bad by attempting to do something good? Was I trying to . . . *repent*? I'd only had Lykke for three days, and I was already losing my mind, perhaps literally or maybe metaphorically—I had no idea. Sanity offered a suggestion: Return Lykke and give up. Insanity reasoned: Why spend the rest of your pathetic life in prison?

One thing I knew for sure: the cops wouldn't dare to stop a nun, and I resembled one if I said so myself. But again, do nuns drive/have driver's licenses? Were the cops even on the lookout for Buck's van, and if they were, what would I say if I got caught? I was apparently a good liar, but I had to create another lie just in case of an emergency.

First, I brought myself up to speed in the news department. I opened the Internet browser on Buck's tablet and typed: "Lykke Fawcett." One article had been posted an hour ago near Fairfax, Virginia, with the picture of Miriam's house. I clicked on the article and the page slowly loaded.

"Breaking news: The Fawcett kidnapper stayed with a hoarder in Fairfax County, Virginia. She held a homeowner, Miriam Turtle, hostage. Turtle described the kidnapper to the authorities, whose composite sketch was released an hour ago. Check below."

There you go, I thought. The end. My heart literally (well, not literally) stopped.

Unwillingly, I scrolled down the page, feeling the cold, salty tears, which dripped on the tablet screen, and my eyes were cloudy as a result. I placed Lykke back in the sheet, feeling I might pass out. Once I examined the sketch for close to two minutes, the tablet fell from my hands.

On the sketch, there was the face of a black man.

For some reason, Miriam was covering for me—*me*, the kidnapper—by lying to the authorities. The cops were still unaware of what the real kidnapper looked like.

Miriam was putting herself in danger but *por qué* (that's Spanish for "why") I had no answer. The sketch showed a black guy with a broken nose that had been in places it shouldn't. His eyes were so narrow you could blindfold him with shoelaces. A scar, like lightning, stretched across his eyes that were peeking from under thick, bushy brows. His lips were of quite an unnatural size as if he blew one thousand balloons and then a football team. His ears were small, with spikes of hair shooting out of them like little fireworks on the Fourth of July. Five-o'clock shadow. Six o'clock bags under his eyes indicating he'd been on a drinking spree after he'd been eighty-sixed from a bar. His name was Barackaba Ma.

Miriam had made him up—a black male kidnapper. In this part of the country, with Confederate flags posted all over the place, Barackaba Ma stood no chance against the police, but since he was imaginary, he actually *did* stand a chance, which meant *I* stood a chance.

Quickly a plan had evolved. If the police captured me with Lykke, I'd tell them I'd found Lykke abandoned by the side of the road, just like that without any strollers or notes, and I was taking her to the nearest hospital.

Scrutiny would follow, of course, and I had to be picky about my vocabulary. First, what was I doing in Virginia—a New Yorker—in the timeframe of the kidnapping, with the kidnapped baby? I could say I was going to North Carolina to meet a guy from a dating website. I imagined Anita telling her next customer: “She was, like, going to North Carolina with a kidnapped baby. Coincidence? I don’t think so.”

My maternal instinct, however, vetoed the thought of giving up the baby because I needed her. There was a reason why I saw a hallucination that day at the park when I thought Lykke was Anubis. My mind knows that babies—and children—make stupid people smarter. Babies help with learning responsibility. They make us adults. Without me, my Mom would be just a fifty-year-old nurse, Dora. Now she’s this woman who is all grown up and stuff. I was hoping the same would happen to me if I never got caught. True, I lost Anubis in the past, but I gave him insulin shots twice a day, regardless of whether I felt like it or not. Sometimes I felt like giving up on him, but I never did. It’s a fact, though, that everything new and exciting eventually wears off, becoming mundane tasks. Of course, Anubis and Lykke weren’t the same species, but according to God, we’re all His children, regardless of our differences, breed, age, and ball size. I mused that once the hunt was over, Lykke would become no more than my daughter, and I would become no more than her mother. We will fight and disagree. But the future was far in advance and a complete blur.

I looked up directions to Richmond on the tablet. My destination, the church, was located off the main road on a lonely street, which was perfect because there would probably be fewer witnesses. The church was thirty to forty-five minutes away according to the map. I fired up the engine and exited the parking lot.

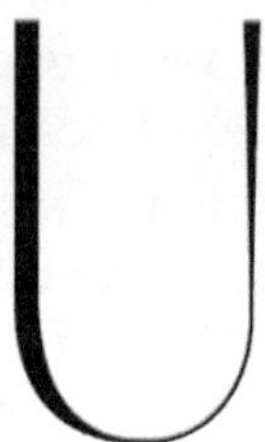

Unusually lucky, lucky duck that I was (*la pata* in Spanish), I found a parking spot right away. I felt like "Dora the Explorer," and Spanish words just kept popping up. I parallel parked between two cars without any problems, despite the fact I hadn't driven in over five years. Lykke seemed suspicious of me as a nun. I'd had to stop one time because she wouldn't stop crying. After I'd fed her formula, she calmed down, and the rest of the ride went smooth.

I looked around—and since I was Dora, it was time to explore. A graveyard peekabooed in the distance, serene and adequately maintained, remarkably quiet, no visitors or birds. When I die, I wish to be cremated—but against my will, I'll be buried since my momzilla had already purchased plots for us both next to Daddy in a cemetery in Brooklyn. Whoever dies first gets to make the decisions.

Farther down, past the cemetery, sat a lake, cobalt blue and still. Maybe it was the same lake Anita was telling me about, where the Loch Ness Monster was on the loose. I can't believe she was naïve enough to even believe in such creature, but who am I to complain if I still believe in Santa Clause? I mean for real—like, what if he actually exists and it's all a big conspiracy? I mean, Anita was young, sure, but a monster? Really? Even me, with all my hallucinations and whatnot, wouldn't fall for such fake news.

Ahead, I spotted the church, which was a combination of several erections with its main building constructed out of red brick. A tower with a bell rose in the front, chimney columns visible in the back. The grass had been recently cut and smelled of a meadow. Trees surrounded the main building, and overall the garden seemed upheld. Air conditioners had been installed in each window to keep your armpits dry in the summer for Sister Trinity and the associates LLC. I didn't know if the "associates" is the right word, but since I was new to all this, I surmised it was okay to assume.

Across the church, stood some sort of a minimart called Fiesta Latina, but the "e" was so dirty you couldn't see it, and it looked like it said "Fist a Latina." Wow, kinky sex advertised right next to a church—that was new. Or if Anubis was alive, I would say, "Well, this is meow."

Lykke had to be fed and changed without any legit money to spend. I thought of the fake bills burning a hole in my pocket and envisioned myself as a single mother who earned minimum wage and lacked government support, which is why she printed her own currency. Upon exiting the contaminated diner, I'd thrown out Miriam's coat in the trash can, but I had pulled out the counterfeit bundle of cash out of it beforehand. What other choice did I have? To be honest, only today, I started wondering how single mothers survive on minimum wage in New York and felt ashamed this topic had never bothered me before. I checked myself in the rearview mirror and adjusted the habit veil over my hair. The habit made me appear unnaturally pale, but I looked decent nonetheless. Catnapping Lykke was adorable in her teeny pink hat and the pink fleece onesie. I just wanted to take and squeeze her. So I did precisely that.

I put on my mittens, stole one bill from the heap of Franklins, and wiped it clean. No nosy parkers were visible anywhere in sight, and I hid the baby under the habit. After exiting the van, I watched both sides of the road before I crossed, like a good Daddy's girl.

I entered the store and noticed a ginger boy nodding at me right away. He was too old to be wearing braces, too young to be having sex/being in charge of the store.

"Sister Mary," he said in a woman's voice and approached me. "You forgot eggs, flour, and butter for your cake." He offered me a paper bag with groceries, while I kept staring at him, wondering if he was the store attendant.

"Excuse me?" I said.

"Your stuff, Sister Mary."

"I've never been to your store before."

"Weren't you just here less than an hour ago, Sister Mary?"

While he was waiting for a reply, I couldn't believe he thought I looked exactly like another sister, who'd been shopping here sometime before and forgotten her bag. I admit too that I felt as if I'd seen the same boy the many times I saw a ginger kid running around: all freckly, skinny, and white like white asparagus. I would have said white like a ghost, but he didn't have raccoon eyes and wasn't wearing a white sheet.

"Oh, right, thank you," I said and grabbed the bag.

I didn't want to sound suspicious since I was headed to the church anyhow. Why not bring the groceries along with the clean habits? The boy hopped along toward the counter while playing by himself. He neighed and lassoed an imaginary bull.

The minimart was perturbingly quiet and empty, which worked fine in my case (the fewer witnesses, the better). I was terrified of offering the fake money to the boy, and my hands shook, but if I played cool, maybe he wouldn't notice that the Benjamin Franklin banknote was counterfeit. I quickly found some baby formula in aisle two and diapers on the shelf underneath. When I placed the items on the counter, the boy eyed me askance.

"That must be some strange party you're throwing, Sister Mary," he said/neighed.

"Yes."

"Did you find somebody to bake the cake?"

"Yes."

"Who did you find?"

"Me."

"Didn't you just tell me you know nothing about baking, Sister Mary?"

"I looked up the recipe on the Internet."

When I said the word "Internet," his eyes doubled in size. *Jesus, what's wrong with this boy?* I thought.

"We're allowed to browse the Internet," I quickly added.

"Maybe I should become a sister. Because my dad doesn't allow me to browse the Internet."

"Not the same story—you need to grow up first."

"My parents are trying to make a baby," he said with a grain of sadness in his voice.

"As God intended."

"They said I'm getting a baby sister for Christmas. That's when they're expecting her. Not the present I wanted for Christmas."

"You wanted a bike?"

"Yeah!"

I knew no parents with a teenage son, and the amount of energy in him exhausted me. "So how much do I owe you?"

"Twenty dollars and sixteen cents," he said, offering his pale hand.

I handed him the Benjamin.

"Wow! I've never seen a real one-hundred-dollar bill before!"

Well, you still haven't, I thought to myself and giggled. I said, "Don't get too thrilled about the bill. Put the bill in the till, and arrange my change." I nervously laughed as the stupid stuff kept pouring out of my mouth. "Fork over my money and hurry up, sonny." He was now laughing with me. I learned kids like rhymes, and I thought that would distract him. "Put away the lettuce, or I'll kick you in the Cletus. *Un caballo* means a horse, and *un cadáver* means a corpse."

"Dad!" he yelled, ignoring me. "Come see a one-hundred-dollar bill! It's *el dinero* in Spanish and 'Spanish' rhymes with 'mannish,'" he added and lifted up Mr. Franklin toward the light. "Wow, no watermarks. How cool!"

Holy crap!

My belly squeezed unnaturally, and my throat got tensed as if someone was choking me. The boy was examining the bill with acute attention to detail. I could grab the fake money and scoot, but realized it was too late when a ginger man approached the counter, a book in hand. He was wearing glasses and was tall like nobody's business. In comparison, the father and son seemed identical, almost clones, except for their heights.

"Hi, Sister Mary," the man said, reading my name on the habit, and closed the book titled: *Throw Out That Basketball. Finally, a Girl! A Book of Baby Girl Names*.

"Dad, look!" the boy offered the counterfeit bill to the man and jumped, trying to reach higher.

The man ignored the boy, and upon removing his glasses, he started cleaning the lenses with the hem of his shirt.

"That must be some strange party you're having, Sister Mary," the man said when he saw what I was buying. He noticed the counterfeit bill and took it, but he probably couldn't see anything as his glasses were still in his hands. *This can't be the end of my movie*, I thought to myself. I had to think of something fast.

"I returned," I quickly said, "to tell you I had a vision. Your unborn baby girl came to me and told me her name."

"No way!" the two of them said simultaneously. That, at least, paused the father from checking the fake bill.

"What is her name?" the father said.

"Page fifty-seven. The second name on that page."

The ginger man put down the counterfeit bill on the counter and opened the book. He seemed excited, or otherwise, the shaking hands would be out of place. He wet his finger by inserting the entire finger in his mouth and flipped pages with an unparalleled passion for a man his age. The boy, in the meantime, frowned and opened the cash register. He took Buck's bill off the counter, placed it in the drawer, and inserted his entire finger in his mouth, after which he proceeded to count my change.

"Matilda," the man said.

"What the fuck?" I said out loud. The boy covered his ears, and I had no idea where the potty mouth came from. "I'm sorry. I meant the duck. Good name for a duck. *La pata*, right, boy?"

"The second name on the page is Matilda," the man said. "That's such an ugly name, and it doesn't go with McManus."

I had no idea what was happening because my dead sister's name showed up—like, was it a sign? So "fuck" was more than appropriate after all.

"I think Matilda is a beautiful name," I said, instantly offended. "I had a sister named Matilda." I stopped and swallowed. "Yes, her name was Sister Matilda."

"We wanted to name our daughter Barb."

"Right, because Barb goes so well with McAnus," I said, trying to offend him.

"It's McManus."

"You can be a McChicken for all I care! We're done here." I turned toward the boy, realizing my face was in heat from being so infuriated. The nerve he had telling me Matilda was an ugly name! I addressed the little ginger boy, "Sonny, you've got my change?"

"Yes, Sister Mary."

"And stop calling me Mary! My name's . . . Gertrude."

I snatched the money from the boy's hands, picked up the bag with my purchases along with the grocery bag for the church, and ran out the door.

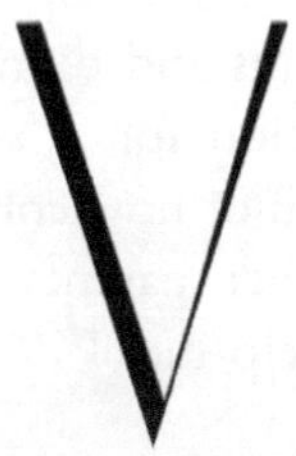

VINDICATION—THAT'S WHAT I SUDDENLY NEEDED. Everything I'd done in the past forty-eight hours was considered shady and suspicious, and I physically could not stand it any longer. I could not defend myself. I had no rights. Most importantly, I could not stand up to the ginger man, who accused—that's right, accused—my parents of having lousy taste calling my sister "Matilda." It's like I was now living in a different period, before Susan B. Anthony, before the first black president, and even before the gays could marry. I was back in time, back to when movies were black and white, to when women could not vote or wear jeans. I felt useless . . . to myself and to society. I couldn't imagine how brave those women were back in the day—who had to keep their mouths shut. I was a criminal without any rights, without identification, without a future. And I still almost punched the ginger man in the face, which would jeopardize my life forever.

My face was crimson when I checked myself in the rearview mirror upon returning to the van. My tears were running so fast I was afraid I would be sodium-deprived in the next ten minutes. My body was literally rejecting this situation, this baby, this feeling of insignificance.

I realized—with shame and sadness—that I would never be happy until I returned Lykke back to the store for a full refund. I had never prayed before, but I did then, in a stolen van. I said, "Dear God? I don't know how to call you. You see, I kidnapped a baby. Here she is. Her name is Lykke—'Lykke' for short. I know it's all a grand plan of yours, and there is a reason why you made me schizophrenic and why I made myself overweight. I have heart problems and didn't get a job as a flight attendant—which is a fancy expression for a 'stewardess,' in case you were wondering. It all seems really minor now compared to what I actually did —kidnapped this baby from her parents. If you indeed exist (don't confuse it with 'exit'), please help me. I doubt I could continue on my own."

Lykke laughed, and it snapped me out of my funk. I don't know why but I looked up into the sky and saw the moon, vague and not bright but clearly a moon in the daylight. I love it when that happens.

I had to be careful now. I could care less back at the store if the ginger man had noticed my rage; how dare he say Matilda was an ugly name? Unlike "Chloe," which means "green shoot," "Matilda" means "strength in battle." Parents who love their offspring choose names considerably. There should be a law allowing parents to change their kids' names around age seven. By that age, we're able to tell whether the kid seems more like a green shoot or shows strength in battle. I mused that once this hide-and-seek business with the FBI was all over, I'd need to purchase a similar book the ginger man was reading (or steal his) to start picking a real name for the kidnapped tot.

Lykke needed a nap because she was getting fussy. She was exhausted from being covered all day, but who wouldn't be? Other than that, she seemed satisfied, and I didn't understand why Calyssa or Lindsay said babies were tough to manage. Those two peas in a pod utilized children as an excuse to avoid facing reality, as did Natalia. My problems were partially over. The FBI was searching for a black male with a broken nose the size of a stapler. I realized I should stop carrying Lykke underneath my clothes, so I retied the sheet above the habit I was wearing and set the baby into it.

I loved the peaceful neighborhood. I hadn't experienced such tranquility since last October when I was in Honolulu. We had actually planned a trip to Vegas, but that Friday night, Calyssa got wasted, and I got high. I was having one of my schizophrenic episodes because I needed an adjustment in medication. Matilda was there with me the entire trip—in the flesh, which was clue number one I was in distress. When I see Matilda, it means it is time to call 9-1-1, because I'm having a focal illusion, aka I'm in danger. I was terrified of rejection and never mentioned my secret to her or to any of my friends. And I never will.

A friar in a hoodless black scapular was working on an evergreen shrub by the entrance to the church. I watched him before going up the steps, but he appeared harmless. I pulled the veil down, half over my eyes.

At the top of the steps, I learned the shrub smelled freshly of manure and reminded me of the way Central Park smells in springs. Ah, how much I missed New York.

"Good afternoon, Sister Mary," he said.

"Hello," I said, taking in that he read my name from my habit.

"Hi, cutie," he said to Lykke and reached out. Lykke extended her arms out, and the friar covered them with his large ones.

"Excuse me," I said. "I'm looking for Sister Trinity. You know where I can find her?"

"The monastery is on the opposite side."

"Thanks."

I took the steps down, rounded the corner, and found another brick building a hundred feet past the garden. Separating the church from the cemetery, a white wooden fence stretched in the distance, weeds growing along the fencerow. Blue hyacinths peekabooed from the freshly watered soil. Someone took good care of the garden. Mom loves gardening, and at home, we have all sorts of plants, flowers, and herbs on the windowsill. She always says gardening was relaxing, but I hate soil. It gets under my nails and dries out my skin, but I'm really terrified of worms—like, *really* really. Plus, dogs pee on the ground, so why touch it?

The monastery stood in complete stillness. No noise. Just three seconds, I reminded myself, and I'm out of there. I'll say hello, give the habits along with the groceries, and say goodbye. Sure, they'll be missing one, but that's the price they must pay for my delivery services, Cheap Habits Express. Approaching the door, I realized I was unfamiliar with the nun etiquette. Do I knock or just walk in? Do I nod and kiss a cross? There was a round brass door knocker, so I assumed knocking was accepted. I banged the knocker three times, one for God, one for Son, one for Holy Spirit. I heard the door being unlatched from the inside while I straightened out, forcing a smile. The door opened a crack, one-third of a female nun in view.

"Yes?" she said noncommittally.

"Hi," I whispered for some reason, "I'm delivering clean habits from your laundress, Anita. And groceries from the ginger boy at the New Deli." I then realize I was like a messiah or at least Santa with all the presents.

The woman eyed the baby for close to a minute and opened the door, but for reasons unknown, I just stood in place as if glued to the concrete floor. She was wearing a habit, but that was the extent of our similarities because age-wise, she was pushing her cart toward menopause. Fear or sadness was written all over her face, while with such an expression, she kept checking out the baby, who was awake and occasionally whimpered. I got suspicious. Maybe I shouldn't have kept Lykke in view like a New York strip steak at a butcher shop for every creepy nun to see. She motioned for me to enter, mumbling something hard to comprehend. I stepped in and noticed how mysterious the monastery appeared from the inside. The light coming from the windows was reduced by a third due to the tinted arched windows. And I knew I was in a place of worship because I suddenly wished to confess that I was . . . hungry again. (Sorry, a little nun-joke/non-joke to loosen the tension.)

"Sister Chloe," she said, "nice to meet you."

On her breast, LGA was embroidered—like the airport in New York? I wondered. The coincidence was uncanny, and what a strange name—was she a pilot?

"Hi, Sister LGA," I said. "I knew a Sister Newark Liberty and a Sister JFK once," I added to keep the conversation afloat. (See what I did there?)

"LGA?" she asked.

"Your name," I said and pointed at her breast.

"Oh," she said and adjusted the top, where there appeared to be e crease. Now HELGA was written.

"Oh," I said. "Here are your uniforms, Sister Helga. I do still like the LGA better." I believe the accent I was trying on came out Irish, but without the beer breath. I offered the totes, which Helga took and placed by her leg.

"Thank you, Sister Mary."

"The ginger boy from the store across the street said someone had forgotten these," I said, offering the grocery bag.

"Who the heck cares?" she said, puckering her lips as if they were a drawstring purse. "Nobody can bake a cake for God's sake. Are you taking part in the nun baking contest? What convent are you with?"

It's like in New York they ask what you do for a living upon meeting you, the nuns ask the same, I surmised. This was a whole new territory for me, so I was lying through my teeth.

"Oh, I'm from Europe," I replied. "We're called Sisters of the Holy Mary. I know it's a silly name. But I'm not entering the contest."

"Do you know how to bake a cake?"

"Do I!"

"Well, do you?"

"I do!" I said.

"Can you help us?"

"I wish I could, but I'm sorry, I can't. I must really be going."

"That's all right." Her voice suddenly changed to a tremble, and she retrieved a handkerchief. "What a stupid contest, anyway. So what if we don't win?" Helga loudly blew her nose and wiped invisible tears. She sniffled and looked me in the eye. "We just wanted to win the first prize, so we could enter a gospel-singing contest next."

"What's the first prize?"

"Three thousand dollars in cash, which means thirty green, beautiful, one-hundred-dollar bills."

"Holy ark," I said. "For a baking contest? You must be joking. If I'd known, I would be baking right now." Helga's eyes opened wider, and I realized why—because I was her rival then. "But I won't," I carefully added.

"We must win," she said. "We are the best choir in the area, Sister Mary. But we can't afford to go to Los Angeles."

"Why did you enter the contest if nobody knows how to bake a cake?"

"Like they say: If you don't buy a ticket, you can't win the lottery. Oh, if I wasn't clear enough: we *did* buy the ticket, and we *didn't* win the lottery." Helga blew her nose so loudly I had to take a step back, thinking of the unsanitary condition of her handkerchief.

"Where are the sisters now?" I said.

"They're praying."

"When is the contest?"

"Tomorrow morning."

"I mean, if it's imperative, I can help."

"Yes, it *is* imperative. I don't know what that word means, though. We must hurry because Sister Mary is working on a cake right now without a clear understanding of what she's doing. She's clueless. She believes the powdered eggs in cake mixes come from chickens that don't drink enough water. Everybody knows powdered eggs are produced like sundried tomatoes and left out in the sun."

"I see," I said. I guess Sister Helga was right: They do know *nothing* about baking and/or um . . . life? "Where is the kitchen?" I asked.

"This way."

While following Helga, I felt like a pushover for being tricked into the nun business. But another trinity of reasons surfaced: (1) I had nowhere to go, (2) It was better to wait for the nightfall to drive in the darkness, and (3) I could help, just like I helped Anita. Being kind is free. Besides, if I baked them a cake, it'd be the most delicious cake they'd ever tasted. I belong to the house of Humblebrag. Babies I may not know, but cakes—and pastries and weed brownies and turnovers—I do. Name a question, I know it. Like, what's the difference between baking powder and baking soda? Baking powder already has acid, which cream of tartar, which is leftover from the winemaking production.

Helga led me past a row of arched windows overlooking a garden, while I was trying to figure out which cake to bake, with the most obvious choice being the red velvet cake, the staple of the Southern cuisine. What if the sisters from other convents bake the same cake? I needed to come up with something exotic (don't confuse with 'erotic').

The ornate brick ceiling was shaped like an arch, ending with Greek columns that were cracked at the base. Pictures of a crucified Jesus and Mother Mary were not uncommon, I gathered, same as pictures of the Pope and black-and-white photos of unknown to me nuns. Lykke said, "Meh, meh," while I laughed to myself, thinking that babies and cakes have a lot in common. Both are produced by a mix of the same ingredients. Then it's all about the timing. *Exact* timing is crucial. Ten more seconds and you end up with a burned cake . . . or twins.

We passed rows of what seemed like bedrooms with their doors open. Set up in each was simple: a bed in each room, ruffled bedspreads with roses or other floral designs on them (something Miriam would sleep on), and the name of the nun occupying the room. Katie 3-52. Helga 3-46. I wondered what that was about. Helga entered a shared room, where several hula-hoops stood in one corner, a piano, a bookshelf, CDs, and lots of issues of *Catholic Virginia* near the TV set. A printer. I wondered if the nuns were printing their own money as well.

Helga turned near a staircase, which led downstairs.

"I assume you're also making money on the side, Sister Mary," Helga said.

"What do you mean?"

"By babysitting."

This was the first time she'd mentioned the baby, and suddenly my feet got cold. I was glad she hadn't asked for an explanation but offered it, so I guess that was better.

"Times are rough," I said.

"Tell me about it. We tried everything. Remember when I said the other sisters were praying?"

"Yes."

"I lied," she said. "They're not praying; they're babysitting."

We descended downstairs, and Helga put her index finger parallel to her nose, as a sign to shush, but I surmised it was meant for Lykke. Helga slowly pushed open the door ahead, which squeaked in response and opened to a small room full of cribs. When the door was two-thirds open, she invited me to peek. Inside each crib, there was a baby or toddler. Several women—in simple dresses seen mostly in the 1890s—were sitting in chairs, knitting—nuns, I surmised. Helga slowly pulled the door to close.

"We're doing the exact same thing," she whispered.

"Is it allowed?"

"Of course, it's allowed. We're helping the community and making extra cash out of it. We'd prefer not to, but we love money. Isn't that why you're babysitting?"

"Yes," I lied, still in my Irish accent. "Why is nobody else wearing a habit?"

"We only wear them when we're out in public."

"Same here," I said.

"I just came from the store and didn't have a chance to change yet."

"Yup. Same here."

It was much darker down here than upstairs, somewhat enigmatic and spiritual, but smelled a bit musty, not gonna lie. I was becoming more and more excited about helping the sisters with the cake. Helga seemed friendly, and they were watching babies here, so nobody would point their finger at me. The FBI was searching for a man anyway.

I stopped in the middle of us walking.

It had dawned on me I was off the hook.

I could scream with excitement but didn't want Lykke to follow suit.

We entered what looked like a kitchen where a lady, wearing a peasant outfit, was reading instructions on a box of powdered cake mixture called Qwik Mix. I would not feed that stuff to a cat—though I'd tried, not gonna lie. The appliances seemed new: an oven, a fridge, a gas stove, and even a microwave. Not too shabby for a bunch of peasant-looking priestesses. The walls were made out of dark-beige brick, where more pictures of spiritual leaders were hung throughout, plus a calendar and the prayers printed on A4 sheets. One window provided sunlight, no lamps, or other illuminating devices visible anywhere. Several candles were distributed around the kitchen, meaning whenever the night fell, the nuns had dinner with their votive objects lit.

"Sister Mary, our troubles are over," Helga told her.

Mary unglued her eyes. "What is it?"

"Sister, also Mary, is a baker who flew straight from Europe to help us bake."

I looked at her askance, wondering why Helga was making stuff up.

"Nice to meet you," I said with the same Irish accent.

"Mother of God, thank you," Mary told me and threw the box of Qwik Mix across the room. She reached for a hug, saw the baby, and withdrew.

"Calm down," Helga told her, tugging on her sleeve.

"This is ridiculous!" Mary said. "I don't understand why none of us learned how to bake. Sister Mary, I've never tried European cooking. Except for once, when I was in Maine."

"That's not in Europe!" Helga said.

"I didn't say I was in Europe, you dope! The woman who fed me the cake was Australian."

"Australia is not Europe either!" Helga hissed.

"Then why on Earth did she make French fries? Isn't French in Europe?" Mary said as I tuned them both out—and began thinking. Like back in the van, I exited my body and looked back. I stood with the baby, thinking, while Helga and Mary were arguing about Europe. I left my body, and I zoomed in on my brain, rummaging through my memories until I found the cake that Natalia had once taught me how to make. It's a Russian cake called Ant Hill, which is mostly butter, sugar, and caramel. How can you say no? Hint: It's easy. You just say no. But you won't after trying it!

"I'll make you a Russian cake," I said when I returned back to my body. "It takes no effort to make, but we still need to hurry. Quickly tell me if you have sour cream, condensed milk, poppy seeds, baking soda, and sugar. The rest of the ingredients I have in the bag I'd just brought."

"We have sugar," Mary said, "but not the rest."

"Sister Mary," Helga says, "we don't have sugar. Remember when Sister Chloe got high on it and started doing cartwheels along the lake?"

"Oh, right," Mary said. "We threw out the entire sugar supply and replaced it with Sweet'N Low. Will that work?"

"Gross," I said. "Go to the store across the street and buy the ingredient; I'll write them out for you. And I'll start here with what I've got. Oh, and buy more butter. We'll need about eight sticks in total for two cakes."

"Eight?" the two of them said.

"Aigh, eight."

"Isn't that fattening?" Mary said. "I was going to make a cake with margarine, that is 90 percent fat-free."

"Sister Mary—why on Earth?" I asked, disgusted. "Cake with artificial sweetener, from a box, and with fat-free margarine? Why don't you let me poop in it for good measure? And have Allen Wrench inseminate it. We want to win the contest, don't we? Butter is the most important ingredient in cooking," my clogged arteries added.

"Not going to argue with you, Sister Chloe," Mary said. "You look . . . um . . . like you know what you're doing."

"Thank you," I said. "Also, don't forget poppy seeds and hazelnuts."

Mary quickly disappeared while I removed Lykke from the sheet.

"Sister Helga, I need you to take care of Trinity—that's her name," I lied.

"Sure thing. She's cute!"

"And she's hungry too."

When I was left alone in the kitchen, I realized it was already five o'clock. The dusk would come at six in about an hour, and I'd lose all the light. I'd never baked under candlelight, and I was not about to start now, so I worked fast.

In the cabinet above the stove, I found white plates and bowls from IKEA. I love that store. Nuns not only saved money but also had class, it appeared. I unpacked the grocery bag and unwrapped two sticks of butter, placing them in a bowl. I stuck the bowl in the microwave for thirty seconds to start melting the butter. Measuring cups were located in a cabinet next to the dishes. I was overly excited because not only was I needed and was doing something for a good cause, I was doing my favorite activity—baking. Nothing else mattered.

After setting the oven to three hundred and fifty degrees, I measured flour equally into two large bowls. Instead of baking one cake, I was planning on making two. It's always a good idea to make two whenever competition or twins are concerned. The secret to this cake, in my opinion, is to make your own dulce de leche from condensed milk. The can of condensed milk is boiled for about two hours, then chilled in the fridge. Condensed milk turns that vibrant caramel color, and the more it's cooked, the stiffer it gets. I prefer making dulce de leche until creamy, not solid, which takes about two and a half hours. Then I mix it with butter and create a sign: "Consume with caution. Warning! Possible cartwheel attack. You become uncontrollable and will roll around the lake."

I found a smile in the microwave door reflection. I am funny when excited. I should work for a morning show or something. Smile—which was proof I felt alive right now. I felt marvelous helping Anita—one person —but now I was ecstatic, assisting a whole gaggle of nuns. Not only would the cakes help them win the competition, but the cakes would also help me repent.

Three hours later, I was done. While finishing the two cakes by decorating them with poppy seeds, the entire convent was watching me. I felt like a two-headed alligator: unique, famous, and raunchy. The sun had ended its journey down the blue yonder, and candles had been lit, which made the atmosphere even more stimulating.

Three other sisters were named Chloe, plus five Trinities, and some odd number of Maries. I told them to call me Chloe to even out the numbers, and nobody argued. One Chloe was black and looked like Whoopi Goldberg, another one was Asian, while the third Chloe was white like a ghost. I'd say white like white asparagus, but, unlike the ginger clerk boy, she was wearing a white sheet.

The sisters were a bunch of gigglers, and I quickly made friends with them, half-forgetting I had to fake an accent. I had already asked Sister Helga whether I could spend the night, and all she did was show me an okay sign with her hand as if what a dumb question I asked. As if I could stay for as long as I wanted. Apparently, all other kids had been picked up around seven, leaving Lykke alone. I lied and said her parents were on vacation, which was why I was babysitting her for a week. That seemed to explain everything, and nobody asked any inappropriate questions. I loved nuns now!

After placing the first cake in the fridge to cool and set, I cut the second cake, distributing it out to the sisters on paper plates.

"The cake for the contest," I said, "should set in the fridge overnight.

The second one is a test, and it won't taste anywhere near the first one, because it's still warm, but at least you could palate it and analyze the flavor. It should still be so delicious, and we'll need to guard the fridge during the night because I swear one of us will try to steal it. Perhaps me!"

The sisters giggled at my joke and began tasting their slices while I watched. There's nothing like seeing your creation being consumed, especially when you know how superb it is and how hard you've been working on it. I wondered if it's the same feeling when you send your kid to first grade.

The giggles diminished to a suspicious level, and my stomach squeezed uneasily. I hadn't tried the cake while making it, due to being in a rush, but now I regretted it. The sisters didn't seem to enjoy their slices, for nobody had said a word for close to two minutes, while I felt disconsolate for being so arrogant. It had become so quiet and strange, it felt like a scene from a scary movie when they'd all decide to attack me and eat me alive. I knew I tasted delicious, according to Kim, but I was still young and unwilling to be munched on.

I swallowed, took a stab at my slice, and carefully put a piece into my—well—pie hole, for lack of a better word. Maybe I was nervous or what, but my tongue discerned nothing but sugar. Suddenly my confidence escaped me, filling me with a farouche void. I longed to weep from feeling this diffident.

"How is it?" I asked timidly, hardly recognizing my voice.

Black Chloe's eyelids began to spasm, the kind of look women portrait in movies upon having an orgasm.

"Oh, give thanks for the Lord," she sang in response. "Call upon His name."

"Make known His deeds," Helga joined, "among the peoples."

"Sing to Him," Mary sang.

The sisters were humming and clapping out the rhythm, while Chloe closed her eyes.

"Speak of all His wonders." She took such a high note I only thought Christina Aguilera was capable of, and my eyes popped open from the wonderment.

I started clapping with the sisters, or otherwise, they'd think I was not enjoying the impromptu gospel performance. They continued citing the Bible, and while I didn't understand how the lyrics were fitting, I took it as a good sign. That was the best vindication.

L

ater that night, when everyone was asleep, I covered myself with a blanket but couldn't wipe the smile off my face. Sleep was the last thing on my mind because it was barely nine. Helga made my bed in the nursery with Lykke, using a rollaway bed. When the sister had finished the first song, Chloe had said with such confidence: "Sisters, we are going to Los Angeles when we win that baking contest tomorrow!"

"Amen!" the rest of them had said and proceeded singing another song, forking at the remnants of the cake.

That's not why I beamed with happiness. The monastery was the perfect home for me right now, a place where I could erase the past and start from scratch. Nobody was searching for me because the FBI was on the lookout for a man. The nursery was crawling with babies, meaning Lykke was safe. Plus, everyone else was Chloe, so who will know who is who anywho? Since I'd told the sisters I was watching Lykke for a week, I had seven days to figure out what to do or where to go. Could I possibly stay with the sisters and devote myself to God? In this case, I'd have to make an excuse for the baby or offer her for adoption.

Earlier, Helga had helped me bathe and feed Lykke. Her experience was invaluable. The sisters weren't getting any nooky, and yet the maternal instinct kicked in regardless. I'd only had Lykke for three days, but it felt longer due to lack of sleep or high blood pressure or the fear of getting caught. But in those three days, I'd learned plenty about myself. I was unafraid to rise to the challenge. I enjoyed being helpful. And even if I was partially insane and terrified of absolutely everything, I no longer felt needy, useless, or unattractive.

After I retrieved Buck's tablet, which I'd stolen from his van, I checked the news. There was a two-minute video with Miriam's house on the background and a caption: "Ghana Boy: Gone Girl." I clicked on the video and turned down the volume. Skip Jones was sitting in the studio.

"After a neighbor called to report a strange woman living next door, the authorities came to investigate. The woman was actually a man. The Fawcett kidnapper had lived in Miriam's Turtle house for two days without the owner knowing the baby had been kidnapped. Take a look."

Erin Wilson—in a bright red coat and a red whore lipstick—smiled to the camera, Miriam's house nebulously seen in the background. Next to Erin stood Miriam with a younger woman hugging her tightly, and gently rubbing her arm.

"Could you tell us more about the kidnapper?" Erin asked Miriam.

"He said he was from Ghana," Miriam said, "delivering the baby for adoption to someone named Brad and Angelina. He said his plane had come early, and he needed a place to stay for a few days."

"And he didn't seem suspicious to you?"

"He seemed like a nice man. He helped me clean the house. Nobody cared for me like that for twenty-two years. But I'm glad my daughter finally came because of it."

The younger woman next to Miriam, turned out, was her daughter, Cecelia. Miriam began to tear up, turned around, and Cecelia clutched her tighter.

"Sorry," Cecelia said. "She won't be taking any more questions. We have a long day ahead of us tomorrow, and my mother needs to rest."

When Miriam and Cecelia got in a black car, Erin turned toward the camera. "The authorities said there are no prints in the house because the Ghana boy was using rubber gloves. Take a look at this footage of the house that we managed to film before the house was taped off as a crime scene. Miriam is a hoarder. By our calculation, over forty cats live in the house at the moment."

Miriam's living room and her junk appeared in view, shot sometime earlier this morning. My heart started fluttering upon seeing my tote bag with an oversized imprint of a black cat, which I'd sewed in myself, the camera zooming in on it and then following a cat—I believe Fluffy—who was watching the cameraman with curiosity. The tote unassumingly blended in with Miriam's jumble, but nevertheless, it was mine. Those who knew me (Mom, Lindsay, Calyssa, Natalia, Sam, Kim) knew how much the bag meant to me. I bragged about the tote because I'd sewn Anubis's face on it.

Maybe I was not that safe anymore.

I don't know if I can go on like this, I thought. I'm scared every minute of every hour. Two minutes ago I was in heaven, now I'm back in hell.

What was I supposed to do?

WHEN I OPENED MY EYES, THE NURSERY WAS MURKY AND inaudible, yet vaguely the first sparks of twilight flickered in the skylight, suggesting dawn. The baby wailed for a second but calmed down quickly after I hugged her and sang a lullaby. I was planning on Helga's help to feed the baby as soon as Helga awoke.

I barely slept—which meant tossed and turned while hungry all night—and the fatigue brought by exhaustion was evident all the way down to my bones. It was also itching inside of my eyeball—like, seriously, body? I shifted in my bed, tried counting sheep, but sleep only came in small doses, and when it did come, I was haunted by nightmares. Every time I opened my eyes, chasing a nightmare away, the dream would clear away, but a strange feeling would linger.

I knew what it was.

I realized I could no longer trust my thoughts or feelings. One minute I was happy, the next scared to death. As hard as it was to think about, it was time to return the baby and go home without going to prison somehow. I knew I had to pay my debt to society somehow, but I'd been volunteering for years and was hoping that would be enough.

Being on the loose had lost its appeal because no longer was I free to run freely. My safety depended on the few people who knew my secret—once they saw my tote from the last night's footage. Dozens of times, my blood pressure had risen to dangerous levels, making me titter on the brink of a heart attack. Bones crinkled, vagin smelled, and now the eyeball itched. Lightning McQueen was defective and needed to be inspected in a garage, along with Sally Carrera and Doc Hudson.

That first day after escaping from Central Park and after making it all the way to Virginia safe, I felt giddy and happy, pleased, and carefree. Turned out, freedom was merely an illusion, a distraction from what was really needed—which was to lose weight. Lindsay wanted freedom from her job and was seeking any excuse she could find, like focusing on the fact that Charlotte swallowed a crayon. Once Lindsay loses her job, I kept thinking, she'd be miserable unemployed. Not that a job is the end of freedom. Same with Calyssa, who was afraid that things were moving too fast and missed her privilege of being single, but had she broken up with Marcus would want to be in a relationship again. Not that relationship, again, is the end of freedom. Natalia, after immigrating, had this freedom to become whom she really wanted to—a woman—and the United States was giving her that opportunity, a place where she wouldn't be judged, or (if judged) at least be safe from prosecution. But instead, she decided to focus her energy on "adopting African children," which, if I may, translates to, "I'm scared of penectomy, because I'm scared of the unknown, but I'm bored and need an activity to do." Again, not that she needed to hurry. It was clearly a tough psychological choice to lose something you've had all your life, her penis. For her, it was like losing an arm or a leg. Or sanity, if you're Courtney Love.

My friends were all trapped in the tangles of their own thoughts, imagining problems out of nowhere to feed the beast that was their hungry and bored mind. That's exactly how I felt just three days ago, and looking back, I realized how it all was merely an illusion. Those were not problems. I'd give up everything just to be "trapped" back in my own life, live with Mom—and I no longer cared about having a job. I wanted my basic needs to be met, like feeling safe, having access to a shower, and even use my mouth to munch on things, like chicken wings.

This time I was trapped for real. Like Dorothy, who somehow got stuck in the middle of a poppy field and couldn't resist falling asleep. Or something more dramatic, like a scene from a scary movie, my hands and feet were tied, limiting my every move. I couldn't go to the doctor or the bank, or even to the DMV for a new ID. What I wanted in the past was not freedom, it turned out, but something else entirely.

Like after sitting in a drive-thru line at McDonald's for hours, I'd finally approached the window. It was my time to order. While the FBI was looking for a black man, it was my chance to request my life back. "With a side of fries, please," I would ask. I had to act. I had to act today.

I looked at Lykke, knowing perfectly well I would miss her teeny nose and large blue eyes. But after everything that I'd done wrong, this was a chance to make it right. I was having focal illusions lately when I thought Whoopi Goldberg was here in black Chloe's body. I could try crossing the street, and a truck could be crossing the street, and my eye would not notice and swoosh—I'm gone—perhaps together with the baby. Just thought of being dead in such a stupid way sent an unpleasant feeling down my stomach. I wanted to go out grand, in style, and be fifteen minutes late for my own funeral. In this case, I'll be thirty years earlier, and nobody will show up.

I had to start taking Clozapine. The worst part of schizophrenia was the nagging voices telling me how cruel I was. Back at the diner, those voices were saying how invaluable I was—and worst of all, I believed them. It was 100 percent paranoia, an after effect of exaggerated self-importance, delusions of persecution, and unwarranted jealousy. According to Dr. Pepper, I was struggling with an overblown ego from fear of being harassed, a state of mind proportionally drawn from my childhood when *I* was the bully. I was now this giant Chloe, thinking nothing would come back and bite me in the ass, not after kidnapping a baby, stealing a car, or using the fake dough. The more the ego inflated, the worse the crash would be. It was time to deflate that balloon for good. Last year when I was "hanging out" with Matilda, my dead sister, I was in a strange stage where reality and hallucinations had collided into a world where I no longer could decipher a fact from a lie. In that sense, Matilda hadn't appeared, and I was partially glad I was sane and could still make my way out of it alive.

THE DOOR TO THE NURSERY SLOWLY MOVED WITH ITS signature squeak, and Helga appeared in view.

"Good morning," I whispered.

In her hands, Helga was holding a baby close to Lykke's age. "Kids are starting to arrive. We need the nursery. Sorry, Sister Mary. I mean, Sister Chloe, sorry."

"No problem. I'm up." Before Helga saw it, I hid Buck's tablet to avoid looking snooty, and as far as I could tell, none of the sisters had a tablet.

She walked in and said, "How did you sleep?"

"Fine. Sister Helga, is there anything for me to wear? I think I left my bag on the bus, and the habit I'm wearing is soiled."

"I'll bring something down if you don't mind watching Ladasha."

While holding Lykke with my left, I took Ladasha with my right, wondering what kind of a name Ladasha was. Maybe it's French from *la dash*, in which case she was really just a dash. But she was cute as a button! Both babies eyed each other and laughed, then looked at me and smiled, then looked around and cried.

I kept rocking them until Helga reappeared, a gray peasant robe in hands. In Helga's other hand, there was a matching mop hat, similar to the one she was wearing. Helga neglected to ask me whether I'd be wearing this outfit commando, which I was planning on doing, as I had no other viable choices. I put both babies in a crib, took the outfit, and went to the bathroom. I'd decided to take a quick shower, and Helga told me the bathroom had stacks of clean towels and that Anita was delivering more tomorrow.

Last night, it had struck me odd the sisters had all the necessities, including A/C, kitchen appliances, and bathrooms with flushing toilets. Today I realized it was not bizarre—it's not like they were Amish. They lived in the twenty-first century and had access to the Internet so they could Google and print lyrics to their gospel songs. There were zero reasons why they had to live like peasants, despite being dressed like ones.

There were five washrooms on the lower level, each with a shower and a toilet. I entered one and locked the door. Clean white towels were folded by the bathtub. Next to the tub, two hampers stood next to each other, labeled "Whites" and "Habits," respectively. On the rim of the tub was a bar of soap.

I undressed and got in the tub. The faucet was brass and old-school, something I'd only seen in old French movies. Three levers labeled "Cold," "Hot," and "Shower" appeared on the bottom. Parallel to the wall, the showerhead sat above in a cradle as would a telephone. I was half tempted to answer, but nobody was calling.

I turned the hot- and cold-water levers, but nothing came out of the hot water faucet. Cold water began dripping, minus the quality I'd expected. I wasn't going to drink it, but I was skittish to lather my beautiful curves under green water with clumps of black hair. The faucet shook as cold water was trickling down without any pressure. I waited for five minutes, watching as a steady stream of icy cold water splattered around the tub. I dressed in my new outfit, and without looking in the mirror, I dropped the soiled habit into the appropriate hamper. I checked out the second washroom: no hot water there either. Ditto in the third. The fourth and fifth were occupied, and unpleasant sounds were coming from both. I was not in the business of taking a cold shower, so there was only one thing to do: ask someone what was happening or spend the day as a filthy peasant.

Mary and Chloe, with steaming teakettles in hands, sleepily greeted me, taking the kettles into their separate bathrooms. Passing through the kitchen, I noticed how other Maries and Chloes waited by the stove, while more teakettles were warming up. Trinity was standing last in line with a bright pink one.

"Sister Trinity," I asked her, "what's up with all the teakettles?"

"We have no hot water, Sister Chloe," she said.

"Really?" I said. "I had no idea."

"We bought teakettles so we could boil our own hot water for the bath. I'd like to apologize—you were so wonderful to us for baking the delicious Russian cake—but we don't have a guest teakettle. Do you mind using a cooking pot? It takes longer to boil, but it's like a tub of its own."

"Thanks, put it on the stove for me," I said.

"Okay, I'll add a ladle for easy scooping," she said and pulled out a slotted spoon from underneath her nightgown, adding, "For myself, I prefer to take a shower. I just run the hot water through the slotted spoon."

"Smart," I said. I meant it, actually. I enjoy finding solutions in otherwise dead-end situations. But there was no way I was using a cooking pot with a ladle to wash my lady parts, primarily since the pot is used to make food and I respect food. I also respect my lady parts. There was probably a problem with the boiler, which was probably broken. It wasn't surprising the boiler was broken since the girls didn't know how to bake either and maybe even were unaware they had a basement. And that's where I went after the conversation with Trinity.

I found the basement door near the kitchen. I glanced in, while the musty smell of fear and regret hit my nose. I couldn't believe I was going to proceed with this—alone in the dark. I shook my head and entered, listening to the door's scary squeakiness. Inside, it looked dark and scary. I returned to the kitchen, grabbed a candle, matches, and returned to the basement. After lighting the candle, I blew out the match and carefully stepped in, quickly realizing the door wouldn't stay open on its own. I stuck my mop hat near the hinge, which seemed to keep it from closing behind me, leaving a teensy ray of light that illuminated the steps.

While I didn't expect to find homeless people sleeping in a corner, or another chia pet assailant ready to shoot me with a fake gun, I felt unsettled. Women are so silly. We're afraid of the darkness for reasons unknown. The candle provided enough illumination, but at what price? I was shaking all over like an unhinged hinge. The sweat slowly dripped down my hand, while the wax slowly dripped down the candle.

A pink door on my left had a sign "Chapel" on it. Well, that's interesting. I twisted the handle and pushed, while the door, squeakily, swung open. A long corridor ahead suggested a gateway to the chapel in case we were being attacked by the republicans and needed a quick way to escape. The chapel sat about a hundred feet from the monastery from what my memory allowed. I entered the corridor because I wanted to see what was in the chapel.

I proceeded slowly, leaving the pink door ajar behind me. Suddenly, hunger attacked me, and I wondered whether that was any good for my body. Fasting, according to the health nut Lindsay, is an excellent thing to practice and not just for religious reasons. Lindsay said fasting changes hormones in your body to make fat more available for fuel—all over your body. Which is why Lindsay is in perfect shape. Fasting causes spikes in Human Growth Hormone, HGH, for thicker skin and longevity because, as we age, HGH declines. Lindsay does intermittent fasting, meaning she eats within an eight-hour-window and drinks water or electrolytes (zero calories, of course) during the next sixteen hours. My opinion? She's got an eating disorder.

The corridor ended with a blue door with a poster of a crucified Jesus. I twisted the handle, opened the door, and slowly entered. Musty and quiet. The steps leading upstairs brought me to the chapel's cellar. Upon reaching the ground floor, I heard nothing. The chapel was haunted, for nobody seemed to be living here or singing any gospel songs. The walls gave a greenish tint, with dawn squeezing through the skylight, casting shadows. The sanctuary, the same with the monastery, had an altar sitting in the distance like an old, wise plumber. I don't know; I always thought plumbers were wise. To fix the boiler, I'd pay a lot for a plumber right now (with Buck's fake currency since I had no legit money on me.

In the nave, near the Tabernacle, instead of pews, several stools were arranged neatly, upholstered in blue satin. Tall, arched windows were laid out in mosaic. Sunlight seeped through the stained glass and reflected off numerous religious statues, including Jesus, Mary, and the various prophets. The air smelled of incense and armpits, but on the second inspection, the armpits smell was partially mine. Even while smelly, I felt holy in this place. I would teach everyone a lesson if I stayed here with the sisters who appreciate and share my affection for butter and sugar.

But they'd probably get tired of me after a month when we're all big and bloated from eating numerous cakes—and then what?

As I approached the vestibule and peekabooed through the stained window in the door leading outside, I noticed the cemetery with the lake visible next to it. The convent I was staying at was on the opposite side of the cemetery, which meant the tunnel in between was quite long, even if I didn't notice as I was walking it.

Okay, that was great. I quickly returned to the cellar and took the getaway back to the monastery, quietly giggling at my little adventure.

When I closed the pink door behind me and turned around, I noticed the boiler: a giant apparatus with an elephant trunk, its elongated body stretching into the black abyss.

"Good doggy," I said and touched it. The boiler was quiet in response. What do I do? I opened Buck's tablet, which I had stuck under the robe, and searched the Internet for an answer. The first thing that popped up was to drain the boiler every few months. The red valve that resembled the one from the picture sat underneath the trunk, so I turned it. Water poured in a manner like it hadn't been drained in a millennium.

The dirty water from the boiler stopped running in about a minute, and I turned the valve counter-clockwise. The next step was to turn the boiler on. The start button was marked clearly, so I pressed and waited.

Yesterday, after the first bite of my cake, Sister Chloe soared into a gospel song, and today the boiler appeared to be doing the exact same, trembling loudly from the pleasure of running. As if it hadn't been used for a while and was finally happy to be of help. The same kind of happiness that was responsible for making me delighted to be of help to the sisters. They knew how to sing, which made me wonder if doing karaoke competitions was profitable, but when it came to fixing around the house, the nuns required someone with tools.

In the kitchen, I passed the row of half-sleeping nuns with their teakettles in hands. I approached the kitchen sink and turned on the hot water faucet. The water came out rusty without any pressure, but soon, as rust was clearing out, the water came out clear and in a steady stream. So steady, I could fill a pot in under thirty seconds. Most importantly, the water was steaming hot. It was time to break into another gospel song with the entire convent.

XANAX TO HEAVEN, I THOUGHT. HOW EASY WAS *THAT*? UPON hearing the hot water was back on, the sisters sang "Hallelujah," and Trinity explained to me they hadn't had hot water for months. They kept waiting for the promised plumber, who was Anita's brother, but since the two had had beef, the plumber never came. The nuns' love for me tripled right then. Chloe offered to take me to the cake-baking contest (apparently seating in the van was limited), but I politely declined the invitation. Besides, I didn't want to step on anyone's habit, I mean toes. If I went, at least two of those skinny sisters would be required to stay. Chloe, Mary, other Chloes, and Maries, plus Trinity leading the way, left for the contest at seven-thirty in the morning with the cake resting on a large white plate. The competition was taking place in Richmond at nine.

Soon after, five more kids got dropped off, one with an "I'm trouble" face, one with a huge nose, and three normal ones. Helga helped me bathe and feed Lykke, which, now that the hot water was back on was a piece of cake. (See what I did there?)

Helga was short on words, and at times I thought she wanted to kick some ass. She handled the babies with care but was stern with the older kids, me, and her fellow sisters. Tough love, some call it. I wondered if living in such solitary confinement was partially responsible for her unfriendly exterior. She seemed content being alone, even if surrounded by the sisters and the babies. Helga was not distracted by the wonders of the TV, by pop culture (aka the Kardashians), by cellphones, by k-pop (Korean pop), or crap (Caucasian rap). Spending extra time thinking was extra time maturing. If silence were not required for finding mental clarity, the spiritual leadership would reside atop the Empire State Building or other high-traffic sights. But no, they choose humbler experiences, simpler clothes, and meeker existence atop of mountains in shabby huts, in isolation; destitute but sufficient, confined but content, taciturn but sagacious.

I loved the idea of being unreachable, perched on a hill in a cabin, surrounded by goats, forest, and a lake. I don't know why I said goats. They're cute? The millennials heavily rely on social media for approval, and depression kicks in the very moment when nobody comments on our posts. Numerous times I found myself sulking because Calyssa ignored my calls, right after posting a picture of her and Lindsay at a party I wasn't invited to. I don't understand why jealousy causes such strong feelings, but this is a problem of the twenty-first century. Each century gets its own set of challenges. Sure enough, in primitive times, food and circumcision were at the center of the discussion, sometimes scurvy if you had vitamin C deficiency, and now, since we have aplenty, we need a new topic to bitch about.

Even though the idea of getting "enlightened" appealed to me on many levels, living in solitary confinements was not particularly tempting. Just look at what happened to Miriam Turtle. Because Cecelia was ashamed of her mother and had left her to her lonesome, Miriam found herself raising cats for nothing rather than to keep her company. My neighbor Agnes was in the same boat. Or at least a kayak. No human wants to live alone, and Miriam was miserable and lonely, counting days before her death, doodling weather reports in her musty notebooks. After Lykke and I arrived, Miriam found herself happier being of help, because she knew how much we needed the shelter, food, and love—the basic human essentials, the basic formula for survival. In a way, we were helping each other.

In comparison, the sisters lived in isolation but remained a community. Maybe that was why my mom kept providing for me, afraid that as soon as I started working, she'd be left all alone with cats roaming the perimeter while Siriporn wouldn't bother to come and clean. Daddy and Matilda both passed away, and I was her only relative left. There was an abundance of Daddy's relatives all over the country, including Aunt Josephine and my cousin Analise, who all reside in the tri-state area. Every day, Mom and I would watch Paula Deen or *Dr. Phil*, but we'd both be playing with our phones, me wondering who *she's* talking to, her wondering who *I'm* talking to. I would be on social media sites stalking Lindsay and Calyssa, getting more jealous the more I stalked. Lindsay was helping Calyssa babysit Grace, but neither invited me and had I never had a smartphone, I wouldn't know about it in the first place. That day I was fuming, felt needy and friendless, and eventually had a fight with Mom over soy sauce. It was one of those times when anything could set me off. The catalyst was an empty bottle of soy sauce. As the adage goes, the less you know, the better you sleep, but with all the technology taking over every aspect of our lives, it's impossible to know less or sleep better. Whenever two people hang out, phones will ultimately appear in their hands, because our attention span and our need for attention are now proportionally correlated.

Could I ever become a nun and learn to live my life without feeling misery and jealousy, enjoying a humble existence and happiness promised by the *Bible*?

THE KIDS TOOK A NAP AROUND ELEVEN, THE CUTE SEVEN dwarfs asleep around me, the Snow White. Staring at the enchanted mirror on the wall in the bathroom, I realized who was the curviest of them all. Don't tell anyone, but I thought it was Helga. While in a good mood, playful and silly, I told Helga I wanted to see the outside garden. She stayed to watch the munchkins and to knit.

Upstairs, the nave was abundantly sunny, promising a fabulous day ahead. I was excited about spending some time in the garden, imagining serenity and quietness so vivid in my mind I could almost touch them. As I was pulling the heavy entrance door to open, I noticed a commotion around Buck's van. I saw the letters FBI on people's backs. The tall ginger man who sold me the formula and diapers was talking to one of them, his son clinging to his leg. The van full of Chloes and Maries plus Trinity was pulling up to the curb. Trinity was holding a trophy in her hands. My hands were shaking, and yet I couldn't let go of the door, stuck like gum caught in the headlights—I mean shoe. I mean dear caught in the gum. I was definitely not myself. I was watching the scene ahead, uncommonly hectic, and unnecessarily crowded for a quiet church street. As soon as the sisters exited the vehicle, an FBI agent—a heavy skank wearing aviator glasses—engaged them in a conversation.

I dashed downstairs without even closing the door and entered the nursery.

"Helga," I whispered, "we have a problem. I have to tell you something, and you're not going to like it."

Helga left the knitting supplies on the chair and stood up.

"The biggest mistake of my life," I said and breathed in deeply, trying to come up with a lie, while tears made my throat tense. "Yesterday, I found a van full of counterfeit currency, and I went across the street to buy stuff for the cake." My voice broke, and Helga approached me, offering a hug.

"Just breathe, Sister Chloe. How do you know the currency was counterfeit?"

"Because there are FBI agents all over the place. They've come to arrest me." With each word, I sounded less and less familiar to myself. With each word, my heart was ramping its speed until it started hurting in my abdominal area.

Loud noises from upstairs announced the sisters' arrival. The ginger man's voice was heard, and someone else's too. Oh, my God. My heart was about to explode, and the itch behind my eyeball reappeared.

"I didn't mean to cause trouble," I said. "Please, help."

"It's okay, Sister Chloe. We're on your side."

Helga lifted up a finger parallel to her nose to shush me and told me to follow her. The FBI agents were going to kill three birds with one giant stone: They tracked the counterfeit currency, rescued Lykke, and sent me to prison. What a productive day for them. On her tippy toes, Helga went up the steps, paused, and stood motionless near the top, from where we could eavesdrop on the conversation.

"*She* was the one who gave my son the fake bill," the ginger man told someone. "Right, son?"

I couldn't see what was going on, but I assumed the little boy either nodded or replied quietly.

"Prove it was me," one of the Maries said. I recognized her accent, which was Jamaican.

"Your name is written on your habit," the ginger man said. "And yesterday, we sold the stuff to you, Mary."

"It does not prove anything," Mary said. "We have five Maries in our sisterhood. Officer, Mr. McManus has been trying to get rid of us for over a year now. He says we're obnoxious when we sing. He intentionally walks his dog in our garden, and she kills our flowers. He always mocks our devotion to God. He belittles us. His atheistic nature cannot comprehend our affection for humanity and our mission to help the poor. He's a bigot."

The ginger man burst out laughing. "You are stupid. You told me my daughter's name should be Matilda, the ugliest name I've ever heard. You knew it was supposed to be Rose Petal or Barb or something cute like Cupertino."

"Have you been nipping, Mr. McManus?" Mary asked. She seemed calm. "Have I offended you personally somehow?"

"You just pretend to be precious and Godly," he said, "while it's clear you have some hanky-panky going on in this monastery."

"Officer," Trinity was now speaking, "can you explain one more time what the van has to do with us?"

"The van belongs to a fellow named Buck Mooney," the officer said. "He's number ten on our 'Top Wanted' list. He's wanted for crimes associated with forgery, money laundering, and counterfeit currency. He's dangerous and, therefore, our priority. We've been chasing this guy for years, and this might be our big break."

"I swear, not me or my sisters know of the man," Chloe said.

"We still have to arrest you, ma'am," the officer said. The ginger man was laughing now.

"Then you have to take me too," said a sister whose voice I didn't recognize. "Because I shopped with her, using the same money."

"And me."

"And me."

Helga stood up and ran toward them. "And me!" she said.

Each sister volunteered in Chloe's defense, while I was silent and remained on the steps.

Suddenly, the monastery became a disorganized disaster, as each sister volunteered to go to jail. Were they all just willing to protect *me* and then each other? Just like that, simple, without understanding the consequences?

"Quiet!" the officer said. "This must be a terrible coincidence. Money quickly exchanges hands. Since Mooney was in this neighborhood, proved by his van parked out front, I'm not surprised a counterfeit bill had surfaced. Sister Chloe, if you pay a hundred dollars to Mr. McManus, we will not arrest you if you cooperate. Right now, we're losing time because the sooner we find Mooney, the sooner it's all over."

"Fine," the ginger man said. "But I'll be watching you."

"And we'll take our business someplace else," Chloe said.

"I'll have my men search the monastery," the officer said. "You two are all set, then?"

"Of course," Chloe said. "Expect your money later this afternoon, Mr. McManus."

"Come on, son," the ginger man said. "And, you, return the money in an hour or else."

"You have a good day, Mr. McManus," Chloe sang from the tip of her tongue.

The huntsmen came to arrest Mooney, I thought, but they will also arrest me in the process. Was this the end? How fitting since I wanted to give up Lykke in the first place. I tried to get out of the kidnapping business without going to prison. Could I still?

By that time, however, I was halfway through the getaway in the basement toward the chapel. Without even thinking, I had grabbed Lykke from the nursery and dashed downstairs, locking the basement door behind me. My ears were pulsating from weird pressure as if I was ten thousand feet in the air. Upon opening the door, I realized the basement was hot, the boiler humming and doing its merry thing. They are FBI agents, I thought, so why am I trying to outrun them? They're trained professionals who catch criminals like me all the time, and they will sniff me out in no time. Unless I can somehow reach the lake and pretend to be a civilian minding my own business.

Once on the opposite side of the tunnel, I approached the door to the chapel and listened. Nothing. I entered the chapel's basement and climbed up the steps. I was terrified of dropping the baby. My hands were shaking, arms heavy. I looked freaking ridiculous. If I got caught, the first thing on my to-do list in prison was to hang myself from the upcoming shame.

I exited the cellar and approached the ground floor. The monastery sat behind us. I had no way of knowing whether the agents had started covering the ground near the chapel or only the monastery. I approached the door and looked through the mosaic window. The two blues collided—the lake and the sky—into one. It was either my escape route or a road to life in prison. I placed Lykke under the dress and held her firmly with one hand. She was crying with her signature meowing sounds, so I whispered, "Please, not now. You've been so good for four days, and *now* you're crying?"

I took a deep breath with my eyes closed. Three more seconds, I thought, and I'll exit. I whispered out loud, "One, two, three."

Slowly, I pulled the door to open. Nobody was on the right, ditto on the left. Birds were trilling in a sequence, repeating one after another right above me, but none pooped, which was good. Ahead was the cemetery, gate to it wide open. I kept talking aloud to calm myself down: "Don't panic, no running. Chest up. Just a peasant with a big chest. That's it. If anyone asks, you don't speak English, or you're in a silent retreat."

I took the steps, one at a time, my feet prickly from a spasm. I held Lykke with my left hand. Sharp pain in the left shin made me lose control, and I almost dropped her. But I quickly caught her with my right. Fear was making me delusional. I couldn't breathe, so I drew short breaths while limping toward the gate, my heartbeat accelerating. A shadow appeared to my right. In my peripheral vision, I noticed the shadow belonged to a woman or a man who liked to wear tight clothes.

"Chloe!" the woman/cross-dresser/drag queen/Ricky Martin said. I swallowed but kept hobbling toward the gate, ignoring her. Everyone here was named Chloe, so maybe she meant the black Chloe. The woman who was speaking was not an FBI agent, so she could suck it.

"Chloe!"

She was running toward me, and I wanted to sprint away, but my legs were leaden as if I was tied with a ball and chain. I approached the gate at the same time as her shadow caught up with me, covering me with darkness. I turned as she was removing her sunglasses.

"Ah" was all that escaped my mouth. I was looking straight at my dead sister Matilda. This time she seemed real. Was she alive all along?

Yellow beams of sunlight made me squint. With my eyes half-closed, I was staring at Matilda in a stupor, wondering whether she was another hallucination. The thing with hallucinations, you have to test them to appraise what value they bring to the table, as usual, it's just your mind putting obstacles in otherwise non-threatening situations or helping you work things through. I opened my mouth, which was surprisingly dry for a humid day like this. Nothing but a squeal came out. I reached for a hug, and she embraced me.

"Chloe," she said, holding me, her voice mollifying me, "are you okay?"

I wasn't. Matilda was not dead, she was real. Unlike a phantom, Matilda's body warmth proved her authenticity. I truly believed life came in all sorts of forms if you open your mind to it. When it comes to the nitty-gritty, to protons and electrons, we are nothing more than light in different manifestations, from plants to animals to stars. Turn off the light, and it will no longer matter what you look like—white, black, tall, or short. My brain had turned off the light and opened its mind to find Matilda, who was just yet another expression of light.

Her voice was different from the voices I constantly heard in my head, which told me how inept, immense, or imprudent I was. Voices are a telltale sign I needed help, but those voices didn't belong to people who spoke them. They were just words of mockery created by the brain. If anything, the brain functions to keep us alive, meaning there must be a reason for the voices as well. Her voice, however, was not of scorn, but of love.

Matilda's hands surrounded me like a fence keeping me against the maleficent mortals, FBI agents, and such. I guess she had never died, and now she found me to protect her big sister, who was suffering a manic episode of a sort. This was exhilarating in itself.

I was searching for words, but the initial shock hadn't worn off yet. Emotions were tightening my throat, ready to erupt in a cry explosion that would last for days. It was hard to picture the believability of such an encounter. I was half sure Matilda was a mirage, a Xenopus outside of African xerosere, a xenial phantom who had learned how to produce body heat. With all my heart, I hoped her touch was genuine. A schizophrenic "episode" happens when I'm stressed and depressed—and I was both—and in front of me stood Matilda. How can this be? I wondered. My hands were shaking while I was sucking in the air in short slurps. When Matilda pulled me even closer, I got a whiff of her hair, a mixture of coconut and hibiscus. It was probably paraben- and sulfate-free. She was all about the environment. She touched the spot where I was holding Lykke underneath my slave garment, and I took a step back.

"I am scared," I said. "FBI agents are all over the place, searching for me."

"I know. What happened?" Her voice was calm.

"I kidnapped a baby."

"You have to come with me," she said. "I am your friend. You trust me. We need to get you to a safe place. Have some electrolytes."

She offered me a bottle filled with pink, healthy-looking liquid. She unscrewed the top for me, and when I permitted by a nod, she aimed the bottle in my mouth. The drink was sweet, cherry-flavored. I savored every drop as if my life depended on it. At that moment, I knew that my life—any kind of life, human or animal—depended on water. While on the run with Lykke, I barely drank, leaving my body dehydrated like a piece of dried fruit. My mind pinged back to when Lindsay explained to me that sometimes we mistake hunger for thirst, a potent but straightforward trick for weight loss I'd stupidly never used. Maybe that's how Lindsay stayed skinny. As I licked the final drops off my lips, with a look indicating satisfaction, Matilda retrieved the bottle and calmly said, "Let's go."

There was no question about it anymore: Matilda was not a mirage. My brain attempted to undo the riddle behind the real reason why Matilda was here. To save me from the FBI? Even if I protested, physically, she was at an advantage to pulverize me. Weakness was settling in my body like a parasite, ready to spread its roots. I had no intention of disobeying, but instead, I wanted to follow her, even if she was taking me to the cops.

I learned later I was not hallucinating. This was part of a bigger plan to save me. Matilda had laced the pink drink with Clozapine, medication for schizophrenia. My mind was slowly returning back to reality after days of hallucinating dreamland, while at that moment, the reality seemed like a mirage. And that's the scariest part of having an "episode": the distinction between true and false is more than vague, with random voices appearing and vanishing, leaving me confused and frightened.

Matilda unhurriedly approached a white Toyota sedan parked near the chapel. I hopped in her wake like Toto after Dorothy toward the unknown and magical. I approached the car as the engine burred to live. Matilda opened the door to the passenger side for me, and I jumped in with Lykke still hidden under the robe.

As soon as I sat, my stomach gave me a kick to announce the guest star: vomit. I swallowed my saliva and breathed steadily to avoid the eruption, while Matilda helped me buckle up. She was talking, but the pitch and speed of her voice sounded off, lower and slower or higher and faster. Like a damaged VHS tape. My chest pulsated, while sharp pain shot through my left arm, and I closed my eyes, trying to focus on my breathing.

We were going slowly, maybe five miles per hour if so. I began petting Lykke under my peasant outfit like I would Anubis. Somehow, such sedative, mindless activity prevented me from freaking out. I assumed Miriam and Agnes found comfort in petting their, well, pets, as well. My hand stroked his body, combing his fur in one direction until his tail went up beggin' for more. I felt disoriented/confused/sleepy. It smelled like a burger and fries in the car, and I wondered if Matilda had gotten a QP with cheese in a drive-thru. The smell made me feel worse.

Our speed diminished as a row of police cars appeared in view with beacon lights a tad too bright. The sound was turned off as if Matilda muted it on the remote control. My mind only registered the picture in scenes of strobe lights that went to black, then more lights, then black. Nobody was paying us any attention or peeking through the window, trying to identify us. We were not men and couldn't be Buck Mooney, nor were we driving the counterfeiting van—so we were in the clear. The SWAT team with guns and dogs was searching the periphery, but the lake was no longer there as if it never existed, just a joke of my jolly imagination. Buck's van disappeared into thin air, as did the monastery. The scenery merged into squares, reminding me of Picasso and Marc Chagall's Cubism—reality folding and unfolding like Japanese origami.

When I opened my eyes, we were sailing along an interstate. Matilda's blond hair hung freely above her perky chest, meaning she was wearing a cone-shaped bra, mimicking Madonna. She had grown since the last time I saw her in October of last year. Matilda was into fashion when she was little, always in hands with the latest issue of *Vogue*. My clothes come from a magazine called *I Gave Up: December Issue*, and that's on a good day. Matilda looked youthful, the yin and the yang of beauty. To look like her, I would kickbox a kangaroo or sell a kidney. She was petite, while there I sat, a giant, unfriendly Godzilla with an ass the size of the Centaurus A galaxy.

She glanced at the navigation system hooked on the windshield.

"In a quarter-mile, turn right on Greenwood Road," the navigation system announced in a female voice. The navigation woman sounded professional, a bit bored.

Is Matilda taking me to the police? I wondered. No, that makes no sense, as otherwise why would she go through the risk of deceiving the FBI just some time ago?

"How are you?" she asked me. "We're almost at a safe place."

My throat had tensed up to the point where I could hardly breathe. Caressing Lykke helped me stay composed, even though my whole body felt stiff, like a whiskey drink on the rocks. Matilda was wearing a navy-colored bomber jacket atop a white tee and skinny blue jeans, paired with a gold necklace that probably cost a fortune. As a real criminal, I immediately appraised it, wondering how much money Sally May would give me for it. Her eyelashes could double as airplane wings: long and thick. Perfect brows, like two domes of blondness, sat above the baby blues, blush to accentuate her cheeks. Matilda used to give me makeovers when we were little, after which I'd look like a call girl in Aunt Josephine's fur coat, Mom's heels, and bright red lipstick, one of Daddy's cigars sticking out of my mouth. I'd come out in that outfit at parties to make the adults laugh. "She's gonna be huge!" Dean Siciliano, Daddy's associate, would say in a heavy Italian accent, not understanding the irony back then.

We slowed down, turned, and entered a parking lot. Right in front of me, Cubism was changing to Suprematism with its abstract geometrical paraphernalia. The building in front of us was a mere blueprint, with pencil lines that were still being drawn by an invisible hand. Soon colors filled the canvas, revealing what looked like a motel. It was a one-story building, shady-looking, and the area smelled a bit of a wet dog. Matilda parked in front of door number thirty-one. The door looked like it had bullet holes around the number three and knife marks near the one. Matilda released the safety lock and exited the car, her navy pumps clicking against the pavement. She checked each direction and opened the door on my side for me.

Feeling a confusing cocktail of vanquishment, embarrassment, and liberation, I exited the car and pushed the door to close. I felt so small I might as well have been Thumbelina, the girl who was the size of a thumb, depicted in the Brothers Grimm's tales.

Several parking spots ahead, a woman was squatting atop a red Honda, her pantyhose down at her ankles. She was taking a dump according to the two brown pyramids rising in the sun. Matilda ignored, while I kept staring at the woman as if I'd never seen anyone pooping on a car before.

"He's a cheater!" she explained with her loud and raspy voice. At first, I wondered whether keying his car would suffice, but apparently, she'd already arranged that. She lighted up a cigarette, while I decided not to intervene by turning away. I as well like my privacy when going number two.

Matilda fussed with the lock for a minute too long but unlocked it. We entered the room most people use for their "sexcapades": wives cheating on their husbands, who, in turn, are cheating on their wives with the maid; politicians getting blow jobs by underage male escorts; perhaps even production of porn movies featuring bimbo starlets. The room was pitch black due to the shades being drawn. Matilda flipped on the table lamp and took a sip of red wine. The bottle had stood open on the dresser. How long had she been staying here before finding me? Matilda locked the room and pointed toward the bed.

"Sit down, Chloe," she said, taking Lykke out of my hands.

I obliged and sat down, and clutched a pillow, hugging it like a teddy bear.

"Do you know why I'm here?" she asked.

"No."

"Do you trust me?"

I nodded. "Yes."

"Did you see Matilda?" she asked. I nodded again, wondering if she meant had I seen her, even though I was staring straight at her.

"Chloe, you are having a mental breakdown," she said.

"Are you not real then?" I asked.

"I am real. I am your friend; you trust me. You took some medication, and your consciousness will return shortly. Remember you wanted this to be over with? Your subconscious made you take Clozapine—you'll be fine."

But the opposite was happening. The background was washed off as if smears of watercolors splashed by a toddler. When Lykke came into focus, she resembled Anubis, just a cute, black cat. I felt embarrassed for having a psychedelic episode in front of Matilda.

"The FBI is looking for me," I said.

"You are safe while with me. Trust me." She put her hand on mine. It felt burning to the touch.

"What's going to happen to me? Why did we come here?"

"You will be fine, Chloe, but first, you must get your consciousness back. What does the baby look like?"

"She looks like Anubis. Because I'm hallucinating again. You're not real, either!"

"I *am* real. How many fingers am I holding?"

"Three."

"Good." She brushed her fingers against my arm, and it felt surprisingly good. "Breathe, just breathe," she added.

I inhaled, sucking the air-conditioned air into my lungs. I concentrated on the coolness it carried along. I paused, listening to my heavy heartbeat heaving in my chest. As I exhaled, a strange sensation passed through my body, my heart pulsating near the temples. My nasal passages were swollen and congested. I gasped for air with my dry mouth, suffocating, stifling, smothering. Matilda noticed my struggle for air and offered me a full plastic bottle of water. I grabbed the bottle and fiercely squished the bottom, sending a jet of liquid down my throat. Some water got in the wrong pipe, activating a gag reflex. I coughed, squished the bottom once again, this time aiming the stream of water at my face. I instantly felt better. Maybe it was the fact that my mind was occupied by something rather than thinking of my futile future of fruitlessness. All I needed was water and oxygen, the very basics of being human, the only organic compounds required for life. Nothing else mattered. I quickly summoned my brain to remember another time in my life when I even thought of the basics, when I was thirsty, or enjoyed a breezy summer day. I missed that simplicity. The older we get, the more cynical and selfish we become. Or was it just me? Yet all the first-world problems seemed foolish and immaterial. I was finally a part of something bigger, a human and a God in one body, indistinguishable.

I sat up. "Thank you. I feel better."

The watercolors on the wall were drying off, transforming the wall into ugly wallpaper, which was yellow dotted with pink roses. I was getting my mind back, albeit slowly, but the past five minutes were wiped from my memories, as was the previous day or past week. I couldn't remember what I was doing, sitting on a bed with Matilda. She was having a glass of red wine from a plastic cup.

"Where am I?" I asked her.

"We're at a motel in Virginia, waiting for Mom."

"My head is splitting. The last thing I remember, I went out with Natalia."

"Oh, dear."

"Is it Saturday?"

"Chloe, you had an 'episode.' Our mom is on her way to take you home."

We were both quiet. It was a strange sensation. As if after sleeping, I felt tired, but the fog in my brain was clearing, which brought contentment impossible to compare to. It was as if happiness erupted in my heart, with its shards penetrating my every cell. Some call this euphoria, mental clarity, a feeling of absolute divinity. I felt alive, a sense I rarely experienced. There was no hate or resentment, jealousy or nostalgia. I was even with God, perhaps being God. I knew answers to every question, philosophical or mathematical. The meaning of life seemed so simple, and yet I never had arrived at that decision. How bizarre! On some level, in a different universe, a thousand years ago, I was sitting above my body, and I was bigger than life. I was the Buddha, I was the Allah, I was everything. Happiness was tickling me, and I was smiling from such pleasure.

"I was ready to leave forever," Matilda said, breaking the silence, "but then your psyche called me and asked for help. You told me that you'd stopped taking your medication and could hurt yourself. I know, none of this is your fault, the mental illness. But I doubt we'll see each other again. I'll be gone forever this time. You should *never* see me again."

"Where are you going?"

"Nowhere. Everywhere. I don't know. I'm scared."

"Why?"

"I know I am dead, but I am afraid to leave you. I'm worried about you. You need to call 9-1-1. Chloe, I am scared about your life."

"You're not happy to be with me?"

"You're always in my thoughts and prayers, but you're not living in reality."

"I think we are both misunderstood," I said. "But it feels lovely to be able to talk about your problems with someone who completely understands."

We both stood up and reached for each other, but quite suddenly, I lost balance. Kneeling down, I realized I was not getting enough oxygen. The pressure in my chest was comparable to being severely kicked in the rib cage. I ran a hand over my forehead, wiping off cold sweat. My hands found the floor, while I was on all fours like a pup.

"Chloe, are you okay?" Matilda said and knelt down in front of me.

I gasped for oxygen, but it hurt to inhale. The reason for my pain was apparent, but I continued to disavow its possibility. I rejected being caught with the baby and have a heart attack on the same day.

"I'm having a heart attack," I managed to say.

"You have got to be kidding."

Maybe I deserved to die after all. I heard Matilda calling for a doctor with the door open, "Help, we need a doctor," but it was amusing for some reason as if every motel had one on the premises. A reel of the past few days was flashing in my head, scene after scene reminding me of my adventure. Anubis's fir, black and shiny, smelled recently washed as I wiped him with a towel. A crowded subway car, the epitome of real New York, swiped the rest of the passengers and me from the platform, and we swooshed under the city streets. Central Park, cold and peaceful, lured me in, toward the playground, toward the swings. The long bus ride, Miriam's house, Sister Chloe's voice singing "Hallelujah," the Russian cake sweet on my tongue. Just like breathing and thirst, memories are vital to our existence. Without memories, we're machines, bones with muscle tissue, and fat. Without memories, we're nobody, nomads, a nonentity. Without memories, we're just dead.

Matilda's hand was holding mine, and I felt her energy generated by the powerful simplicity of touch, the essence of humanity. And I fell in love. I had memories, I had a great life, I had friends.

All the layers were now stripped off, and I stood bare. The real me, not a kidnapper in disguise. In front of me was the eternity, a tall endless mountain full of uncertainty and thorns, and behind me was my past, quite a quarry of qualms and doubts. I was finally me, back in my own soul, and bizarre as it sounds I felt content. Can I go back to my old life? I wondered.

With all the problems, negative emotions, disease? Or was a new life better, that feeling of being above all and ruthless, like a warrior woman?

I had to make a decision.

Do I persevere, or do I fall?

"I'm glad I got to see you," I whispered, not yet sure of my decision. Two more steps and I approached the cliff, a valley in front of me, inviting me in. One more step and the void would slurp me in as if I were nothing but a bottle of water until every drop of me consumed.

My zaftig body was pulling me down with great zeal toward ground zero. I was having an out of body experience, hovering above myself, belatedly realizing I wasn't as huge as I'd thought—my body was perfect. It was too late for regrets. In my next life, I will learn to love myself as I was. Whether I was going to end up white, black, Asian, or Hispanic; petite or large; rich, poor, or anywhere in between. It was so easy to love myself now —when looking at myself as an observer. My ears looked small and perfect; why did they ever bother me? Why did I ever hate this beautiful body—my light, my energy? Why did I ever doubt the Universe—the God that created us all? I was perfect in every way. Too bad I wasn't going to enjoy that body for much longer.

I'd heard people in deathbeds express their regrets and realized that's what I was doing.

Farewell. I'm ready for takeoff.

"Heart attack," I heard Matilda say in her phone. Her voice was vague and unfamiliar, distorted, and its volume was diminishing by the second. "She took a double dose of Clozapine and a sedative. At a motel. Greenwood Road. I'll stay on the line."

I couldn't hear it anymore because I'd gone deaf.

Maybe it wasn't really up to me to decide whether I should die.

Because someone always cares for us. Someone always loves us—even when we don't love ourselves or can't make our own decisions. That light, that energy is within us. I just wished I'd felt love for myself before.

I took a step forward, toward the black abyss—and the wind swept me into the void.

ZEN—THAT'S HOW I FELT—FLYING ON CLOUD NINE. I WAS alive, heavily sedated, and therefore quite happy. Because it was all over with, and I was safe. No more running from the FBI or running away from my health problems. No more Lykke Fawcett. No more lying.

The thing about memories is: they aren't real.

Not to say they aren't true, they are, but they are only accurate to a certain degree, to the extent of our ability to remember. Most memories are exaggerated, forgotten, or mere imaginations. Bad memories get tainted with bias, fears, insecurities, and soon become our worst nightmares, and good memories are just pictures of certain positive emotions, but also inflated from prejudice. It's no longer memory but merely a memory *of* a memory, and from that moment on, the truth twists further and further into an unrecognizable pretzel. If a witness told the same story over and over for the next several years, sometimes out of boredom, if nothing else, the blond becomes a brunette, a pocketknife turns into a sword, and the dildo was actually a bagel with lox.

The memories of that first night at the hospital—when I felt alone, terrified, confused—perhaps differ from the memories of the hospital staff.

The nurse was a young skinny brunette, who was throwing shade at me while I pretended to be asleep.

"And she was by herself in that motel," she was telling another nurse. "Drank red wine, pooped on someone's car, and was lucky enough someone called an ambulance. Of course, she's a hooker, one of those you can get at Costco for 90 percent off."

Or maybe that was untrue. Unconsciousness never returned, though I dearly hoped it would, and I remember an awful lot through the hazy state of being on painkillers.

Let's get one thing straight: it turns out I did not have a heart attack. It was a panic attack in disguise. The very same panic attacks Agnes fakes for attention. It was not anything I chose to have. The brain has much more power over us than we imagine. It protects itself by having you freak out and go to the hospital rather than die alone and be nothing but a meal for the worms.

Back at the motel, I was laughing for reasons unknown, though unaware of where I was or who I was. Lykke was meowing, a hallucination brought on by the panic attack. It was the first time I saw the baby as a strange specimen I was not allowed to touch, let alone hold, hide, or dress. Or kiss. Or bathe. It was also the time I realized I had a full-on schizophrenic episode with my sister Matilda watching me. I couldn't recognize myself in the mirror. I had changed—and it felt bizarre as if I were a stranger to myself because, at that point, I was. I wasn't sure who I was anymore.

Mom was at the hospital holding my hand in a few hours, and as far as I remember, she didn't pull out her phone once. When I got sedated, things started looking even better.

With Mom by my side, I was soon back in New York and booked to a psych ward, but only for two weeks. The medication was helping me gain my memories back, and finally, I felt like an old self. My identity, that Chloe I used to know, returned back to my consciousness. Those several days, while I was on the loose, were missing from my mind—a complete blank—and not until later, while under hypnosis by Dr. Pepper, did I begin to understand what had happened to me and how scary it was or how fatal it might have been.

Calyssa visited me at the psych ward too. She was wearing jeans and a gray sweater, while I had on my Wonder Woman PJ's together with my kitty slippers. They're completely black, with a white spot around the nose.

The two of us did not discuss my "episode," not only because I was embarrassed by it, but also because I had no recollection of what had happened to me. Dr. Pepper said memories would be triggered by the "outside" sources (rain, for instance, or specific colors), and eventually, the pieces would fall together, connecting all the dots. I just had to give it time.

"What happened to the ring?" I asked.

"Which ring?"

"The twenty-thousand-dollar ring, the one that you swallowed."

"I pooped it out."

"Oh," I said, as the image of her pooping out an expensive diamond ring materialized in front of me. That picture stayed with me for days—I'm unsure why—it's quite puzzling. There's something dazzling about things so bedazzling coming out of places they shouldn't, and that includes Calyssa's chocolate factory.

She sighed loudly, suggesting a change of subject was due.

"How did you manage to poop it out?" I pushed on instead. "Weren't you afraid it would get flushed with the brown pyramids?"

She pursed her lips. "I'm not giving you tips, Chloe. If you're stupid enough to have it in your ass to begin with, you deserve to poop into a colander for three days in a row. It's not like I could Google 'How to safely remove a ring from thy colon?' Because I have fucking tried."

Of all topics, we were discussing her poopzillas, and it made so much sense why we were friends. Once you know, you *know*, so to speak. Being in her company was like the Earth being in the sun's orbit, so fitting.

"So, you didn't lose your job?" I asked.

"Nope. The woman who'd bought the ring canceled the transaction a couple of days later. How rude."

"How *rude*?"

"Yeah, rude. I was going to get a big commission and preordered a new bed. I mean cash is all I think about, now that I'm working in retail. Girl, I need that cash. I have to pay for my unemployed cousin and all the household expenses. You copy?"

"Yes, that makes sense. What happened with you and Marcus? Why did he want to take you out to a fancy restaurant?"

Calyssa told me she went to that fancy restaurant, and Marcus said he loved her, just like she expected, and she said she loved him in return and that it felt right.

She added, "I feel like I was caught up in my life, and sometimes all I need is to chill. You know what I mean? I'm, like, here, doing this, then there, doing that. Taking care of baby Grace, listening to my cousin Christina, then trying to manage time between my job and Marcus."

I said, "You're blabbing again. You need to chill."

When Calyssa left, I resumed brooding about my "episode," so instead, I switched the channel in my brain. I watched that scene with Calyssa and the colander over and over and over again.

Natalia visited me a day later. She was slurping on a green smoothie, her hair in a tight bun, a leopard leotard for an outfit. She brought me pieces of carrots and celery in a Ziploc bag with the ranch dressing in a teensy container. Little did she know I had decided to avoid animal products, especially the ones loaded with sodium, and the ranch was dairy, a big no-no for me.

Seeing me in my most vulnerable state, Natalia decided to come clean and confessed to me why she was trying to give money to the hungry African children. She was seeking a distraction from her life because she owed big bucks to the IRS. That was totally out of the blue for me.

"Like the Internal Revenue Service, IRS?" I asked her to clarify.

"No, like the Immature Raving Savages. Of course, the Internal Revenue Service. They caught me lying on my taxes, freaking assholes, and issued me a huge fine."

"Huge" is an ambiguous number, and when it comes to money, it means nothing to me. When it comes to a penis, however, as in Kim's penis is huge, no further clarification is needed.

"How much is 'huge'?" I asked.

"Huge—just trust me on that one. As huge as the debt of Luxembourg, probably."

"Why did you lie on your taxes?" I asked.

It was not the question Natalia wanted to answer, clearly, because she inserted a drinking straw in her mouth and loudly sucked on the smoothie, picking up every drop from the bottom of the plastic cup. I decided not to press her. Gambling for a living, which is what Natalia does, some assets could be hidden—clearly—just not from the IRS. That story was her most embarrassing moment, I could tell. She avoided eye contact the entire time. Natalia was not the type who likes to be embarrassed. She's always right, she looks beautiful, and she does no wrong. Well, that was true until now.

That all made sense why Natalia was sending money to the kids in Africa. She felt forced to do something right to offset the bad, and she also needed a distraction from her transgender process. Basically, she was lending the money to get this noble feeling in return for self-validation.

It was now time for the penectomy, a surgical procedure that removes the male reproductive organ, but she was not ready to say goodbye to it yet. She said once she paid the fine, she would start saving for the expensive surgery that cost two hundred and fifty Benjamins (twenty-five thousand dollars).

It annoyed me in the past that most of our conversations ended up talking about her and her surgery, but this transition, I had come to accept, is a massive part of who she is, and I shouldn't blame her for needing support. That's what friends are for, after all. That's what Natalia was doing for me while I was all alone at the psych ward.

Natalia clearly was done with the confessions, because she flipped her phone in my direction so I could see the screen on which I saw a floral slip dress. She said, "Do you like it? I need something for my date on Friday."

"Who is your date with?"

"Some guy!"

Lindsay came for a visit a few days later wearing black leggings that made her skinny legs appear nonexistent. Her down jacket was silver and puffy, which created an interesting contrast to the legs. Her blond mop was parted in the middle and secured on either side of her head with bobby pins. Her boots were UGG's in brown and looked brand new. My new goal was to lose thirty pounds by summer—unrealistic, but I didn't care—and I wondered whether soon I'd fit into Lindsay's clothes.

After some small talk and yada, yada, yada, Lindsay offered me a prosciutto sandwich she'd made. It was on a long French baguette with arugula sticking out the sides, with slices of red tomato and white mozzarella.

"Did you stop eating vegetarian?" I asked and took the sandwich to show my appreciation. I had no desire to chomp on meat, but I placed the sandwich by my bed and said I'd save it for "later," which meant the trash can.

"Vegetarian-schmegetarian," she said and bit the sandwich. She chewed for ten seconds, swallowed, and said, "I mean, I was trying to figure out *why* I was vegetarian. Was it about health, or was it about the animals? I looked at my tofu-shaped rug and realized I was probably allergic to soy anyway. Did you know Asians have a special enzyme that breaks down soy?"

"No."

"Well, they do. I also tried making seitan, which is a product made out of wheat, so basically gluten. And I've been trying to eat gluten-free for a while. Like, this sandwich is gluten-free and made with brown rice flour."

"A gluten-free baguette?"

"Uh-hum," she mumbled while taking another bite.

"So, how does it tie in with not being vegetarian?" I asked.

"Well, that's just it. There was no reason for me to be a vegetarian anymore—it was inconvenient, expensive, and animals were being slaughtered anyway whether I ate meat or not. I needed a distraction for my mind, something to focus on—because I was simply bored to death. This nanny job is so slow." She stretched the word "slow" to prove her point.

"I remember," I said. "I even pointed out that you have all this time on your hands."

"Excatly," she said, using the word I made up, which made me smile. Ex-*cat*-ly. Get it? That's how I knew she cared.

"I had to be honest with myself," she went on. "I need a new job. This is why I'd made up that whole story about Charlotte eating a crayon. Remember how I mentioned she choked on it?"

"Yes, vividly."

"All made-up. I had to save face, in case I decided to suddenly quit. I didn't want you to think I was an impulsive quitter—so I had to have a reason, which was that choking, for example."

"If you quit your nanny job, where will you live?"

"I'll find a bedroom someplace. Not a big deal. It's New York City, a land of opportunity!"

We chatted about this and that for a while until four. Then Lindsay kissed me goodbye and picked up her handbag. Before stepping out the door, she turned around and said, "You know what sucks in our society? That it's frowned upon to talk about mental health. I wish people were more open to it."

A

h, memories! What I now remember differs from what happened in reality. When I asked my mom if she knew where Matilda was, she replied, "She passed away many years ago, sweetie."

"What about the baby?" I asked.

"There is no baby, just the cat."

"I don't understand."

"Remember, I am your friend. You trust me, right?" Now, she was talking like Dr. Pepper. He has couched her to repeat those words like a mantra, which sends my psyche into the right place. Sometimes I cannot decipher what's real and what's not. If Dr. Pepper or Mom used those words, it meant this was the reality and not an illusion.

"I kidnapped a baby," I said.

"You can trust me, Chloe. You had an 'episode.' You did not kidnap a baby. It was a cat." A black cat resembling Anubis was sitting on her lap. He was not Anubis, because he was missing a streak of white on the collar.

What she had said wasn't sinking in.

It was now the nighttime, and Mom was gone, and my thoughts took me back to Lykke. It was as if I was high when I took her. Those days with her in my hands now seemed untrue, because they weren't true, according to Mom. This is why the brain is perhaps the most misunderstood organ.

There's nothing for me to say, except that when I thought I was on the loose with a baby, I had kidnapped a black puss instead.

When I was released from the ward, I was seeing my psychiatrist, Dr. Pepper, regularly. The very first time I saw him since the ward, he listened to my entire story and said, with relief, I could sense that I didn't kidnap a baby. I wasn't getting how my mind could just make up a baby, but Dr. Pepper perused the point: "You were not taking your medication, and the kidnapping story of Sia Shirtley consumed your mind. That's all you talked about during your appointments. I know how to distinguish reality versus a hallucination. You compared parts of your story to children's books, which is proof your mind fabricated them."

"I don't understand," I said.

"When you opened a savings account in Newark, you compared it to *The Wonderful Wizard of Oz,* Noah's favorite book. The banker looked like the Tin Can Man, the cashier was the Cowardly Lion, and Stinky—how you called him—was the Scarecrow."

"Did I open a savings account?" I asked.

"Not that we know of."

"What about the witness who saw me?"

"Which one?"

"Glamazon."

"Describe her for me, Chloe."

"She was black with long nails and kept calling herself Miss Fine."

He exhaled loudly. "Miss Fine was the witness from Shirtley 's case. You brooded about for months, and your psyche wanted to connect with Sia and her parents and everyone involved in the story. Remember, your mind was playing tricks on you. When you were on the bus to Washington, you compared yourself to the Gingerbread Runner. When you went to pawn Miriam's phone, you said you felt like Jack from 'Jack and the Beanstalk.'"

"What about Miriam? Did I stay with Miriam?"

"You stayed somewhere. I'm not sure where. You did not compare Miriam or her living arrangements to any book, except you said she took Lykke to Hogsmeade's, which, I learned, upon looking it up, is a settlement from the Harry Potter series. Evidently, she reminded you of your neighbor, Agnes. They're both hoarders in your story and have multiple cats. I assume Miriam's house was real, and I believe she may have had cats, even the one rotting in the fridge. But it could have been an illusion. What we know for sure you did stay somewhere for two nights, and it's still a mystery."

"But I saw the cops around her house," I said. "How could she not be real?"

"You refer to the FBI agents and cops in your story as the huntsmen from 'Snow White.' I believe it was mostly your imagination. When you went to pawn Miriam's phone, Sally Maye reminded you of Natalia, with the same physical attributes. That made you feel safe."

"What about Regina and Vijay?"

"You compared the limousine ride to the movie *The Lady and the Tramp*. Regina as Lady, and you as the Tramp. You were not in that limousine, for sure. Regina had all the characteristics of your friend Lindsay. The same hair and slim body. You longed for your friend to be there, and your imagination created her."

Needless to say, Regina's bracelet that I stole from the limousine was never found.

I said, "What about Buck Mooney's car, the one I was driving to Richmond?"

"Your mind did wander through that story. There are too many references to the movie *Speed* with Keanu Reeves. You called yourself Annie at some point. And Buck did look a lot like your boyfriend, Kim."

Just when you think you know yourself, I realized, there's still plenty to learn.

Dr. Pepper said I used word Nottingham where I found Anita, who looked like Calyssa, and since I missed Calyssa, my mind had made her up, just like it made up Lindsay and Natalia. Nottingham is a town from *Robin Hood*, yet another cartoon.

Yet, another fictitious settlement.

In fact, Anita worked in a Merfolk Diner, and Merfolk is a fictional underwater kingdom from the movie *The Little Mermaid*, something I've watched with Noah a million times. He used to dress up as Sebastian, the crab, and I was Ariel.

Dr. Pepper brought up another point to consider: I was following the scenes from my memories like Baby Bink does in the movie *Baby's Day Out*. Anything I'd seen, watched, and heard ended up making its way back. For instance, when I met Lazy Susan, it was because she looked like Paula Deen, my favorite chef who I always watch on TV. After watching *Sister Act* with Miriam, I ended up in a monastery, and Sister Chloe resembled Whoopi Goldberg.

All makes sense.

Dr. Pepper pointed out I compared myself to Thumbelina, a cartoon character when Matilda took me to that motel. He didn't believe I stole Buck's van, but he offered an explanation that I may have taken a bus.

Nobody will ever know.

Plus, I ended up in the monastery, which is where it all ended in the real story. It's where Sia Shirtley was found and where Ama Takayoza was arrested. The faces I saw in the monastery also belonged to the nuns I'd seen on TV—to the very last zit on Sister Mary's face. But I was not in a real monastery from what he could tell.

Last, who called 9-1-1? Well, apparently, I did. Matilda, who guided me, was the reincarnation of the one sane cell left in my brain, and "she" helped me stumble on a telephone booth to call an ambulance.

For that, I was grateful.

And just like that, my life was now different.

It was an unsettling feeling. Something kept nagging at me as if there was some unfinished business. I know I didn't go to prison, but did it even matter? Was I a prisoner of my own mind all along? My mom, my friends, all other girls, and boys with broken hearts, we lie to ourselves how ugly, unwanted, or stupid we are. Is it really freedom walking on the streets and being part of "society"—while inside, you're nothing more than pain, hurt, and guilt?

I was back to being white, straight female, and everything appeared normal. But it was not. I *was* a minority. How many people can you name offhand with a mental disorder? That's something I have to live my entire life with. Just because you can't see a disturbance on the surface, it doesn't mean you have the right to judge people because they're doing something you're not used to. They can look happy because it is embarrassing to be vulnerable. The problems may only be apparent if you take a glimpse inside (which for me was inside Miriam's house). In our own little ways, we all belong to small communities that are far broader than race or religion. You may be anorexic, morbidly obese, gay, an illegal immigrant, have breast cancer, or have small boobs. Maybe you can't afford a diamond ring at Calyssa's store that cost ten thousand dollars or Natalia's surgery that cost twenty-five thousand, or perhaps you can't afford your next meal. I often hear things like, "Oh, poor rich girl who can't get pregnant—I wish I had such problems."

Do you? Do you really? Leave her alone and focus on yourself. What's meant for you will happen. The rich girl who can't get pregnant will see you on the street and think, "God, I wish I had her beautiful teeth." Even the Kardashians have problems! And Oprah. We're all the same. I wish we could turn off the light and get to know one another. No race. No status. No bullshit.

Even after my newly found, I don't know what to call it—enlightenment?—disappointment?—understanding?—I wanted to call it quits with Kim after being released from the psych ward. I figured he wouldn't want to date a girl with a mental disorder. I mean it's clearly no joke and what if it happens again? What if the disease escalates or what if I became dangerous? I mean, I took a cat from the playground who could have easily been a baby—and end up in prison for life, dragging his reputation down together with me.

I invited him over and made dinner. I asked him not to interrupt, and I started from the beginning. Kim listened until the end, when I said, "So I guess, this disease is me against the world, against you. I don't think we should see each other anymore."

He put my palms in his. "Thank God," he said. "Chloe, I'd much rather date you than any girl without a mental disease. I mean, who is 'normal,' anyway?"

"Lots of people."

"Listen. We are not getting married. Maybe we will—I don't know. We are here now. We like each other. Why make it so complicated?"

"I'm just thinking of the future. If we put all this energy into dating and become closer, it will only be harder to break up in the future."

"You're already thinking of us breaking up?" He squeezed my hand tighter. "My mom is bipolar. Did I ever tell you that?"

That took me by surprise. "No. We never talked about your family. Why didn't we?"

"Same reason you didn't tell me about your schizophrenia."

We didn't break up. Kim told me about his mom and messed up situations she was in when he was growing up. He'd seen it all, so to speak. Ironically, our breakup conversation brought us even closer. I am happy I was brave enough to have this conversation because, in the past, I'd do what all other guys did to me—ghost Kim and block his number. He'd never know what had happened, and maybe that would torture him until the day he died. But that's where our society came to. I really wish like Lindsay said, we could have open discussions about things that are hard to say. Like our feelings, our dreams, our fears.

By the end of June, I lost thirty pounds, which was my goal. I was taking a different type of medication that didn't raise my cholesterol or triglycerides, but the main change was that half of my meals were vegetarian, and I frequently visited the gym. Once, Kim and I worked out together, and I used a stationary bike while looking at his skinny arms lifting fifteens in front of a mirror, seat rubbing against my crotch, faster and faster and faster as I pedaled, I couldn't take it any longer, grabbed him, and took him home. I had no idea workouts could be so arousing. Since then, I don't invite him to work out, because when I work out, I . . . um, want to work out, for lack of a better expression.

The little black kitty cat I'd snatched from Central Park thinking she was a baby had to be returned to the shelter. I didn't want just another cat. I missed Anubis. This one was female, and I named her Tia, short for Tiana. Unfortunately, we've never found Anubis, but for whatever it's worth, I believe he's still alive and that one day he'll return.

EPILOGUE

Agnes was banging her ceiling with a broom again, and that was enough to set me off. It was a hot summer day, June twenty-fifth, and our central A/C unit on the roof that provides cold air for the entire building wasn't working because a pigeon had apparently settled inside of it somehow and died. The stench was unbearable. Not only it smelled like anus for days, but the fan I was running in my living room was helping zero. The A/C guys had been working on the unit for five days straight, but I didn't know how much longer of this heat I could take. Mom was on vacation in London, regularly sending me pictures of homeless people, buildings, and dinner plates. At least she was having fun, and for the first time, she was not worried about me, which was a relief. Kim was out of town too, and my friends were all working. I was bored to death. The book *War and Peace* was my only salvation. I had opened my windows, praying for a breeze, even though it helped very little. My TV was off, which is why the banging on the ceiling was out of the blue.

It was clear to me Agnes was bored and in a bad mood. I unglued my sweaty butt from my leather couch—which gave a smooching sound—put on underwear, a pair of PJ bottoms, and a tank top. I was ready for a fight. I grabbed along a rolling pin, put on my cat slippers, and took the elevator one floor down.

I knocked on Agnes's door with the rolling pin. I was now forty pounds lighter and wondered if Agnes would confuse me with the skinny Japanese Chyna, which would be a compliment, actually. I heard boots approaching from the other side of the door. I heard lock after lock getting opened. The door swung, and Agnes in curlers appeared. Her face was as sweaty as mine, and for the first time, I saw the light in her apartment. She, it seemed, had opened the windows much the same way I did to let the breeze in. It didn't even stink as much as it did before, which was helpful.

"Agnes, why are you banging on your damn ceiling? I'm not even watching TV!"

But she couldn't speak. Her face was becoming whiter, and her eyes seemed devoid of life.

"Agnes, are you okay?"

She couldn't speak, but she shook her head for a no.

Thankfully, I had my phone in my pocket, and I dialed 9-1-1 right away. Agnes leaned on me as I helped her step toward the hallway, where it was cooler, after which I kneeled together with her. The 9-1-1 operator thought Agnes was hyperventilating and suggested she breathe through pursed lips. I put the phone on speaker to make sure Agnes heard the instructions. Agnes followed the advice and breathed through pursed lips until the paramedics arrived and took her off my hands. I told them I would contact her daughter because my mother was a nurse and knew her family. I sounded so grown up!

I realized Agnes hadn't been banging to annoy me, but to save her life. A cry to save herself. Thank God I was home! Why she didn't use her own phone to call 9-1-1 was a mystery, but I thought I'd better check her phone in case it's broken.

While the moment presented itself, I entered her apartment. I was hoping to find her daughter's phone number on the fridge. This way, I could contact her without bothering Mom and avoid weeks of listening to her discussing the story with Aunt Josephine. I saw an old phone, red with a rotary dial. When I picked up the receiver, I realized there was no dial tone —which explained why Agnes couldn't call the ambulance herself.

Junk was all over the apartment, of course, just like I imagined, and her cats scattered in all possible corners as soon as they sensed me. Looking around, I smelled sadness and rotting foodstuffs, cat urine, and lots of dust. I covered my mouth from such a surprise. No wonder her daughter never visits, which is not to say she shouldn't. I made a mental note to always check on my Mom once I live alone—every day, even if needed. No human should be living in such unsanitary conditions.

One black cat was staring at me, utterly unafraid of the stranger. As I approached the fridge, the cat approached me and wound its tail around my leg, meowing in a soft voice.

"You'll be okay, kitty," I said as I picked it up. "I'll feed you while Agnes is gone." His green eyes looked straight into mine. I noticed a white streak on the collar. Black fur.

I believe my eyes popped out from their sockets. Because I was holding my cat Anubis. He was much skinnier than before, but it was definitely him. He was meowing weakly as if he hadn't been fed in months, but he was not inadequately taken care of. Agnes didn't know he was diabetic.

"I didn't lose you," I said, looking at him, still at a loss for words. "I've never lost you. You never ran away from me. Agnes stole you. My poor thing!" I hugged him tightly, while I looked for Agnes's daughter's phone number on the fridge—which was written on a piece of paper, secured by a magnet that said "Vegas."

At that point, I knew everything was going to be okay. Agnes had another panic attack, hoping to get her daughter's attention. Everything—absolutely everything, just like I wanted back at the "monastery," or wherever I was at the moment (some sort of safe place), hoping for the simplicity of life. It was there—it always had been there—I was just unable to see it.

In the end, I was given another shot at life. If I took care of my health, hopefully, everything else would fall into place. I am happy about one thing that I did not kidnap a baby. I could not live with myself if I had. And maybe that's good to know that even in your darkest moment—when even your brain, your main organ, can't think straight—if you're a decent person, you will do the right thing.

THE END

ACKNOWLEDGMENTS

I would like to thank the following people: my southern dialogue director Michael McMurtrey, book designer Jessica Smith, cover designer, Victoria Graham, and my editors, Crissy Cutting and Andrés Martinez.

ABOUT THE AUTHOR

Jeremy Taylor was raised in Siberia and Kazakhstan and moved to the United States in 2007 at the age of nineteen. He received political asylum on the basis of being gay and now lives and writes in West New York, NJ.

Find out more on his website:
WWW.JEREMYTAYLOR.ONLINE

x.com/jeremytaylor_ny
instagram.com/jeremy.taylor.ny

BOOKS BY JEREMY TAYLOR

Once Upon an Apple Martini

Diary of a Mad Gay Man

The Cornerstones of Happiness

One Hundred and Eleven People I Can't Stand

Smart Casual and Other Expressions I Hate

Noodles with Grandma and Other Stories from Our Homestead in Kazakhstan

HIS FAVORITE BOOKS

I Hate Everyone Starting with Me and Diary of a Mad Diva by Joan Rivers | *My Horizontal Life: A Collection of One-Night Stands* by Chelsea Handler | *Are You There God? It's Me, Margaret* by Judy Blume | *R Is for Ricochet* by Sue Grafton

HIS FAVORITE TV SHOWS

I Love Lucy, Crazy Ex-Girlfriend, Kim's Convenience, Schitt's Creek, Friends, Sex and the City, Broad City, Emily in Paris, The Good Place, Young & Hungry, Workin' Moms, Desperate Housewives, The Kardashians, Foundation

www.ingramcontent.com/pod-product-compliance
Lightning Source LLC
Chambersburg PA
CBHW021621030826
48979CB00035B/1397/J

* 9 7 9 8 9 9 0 5 1 8 9 0 2 *